"Doug's stories exist in a space where reality is labile, a space that has its own rules and expectations, and commands a sort of mental poetry."

– Eileen Gunn, author of *Stable Strategies*

"It's legitimate SF, and it's 'mainstream,' and it's metafiction: I don't know anyone else doing quite what Lain is doing; fascinating work, moving, strikingly honest, powerful."

– Rich Horton, *Locus Magazine*

"Philip K. Dick would have admired Douglas Lain's 'The Sea Monkey Conspiracy,' and would have been unsettled by it, for the same reason—he would have seen himself in the alienated young narrator/protagonist. He might have argued that it's a sequel to—and perhaps better than—his 1979 story 'The Exit Door Leads in.'"

– Paul Williams, author of *Only Apparently Real, The World of Philip K. Dick*

"Reads with compelling immediacy, an unnerving combination of masks, secrets that distort and finally shred one's identity..."

-Sherwood Smith, *Tangent Online*

"A must-read for originality and perceptive social satire."

–Daniel E. Blackstone's *Firebrand Fiction Column*

"Exquisite... savvy.... and sophisticated.... Lain is a master at imbedding information for the reader to discover on subsequent readings."

– Therese Pieczynski, *Tangent Online*

"Anything involving magic and cons of any sort, even ones that work against the space-time continuum, appeals to me, and this one has the added benefit of being written well. It's entertaining, thoughtful, thought-provoking..."

– Matthew Cheney, *The Mumpsimus*

"The wonderful autobiographical inserts leave the reader wondering whether Lain has written the story or the story has written Lain.... One is never quite sure if the main character is sane or not, nor is the reader ever clear about what is real and what is illusion."

– Forrest Aguire, editor, *Leviathan 4: Cities*

LAST WEEK'S APOCALYPSE

LAST WEEK'S APOCALYPSE

STORIES BY DOUGLAS LAIN WITH AN INTRODUCTION BY EILEEN GUNN

NIGHT SHADE BOOKS
SAN FRANCISCO & PORTLAND

Jacket art © 2006 by Gee Vaucher
Jacket design by Claudia Noble
Interior layout and design by Jeremy Lassen

First Edition

ISBN-10 1-59780-034-1
ISBN-13 978-1-59780-034-1

Night Shade Books
Please visit us on the web at
http://www.nightshadebooks.com
Printed in Canada

This book is dedicated to my wife and first reader Miriam.
She is more than I deserve.

CONTENTS:

CRANKING THE WHEEL OF REALITY

AN INTRODUCTION BY EILEEN GUNN

I have to admit I don't know a whole lot about Douglas Lain. I already told the Homeland Security guy everything I could remember, so don't bug me about it, okay? I know nothing about his personal habits, except what I can extrapolate from the fact that he lives in Portland, Oregon: he drinks coffee (but probably not from Starbucks) and is tolerant of damp.

I do know this, as well: he writes what he sees.

He sees a world in which baffled aliens relentlessly pursue married men with small children ("Music Lessons"), and in which baffled aliens *are* men with small children (" 'Identity Is a Construct' "). I'm confident that's reality as he knows it. (Doug has four children. At least some of them are small.) He describes his reality in the gentlest of terms, with a stunning command of dialogue and a knowledge of the way men and women talk to one another when they really are speaking of something else entirely.

Doug's stories exist in a space where reality is labile, a space that has its own rules and expectations, and commands a sort of mental poetry. Lain-space is governed by shadowy, irrational forces that most humans never encounter directly, kind of like Homeland Security. Familiar objects morph, and nothing is necessarily what it seems. It has a mid-scale paranoia index: the underlying threat is interior—psychological, not physical.

"The '84 Regress," which I bought for the *Infinite Matrix* webzine, was the first Doug Lain story that I ever encountered. Starting to read, I was struck with a familiar thought: the writing was too good to be true, and I'd be disappointed. But I wasn't disappointed. Maybe I worry too much. The writing is, in fact, exactly good enough to be true, which is especially important in a story that bends reality to its will.

"The Suburbs of the Citadel of Thought" gets into seriously metafictional territory, in this case something akin to high-wire walking in clown shoes. Reading it, I worried sometimes for Doug's sanity, and other times I feared the imminent demise of his narrative skills. It is a *tour de force* that manages to be compellingly readable as plotted fiction, while at the same time it meditates on the relationship of the dead to the living and undercuts its own fictive credibility by analyzing the creative process from the viewpoint of a writer who thinks too much. (Warning to amateurs: do not try this at home.) I like it as a writer, I like it as a reader, and I like it as someone who has for nearly fifty years been a fan of disintegrating realities.

"Music Lessons" is both scary and wondrous: it offers both a sense of the imaginative life of an idiosyncratic contemporary composer, and a Le Guin-like glimpse of an alien reality in which there is no boundary between sleeping and waking, or between music and speech. It's hard to say which is stranger: the human or the alien.

I confess that I'm enchanted by the women in Doug's stories. These women are well grounded in reality. They dress imaginatively, and they're exasperated but not intimidated by a husband or boyfriend who lives in another universe. They cope well. If you found yourself trapped in Lain-space, they are the people you'd want with you.

Lain-space, I expect, is waiting to trap the unwary at any moment. The manuscript of the book you hold in your hand, for example, escaped from a sealed box, leaving three very ordinary cookbooks in its place. Wrong box, I thought, when I opened it: somewhere, some Lain family-member is opening a birthday present and finding Doug's manuscript, instead of the Bass-o-matic cookbook that they had been hoping for. No doubt they had already given him a heads-up.

I emailed Doug, and I could hear the cogs slipping on the wheels of reality. There was no other box, came the reply. No one was missing a birthday present. He'd never heard of the cookbooks. Was I sure it was the same box?

I felt like a character in a Doug Lain story. Was there ever really a box?

"Was it an Office Depot box?" he asked. "Was your name written in darker ink than your address?"

I sensed that I had lost his trust, and had to pass the ink-colors test. I rolled my eyes and answered. Yes, my name was darker than my address.

It was the right answer. He said he would send me another box. I could tell that it was my responsibility to make sure it contained the manuscript of *Last Week's Apocalypse*.

A few days later, I got a box in the mail that looked just like the first box. It contained dozens of brown glass vials labeled with the titles of Doug's stories, each vial filled with pink pills. I took two capsules of "The '84 Regress" and began this essay.

It may be that, as I write this, a Homeland Security agent is looking all over the place for a book called *American Desserts* (one of the books in the box—doesn't it sound like government issue?). Nearby, perhaps, the agent's spouse or child is being subverted by "The Headline Trick," a story that makes a satiric connection between the flow of money to the wealthy and the Bush government's policies on Iraq, the environment, and public education. As you would expect from a Lain narrative, there's a somewhat nonlinear relationship between the different parts of the story. I'm pleased to note that it indicates that even ATMs are repulsed by the general trend in US politics.

As I told Homeland Security, Doug's a normal-looking guy: medium height, brown hair, plaid shirt. On the outside, he looks pretty much like everybody else in Portland. If he's escaped into Lain-space, it should take them quite a while to track him down.

So you have time to read this book before the trial. I recommend it.

Eileen Gunn
Seattle
July 2005

THE '84 REGRESS

LIFE IN THE 80S

Life in the eighties isn't all bad. Television, for instance, is better than you might remember it being; there are fewer stations, fewer commercials, and everything is slower, slowed down. There aren't ATMs or FAX machines; there aren't any e-mail messages.

Driving on the interstate, counting the yellow dashes that zoom by, it all makes sense. The last sixteen years were just a series of bizarre nightmares, everything was just as unreal as it felt, and the year 1984 never ended.

Let me repeat:

The year 1984 never ended.

It's my own unified field theory. Generation X, the Clinton presidency, Jay Leno, my relationships with women—all of it makes sense now.

THE BREAKUP

Cindy and I broke up in 2001.

The problem was that Cindy didn't know how to argue, or more to the point, she didn't know how to sublimate. She'd been through therapy just like everyone else, and she took her medication, but she could never stick to the issue at hand. I'd start in about how she squeezed the toothpaste tube, or complain about her haircut, but she always tried to figure out what was really going on.

"You don't care about my haircut. You just don't want to marry me," she said. She didn't understand how the game was supposed to be played.

"It's your hair. It's your hair. I know you don't understand, but it really is your hair."

She looked great actually, her hair was fine, but when she stood there looking at herself in the mirror, in her mother's wedding dress, and with her hair pulled back and her tan face shining, suddenly I couldn't stand her.

I took my pill. I took my pink pill and smiled.

"You should try on the tuxedo," she said.

"I can't," I said. "Because of your hair."

Cindy and I broke up. We broke up because she didn't know how to argue.

THE SMITHS

I left Cindy and moved into a studio apartment. I moved into a tiny room with yellowed walls and a shared bath.

I met Mrs. Smith the first day.

She knocked on the plywood door to my place.

"Hello neighbor," she said. "Can I borrow some butter?"

She was on the young side of middle aged, maybe thirty-seven, but she still looked young somehow, acted young. She wasn't really fully dressed. She was wearing a pair of men's boxer shorts and a sports bra. Her hair was a solid brown, darker than it would naturally be, and her body was trim and fit.

"Butter?" I asked. "I'm not sure. I just moved in."

"No? Well I think I might have some. Why don't you come over and borrow some from me."

"What?"

"Welcome. I'm saying hello to the new neighbor and welcome. Come on over. I'll introduce you to my husband."

She led me to her apartment, to their apartment. She and her husband lived in a much bigger place than my own, and much more expensively decorated. She opened the front door and led me past overstuffed chairs, through a hallway with track lighting, and into the front room.

A man who I assumed was her husband was resting on the perfectly white sofa. His socked feet dangled over the armrest and his head was propped up by throw pillows. He was working on a Rubik's Cube.

"Winston, the new neighbor is here," Mrs. Smith announced to the man on the couch and then she turned back to me.

He didn't say anything. A mechanical ticking sound filled the silence. The Smiths had a large reel-to-reel tape recorder underneath their glass coffee table and the red light was on; the VU meter was swinging back and forth in tiny arcs as Mr. Smith turned the colors on his Rubik's Cube.

"Are we recording this conversation?" I asked.

"There's nothing I can do about that. That's not ours," Mr. Smith said.

"Whose is it?"

He didn't answer. "You're diagnosed, right? What they got you on?"

It was a rude question. Not that I had anything to hide, exactly. "What about you? You've been diagnosed too, right?"

"What are you on?" Mr. Smith asked again.

"Ritalin mostly. I'm distractible," I said. "But I'm okay, really. I can work. I was even going to get married."

"You're a voter then?" Mr. Smith asked.

"Yeah. I'm a voter."

"We're not voters," Mrs. Smith said. "Most of the tenants here aren't voters."

"We used to be voters," Mr. Smith said.

I shrugged. Being a voter wasn't something I took too seriously.

"Do you think we could, maybe, borrow a few of your pills then?" Mr. Smith asked.

"Just to try them out. Just a few of them," Mrs. Smith asked.

"My pills?"

"Two or three is all."

"Hey, listen…I'm on a routine, if I gave you anything that would disrupt the schedule."

"Just two?" Mrs. Smith asked.

"No," I said. "I don't like you even asking."

"Just one?" Mrs. Smith asked. She put her arm around my waist, trying to hold me. I jerked away and stumbled back, catching myself from falling. I brushed past the overstuffed chairs beneath the track lighting.

"You don't have to go," Mrs. Smith said as I opened the front door. "We'll be nice."

I didn't say anything to her, but half stumbled and half ran back into the hall. I leaned against their door and immediately reached inside my jacket pocket for another pill. I reached inside but there was nothing there. The pills were gone, the bottle was gone. They'd lifted them off me.

"Hey!" I yelled at the door. I pounded with flat palms on the wood. "I'm on a schedule! Open the door!" I pounded and pounded. "I need my medication. Open the door."

"You'll be better off without it," Mrs. Smith said from behind the plywood door.

"I need those pills!"

"No. We need the pills. We need them!" Mr. Smith shrieked from inside. "We don't have a future without them!"

GROWING UP STONED

I fidget with the radio dial, seeking out static. Cindy tells me to watch the road, but I can't help myself. I can't keep my fingers from nervously drumming. I lock and unlock the driver's side door and finger the stick shift.

I was diagnosed, at the age of eight, with attention deficit disorder. They put me on Ritalin, and it was almost fun. I'd get totally stoned on these chemicals, with full sanction from my parents and the school district, and then take off on my Bigwheel. Pedaling faster and faster I reached speeds unimaginable.

Now I'm clean and I feel sluggish. Worse, I can't keep my hands and eyes from wandering.

"It's not you. It's this boredom we're living through. The tedium of all these billboards and exit ramps," Cindy says. "Keep your eyes on the road."

I take a package of spearmint gum from the glove compartment, chew up a wad, and swallow.

I hope for a placebo effect.

WITHDRAWAL

At first I thought I could handle it. I didn't want to explain anything to my doctor, didn't want to end up begging for a refill at the pharmacy, or going to Cindy so that she could let me raid the old apartment for an extra bottle. I didn't want to face Cindy at all. Whatever distractions came up I'd just have to cope with, and then after work I'd go by the Smiths and get my pills back.

But, within an hour of my arrival at work, I was emptying my desk drawers, sorting through the first aid kit in the employees' kitchen. I even asked the secretary for one of her pills.

"Why are you staring at me?" she asked.

Sheila was in her thirties with frizzy blonde hair and she was always in the same red turtleneck and brown skirt. She was practically invisible; she liked to be inconspicuous, but I was determined to draw her out. She had something I needed.

She stood next to the filing cabinet, pulled the top drawer half-open, and then stopped.

"Do you have any pills?" I asked.

"What?"

"Withdrawal," I said. "I'm going through withdrawal. Do you have any extra pills?" I asked.

"I took my daily allotment already," she said.

"Please."

I crossed the room and stood next to her at the filing cabinet. I took her by the shoulder and pointed her toward my cubicle.

Sheila sat down at my desk. She pushed my cup of number two pencils, my Swingline stapler, and the solar-powered calculator I'd stolen from the marketing department out of her way and pressed her cheek against the coolness of the metal desktop.

"What do you want from me? I don't know anything. I'm not anybody important."

"I need your pills. Just a few pills, that's all." I was deranged already. Streaks of transparent gold and cellophane red wavered in front of my eyes and when I looked at Sheila, she looked younger than she had before. She'd changed. She was sixteen, maybe seventeen, years old.

"Your phone is ringing," this teenage version of Sheila said.

It was, it was ringing like a bell rather than trilling out its usual computer-generated farts. When I didn't move to answer it Sheila picked up the phone herself and handed me the receiver.

Mrs. Smith was on the line.

"How did you get my number?"

"It's on the bottle."

"What do you want?"

"How are you feeling? A little funny maybe?"

"I feel fine."

"You don't, but you could. You want to feel better? Why don't you come over?

Take some time off work?"

"I'm on a routine—" I started, but then I caught myself. I didn't want to beg and wasn't going to justify anything.

"Come on, pay a visit. I've got something to show you."

IN THE MIRROR

Cindy stares into the mirror above the bathroom sink and runs her index finger down the curve of her neck. She lets her clean white towel slip from around her midriff and fall to the tiled floor.

"It's the only perk of coming down," she says.

"What's that?"

"Youth."

I pull back the thin coverlet on the motel's king-sized bed, grab the remote control off the nightstand, but don't turn on the set.

"You look beautiful," I tell her.

Cindy shrugs her shoulders and sucks on her finger. She cups her breasts and arches her back, displaying herself to herself.

"I've got perfect breasts," Cindy says.

"Yes."

"I've got perfect skin."

I agree with her, but all I can think about is getting another fix.

"Do you want to fuck?" Cindy asks.

At nineteen she's beautiful, her skin is perfect, and my own twenty-two-year-old body is a good match: a flat stomach, thick shoulders, but sex is the last thing I want.

"I don't want to do anything," I said. "Except get stoned again."

Cindy picks up her towel and holds it up to her chest, barely covering herself. She starts out of the bathroom but then turns back to her reflection.

"Let's hit the road." I say.

Cindy doesn't stop staring but just nods at her reflection.

"Let's get going."

"You know..." Cindy says, "I can't stand myself like this."

COMING DOWN

"Hi," Mrs. Smith said. She pushed open the plywood door and stood in the frame, blocking my path and exhibiting herself for my appraisal. She was wearing a peach-colored silk robe that stopped at her thigh. "You came," she said.

"Yeah." I wasn't sure what I was affirming. "Let me in."

She moved aside, just enough for me to squeeze by, and I staggered into the darkness of the apartment.

The only source of illumination was a spotlight aimed at the center of the room. A metal folding chair had been set in the beam, and Mrs. Smith went to it and sat down.

"They're filming us now. They keep demanding more details," she said. "Have your eyes adjusted yet? Can you see the camera?"

I could. There was a vague triangle in the corner, and a blinking red light.

"I keep it dark so they won't see me," Mrs. Smith said. She opened her peach-colored robe and pulled my prescription bottle from her inside pocket.

She shook one of my pills into her hand, broke open the capsule, and took a taste of the drug. "My husband is a good man, but he does what he's told. He does whatever the Brotherhood tells him. They tell him to stop taking pills, so he does. They say they want to record us, to videotape everything, and he lets them. Of course he let's them. What else can he do?"

"Give me my pills," I said.

"They won't help. You're off the routine; the pills won't work fast enough. But, I've got some smoke. Why don't you do some smoke and calm down?"

I sat next to her, on the floor, and she produced a paper package from her robe. She sprinkled green leaves onto a rolling paper and twisted it into shape for me.

"Hold it in your lungs," she said.

I took one drag after another, and the symptoms of my withdrawal intensified. I leaned back, letting my head rest on the metal seat of the chair, and watched the purple fog above my head.

"I'm withdrawing," I said.

"Look at this," Mrs. Smith said.

I opened my eyes, adjusted myself into a more upright position.

And then Mrs. Smith handed me a microwave oven. Neon-colored, bright orange, microwave oven.

"What's this for?" I asked.

"Just keep your eye on it."

The incongruity of this major appliance went beyond the fact that it was unexpected; something about the microwave was wrong. I couldn't quite believe that it was really there, that such a microwave oven could even exist.

"What's wrong with it? There's something wrong with it, but I don't know what it is."

"Open it," Mrs. Smith suggested.

Inside, sitting on the rotating glass plate, was a smaller microwave oven—an older model. The older microwave had only a single dial. And, as I sat and watched, this older microwave grew. It grew until it filled the inside, it grew until the outer microwave started to groan from the pressure.

"Keep your eyes open," Mrs. Smith said.

The outer oven gave way, it cracked along the corners, and the black box inside emerged.

"What?" I asked as a trickle of orange plastic flowed onto my hands, into my lap. The inner microwave replaced the outer facade; all that was left of the newer model was a pool of melted orange plastic.

Mrs. Smith plugged the black microwave into the wall, and dropped a plastic grocery bag into my lap. Inside the bag was a Swanson's TV dinner.

"Let's see if it will cook," she said.

I tossed the TV dinner inside and without setting the temperature, without the option of setting anything, I pressed the start button. We watched as the cardboard package spun around and around.

"It still works," I said.

"Yes." She pressed the release button and the microwave popped open, and then she peeled back the paper lid of the TV dinner. Steam wafted up and the brown goo inside was bubbling.

CAN'T DRIVE 55

The future is a hallucination. I see it shimmering across the horizon, a city of cylinders and squares, and I'm amazed at how it floats. The future is unreal; it's red and green, like Christmas.

The Yugo has a television screen where there once was a speedometer, and there is a jet stream where the exhaust pipe used to be.

"We're flying," Cindy says. She's strapped in next to me, wearing a spacesuit and talking through a small slit in her helmet. "Flying."

The future is a hallucination, a joke, but I press down on the gas anyway. I want to reach this glimmering city on a hill before it fades into the ether, before it reverts back.

THE PINK POWDER OF OPRAH WINFREY

I broke into Cindy's apartment, my old apartment. Slipping a credit card between the door and the frame, I was in, and the first thing I did was head to the bathroom, to the medicine cabinet.

I scanned the dozens of bottles inside; brown vials full of little pink pills. I read the labels, starting at the top there was Aging, Continuity, Memory, and so on…

On the bottom shelf, the labels were more specific:

The Internet, Beanie Babies, The Clinton Administration, Howard Stern…

I took "Desert Storm" and "Generation X" from the bottom row and read the fine print. I was supposed to take these pills twice a month, on an empty stomach. I grabbed another bottle, one called "Oprah Winfrey," and pressed down on the childproof top.

I pulled the gelatin shells apart, and considered the powder. I licked the tip of my index finger, and took a taste.

"Today we're going to talk to the parents of kids who can remember their past lives," the television blared from the living room. I closed the medicine cabinet and went to see what was on.

A thin Oprah Winfrey walked the steps up into the audience. "These children can remember family and friends from a time before they were born."

I approached the set and turned it off but Oprah kept talking. I grabbed the electric cord, yanked it hard, and found that the television wasn't even plugged in.

"You go, girl!" the television blared, and then shut off abruptly. I took another taste of the pink.

"It's me..." Oprah told a child in a body cast. She was standing over him in his hospital room, and his mother wept as Oprah shook the boy's fingers, the only part of his body that wasn't sheathed in plaster. "It's me...Oprah."

I walked to the bathroom and washed Ms. Winfrey off my hands; I turned the bottle upside down over the toilet.

The capsules floated in the blue water; they bobbed up and down inside the bowl for a long time before I gathered up the nerve to flush.

WITHDRAWAL, POP MUSIC

There was a specter haunting the end of the twentieth century, a specter that I'd always known but couldn't name. But, once I flushed Oprah Winfrey, suddenly I knew the words. I watched pink powder swirl in the toilet, listened to the sucking sound, and remembered the lyrics to every Top Forty pop song released between 1980 and 1984: Purple Rain, Too Shy, Stray Cat Strut, The Safety Dance, I Melt with You, Hello, Cars, Down Under, 99 Luftballoons...

Every single scrap of Pop Music, including Pop Muzak, was playing across my brain, and all of it made sense.

Video killed more than the radio star, I realized. I wanted a new drug, but had to whip it. Someone was watching me, and they'd blinded me with science.

I sat down on the tiled floor, and tried to clear my head of the politics of dancing.

"Just say no," I told myself. "Just say no."

Slowly, and amidst a cacophony of inner pop, I cleared my medicine cabinet. One by one I dumped the contents of the brown bottles into the toilet, and flushed.

"I'm still standing," I said, staring into the mirror and trying to recognize the face that stared back at me. It was a young face, unmarked by time. I was changing, like a microwave oven, but I kept going, kept flushing.

"Let's go crazy," I told the young man that looked back at me from the mirror. "Burning down the house."

DRIVING SINCE THE SEVENTIES?

"I think time must have stopped before we were born," I say.

"Oh, gag. Spare me." Cindy rolls down the passenger window and flicks her ash. She's smoking cigarettes, even though she doesn't...or didn't used to, or isn't going to, smoke.

"How do I look?" Cindy asks. She pulls up the bottom of her shirt and ties a knot under her breasts, and I find that I've got another erection. I wish that I'd grabbed her when I'd had my chance in the motel.

"You look good," I said. "Sexy."

"Thanks." She takes another hit off the cigarette and leans back, resting her elbow half out the window.

"But you're not listening," I said. "This static feeling has been going on for a long time. Since the seventies for sure."

"Whatever," Cindy says.

ORANGE POWDER AND RONALD REAGAN

I made myself dinner, boxed macaroni and cheese, and watched Big Bird on television as I waited for Cindy to come home from work. I watched *Sesame Street* because the cable wasn't connected anymore.

"This is the year 1980. You're in the wrong time," Big Bird said.

"I'm cursed. I can't return to my own time, to my mother and father, to my Egypt, until the curse is lifted," some kid pharaoh explained.

It was a rerun. It was the episode where Big Bird gets lost in the Metropolitan Museum of Art.

I stirred orange powder and margarine into the noodles and sat down in front of the television set. Was the apartment regressing? It was impossible to tell, everything Cindy and I had was old to begin with.

"Will you help me solve the riddle?" the prince asked.

I was afraid to eat my dinner. I read the list of ingredients on the back of the box, and worried that the orange powder might have gone bad.

After *Sesame Street* and the pledge break I switched over to NBC. The network didn't come in perfectly, but after adjusting the antenna I could just make out what it was I was seeing.

The presidential debates were on. Walter Mondale and Ronald Reagan were going to have it out on taxes, defense spending, and the death penalty. I watched the fuzz build up on the screen, the reception wavering, and waited for the candidates to be announced.

The front door creaked as it opened and I could hear the sound of Cindy's keys jangling as she put them down on the front table.

"Hello?" she asked as she stood in the front hall. "Who's there?"

"I'm watching television," I said.

Cindy didn't take off her raincoat but stepped into the front room, dripping onto the hardwood floor. She unzipped her coat, and I could see that she was dressed in her usual khaki skirt and green turtleneck, but she looked odd. She looked false, too young for her outfit.

"What are you doing here?" she asked.

"I told you. I'm watching TV."

Ronald Reagan ambled up to his podium, smiled at the audience, and flipped through his notes. Walter Mondale's podium remained vacant.

"Well, I'm glad you asked that," Reagan said. Nobody had asked a question yet, and Mondale's podium was still empty.

"There you go again..."

"Mr. President," one of the journalists on the panel interrupted. "Mr. President."

"I refuse to make age an issue in this campaign," Ronald Reagan said. "I don't want to take unfair advantage of my opponent's youth and inexperience."

"Mr. President, the opponent has not...Mr. Mondale has not arrived."

"Well, I..."

Cindy stood in front of the television screen, waving her hands in front of my face; she was insistent. "What do you want?"

"Well, I..." Ronald Reagan said.

Cindy turned off the television and crossed her arms. "What are you doing here?"

"I have something..." I started.

Cindy brushed her fingers through her damp hair and sighed a put-upon sigh.

"I have something to show you."

MS. PAC-MAN AND THE MEN IN BLACK

It only took a few hours for Cindy to come down. She'd been skipping her medication, forgetting her schedule, for days already. She told me how much I'd hurt her, told me that she wasn't sure she wanted to see me anymore. I agreed with everything she said, but I didn't leave. I told her I wanted to talk it out, and I waited for the drugs to wear off.

Without drugs Portland was different. The light rail system was gone, and instead of Starbucks, Blockbuster, and the Gap, there was a record shop, a sports bar, and a 7-Eleven. And nobody looked right, everyone had big hair.

Cindy started to get dizzy, she saw streaks of color. She said she wanted something cold to drink.

"Do I want a Slurpee?" Cindy asked. "Yes. I want a Slurpee."

An electric chime sounded as we entered the convenience store.

"Do you have an espresso machine?" I asked the clerk.

"No."

"Not a real espresso machine, but one of those automatic jobs with the stale coffee and the chemicals? You know, one of those cappuccino machines?" I asked.

"Are you on drugs?" the kid asked, quite seriously.

"See anything different?" I asked Cindy. "Anything seem strange?"

"I want a Slurpee," Cindy said.

There were two video games in the far corner, Donkey Kong and Ms. Pac-Man. Two men in business suits were hunched over the controls.

"Are you on drugs?" the kid behind the counter asked. "Are you voters?"

"One Slurpee, please."

"Get it yourself," the kid said.

I went to the back of the store, and while I filled a paper cup with red slush I watched the video game screens. Pixels of light dashing around. I closed my eyes and listened to the repetitive music and bonking noises.

"What's up, Mister?" one of the men asked. He'd stopped playing and was coming my way. He was about six feet tall and he wore a black suit, a silver badge, and almost no expression. "You okay?"

A pink ghost devoured Ms. Pac-Man and the game ended.

"How's your girlfriend? She feeling a little woozy?" the man asked.

"She'll be all right."

But they didn't let it alone. The man playing Donkey Kong stopped. He stepped back from his machine.

"You know what time it is?" the Donkey Kong player asked.

"It's a little after ten."

"What year is it?" the Ms. Pac-Man player asked.

"I don't know."

The Ms. Pac-Man player grabbed my elbows and pulled my arms behind my back. He spun me around and forced my face down onto the glass surface of the video game maze. The top players' initials flashed across my cheek. FUC, BLT, and CDL held the high scores.

"Take a guess."

"I'd say maybe 1983 or '84," I said.

"I'll get the girl," the Donkey Kong player said.

The Ms. Pac-Man agent slammed my face against the glass again, and I was afraid the screen would break, but then he pulled me up and looked me in the eyes.

"You stopped taking your medicine, didn't you?" the Donkey Kong man asked Cindy as he pulled her over, sent her sprawling against the Slurpee machine.

"You need to start over," the Ms. Pac-Man agent said. He grabbed my arm and tore my shirtsleeve open.

He held the syringe up in front of me, showed me the symbol printed on the side. The Starbuck's mermaid smiled from the needle.

"You said before that you wanted some espresso," the Donkey Kong man asked.

"No," I said. "Not really."

"That's what you said."

"I'll have an iced latte," Cindy said. Her eyes were dull, unfocused. "Or a Slurpee?"

"Just sit down and the barista will make you a grande iced latte," the Ms. Pac-Man agent said. And he plunged the needle into my arm.

I sat down on the tile floor and listened to the sounds from the games: I head Donkey Kong shake the rafters. I heard Ms. Pac-Man as she consumed the dots.

A CUP OF COFFEE AND THE MORNING PAPER

I was drinking a double mocha and chewing a stale scone when I came back to consciousness. What year was it? The air conditioning and natural lighting confused me as I looked around for some sort of clue. It looked like it was morning already.

"When is it?" I asked.

"What?" Cindy asked. She was sipping an iced latte and tearing a paper napkin into little bits.

I went to the counter, to the newspaper rack, and bought a copy of *USA Today*. It was dated January 23, 2000, but the front page photograph was of Ronald Reagan. "His legacy lives on in campaign 2000," the caption read.

I used my visa card, signed my name on the dotted line.

What year was it? It was impossible to tell. *USA Today* reported corporate mergers and the deregulation of television and quotes from the campaign trail, but it didn't mention whether Donald Duck was seventy or eighty-six. Madonna was making a movie, the Back Street Boys were at the top of the charts, and George Bush was not going to apologize even though he was very sorry.

I flipped through the paper and drank my mocha, but the news didn't help me decide anything.

"I'm thirsty," Cindy said.

THE CRATER

My apartment building was gone, the whole street was missing. Instead there was a giant crater and a few shards of glass. Even the foundation was gone.

"What year are we in?" I asked.

"This is where you live?"

"There was a building," I said.

"It's two thousand and something," Cindy said.

"What?"

"It's 2001."

"Yeah, only the paper said it was 2000. We're still a year off," I said. "Do you remember the man with the syringe?"

Cindy shook her head no, and then kneeled down and started sorting through the gravel. She found a rusty nail, a silver lighter, a bicentennial quarter, and a piece of a Rubik's Cube. The red and green stickers were burnt around the edges.

"Remember? At the 7-Eleven?"

"How is this helping?" Cindy asked. "Who cares what year it is anyway?"

"Maybe there was a war."

"What do you mean?" Cindy asked.

"I don't know. Maybe there was a nuclear war. Maybe we're all dead."

Cindy flipped the bicentennial quarter, it came up heads. She peeled off the green sticker from the piece of Rubik's Cube. "You're dead the moment you start thinking like this. You're dead the moment you break the routine. Dead. Deranged. Done."

"A lot of people live without the routine. Lots of people are unmedicated."

"Nonvoters," Cindy said. "We're nonvoters now."

COLD TURKEY MERRY-GO-ROUND

That night we stayed in the office, hid in my cubicle. We drank instant soups out of paper cups and tried to distract each other with games like Twenty Questions and Name That Tune, but both of us kept thinking about pills.

Cindy and I were withdrawing again.

"When I was about five years old my father, my real father and not my Dad, took me to an amusement park," Cindy said. "He wanted to ride the merry-go-round, but I didn't want to."

"Who sang that song about talking in your sleep?" I asked. "Was that the Romantics?"

Cindy didn't answer, but turned her head away and grabbed a plastic wastebasket. She vomited up chunks of noodles, brown meat.

"Are you okay?" I asked.

"Oh Christ," she said, wiping her mouth with her woolen sleeve. "I'm all rubbery. I can't decide if I'm hot or cold."

She was bright red, and hot to the touch.

"I'll get you some water."

"Why don't we take a pill. Shouldn't we just take a pill?" she asked.

"No."

Cindy wiped her mouth, took another sip of cold soup, and started again.

She fiddled with my solar calculator, turned it upside down and spelled out "BOOB" and "hEll."

"I was terrified of the rides, all of them. I just stared at the different machines and cried," she said.

"What?"

"When my Dad took me to the amusement park."

"Oh, yeah."

"But the worst one, the worst ride was the merry-go-round. There were these miniatures along the top of it, wooden figurines of Dutch girls that rotated back and forth as the ride turned, and I thought that the dolls were real. I convinced myself that they were the shrunken bodies of the children the merry-go-round didn't like."

The office was different; there was a dome-shaped light sitting on top of a swatch of red carpet where there had been a FAX machine. And there were no computers anywhere.

"Listen to me," Cindy said. She squeezed my hand and I sat back down, only realizing after the fact that I'd been about to leave.

"Listen," she said. "It wasn't so much that I thought I'd be turned into wood, it was more like I thought I was already up there," Cindy said. "I imagined that I was already made of wood, that I was just a doll."

I took another sip of soup, and burned my tongue. The soup was hot; it had cooled, but now it was steaming again.

"He, my dad, decided to ride by himself. He said that he was going to have fun, that he was going to show me that there was nothing to be afraid of," Cindy said. "And I just knew that he would die, that he would freeze solid and the park people would have to find a spot for him up there, up with the Dutch girls in their wooden dresses. And I knew he wouldn't really fit."

"But he didn't die. He didn't die and everything was fine."

"Didn't he?" Cindy asks.

I didn't say anything. I was too busy vomiting into the plastic wastebasket.

"I don't remember what happened after that, it was a long time ago."

"It wasn't as long ago as you think," I said.

STREET FUTURE

In the morning we decided to leave town. Cindy's Yugo was parked in front of the high school, about two blocks away from my office.

A teenage boy, a punk kid wearing army pants and a pink muscle shirt, was sitting on her car. He was cross-legged on the trunk and smoking a cigarette when we arrived.

"Move it kid," I said.

"Who are you supposed to be, my grandpa?"

"Just get down from there," I said.

"You in the present?" he asked. "You need some future?"

"Come on, we've got to go," I grabbed his arm and started to drag him off of the trunk. Cindy grabbed my wrist, and shook me loose from him.

"Wait," she said, "he's trying to help us out."

"Listen to your lady. I'm not loitering, I'm talking business," he said. He took another drag off his cigarette and then flicked it into the street.

"What kind of business?" I asked.

"You know that future everybody says won't ever get here? Well, this is it." He held out a joint, a vial of some pinkish crystals, and a few capsules.

"I don't want any," I said. I grabbed Cindy's hand and tried to loosen her grip on my other arm.

"Look at yourself; look at your lady. She's hurting, needing. You two aren't going anywhere without a fix."

"Yeah?"

"You're a voter, right? The year two thousand and all that?" he asked.

"Sure," I said. "I guess."

"You've been doing the wrong stuff, that's all. They've got you hooked on all kinds of bullshit. Listen, I'm not selling their future," he said. "I've got the year 2000 in this vial, the real 2000 with flying cars and Art Deco and robots. This is the shit," he said.

"Flying cars?" I asked.

"And robots," he said.

"How much is it?" Cindy asked. "How much do you want."

ON THE ROAD

We're like tourists. We stop at rest areas and roadside diners and take pictures of asphalt and urinals and neon signs that read "no vacancy." Except now I can't wait for the next exit ramp, I can't keep driving anymore. I pull over at random, stop on the shoulder of I-5 and get out.

I lean inside the car and turn on the emergency blinkers.

"What are you doing?" Cindy asks. "Somebody might stop for us."

I lean back inside and turn off the blinker, but before I pull myself out again I flip on the radio. Boy George is singing "I'll Tumble 4 Ya," and I spin the dial.

"Get the camera while you're in there," Cindy tells me.

I hand it over and Cindy takes a picture of the highway in front of us. I put my arm around her and pull her to me. I want to be as close to her as possible. I want to live happily ever after.

We get back in the car and just sit for a minute, unsure what to do next.

"Let's smoke some more," Cindy says. She holds up the vial and starts to unscrew the top.

"You sure?"

Cindy doesn't reply, but pulls out a metal pipe, takes a hit, and then passes it over to me.

I watch pink smoke fill the front of the car, and then take a drag myself. With water in my eyes I decide to go again, to continue. I put the key in the ignition, listen to the engine turn over, and press down on the gas.

Cindy rolls down the passenger window and peers out, looking through the lens. "Smile," she says to the flat landscape, the patches of brown weeds and barbed wire fencing.

The tires lift up from the road, and I watch the gas gauge transform into an altitude gauge. I take another hit off the pipe and lean back in the ultra-conforming gelatin-lined driver's seat.

We float away, zip off toward the horizon, and Cindy presses down on the button of her instamatic, takes a snapshot of the ground as we lift away from it.

"Smile," she says.

ON A SCALE OF ONE TO THREE

Please indicate your level of agreement with the following statements on a scale of one to three where one equals a firm Yes, two equals Maybe, and three is a firm No.

1. "I sometimes find myself laughing at other people's misfortunes, even though I'm not very proud of that reaction. Maybe it's just a way of saying 'There but for the grace of God go I.' "

One, two, or three?

Ronald Reagan was the president, Van Halen's suicidal anthem "(Go ahead) Jump" was at the top of the charts, and I was fourteen years old and afraid. What I feared most was a sudden burst of light—a light brighter than the sun—and a roar of radioactive wind.

I was obsessed. Over a breakfast of Cream of Wheat, or during a family argument about my grades, I would find myself freezing. I would simply stop and listen for the blast. Waiting for the heat and then the quick disintegration, I would pause.

My mother worried that I had a personality disorder.

2. "People tell me that I express myself in an odd way—that I say things that are too deep for them, or that I don't explain what I mean."

One, two, or three?

In the summer of 1984 my parents decided we needed a family vacation. My father would take a break from his arthritic patients, and we would leave town for a couple of weeks. They decided to do something about my personality problem, my obsession, by renting a Winnebago and setting off for the Trinity test site in Los Alamos, New Mexico.

"The blast, as you'll see, was small. Certainly not apocalyptic in size," my father told me.

"They'd be bigger now. It's a matter of megatons versus kilotons," I said.

"They've got gift shops by the blast site. The radiation is long gone. You can even buy souvenirs made from the melted sand. You'll see."

A 165-pound man standing in the open one mile from a half-megaton nuclear explosion would absorb ten thousand rems of initial nuclear radiation, would be seared by heat amounting to 500 calories per square centimeter, and would be sent flying through the air by the blast wave at a rate of well over 100 feet per second.

3. "I don't believe in feeling guilty about what I've done. There's nothing to be gained from it. 'Don't look back'—that's my motto."

One, two, or three?

The Winnebago was huge. A full kitchen, two tables in the center, a toilet, and even a cable television hook up was contained inside the plastic walls of my parent's rented road slug. We took off for Los Alamos with the air conditioning on full blast. As we sped towards the Trinity test site at forty miles per hour the only sounds were from the air vents. I demanded complete radio silence. I was frozen, listening.

4. "I don't like spending time alone, and I avoid it as much as possible."

One, two, or three?

Years later, after the Cold War was over, I would still be obsessed. Even without nuclear Armageddon hanging over me, I would still find ways to stop, find reasons to freeze in my tracks. I would look up at the sky and worry about flying saucers, I would think about the ozone, or I would simply stop and listen to my own heart beating.

When I was fourteen I had Reagan, I had the button, and my panic attacks made sense.

5. "Emotionally I am a very calm person. I seldom have strong feelings of any kind—angry, miserable, or ecstatic."

One, two, or three?

Outside of the San Cristobal reservation our road slug took up two parking spaces at a rest stop diner. We left our diet sodas and bags of potato chips in the trailer. We switched over to burgers and fries.

Over this lunch of fried meat and iceberg lettuce I informed my parents that the military often illegally dumped radioactive waste on Indian reservations.

"The only good Indian is a dead Indian," my father joked. He loved to rattle me with nigger jokes and other racist quips, even as he voted against Ronald Reagan. He'd get my blood boiling and then point out that it was he, not I, who'd marched on Washington with Martin Luther King, Jr.

"The Native Americans are getting a free ride from our tax dollars. I have trouble feeling sympathetic or guilty about their supposed plight," my mother said. She wasn't kidding.

I looked around furtively, afraid that the locals would shower us with tomahawks and poisoned arrows.

6. "Even though I'm not sure I should be, I find myself fascinated by violence, weapons, and the martial arts. I like films and TV shows with a lot of action and violence in them."

One, two, or three?

On the streets of Alma, New Mexico, there was an odd mix of upscale restaurants and small gas stations with rusted storage tanks.

My parents and I were exiting one of the restaurants when we caught sight of two old Hispanic women huddled together by the gutter. One was squatting over the curb and vomiting blood into a drainage grate while the other grimaced and watched.

Neither woman spoke English, but their pleas for help were obvious enough.

"Honey?" my mother asked.

"What?" my dad replied.

"Don't you think you'd better…"

Dad shrugged and approached the two women; he gestured towards the woman whose white sweater was slowly turning pink, and leaned over to listen to her chest—to her pounding heart. Dad smiled, glanced up at the woman, and then stepped back as she began retching again.

"Hospital?" my father asked.

"Mucho penoso," the woman replied between heaves.

"Haas-pit-tall," my father repeated to the woman in the gray sweater whose wide eyes and nodding head indicated anything but comprehension, and then gestured to the sick woman and started over.

"Donde hospital?" my father asked.

"Muy lejos," the old woman in the gray sweater said.

The sick woman agreed, her vomiting subsiding for a moment. "Muy lejos!" the sick woman said and then began to hyperventilate.

"Donde hospital?" my father asked. He leaned over again and, careful not to brush against any blood, put his ear to the sick woman's chest again. "Go to the hospital," my dad said.

"Médico?" the woman in the gray sweater asked, and pointed at my father.

"Yes," my father said.

"Hospital muy lejos!" the woman in the gray sweater said, emphatic now.

"Right. Take her to the hospital."

Dad ambled back over to us.

"What's wrong?" I asked.

"Oh, well—she's just having a small heart attack. If you guys want to go to a movie tonight we'll have to hurry. Los Alamos is still two hours away, and it's almost seven."

The sick woman was vomiting again, gushing. Dad turned towards them and tried to wave them away.

"Hospital. Get her to the hospital," he commanded. And then we left, getting into our rented slug, slowly backing out onto the street and then speeding forward and away.

7. "I believe that in some situations you may have to step on someone else's toes to get where you're going."

Yes, no, or maybe?

The first atomic bomb was tested at 5:29:45 A.M. Mountain War Time on July 16, 1945. The bomb tested released a 19-kiloton explosion in the desert outside of Los Alamos.

Included on our Trinity Site tour was Ground Zero—the spot where the atomic bomb was placed on a 100-foot steel tower and then turned into a mushroom cloud. A small monument marked the spot. This monument was surrounded by a chain-link fence and this fence was marked by a small yellow sign which indicated that the area was radioactive.

There were also green balls of melted sand at Ground Zero, but these weren't for sale. In fact our tour guide told us that the green glass was still hot (radioactive), and wasn't to be touched or picked up.

So there was no gift shop, but there were portable toilet facilities available, and hot dogs and sodas were sold from vending carts in the parking lot.

My dad brought a camera, which technically was allowed, but the camera seemed to make the soldiers nervous. The men working on the White Sands Missile Range sneered at us from behind barbed wire, and they would scream at us if Dad pointed the camera in the wrong direction. After awhile our tour guide asked Dad to put the camera way.

Still, I felt safer after walking through the blast site. I came to believe that the bomb was a part of history, and I felt that nukes, like lightning, could never strike in the same place twice.

8. "Occasionally I make up stories or distort the truth, just to see how other people will react. Sometimes the truth is too much to bear."

Yes? No? Can you even tell the difference anymore? Can anyone?

Calculate your total score as follows:

In columns A, B, and C count the number of Yes answers, No answers, and Maybe answers. Transfer these numbers to appropriate boxes. Multiply by two.

THE SEA MONKEY CONSPIRACY

I was eighteen years old, a freshman at Eckerd College, but rather than undergoing dream analysis or guided regression, I was instructed to play. The graduate student pulled out a trunk of therapeutic toys: wooden horses, flexible plastic people, a toy house with green shutters and a doorbell that would ring if you pressed the button vigorously.

I made the Papa doll watch television while the Mama doll did the dishes and the boy doll slowly and deliberately took apart the moorings of the house. The frame collapsed, folding in on itself, and I stepped back and pondered.

"Why did that happen?" the graduate assistant asked. She wrote something on her clipboard and pulled a lock of hair back behind her ear. "Why did the boy do that?"

"He doesn't believe in the house," I said.

"Why doesn't he believe in the house?"

"Because it isn't real. Look, it's just a toy. See? I can take it apart here, and there's this corner that moves out like this, and that's not supposed to happen in a real house," I said. I moved over to the color form set. "Do you have anything else I can break?"

The graduate student smiled and then handed me a remote control. I was left alone to watch television and doodle.

I watched CNN and CSPAN and the network news shows on videotape, and I wrote down my responses, my feelings, just like they asked.

"Smart bombs don't take good pictures," I wrote.

Next there were clips from *Mr. Roger's Neighborhood*, *Sesame Street*, and *3,2,1 Contact*.

"I'm special," I wrote.

"X is for X-ray."

"Fish can only live underwater."

***

The road trip to Eckerd College felt more like a family vacation than a goodbye. Despite the physical fact of the three of us jammed in with my steamer trunk, my desktop computer, and a few dozen books, we weren't really together.

We stayed at Holiday Inns and Best Westerns. Each room smelled of air freshener and every room had a balcony and was near the swimming pool or the ice machine.

We took turns in the bathroom, took turns at the gift shops, took turns reading bestsellers or watching golf tournaments on cable TV.

"You understand that this will be tougher than the army?" my father asked. He turned back from the wheel, glanced at me in the back seat, surprised me with his attention.

"What?"

"You'll have to really apply yourself. If you'd joined the army it would have been easier, but now you'll have to apply yourself, make your own way," Dad said.

He'd never told me that he wanted me to join the army. My father was a psychiatrist with a private practice in Denver, not a military man.

"I should have joined the army?" I asked.

"It was an option," Dad said.

"Not one that I ever considered."

"Well, it's too late now."

I bought some postcards and a *Writer's Digest* magazine at a 7-Eleven in Nevada. All of the postcards were the same. There was a faked photograph of a rabbit with antlers on the front, and a description of the species "Jackalope" on the back. I filled out each card, sent the same message back to every friend and acquaintance.

This is me. I'm an exotic species rarely seen except by drunks and small children.

I tried to think about creative writing, about the degree I'd be working for once I arrived. I read my *Writer's Digest* and was assured that I could find the right agent, informed that I could sell my magazine articles, and admonished to protect my intellectual property rights.

"Hey, Dad, did you know that every story has to have characters?" I asked the front seat.

My father didn't reply, but turned on the air. We were almost there, had already crossed the Florida State line, and the humidity was oppressive.

"You could have joined the army," Dad said. "I told you that. I know I told you that."

"Mom, what is he talking about?"

"You know very well what your father is saying."

"Yes, but I don't know why," I said.

And they, both of them, relaxed. I'd said the right thing, for once. Dad turned on the radio, spun the dial until he found something upbeat and bouncy. Dad blasted Salsa music out the back speakers, keeping me from asking him what he'd meant, keeping me from asking anything.

***

When I signed up for the study I didn't think it had anything to do with me. The psychology department was offering a hundred dollars a week if I'd tell them what I thought of the situation in the Persian Gulf and attend some therapy sessions.

That sounded easy enough. I was against the coming war, against wars in general, but I didn't feel strongly about it. I just liked the idea of studying for exams during the day and then stopping off at the psychology department to fill out forms and look at inkblots.

I signed up, agreed that the university was not responsible for any physical or psychological injuries I might sustain during my participation in the study, and it wasn't until the package with the Sea Monkeys and John Philip Sousa LP arrived in my mailbox, wasn't until the cartoon missiles flew across maps of the Middle East on television, that I knew I'd made a mistake.

***

I opened the official Sea Monkey Handbook, skipped past the explanation of their origins, and followed the instructions.

The first step was to add the water purifier, the package of dust that would neutralize the poisonous metal oxides from the plumbing. I tore the packet open with my teeth, dumped the contents, and then stirred with the plastic feeding spoon that came with the tank.

Sousa's "Stars and Stripes Forever" played on my old turntable; majestic trumpets sounded as I read aloud from the Sea Monkey Handbook:

Now that you've completed the first step, your MAGICAL MOMENT is about to begin. You will now bring the Sea Monkeys to life!

I poured the contents of packet number two, the dehydrated Sea Monkey eggs, into the miniature tank and waited for instant life.

And waited.

I looked down at the manual again.

You must let the water purify in stillness for thirty hours before proceeding to step two.

"Stars and Stripes Forever" reached a crescendo and I blushed.

I'd killed the Sea Monkeys.

***

Frannie was skeptical as she lay down on my cot, pulled off her short-haired blonde wig, and ran her fingers through her own spiky copper colored hair. She was an art student working on an MFA in photography and she lived upstairs.

We'd spent a lot of time together in the first few weeks. Having both arrived a day ahead of schedule, the only students on campus that first day, we'd strolled along the inlets and docks near campus, explored the concrete bunkers that made up the college itself, and ended up in a sort of romance.

There were no ivy-covered halls at Eckerd, no hundred-year-old brick buildings with famous quotations etched along the latticework; instead there were concrete boxes with metal stairs up the sides. Eckerd was a generic place, an anonymous institution. Only the palm trees and the tough, tall grass made it tolerable.

"It's not an appealing place," Frannie said.

"You don't think so?"

"How did we end up here?"

"Did you go to high school?" I asked back.

"Yes."

"Me too…I think that was our mistake."

We went to pick up our mail, not that we expected there'd be any. The mailboxes were by the front gate; one whole wall of the student center was taken up with mailboxes, rows and rows all the way to the ground.

"How will people with the lower boxes open their mail during the winter?" I asked Frannie.

"What?"

"How will people get their mail when it snows?"

"When it snows?"

I was out of my element in Florida, and by the second month I was sunburned and nauseous. I was sunburned, nauseous, and paranoid.

"Why would the psychology department send you Sea Monkeys?" Frannie asked as she lay across my cot and pulled off her wig.

"Why would they send John Hinckley a copy of *The Catcher in the Rye*? Why would they flash subliminal pictures of skeletons during the *Late Show*?"

"Are you really telling me this, or is this one of your story ideas?" Frannie asked.

"I don't know. Can this kind of thing really happen?"

But I knew it could happen, had happened. At the university library there were hundreds of documented examples, case histories of CIA and psychiatric experiments that utilized exactly the kinds of technologies and techniques I'd experienced. Tape loops, psychedelics, electric shock, isolation, and so on…

The real question was whether this could be happening to me.

Was my mind not my own? Was my life, despite its mediocrity, directed by others?

***

I was working on a word puzzle, searching for "aspirate" and "phosphorous" in the jumble of letters that the new graduate student provided me. This one was older than the others were, in his late twenties he looked more like a professor than a student, but once the session started it became clear that he was just working for his degree like all the rest. He was following orders, reading from the prepared script.

I clicked my pen, tapped my teeth with the inky end, and listened to him read from his clipboard.

"Since World War II the United States has been the primary global power. This, in itself, is an explanation of its role as a source of global terrorism," he said.

" 'Annihilate,' " I said as I found the word.

"Despite a national ideology that includes protection of human rights, equality, and freedom, the United States has employed censorship, murder, and torture to protect the national interest."

" 'Contagious,' " I said.

The letters were clearing a path for me. The words emerged, one by one, as I listened to the grad student. It was remarkably easy.

" 'Jingoism.' "

"What the neocolonial project relies on, what must be delicately maintained at home and brutally enforced abroad, is a complacent public. What must be suppressed, if our democracy is to survive, are demands for participation in the decision-making process." The student paused, took a sip of diet cola, and looked up at me, noticing my progress.

" 'Invertebrate.' "

"Good," he said. "You can stop searching now. Just listen. 'There is no contradiction between the national ideology of freedom and the practical reality of US aggression. Rather, these discrepancies merely reflect the complexity of true democracy, the ambiguity of freedom.' "

"Ambiguity of freedom."

"When you go back to your dorm you are to take notes. Please watch the evening news on channel four and take notes," the student said, and then flipped the page on his clipboard. "Now, think about the Sea Monkeys and be very quiet."

I did as he asked. I pictured the Monkeys twirling around in their tank, bouncing to the music of the graduate student's voice. Sea Monkeys danced to US atrocities.

***

"Take my picture." Frannie handed me her 32mm camera.

We were standing outside the Federal building, mingling with the street protesters and banners. We were in the thick of the dissent, mingling with the "No Blood for Oil" signs, but only so Frannie could get her homework done. The protest was just another assignment.

"Take my picture," Frannie demanded.

I aimed, looked through the lens. Frannie was dressed like a secretary from a Hitchcock film, like a Norma Jean or an Audrey Hepburn, and somehow the giant puppets and magic marker signs in the background complimented her pose.

She stared up into the sky and I zoomed in; framing her skeptical but frightened face with skyscrapers.

"Now you should dress up like a French maid," I tell her.

"Okay."

"No, wait. Put on the bikini and smoke a cigarette."

She stripped mechanically and in full view, right out of her underwear, and then stepped into the yellow bikini bottom and pulled the top across her chest. She grabbed her purse and fished out a package of Virginia Slims. The anti-war people closest to us, a couple of post-hippie kids in Birkenstocks and tattoos, seemed to forget their militant rage as they stopped chanting and gawked.

"Do I look like an advertisement?" Frannie asked.

"You do, only you should spread your legs and take a strap off your shoulder."

"Okay. Now take my picture."

***

The hypnagogic images were not my own:

Vietnamese refugees pounded by US bombs, hundreds of Panamanians summarily executed, Nicaraguan children blown to bits by a US-sponsored attack on an elementary school, all of it runs through my mind as an abstract. Without persistent guidance from the graduate student, without her narration, I wouldn't be able to distinguish one atrocity from another.

I woke up at the airport, found myself sitting in an orange plastic seat, watching 747s land and take off. I had a gun in my hand. It wasn't concealed, it was sitting in my lap and I fingered the safety, flipping it on and off.

To my left the student, this one an attractive blonde in a denim skirt, was talking to a man in a black suit; a fat officious man who looked uncomfortable in his clothes.

He listened to the student's questions, shrugged, and then glanced over at me. He pointed me out to the blonde student, told her that I was awake again.

"What are you doing up?" the girl asked me.

"Hmmmm?"

"The Sea Monkeys—," she started.

"I'm tired of the Sea Monkeys."

"The Sea Monkeys are swimming," she said.

More men in black suits clustered around me, about five or six of them, all of them pointing at me and reaching for their pockets.

"I'll play with the Sea Monkeys," I said.

"Good," the student said. She made a hash mark on her clipboard. "Good."

"I'll play," I said.

***

Sousa's "The Liberty Bell" was the theme song for Monty Python's Flying Circus, and I couldn't listen to it without laughing, without imagining a Giant Foot falling from the sky and squashing the orchestra.

I filled the tank again, dumped in the water-purifying powder, and waited. I put the miniature tank on the windowsill and waited for the oxides to be defeated, for the impurities to dissolve.

I loaded my 32-caliber pistol as "The Liberty Bell" came to an end. The next number was the "Star Spangled Banner."

I like Sea Monkeys. I've always liked them.

When I was a little kid I thought the Sea Monkeys represented the perfect family—smiling, smooth, and royal. When I was eleven what I noticed was the strangeness of their bodies; the way their cartoon arms had no joints and how the red freckles, the spots, decorated their bodies. Later on, when I was twelve or thirteen the fact of their neutered nakedness was what fascinated me most. But all along there were the King Monkey, the Queen Monkey, and the Prince floating on the back of my Captain America and X-Men comic books. They were always perfect, perfectly smooth.

I fantasized about them, wanted to be a Sea Monkey, thought I secretly was a Sea Monkey. My father, I convinced myself, was actually the King or President of Atlantis, my mother, of course, was the Queen. We were hiding in the United States, in disguise, but one day our fins would reemerge, our tails would sprout, and we would dive back into the Atlantic Ocean. We would return to our depths.

Or, I was the son of the King of Atlantis, but my family didn't know it. I was somehow switched at birth, abandoned with this terrestrial family, but would one day be reclaimed by the Monkeys.

***

Frannie and I were in bed, crammed together in my small cot, wrapped in bed sheets. Sweating, uncomfortably rearranging ourselves, tangling and untangling, we were both fully dressed. Both of us shy and unyielding.

"They say I'm making progress," Frannie said.

But, this disclosure came late.

We'd been wrapped together for hours, and I was tired; tired of listening to her questions and answers about the war, tired of our guilt. Each time she put her mouth against my ear I'd start, grow erect, and then she'd whisper words like "Napalm," or "Hiroshima," and I'd close my eyes again, feigning sleep.

"I'm getting rid of my exterior in order to make room for the facts. My therapist said it's normal, healthy even, to feel flat and false and to work on getting rid of your masks. She talks about masks a lot." Frannie said.

"She's not a therapist. She's just a student," I said. I kicked off my shoes, pulled at my collar, and then sat up to adjust the pillow.

Here's what Frannie said as she, finally, started to take off her clothes. Here's what Frannie said before she let me touch her that night, before we both gave in to each other.

"It's not enough to know the truth of our guilt. We have to be destroyed by it. They're going to make us into clean slates. We have to be clean slates."

I nodded as I pulled off my blue jeans.

"I'm making progress," Frannie said.

***

On August 2, 1991, Iraq invaded Kuwait.

John Philip Sousa was born on November 6,1854.

A Sea Monkey is a gift from modern science.

My creative writing professor read these sentences slowly and then turned my paper over, pretending to hunt for the rest. "Is that it?" he asked.

"Should there be more?"

"I would think there would be more."

"I tried to make every word count."

My instructor pulled on the sleeves of his tweed jacket and put the paper down. He looked around the room for a raised hand, and when he didn't find one he cleared his throat and looked at me expectantly.

I didn't say anything.

"It's very factual, I guess," he said.

"Except for the last sentence," I said.

"What?"

"The Sea Monkeys aren't necessarily a gift from science. That's opinion," I said. "That's just my opinion."

***

"How are you feeling?" the female graduate student asked.

"Captured."

"Sorry, but it's necessary."

The straight jacket was uncomfortable, but the student did press a button next to the glove compartment and my seat belt slackened and I leaned forward. I opened the glove compartment with my mouth, and a pile of tapes, unmarked black cassettes, fell into my lap.

"What are these?" I asked.

"We've been monitoring you while you write your reports about television," the student said. "Would you like to hear what you've been saying?"

She popped in one of the cassettes. "That's the CBS eye," a voice said. It was my voice. "That's Bugs Bunny in a dress."

"Listen, I'm going to untie you and then I'll be giving you a gun."

"Okay."

"Your target is coming in on flight 231."

"Is that where we're going now?" I asked. "The airport?"

"Yes."

"Why?"

"This is part of your therapy. This is going to help you feel better."

"Matlock is winning his case," my voice, preserved on magnetic tape, squeaked out from the van's speakers.

***

Frannie and I were at a coffee shop, a Coffee People where some friends of hers worked and we could get mochas for free. She was dressed like a seventies porn star, with a rainbow-colored halter-top and hip-hugging jeans.

"I'm thinking of dropping out of the photography department, out of school entirely," Frannie said.

"Why?"

"It's too humiliating," Frannie said. And then she told me about her dream.

***

It started with a toy, a talking robot with an eight-track voice that asked her personal questions and then rejected Frannie's answers.

"Is it true that you feel no guilt? Press the red button for Yes, blue for No, green for Maybe, and yellow if you don't understand the question," the robot instructed.

She was alone in the playroom, she was about three or four years old, and alone with the Legos and action figures and the little eight-track robot. She felt she'd been left alone with this robot every day for weeks, and every day she would press the wrong buttons, and she'd get a mild electric shock.

"Do you feel guilty when you're alone? Press the red button for Yes, blue for No…"

After weeks with the eight-track robot, weeks of interrogation in the guise of play, the machine was finally taken away.

"You're not making any progress this way," the man in the lab coat told her. "We're going to try something a little more extreme."

"Is it going to hurt?" she asked. A lot of what the man in the lab coat did to her hurt.

"That's up to you, Frannie. I'm going to let you play with any of these toys that you like. We're not going to test you anymore, and you can just play. But, we are going to leave this box in here with you, okay?" he asked, and then turned away before Frannie could answer. He walked toward the door and started stroking his beard and staring at his charts.

"What's in the box," she asked him.

"You're not to touch the box. Understand? Don't go near the box and you won't be punished," he said.

"Okay, but what's in it? Is it a present?"

"It's not for you," he said, and then he was out the door.

Somehow she knew that some kids leave the box alone at first. In the dream she imagined a kid coming to that little playroom for weeks and minding his own business for a long time. But she also knew that no kid could avoid the box forever.

She went for it right away.

It was a square box, just big enough to hold a coffee cup or a snow globe, and it was wrapped in paper with little fish symbols all over it. It didn't make any noise if you shook it, but the wrapping paper wasn't taped on and she thought she could probably unfold the outer layer and open the box without causing any damage. She could make her crime undetectable.

Inside there was nothing but darkness. She held the box up to the light, turned it upside down, but somehow it was impossible to see inside.

It occurred to her to put the box back, to refold the paper into place, and put the box back on its shelf and try to put the whole thing out of her mind. It was probably empty. It was obviously a trap.

But she reached inside, put a clenched fist down inside the cardboard, and then spread out her fingers.

***

"What was inside, Frannie? What do you find?" I asked.

"It's a trap. A rat trap. I spread out my fingers and hear a metallic snap, and then feel the pain and see the blood. After the trap goes off I can see into the box with ease. My small hand is stuck in a big mousetrap. My index and middle fingers are cut and bleeding and held fast," Frannie said.

***

I was always on the outside of my family. I was always at the periphery trying to figure out what was going on at the center.

When I was fourteen I went to Vail, Colorado, with my family. It was a business trip disguised as a vacation.

"I wonder who designed this resort," my father said to his colleague as we unloaded the station wagon, tightened our ski boots, and clomped off, heel to toe, for the gondola. "It's like something out of *Brave New World*," my dad said.

I dropped my skis in the snow and looked up at the wires and gondola cars as I struggled to get my equipment realigned and propped on my shoulder.

"You talk too much," my father's friend said. He was dressed in a black, skin-tight snowsuit; he looked like Jacques Cousteau or like some sort of high-tech soldier. His goggles were mirrored and his skis were thin and flexible, not downhill skis but cross-country. "You people in research talk too goddamned much."

"It's just an observation," my father said. His ski suit was the opposite of his colleague's with lots of padding and made of bright red fabric. "Ski resorts are, in themselves, interesting experiments in manipulation."

Dad's friend quickened his pace causing both of us to gallop clumsily behind him, stumbling and tilting back and forth as we tried to catch up.

"I come here every winter," dad's friend said, "and I come here of my own free will."

We reached the line for the gondola and dad fell silent. We made our way to the front, through the maze of people, the system of lines and checkpoints, and I watched the red and yellow gondola cars swing over our heads; watched the people step into each box, watched them spin off into empty air.

I stepped forward—heel to toe, heel to toe—and put my skis in place at the back of the gondola car. I turned to speak to my father, but he was still in line, watching me. He'd let me get ahead of them, let me go up on my own.

"I'll meet you at the top," my father said, and shrugged. "Mr. Jenkins wants to talk."

"What?" I asked, pretending I couldn't hear his instructions over the din of the machinery.

"Go on!" Dad yelled. "Go on!"

I opened the door to the gondola, stepped inside, and sat down on the metal bench to my right. I was alone inside a metal box, and I shuddered as one of the lift attendants stepped forward and closed the door.

I closed my eyes as the car was shifted onto the wire, as I was moved along and then jerked forward, into empty space.

***

Frannie was dressed up as a college student. She had a knapsack over her shoulder, a Yale University sweatshirt tied around her midriff, and a pair of torn jeans and a half T-shirt on. She wore a pair of Lennon-specs and bright red lipstick.

"My roommate is going out for the night," she said.

"Yeah?"

"I'm all alone," she said.

I took her picture, a shot of her perched at her desk, leaning on her desktop computer, and then watched as she started to undress. I put down the camera and went to her, put my arms around her waist and my lips on her neck.

"What are you doing?"

I didn't answer, but put my hand between her legs, underneath her unzipped jeans.

Frannie didn't say anything as I shoved her onto the cot, as I kissed her mouth and face. She didn't respond at all as I unbuttoned my own jeans and pulled off my own college sweatshirt.

I embraced her, took her breasts in my hands, and pressed up close.

Her skin was cold, covered in goose bumps. Her body was stiff, unyielding.

"What are you doing?" she asked.

And it dawned on me, finally. Frannie had been dressed up like a college student and I'd taken her picture. She'd started to undress but only so she could change into something else, into somebody else. It was just a part she was playing, the sexy coed, but I'd taken her seriously.

"Frannie?" I asked.

She didn't say anything, but got up and went to her dresser. She put on a terry cloth robe and unzipped her knapsack.

"I'm sorry," I said. "My timing is bad."

Frannie didn't reply but began to take off her make-up. She tore open a wetnap and ran the pad over her lips and cheeks. She took off her black-haired wig.

Finally, when her make-up was gone, when her lips were clean and nearly invisible, she looked in my direction.

"We're finished for today," she said. "I'm done."

"Frannie?"

She didn't even look at me.

***

The flight attendants unlocked the doors to the walkway and people ambled in from the landed plane. I watched them, tourists blankly staring past each other as they deplaned, husbands and wives returning from business trips who were surprised to discover that their families weren't there to greet them, and then the men in black suits behind them.

"Who should I shoot?" I asked.

"Do you think you're supposed to shoot somebody," the student asked me.

And then he stepped out from the gangway. He was just like the others, just a man in a black suit, but I knew that he was the one I was supposed to hit. It was my dad getting off the plane. I aimed my handgun at my father's head, and contemplated filling him with holes.

"Son," Dad says, "what have you gotten yourself mixed up in?"

"Are you my target? What's going on, Dad?"

"The Sea Monkeys are swimming," the student reminded me.

"How do you plan on setting up a control?" my father asked the student. "Are you going to find somebody else from the agency, enroll their kid, give them a gun, but not condition them?"

"You'll have to bring up your concerns with the department head," the student read from her clipboard. "We have a signed release absolving us of any responsibility," she said. And then she turned to me. "Shoot the target."

I raised the gun again, this time not aiming too carefully but pointing it in her direction, and pulled the trigger. The student flinched as the gun clicked away. There were no bullets.

"I can't believe the university funded this," Dad said. "Didn't we learn anything in the seventies?"

"You'll have to take up your concerns with the department head," the student repeated, but her heart wasn't in it. She was rubbing her forehead, examining the spot where the bullets would have penetrated her skull if there had been any bullets.

"Is this going to be discussed at the conference?" my father asked.

"We have a signed release absolving us of any responsibility."

Dad kneeled beside me, shook me hard, and tried to get me to hold his gaze. "What's the trigger phrase?" he asked.

"Sea Monkeys."

"Son, listen close. I'm going to tell you something about the Sea Monkeys that you need to understand," he said.

"I'm tired of Sea Monkeys."

"When you get back to your dorm the Sea Monkeys are going to tell you to call me. When you get back to the dorm you are to call me on my cell phone," Dad said.

"I almost shot you," I say.

"Never mind that. Just think about the Sea Monkeys."

***

Frannie was packed and waiting for traffic. She'd dressed in a plaid skirt and white blouse and in a long, light blonde wig. She stood at the curve in the highway, with her hands behind her back and a duffel bag at her feet, and I was reminded of the Beatles' song "She's Leaving Home." I was reminded of Natalie Wood in *Rebel Without a Cause*. She was going to hitch without using her thumbs, going to catch a ride based on a stereotype.

"You're not only leaving the university," I told her. "You're also leaving me."

"You'll take care of my plants?" she asked.

"I can't promise that."

"I have to leave. This is getting to be too much for me. I can't go on with this, with the program."

I take her hand in mine, and then grab her and pull her close, but she's stiff in my arms. Unmoved.

"What was that about?" she asked.

"I don't want you to go. I don't want you to leave me."

"Do you really think this is about us? Can you even remember what our relationship was like before the project?"

I couldn't. All I knew was that Frannie was my girlfriend and she was in the art department and I was supposed to help her with her thesis. I was supposed to take the pictures.

"I'm in love with you," I said.

"That's very nice, but I have to leave now. I'm going to get away and you're not going to stop me."

I had no intention of stopping her.

Frannie stood at the curve in the highway, with her hands behind her back and a duffel bag at her feet. I aimed my pocket camera at her back and pressed the button.

***

I watched CNN, CSPAN, and the Disney Channel and took notes in my green spiral notebook, just like I was instructed.

The victory parade makes me sick. Yellow ribbon, tanks, healthy white people eating hot dogs and waving flags, I watch this on television and wonder what it has to do with bombers, metal death, bulldozers.

Even Sousa is better than this.

Something was wrong with me. I wanted to tell the other students in the lounge, the kid with the green hair and Buddy Holly glasses or the one with the briefcase, about the US Ambassador who gave Hussein the green light to invade Kuwait, or the Russian peace proposal, or about how we bombed the water supplies. In Baghdad oxides are the least of the problems. But I couldn't say anything.

Instead I listened to "Stars and Stripes Forever" and wondered if it was coming from the TV or from inside my skull.

***

Back in my dorm room I called my dad.

"Son, you need to quit school now."

With every round of mortar and every Stealth attack on the TV, it became clearer. The images on the screen were merely reflections of my inner state, my own hidden motives and impulses. I'd done something, or would do something, that made the killing on the television screen justifiable. There was something about me that made all of the atrocities inevitable.

"The Sea Monkeys want you to go home for a while," Dad said.

I was one of the victors. I was one of the people who dropped the bomb on Hiroshima, napalmed Vietnam, supported the Shah and Marcos and Pinochet.

But none of it could touch me.

"I'll be wiring you the tickets, the airline tickets, tomorrow morning."

Aspirate. Annihilate. Contagious. Jingoism.

There wasn't any me to touch. I was not I.

"Son? Are you there?"

No.

"What did you do?" I asked.

"What was that? What did I do about what?"

"What did you do…during the war?"

***

Looking at her pictures, the photographs that she left behind, I realize that even though Frannie could make herself glamorous she was never beautiful or even pretty. She was just ordinary. In most of the photos she looked terrible. She looked confused and tired and sort of frumpy.

I missed her terribly.

How had she done it? How had she gotten away? She'd been eliminating herself, following the instructions, but somehow she still managed to escape. She'd gotten away from the project, from me, from the flash and the click of the shutter.

How?

I put her photographs aside and opened my green spiral notebook:

On March 2nd the 24th Infantry Division attacked the Hammurabi Division as the Iraqis fled. Our boys destroyed six hundred vehicles in this attack, and there were reports that the bodies of the Iraqi soldiers were buried in the trenches. There were reports of people buried alive, attacked from behind, bulldozed into the earth.

Looking at the photographs, listening to John Philip Sousa, reading my notes in the green spiral notebook, I thought, again, of the Sea Monkeys.

The Sea Monkeys in their tank, the Sea Monkeys and the instruction manual, were all I had left. They were my last hope.

***

I turned on the Sousa music, marched back and forth in my dorm room, and conjured up my own version of a Sea Monkey, watched as this cartoon version, with his crown and his freckled fins, bobbed up and down to the martial beat.

I shut my eyes tight, sat down on the cot, and asked the Monkey what to do. Asked for my instructions.

"Open packet two. When the Sea Monkeys are born you will experience instant life," the shrimp said. "When the Sea Monkeys are born you will not go back to the psychology department, you will not call your father, you will not watch CNN or CSPAN, and you will throw your notebook away."

"How can I do it? Where will I go?" I asked.

I opened my eyes and picked up the Sea Monkey manual. I hurriedly flipped to the back of the booklet and read the Emergency Instructions:

When born your Sea Monkey has but ONE eye, right in the middle of his "forehead." As he grows older, he grows two more eyes on each side of the middle one, making him a three-eyed "freak" of nature.

Your failure to SEE them is one of the most common reasons for thinking they did not hatch.

They will NOT hatch ON TIME if you fail to WAIT long enough.

Put the container in a light, warm area and let it stand undisturbed. You will have your Sea Monkeys soon.

THE WORD "MERMAID" WRITTEN ON AN INDEX CARD

The three-by-five index cards feel good in my hand. I write the words "swimming pool" with a Sharpie and then toss the card into the chlorinated water, aiming for the middle. Watching it float there, feeling sweat rise up on my neck, I have a moment of peace. A moment, and then I dive in after the word.

Getting the Navy shrink to believe me was easy. All I had to do was imitate a television set. Just flip from one subject to the next, without transitions, every thirty seconds, and I was officially crazy—schizotypal with manic and suicidal ideation.

In the middle of the pool I've got the card in my hand, more proof of my disorder, and I can't decide if I feel more like Dustin Hoffman in *The Graduate* or Ric Ocasek in The Cars' video for the song "Magic." You know the one where Ocasek imitates Christ by walking on chlorinated water while girls in neon bikinis jump in after him, splashing and smiling and sinking away?

I'm holding my breath. I've been at the bottom of the pool for over a minute and I'm looking at the filtration duct, wondering if I could jam my foot in and get stuck. The water is blue, like toilet bowl water, and the sky is clear and beautiful like a Sunkist commercial. I need to breathe. I need a drink even more.

Heaving myself up and over the edge, spread out on the concrete and watching the droplets evaporate, I reach for my bottle. It's whiskey—single-barrel whiskey from my mother's liquor cabinet. I put my finger in the neck, and then roll back into the water. At the bottom I take my finger out and thrust the bottle to my lips, but I can't drink and hold my breath at the same time.

Determined, I breathe in chlorinated whiskey, watch a cloud of brown come coughing out of my mouth, and then rise to the surface involuntarily.

Jam the foot first, then drink the whiskey! I can never get the sequence right. Everything I try is always out of order.

On the concrete again I try to rearrange everything in my head.

Am I here because of the Navy, because I couldn't hack basic training? Am I here because of Dad and all of the different things he couldn't hack? Or am I here for some other, undefined reason?

***

My mother doesn't want to leave me alone, she takes me along with her everywhere.

Today we're looking at Island property even though my father already bought the condo we're living in. I guess it feels strange to her, controlling the money, so she's just falling back on old habits. Not even her own habits, but Dad's.

Dad was always hunting for another good investment, never satisfied with what he had.

This condo is brand new and full of high-tech conveniences. A few buttons control the lights, home entertainment center, ice machine, and Jacuzzi, and the walls are made of cold, artificial stone. The lights are multicolored and the realtor has the living room set to aquamarine, the color of pebbles in a fish tank. The home entertainment center is playing "Classical Gas" over and over as the salesman gives Mom his best pitch.

"There are plans for new development. This will be the cultural district in two years," he says. "We've already sold ten units here. It's a sound investment."

"Seven hundred is steep. Is that what people have been paying?"

I leave the living room, drag my fingers along the stucco wall of the hallway, and head to the bedrooms. I admire the interior decorating.

They've furnished this condo with fictional lives: knickknacks and postcards, bookshelves full of popular hardbacks with colorful sleeves. Each bedroom clearly reflects the sensibility of its pretend occupant. The bedspread in the second bedroom shows Luke Skywalker and Boba Fett, and the master bedroom has a copy of *Jonathan Livingston Seagull* open on the pillow.

The pretend family that lives in this newly constructed condo-unit is not only exceptionally neat, but also unstuck in time.

"Are all of your prospective buyers elderly baby boomers, or is this setup just for Mom?" I ask the realtor.

"What?"

"I noticed the Transformer Action Figures in the kid's room. All the toys are straight out of 1983."

The realty company contracted out to a company called Life Designs.

"They specialize in pseudo-environments and corporate space development for high-stakes development projects," the salesman tells me. But it's all by rote and he clearly doesn't want to pursue the subject. He's focussed on my mother, on reiterating square footage and amenities as she drinks the complementary coffee from a plastic disposable cup.

She's flipping a packet of nondairy powder back and forth and stretching her legs under the glass table.

"The furnishings are optionally included," he tells her.

"Even the Transformer Action Figures?" I ask. I've got my right hand buried in the flower display on the entryway table. I'm waiting by the door and fondling the glass beads in the vase.

"Don't do that," the realtor says.

I move my hand back and forth, rattling the beads inside the vase.

"The beads are not complementary," he says.

"I wasn't going to take any," I say.

"Everyone steals them. We have to refill the jar every other day. Please take your hand out of the vase."

"I wasn't," I say, and hold up my empty hand. I stuff my left hand into my jeans and fondle the thirty or so beads I've already deposited there.

"I'm going to count them when you leave." He tries to smile at me, make it a joke, but he doesn't quite pull that off.

"I wasn't—"

"Everyone takes them."

I stick my right hand in my windbreaker and slowly rotate the action figure I've got stowed there; I click its limbs into the shape of a jet.

***

I write the words "Sea Otter" on an index card and stick the card to the glass of the exhibit.

Sanibel Island's aquarium is empty today. The tourists are gone for the season, and on Tuesday afternoon the Island kids are in school. I scrawl the words "Jelly-fish" and "Octopus," and unroll invisible tape from the dispenser. I write the words "concrete" and "coke machine."

Animals have simple lives. It would be much less complicated to live in a man-made tidal pool behind glass. I'd only have to use one or two index cards in my entire life.

I sit on the ground, next to a wooden bench with a donor's name on a plaque, and I spill a handful of the glass beads on the weathered planks. I spread the baubles out. All of them are clear glass, all have a bubble in the center. I try to arrange them by size, but somebody sits on the bench next to my display. She just plops down, not even looking. I glance up at her; she's about my age, maybe twenty. She's wearing cat eyeglasses and has the kind of black hair that's obviously dyed.

She's kind of pretty. She's got a faraway look in her eyes like she just got out of her parents' Winnebago, or like she's on Thorazine. I look at the shapeless but short dress she's wearing. It's gray and black with square patterns of stripes, and I can't decide whether or not it's a hospital gown.

I go back to arranging the beads on the bench but stop again when she reaches down and takes one. She holds the bead in her palm and stares, her eyes flashing back and forth on it, scanning. Then she pops the bead into her mouth. She doesn't say a word, but takes another bead, and another, and swallows them dry.

I stand up and step away from her. I feel the cold metal railing around the Sea Otter exhibit press into my back. She looks at me from the bench and smiles as if nothing strange is going on.

"I've seen you at the Palms," she says.

The Palms is the name of the condominium complex where Mom lives.

"I'm Annie. I'm in unit 11. By the pool?"

"My name is John," I tell her. "I'm staying in unit 23 with my mom. I got discharged from the Navy because I'm crazy."

Annie swallows another bead and I wonder if I should offer her the transformer to go with it.

"I've seen you at the Palms," she says.

***

Mom doesn't like it.

I'm smoking in the condominium unit and watching the evening news. I breathe out puffs, watch the smoke stream away, up to the vent in the ceiling, while, on television, a smart bomb is filming it's target as it comes down. The Gulf War as *Candid Camera*.

"They've lit the oil fields on fire," I say.

Mom is in the kitchen by the dishwasher, and doesn't hear.

"They've set the fields on fire."

My mother, her arm wrapped in bandages, not because she's suffered any injury but because of the nerve damage, because of the phantom pain in her arms and legs that comes from years of unbalanced insulin levels, my sickly mother in her blue terry cloth robe and bandages, storms into the living room and stubs out my Marlboro.

"You may not smoke in the house. I understand that you're mentally unwell, but there are limits."

"This isn't a house," I say.

"In the condo. No smoking."

"They set the oil fields on fire," I tell her.

"I'm glad you're not over there," she says and then takes my seashell ashtray to the kitchen. "I'm glad you're safe."

***

I joined the Navy for the discipline. I needed somebody telling me when to get up, when to sit down, when to eat, when to move, and when to remain absolutely still.

"Discipline." I write the word on an index card but I don't know where to tape it down.

Iraq invaded Kuwait during basic training. Back in August I heard about Saddam Hussein for the first time. I heard that we'd probably be going to war.

It was a surprise, but I didn't really feel anything about that prospect one way or another. I didn't care about going to war or not going to war, about killing or not killing, living or dying.

My problem was unstructured time. I couldn't handle unstructured time. The Navy solved that one for me.

"I can't take making my own decisions and my own way and all of that," I told Dad.

"You were accepted into every college you applied to."

"Yeah, but that's not for me. I'll just end up wandering into traffic."

Dad understood. We had a lot in common. He told me that if it hadn't been for Mom and me, if he hadn't had to find a job and pay a mortgage, he'd probably have been an addict. He would have killed himself with drugs years earlier.

"Pressure is what made me recover. Responsibility," Dad said. "Some people need to get trapped by life, otherwise they don't stick with it."

I write the word "Life" on an index card. I write the word "Father." But I don't know where to put these cards either.

And I'm out of tape.

***

Annie, the girl I met at the aquarium, told me she was a mermaid. Predictably enough we ended up having sex on the beach.

I got sand in my hair and in my mouth, and the water was cold. I swallowed salt water while I shivered and pressed against her, a stranger. Her tongue and mouth, and salt and sand. With my hand between her thighs the world stopped making sense; I couldn't keep track of who was who and what was what.

Then it was over and I watched her eat a beer bottle—a Budweiser bottle, label and all. She broke it into pieces and swallowed them down. She told me that she was a mermaid, a Siren, and that she could taste people's souls when she ate their garbage.

"That's where you keep it, your soul. You keep it in your stuff—mostly in the stuff you throw away," Annie said.

She folded up the words "King of Beers" and chewed them up.

Annie is older than I am, and she's done more. At twenty-two she's been a waitress, a student, a drop out, a tour guide. She's lived all over the country. She grew up in Connecticut, moved to Florida to go to college, and when she dropped out she sort of drifted into life on the beach. An aimless life, taking up odd jobs, odd friends, odd ideas.

She lives two buildings over from my mother's condo, in a unit that looks like all the others. Yellow walls, picture postcards behind glass and framed, clean linen and blue tiles in the kitchen. She even has cable television, but she doesn't have any money. I bring her TV dinners and ice cream, cartons of milk and breakfast cereal.

I don't know whose condo it is, or how long she'll stay.

"Your father was a doctor?" she asks.

"An anesthesiologist."

"How did he do it?"

"He overdosed. Put himself to sleep."

We've made dinner. I contribute frozen fish sticks and she serves up ten rusted pennies. We wash back the meal with tap water drunk from disposable plastic cups and watch golf on television. I try a penny, fascinated with her trick, but it tastes awful and I spit it out.

"Medical school fucked Dad up," I say.

The Denver University Hospital kept cadavers in the basement. About thirty bodies were stored in a shallow concrete pool filled with formaldehyde. The bodies were neatly placed in rows, fitted together by size, and stored for dissection.

"Dad's class was taken down in groups of four. Each dissection team was sent down to pick out the body they'd work on. The instructor liked to let his students pick," I tell her as the middle-aged guy on the screen taps his orange golf ball into the hole. "Dad told me that the pool terrified him. He was sure he was going to fall in. He wanted to jump in. His life felt cheap. Those dead people stored like canned vegetables, like overripe tomatoes. Life lost its glamour. He was just another body waiting for eventual dissection."

Annie puts her arms around my waist, snuggles against me on the couch. She lies down, using my right leg as a pillow, her cheek against my thigh. I like her like that. I feel quiet and domestic even as I watch her eat another penny.

"Mermaids don't have to breathe," Annie tells me. "We're like the bodies in the pool."

***

I never had any trouble following orders. Getting up early and running and jumping, the pull-ups and sit-ups and marching, it was fine. I wasn't the fastest runner, but I wasn't the slowest, and the morning air, the slow burn, the way I could really feel it when I breathed, was good.

Rifles were to be cleaned and reassembled and fired. Bayonets belonged in the belly of the training dummies. When I put the rifle butt to my shoulder and held the gun steady I just had to really look and empty my mind and I'd hit the target.

Better still were the swim tests. All I had to do was stroke and kick, jump or dive, or just tread water. If there hadn't been any classrooms, if there hadn't been any discussion or questions, no chalkboard, no ideas, no study guides, I'd have skated through basic.

The United States Navy has some core values. It was important to know, but hard for me to understand. For the first time in life I felt really connected to my body, flexing and flexible. But, when I'd sat down in a wooden desk and the commanding officer started in about how the Navy has met all its challenges, and how "America's Naval service began during the American Revolution, when on October 13, 1775, the Continental Congress created the Continental Navy," I hit a wall. I listened to the CO but I couldn't connect his words to the room I was in, to the way my legs felt, to the way my back bent. Total disconnect.

"Certain bedrock principles or core values," the CO said, but there was a spider walking along the concrete floor. There was a spider right beside the CO, crawling up the blackboard. A big fat spider.

And the CO went on about honor and faith and allegiance. The CO said "courage" and "commitment" and "respect" and "spirit" and "dignity" and "moral strength" and "decency" and all the while the spider climbed the wall. A bug was crawling up the wall, and my legs were tired, and I could feel my heart beating, I could hear my breath, and none of it made sense.

I raised my hand, and that was the beginning of the end of my time in the Navy.

"Do you ever have to shit?" I asked.

"What's that, Recruit?"

"Now that you know the code of honor, do you still have to shit or piss? If I pledged my allegiance would I still want to fuck?"

"Get out of my class, Recruit—"

"Sir, there's a big black bug crawling on the wall. Right behind you. How does that fit in with the code? It's a fucking bug, sir."

The CO walked to my desk and started barking at me. "You will find the exit, Recruit, in the back of the classroom, and you—"

"Are you going to kill it? How can we create a code and follow it for centuries when we can't even keep insects out of the classroom?"

My CO gave me a slap. It was so hard that it knocked me out of my chair and I stopped talking, stopped asking, for a moment. Then I started up again.

And I kept talking, asking, until I ended up in the infirmary. I listened to my own words, to the nurses and doctors, and everything seemed to come apart. The words that we spoke and the world I lived in separated.

I babbled on about it, just sort of listening to the sounds and admiring the concepts in themselves, and they injected me with serum, and after a while I slowed down. I discovered that when I talked less, when I only spoke when spoken to, they treated me better.

They'd let me out of bed. After a few days they let me walk the halls of the hospital on my own.

I found the index cards on my way back home, after my discharge. I was at the airport, and between flights I wandered in and out of newsstands, restaurants, gift shops. I found the index cards next to a windup airplane with a propeller that could spin. I bought them straight off, not quite sure why, but when I arrived in Florida, when I found a Sharpie and some tape in mother's desk drawer, I figured it out.

Washing my hands didn't help, and neither did turning doorknobs exactly three times, but the index cards worked. I could reconnect words to the world one at a time.

***

I'm drinking tomato juice and vodka under a cloth umbrella by the pool. My sister Shelly arrived yesterday; she drove her Mercedes Benz station wagon down from Kentucky because she wanted to help. Now she's sitting at the end of my recliner and squeezing my foot, making human contact. What self-help tape has she been listening to this week? What seminar does she have in mind for me?

"Don't get me wrong," Shelly says, "this war is terrible, and I'm glad you got out of it."

"My juice is bland." I shake my plastic Dixie cup at her.

"What are you going to do now? Get a job?"

There is a ceramic container filled with NutraSweet on the table to my left. I take one of the blue packets, flip it back and forth, and then tear it open and pour it on my ice.

"Have you thought about college?" she asks.

Shelly's six years older than I am. She's married and employed. She works for the phone company and her husband, Ted, works for the IRS. They're a conspiracy, both of them.

"No, not college."

"There are treatments. If you're out of control you could go somewhere for help. The family could afford that."

I pat my sister's hand, and then empty the ceramic container. I dump the blue packets onto the table and then tap the dish against the metal frame of the table. I break the ceramic into pieces, scoop up the shards, and drop them in my plastic cup. I take a gulp of the melted ice, and taste NutraSweet and blood.

"What are you doing?" Shelly screams.

"I'm okay," I try to tell her, but nothing will come out. And then I'm rolling on the concrete, my hand at my throat. I'm writhing and kicking over deck chairs and the blood is spilling out of my mouth, down my throat.

I wonder if I can still breathe.

***

There are stitches and a tube in my throat. I'm propped up on an electric bed, and the television is on. Shelly and Mom are watching CNN and I don't have enough energy to change the channel.

"We have Bernard Shaw in Iraq, reporting from al-Amiriya, where Iraqi forces suffered major casualties today. Bernard?" the anchor says.

I reach for the remote; it's magnetically attached to my bed frame, but I can't reach far enough.

"You awake?" my sister asks.

I nod, and mime writing, using my hand as an index card. I want to figure out what's happening, find the right word.

Mom seems to understand. She rummages around in her purse for a pen, but then stops and just sits there watching the TV with her mouth open and her hand in her purse.

I'm stuck in the bed, unable to reason. I signal for a pen again, and Mom hands over her fountain pen and her checkbook. I shake my head. I wanted a Sharpie.

"You lost a lot of blood," Mom says.

"You should be dead right now," Shelly says.

The man on the TV set is talking:

"The state of people generally is one of pure shock. They're walking around like zombies, Peter."

"Did you want to die? What did you think you were doing?" Shelly asks.

I write on Mom's six hundredth check, fill out the line for a dollar amount with a message instead: "It was supposed to be a trick."

"Some trick," Shelly says.

"It was supposed to be like pulling a tablecloth off a table and leaving the dishes behind, in place." I write on the back of the check.

"But it didn't work, did it?" Mom asks. "Instead you nearly broke everything." And she takes her checkbook away.

***

The bottles of Prozac, Clozaril, and Depixol look good in the morning sunlight. It's interesting to look at them, set on my bedside table with their sticker labels and childproof lids. I write the word "cure" on an index card and tape it across all three of them, but then decide I don't like it. The card reflects too much sunlight and obscures my view of the brown plastic.

I take the card down and crunch it into a ball.

Using my thumb I pry the lids off the bottles and dry swallow the pills. I put on Bermuda shorts, comb my hair, apply sunscreen and deodorant, and head for the beach.

***

Everything seems very clear and brightly lit.

Annie takes my hand and leads me through the crowd of tanning tourists—supine teenagers and egg-shaped parents, all greased up and baking in the sand. She picks up a piece of litter, a Pepsi-Cola paper cup, and walks towards the water. Letting her guide me, watching her eat the Pepsi logo, I'm not impressed. Her mermaid fantasy fits in too neatly. It's just another part of this mad system. A system that gets people to travel thousands of miles so they can expose their bodies to a light that's growing steadily brighter, steadily hotter.

Annie is eating the Pepsi cup, ripping the waxed paper along the seam and biting down. I try to get enough sound from my sore throat to object.

"How long can you stay in that condo?" I ask her. "What are you going to do after that?"

She doesn't answer, but walks me to the water's edge. The tide slides up onto our feet, and she finishes her Pepsi cup. She steps out of her modest black and white one-piece swimming suit.

How can she be so pale, her legs and ass both the same shiny white? And she's so thin, her ribcage pressing against her skin. She adjusts her cat-eyed glasses and scratches at her pubic hair, while I just marvel.

"Do you need any money?" I ask her. "I could probably get you some money."

"Let's go in," she says. "I'll show you."

"Show me what?" I ask.

A few yards away one of the housewives looks up from paperback distraction, and spots us. The housewife puts her hand up to block the sun from her eyes and, seeing Annie, starts to reach out for her husband but doesn't. She doesn't want him to look after all.

"We've got to go," Annie says.

"I'm not so sure."

"Come on." Annie reaches out for me, water dripping off her arm. She's up to her waist in the ocean. She's up to her chest.

"I don't think so," I tell her.

"Come with me," she says. The ocean is up to her neck, and then she's under. Her arm stays outstretched, her hand grasping for me for a few more seconds, and then she's gone. I wait for her to come back up, scan the horizon to see if I can find her somewhere, but the sun is too bright.

After a few minutes I decide that she's not coming back, that's she's gone for the day.

I pick up her swimsuit and carry it back to the condominium complex. I hang it over a deckchair to dry, and then run my hand across the fabric and remember that the suit never got wet.

The sun is bright, the swimming pool is glittering and sparkling, and everything seems very clear and positive and light. I sit on the concrete and dangle my feet in the water. I watch the palm trees and long grass, feel the sweat run down my back, and feel glad that I remembered to put on sunscreen. Feel glad that I feel glad.

I swing my legs back and forth in the pool, totally content. Back and forth.

After awhile I feel a knot of hunger in my stomach. I look down and see my feet are wrinkled up. I look up again and my eyes are sore.

I stand up from the pool, check my underarms for stink, and head back to my room.

It's time for my afternoon dose.

***

Prozac. I'm just guessing but I think it's what is making me feel so good.

The other two drugs, Clozaril and Depixol, these are the antipsychotics responsible for my lack of interest in index cards and labels. The antipsychotics are why everything seems so calm and clear.

It's seven o'clock in the morning on a Tuesday, March 6, 1991, and I'm calm and focused. I'm dressed in Bermuda-short bathing trunks and an OP sweatshirt. I'm wearing thongs, eating Wheaties, and watching CNN.

On the screen there are burned out cars, jeeps, tanks, and buses.

"There are also indications that some of those bombed during the withdrawal were Palestinians and Iraqi civilians. Families trying to flee the destruction," the reporter says.

"We'll be right back." The anchor is unfazed, a sociopath. Neither he nor I have any kind of response. He adjusts his tie and some paper on his desk while the camera pulls back. A bowl of Wheaties fills the screen.

I eat my Wheaties.

Watching CNN I feel just fine. Now there is a commercial for an amusement park on the screen, a water slide, and it's very clear to me that the world is destroying itself.

But napalm, cluster bombs, uranium-tipped shells, these are all just fine. I understand, and I'm not upset, and I'm not hallucinating.

I can't hallucinate anymore. I can't get upset.

The prescription bottles are next to my juice glass; I'm drinking a small glass of freshly squeezed orange juice this morning. It's very sweet stuff, and I only drink a little bit, just enough to swallow the pills. One, two, three.

I switch to NBC, to the *Today Show* with Jane Pauley. She's listening to an expert:

"On many occasions Iraqi soldiers tried to surrender to American forces."

"Thank you, Doctor Parenti," Jane Pauley says.

My cereal bowl is empty, and I've finished my juice. I clear my dishes, put them in the dishwasher, and then sit down at the coffee table. My sister has left out a variety of college brochures, and looking them over I decide to get to work on them, to get back on track.

Some of the institutions are far away, like Evergreen College in Washington State, and some are very near, like Eckerd College, but all of them are presented well. On the glossy eight by ten pages they are perfectly acceptable, it looks like any of them would suit my needs. Picture perfect colleges with palm trees or pine trees or ivy along the facades. All have a variety of prestigious faculty members and dozens of interesting departments.

I fill out the forms in the back, the application forms. I fill out all six applications and then try to think up my answer to the essay question. I wonder if my SAT and ACT scores are still available by mail.

I feel clear and calm and good. And while the war rages on, as the world cycles through its ending, I start my essay for Eckerd College.

"I do not want to go to Eckerd College. I do not want anything. I've gotten beyond all of that," I write.

***

Annie's still awake, or maybe awake already, when I knock on the door to her unit. She flings the door open wide, knocking into me and pushing me off the welcome mat. She's in her swimming suit and has a sea gull feather Scotch taped to her forehead. It's a tiny feather, mostly just a bit of white fuzz.

"I'm going to college, applying for college. I don't feel anything. I wanted to say goodbye."

I write the word on an index card and hand it over to her. She takes the card and sticks it into her mouth.

"Tell me why you were kicked out of the Navy," Annie says.

So I tell her. About the Navy's Code and the index cards. I tell her that Sharpies make nice fat lines, and that it's easy to read words that are written in fat lines with dark ink, easy to understand.

"I start to feel disconnected but writing stuff down, labeling stuff, that helps."

"Want to know how I became a mermaid?" she asks. "Do you want to know why I don't have to breathe?"

Annie used to do LSD. She used to do LSD and Crystal Meth and Cocaine and Heroin and maybe even Airplane Glue. She was a party girl, a real good time, and she would go to her dealer's place and stay up for days listening to the stereo and snorting coke or meth, or putting tiny squares of paper on her tongue.

"I ate a dollar bill," Annie says. "I was hungry. I hadn't slept in two days and I was hungry too and because I was too tired to go to the 7-Eleven, too tired to move from the shag carpet, I decided to eliminate the middle man."

She crawled across the carpet, found somebody's purse, rummaged through it, and ate the money inside.

"Money buys food. Money is food," she says.

"But, what happened. How did eating a dollar bill do anything?" I ask.

Annie closes the door to her unit, and steps into the night air. "You've got to get in the water," she says. She's humming tunelessly under her breath and walking gingerly along the boardwalk in her bare feet, pulling me along behind her, she's got me by my waistband.

"I wanted to say goodbye."

Annie tells me that I always get everything backwards. She laughs at me, imitates the way I talk with my damaged throat. I write the word "ocean" on an index card, but Annie grabs it from me. She grabs my index cards, tosses them into the water, and then drags me in after them.

The water is cold, but I go along with her.

Annie takes off her swimming suit when we're far enough out that I can't find the ocean floor. She flings her black one-piece over her head, whipping out a light spray as she spins the suit, and then watches with blank eyes as her suit falls and sinks away. She swims over to me, puts her hands on my back and then slides her hands down and pulls off my trunks. She flings my bathing suit by its inner lining.

Annie dives and finds me under water. I feel her under me, grasping blindly, cupping my knee. I'm treading water, trying not to kick her, and she pulls me down; pulls me under.

Beneath the waves, Annie's arms wrapped around my middle, hands locked together tight, I sink fast. We touch bottom in seconds—fast enough that I worry about the bends.

She's got me in a hold I can't break, and she's much stronger than I'd have expected. With my arms bent behind my back, staring into the dark, I start to jerk and struggle. I don't really want to struggle. It isn't voluntary. I've run out of air, and can't stop myself. I jerk back and forth, try to get my arms free, kick my legs, but I'm stuck.

I lose control, trembling and jerking and anything to get free. I let out a scream and seawater fills my throat. I scream, but, despite everything, I'm all right.

Annie strokes my hair as I sit down on the sea floor. I'm breathing salt water. I can feel the fluid in my lungs, but it doesn't hurt. I don't need anything. I'm fine.

I'm breathing underwater.

Annie kisses me, wraps her legs around my waist, and I reach out and touch her face. She's still got a feather there, on her forehead. The Scotch tape hasn't given way.

***

Now that I can breathe underwater I can also eat trash. I'm not as good at it as Annie, broken glass and metal pull tops are still indigestible, hard to swallow, but I can eat garbage without too much trouble. I've learned how to eat trash and find hidden messages with my tongue. I can find hidden messages in anything.

It started with my breakfast cereal. My Cheerios were talking to me as I crunched them without milk. My teeth chattered, punctuating the cereal's monologue:

"Sucked from the earth by a machine. The dirt is dry and pulled and twisted and boxed in. Boxes. Seeds that can't sprout and plants that can't seed. One type of stem and root and leaf and sun for all. All of us the same. All of us speaking with one voice, sucked from the dry earth to be eaten, dry, by one man. The same man in the same room with electricity in a box, eating the dry and desiccated earth. Sucking up dirt from his bowl."

Stirring Cheerios with a stainless steel spoon, I'm shaking. The mental effort required to keep breathing in and out is exhausting. Such an optimistic endeavor, sucking air through my nose. I put my head down on a green place mat made of woven cloth, feel the weave leave an impression on my forehead, and hold my breath. I find that holding back, trying to quit, takes more effort than continuing.

I let go, let the habit of living carry me forward. In and out, in and out.

Is this what Annie feels, is this the kind of thing she hears when she eats an aluminum can?

I reach into the kitchen trash and pull out a coffee filter with wet grounds still stuck to the paper. I put the filter in my mouth, bite off a piece, and chew.

"Twisted chemical addiction to plastic love. You will come back. You will continue to continue. Bodies in ditches. Hacked up love. Chemicals that twist and twist. Dark blood welling up in streams of happy, repeating, fractured love. A corpse in your mouth, going down smooth."

***

I stop eating. It's easier that way. I can't take the manic depression of chewing and swallowing.

My stomach growls with relief and I sit on a cold metal bench at the entrance of the miniature gold course. I watch my sister get her hand stamped for admittance. I hold out my own hand.

"We're up," Shelly says, and gets ready to putt. Mom smiles at her, watches with anticipation. But what's really making Mom feel better is the mail. Mom's glad about the mail. She helped me lick the envelopes earlier that afternoon, and walked with me to the post office.

"We sent out his applications this morning," Mom says. She aligns her orange golf ball on the rubber mat, on the tee-hole, and then swings her putter too hard and sends the ball flying into a miniature windmill on another hole.

"Mom, he's stopped taking his pills. He needs professional care," Shelly says. "We can't just pretend that everything is okay because he filled out some application forms."

I putt. My green golf ball rolls smoothly down the first lane, right up next to the hole.

"I read his application essay. It was good. I think he'll get in. Don't you think you'll get in?" Mom asks me.

"Yes. Just one more stroke."

"When was the last time you took a bath? When did you last eat? You look terrible," Shelly says.

I drop my club and approach the windmill across from us. Eternity is a circle, watching a windmill spin. I stop it with my hands, and then let go and watch as it starts around again.

"Fore!" Mom shouts. She hits her ball and I see a flash of orange and feel a knob of pain on my shin. The ball bounces off my leg and back into our lane.

"His throat hurts is all. That's why he's not eating much. But we sent out the applications today and he wants to go to college. You want to go to college, don't you?"

I start to answer, but the words aren't there for me, the world and the words don't connect. I'm too hungry to talk, too empty. I pick up my golf ball and put it in my mouth, feel the dimpled surface with my tongue, and then spit it out into the hole.

"Children with slanted eyes choke on rubber bands in the happiness factory," I tell Mom.

"What's that?" Mom asks. She stops lining up her shot and turns to look at me.

I say it again. Then I put the handle of my club in my mouth and find something more.

"For our amusement," I tell them both.

My sister puts her hand on Mom's shoulder, hugs her as Mom starts in with her tears. I watch them pat and comfort each other as I line up for the next hole.

***

My bedsheets are terrifying me. I pull the corner of fabric out of my mouth and just lie still in the darkness, unable to move. Petrified by visions of mutilated bodies, people destroyed by weaving machines.

***

"I'm against the war," Shelly says. "It's not like you're the only one who feels anything."

We're watching CNN and she's looking at the rough draft of my application essay, at my handwriting.

"Just because you're against the world—the war—that doesn't mean you can stop. That doesn't make it noble when you don't eat. It's selfish. Think about Mom."

I change channels and take the essay from her when she gets up from the couch. Shelly leans over, hands me the pages, and stares into my face.

"You won't even look at me," she says.

"Could you fetch me index cards?" I ask, but she doesn't answer. She straightens up and leaves me alone on the couch.

"I'm going to the beach," she says.

I prod at the bowl of Grape-Nuts cereal she brought me, the mass of soggy grain, and then push the bowl aside and look at the screen.

The dead person on television, a cartoon ghost with bulging eyes and veins, has a spray bottle that turns people inside out. Everything on the show is turned into its opposite.

Reading my application essay I'm not sure what to do with it. It's obviously a call for help this thing that I first wrote in long hand and then neatly typed into my mother's PC—it's deranged in its sincerity.

This is my response to the war, to the world, to my failure. This is my attempt to articulate a future, to connect words to the world. I tear it into strips and put them into my mouth while, on the television, a cartoon girl robs a bank while the dead man watches in horror. He doses her with his spray bottle, but she stays crooked. Changed once by the stuff she won't change back. The ghost runs in circles, waving his hands, while the cartoon girl looks at her fingernails.

My essay tastes like chalk, like India ink and chalk and pencil shavings. I chew and the taste changes, now it's beer and photocopy ink. White-out and whiskey.

On television the cartoon ghost falls onto his back and then floats and grows wings. He sprays himself with the magic potion and turns into a devil.

I taste college. It tastes like pretzels and bathroom cleanser. Awful. I put my fingers to my nose, clamp it shut. I take a deep breath through my mouth and then hold it in. My cheeks puff out and face grows hot, but I don't exhale. I don't want to taste anything more. I watch television and wait to black out, but instead of fainting I just relax and open my mouth.

"Beetlejuice, how are you going to fix it now?" a cartoon girl asks.

I open my mouth but I don't exhale. I've eaten my future and now I don't have to breathe.

***

Annie and I are getting some sun, slathered in tanning lotion. My legs have a thin layer of sand stuck to them, and the towel I'm sitting on is half-buried in the beach, but I've chewed my index cards up into pasty wads.

"Sand Castle." It tastes like plastic heated by the sun, a toy shovel that's gone soft.

Annie is wearing a silk bra and a pair of panties instead of a bathing suit. She's covered with feathers and Scotch tape, but the tanning oil is making the tape lose its grip; her Siren identity is coming apart, dripping onto the beach.

"You shouldn't try to understand what you eat," Annie says. "You might hear words, but the important part is how it tastes, what it does in your gut, how it changes you as you digest it, metabolize it."

I write the word "metabolize" on an index card. It tastes like acid and red meat.

I open the picnic basket we brought with us and take out the *New York Times*. Tearing out images of dead soldiers and the Domestic Stock Index, I hand them to Annie. She blows sand off the newsprint and stuffs the clippings into her mouth. She drags me by my waistband, pulls me to my feet and into the water.

I bob up and down, holding my index cards over my head, and trying to find the ocean floor. I watch Annie take off the panties and bra, watch as she lets her clothes get washed out to sea.

"Mermaids don't have to breathe," Annie reminds me.

"But I'm not a mermaid," I tell her.

Annie asks me to take off my swimming trunks. She tells me to throw my index cards away. I look at her, past her, at the coming wave, and realize that the ocean is going to knock me off my feet anyway. Eventually, I'll be going down. I can't avoid it forever.

"But you don't have to do it alone," Annie says.

As quickly as I can I scribble the word "Mermaid" on an index card and then stuff the card into my mouth. The water hits me, I'm thrown off my feet, salt and seaweed and force, and I let go of the Sharpie and sink. I try to chew the word "Mermaid" but a rush of water washes the word away and fills my mouth. I let it push me, let the water pull me off the shoreline and into the open ocean.

And my mouth is full of seawater:

"Broke perspective without a center. Spinning without thinking. Ice cold sun. Drowned self. Total submersion. Death."

I sink to the ocean floor, to the bottom, and then reach out, blindly, and grab Annie's hand.

MUSIC LESSONS

PSYCHIATRIC SESSION, DR. WILLIAM HOWSER, 11/2/98:

Q: Tell me about the sound.

A: I've given you the wrong impression. It wasn't a sound. It was more of a concept. I heard it inside my head. I didn't really hear it, but I thought it.

Q: How old were you?

A: I guess I was about four…three or four years old. I saw the gorilla, no, the man in the gorilla costume. He was standing in the doorway.

Q: And he made this sound?

A: No, he just stood there looking menacing; there was this gorilla man in the doorway, and there was fog throughout my room…I don't know, maybe I had a cold and the humidifier was on.

Q: You were afraid.

A: Yes. I pulled the sheets up over my head; I tried to go back to sleep and then wake up again. You know the trick? It was like, "This is a dream, I'll close my eyes and then when I open them the gorilla man will be gone and I can go tell my parents that I had a bad dream." So I pulled the sheet over my head and I closed my eyes.

Q: And when you looked out from under the sheet?

A: He was still there, of course, only now he was in the room with me. And the smoke, the steam from the humidifier, was everywhere. I'd been holding my breath, and when I looked up again and saw him standing at the foot of my bed I let out a gasp and tried to scream.

Q: Did your parents come to you then?

A: No. I tried to scream, but I couldn't do it. I opened my mouth to scream, but instead of sound this bubble came out of my mouth. I screamed and screamed, and when there should have been noise there was only this inflating bubble. And then it popped.

Q: It popped.

A: And that's when I heard the noise. Not the screaming noise, but the sound I was telling you about before.

Q: The sound you say had such a big influence on your music. The sound that wasn't a sound.

A: It was just an idea really. It was what you'd hear if you could hear between the notes.

Q: Silence?

A: No. Something. A sort of deep hum. I got close to it with my tape music.

Q: Why did you think of this today. Last week we were talking about your mother's illness, and today you tell me about this sound. How do you think these two things relate?

A: I saw him again.

Q: Who did you see?

A: The man in the gorilla suit. I saw him when I was in Pittsburgh on Friday.

***

Monday was a day plagued by bees. I woke up in my work studio, lying by an open window, to find that a crown of bees, half-dead and dawdling, had converged around my hair.

I couldn't remember how I'd arrived at the studio apartment from the Symphony Hall, and I had no idea why I'd chosen to spend the night on the floor of my little room rather than at home and in bed with my wife.

"I'm all right," I told Meredith.

"You're in your room?"

"Yes," I said.

"I thought so, but when I tried to call last night I just got your machine."

"I'm okay."

"That's good, but where were you?" she asked.

I squashed one of the bees with a paper towel. The insects were so dazed that all I had to do was lean down and pluck them up one by one.

"I was hanging out with some bees," I told her. "I'll be home soon."

There was a bee in my car, buzzing around the windshield. I drove slowly, thinking about the sting.

It was midafternoon by the time I got home. I walked into the high-rise, crossed the lobby, and entered the elevator. The sound of the leather soles of my loafers crunching insect shells, a repetitive popping, distracted me from pressing the button for my floor.

Dried dead bees, perhaps a thousand of them, carpeted the floor of the elevator. I glanced at my watch and noted the time. It was 2:15 P.M. which meant the drive from the Hawthorne district to downtown Portland had taken four hours. I hadn't driven that slowly.

"Where have you been?" Meredith asked.

"I'm not sure."

"Well, I got Jacob down for his nap without you. It took forever," she said.

"I'm sorry. I must've lost track of time."

My wife and I rely on each other. She helps me keep the noise out and the sounds in, and I try to do the same for her.

Both of us are essentially cowards, and little things will set us off…send our heads spinning. A psychological study on the effects of television on children, a plague in Bangladesh, the death of a colleague or a distant relative, these things can have long lasting and detrimental effects on one or the other of us. And when this happens the other person's job is to stay stable, to hold onto the earth. We can't both breakdown at once.

"I've been sitting at home nurturing an anxiety attack," Meredith said. "I've been reading about the corpse print again."

Meredith isn't particularly religious, she's an agnostic really, but around that time she was reading about the Shroud of Turin. The Shroud is this sheet that covered Jesus after the Romans killed him, and what's significant about it is that it has this image on it. There's no paint on the sheet, the image seems to be a discoloration of the fabric, and nobody can say how or why it's there.

I hung up my coat on the rack by the door, and went to peek in on my son while he slept. I sat by the side of his bed, a small twin bed shaped like a cello, and watched him breathe.

Meredith stood in the doorway and whispered in at me, "He was floating. That's what they think."

"What?"

"The corpse. We're talking about a floating corpse," she said, holding up her book and pointing at the shroud. "What if they're right? Not the medical experts, but the Christians. I mean, what if he comes back." She moved over to the side of the bed and sat down next to me. I put my arm around her.

"That would be good, right? We're talking about Jesus after all."

She shrugged my arm off her shoulder, and turned to face me. "The man is dead. What we're talking about is a zombie situation. I don't want a zombie in the apartment."

"You think He'd want to visit?" I asked.

Jacob stirred and kicked off his sailboat blanket. He turned his head away from us and a Matchbox truck slipped out of his hand and onto the floor.

"He fell asleep while playing?" I asked.

"No, I rocked him to sleep but he wouldn't let go of that car."

I grabbed the toy off the floor and stood up to leave, waiting for Meredith to follow me out into the hall.

"What are you really worried about, sweetheart? Maybe you shouldn't keep reading that book."

"No, I want to know about it. But my life is complicated enough. I don't need gray corpses floating around the living room," she said.

"You're really afraid?" I asked.

"You didn't come home last night and I know you were just working, but I've been reading this book and when you consider what else has been happening," she said.

"What? What's been happening?" I asked her.

"I don't know. I mean look at him," she said, holding up her book again.

I took the book away from her and tried to smile. With all the sincerity I could muster I told her, "Jesus loves you, Meredith. He won't hurt you, even if He is a zombie."

"Great."

"I'm serious."

"But how do you know. How do you know what they're up to?"

"They?"

"I just want reality, that's all."

"That's a tall order," I told her. "Reality? What is that exactly?"

She smiled. I'd done my job without faking it too much. I held her in my arms, and stared down at my hand on her back. I looked at my son's toy truck while trying to make everything all right.

"Jesus loves me?" Meredith laughed.

"Sure. Yeah. That's what they say."

"All right."

"I'm fine. Everything is fine."

But I wasn't.

My son's truck was yellow, and painted on the side, for no good reason that I could discern, were two little bees.

"It's fine. I'm fine," I told her. But I was staring at my son's truck, at the words printed beneath the bees.

"Join Us," the words read.

Jesus.

***

SOURCE UNKNOWN, DATE UNKNOWN:

Q: How do these separate ideas connect.

A: It's a sampling, not a map.

Q: "Johnny B. Goode" is quite enjoyable. Mozart is interesting and also quite enjoyable. But I don't understand. Explain please.

A: Chuck Berry composed and performed "Johnny B. Goode". He's a rock and roll star. It's a rock and roll song.

Q: Will you please hold the baby bear?

A: That's not a real bear. That's a cartoon bear. How can I hold that?

Q: Will you please hold the baby bear?

A: No. That's just a picture, that's Boo-Boo. There's no baby bear here.

Q: What is rock and roll?

A: It's a popular musical form derived from blues and jazz.

Q: Look at the screen. Don't worry about that, you don't need to think about that. Look at the screen. What do you see?

A: It's just a bunch of waves, some red waves and…

Q: Do you hear that?

A: What is that noise?

Q: Please tell me about Mozart.

A: What do you want to know?

Q: What does Mozart mean?

***

I was maybe seven years old, and while the violin was not new to me, I was not a prodigy. Out in the backyard there was plenty of room, plenty of distance between me and anyone who might be trying to listen.

I sat on the root of the maple tree and looked up at the apartment house that I lived in with my parents. My father owned the house and while there were several other families who lived there, we didn't really interact with them.

I was alone in the backyard. I was bowing back and forth, doing variations in the key of C, when I spotted the bee.

It was huge and at first I thought it was a hummingbird. But, as it circled around my head, I spotted the yellow and black fur and I jerked back, falling onto the grass and letting my violin slip gently to my side.

The bee came down, hovered right over my nose, and then lifted up and to the side. It didn't fly away, but just hovered about two feet to my left. After a few minutes I decided there was nothing to do but ignore it.

I improvised in the key of C and I saw the bee bobbing in the air, moving up and down to the music. I'd let off a long, high note, and the bee would jet off, up into the air. I'd sound a low note and the bee would sink. A quick burst of a song, I tried Mozart's "The Magic Flute," and the bee was everywhere; weaving up and back and darting all around.

I played for hours, bowing along to a dancing bee.

I don't remember when the bee left, I don't remember how long I was out there. All I remember is that when I came back in it was dark. My parents were furious, hysterical. I'd been gone for eight hours, they said, and they were on the verge of calling the police.

When I told them about the bee they just looked angrier.

"Don't lie to us," my mother said.

"What, do you think we're stupid? I looked all over the backyard for you. You think I didn't look in the backyard?"

"Where were you?" my mother asked. "Why did you scare us like that?"

All I could do was tell them about my bee, and tell them my violin playing had really improved. Eventually my parents stopped asking me where I'd been and started examining my head, my arms and legs. Suddenly it wasn't anger, but stark fear that moved them.

"How many fingers am I holding up?"

"What's the last thing you remember, sweetheart?"

"I was with a bee. A huge bee. And we were dancing."

***

RADIO PROGRAM, TALKING MUSIC, 11/5/98:

Q: Do you envision yourself ever returning to your work with machine music?

A: Well, I never was much of a tech junkie. I mean Steve [Reich] worked on those electric circuits and channel selectors…

Q: The phase-shifting pulse gate?

A: Right, and he did those pieces with swinging microphones and feedback.

Q: What did you think of those pieces?

A: Well, that stuff was interesting…I mean that was interesting to me because we were both working with tape loops in the sixties, and phase-shifting was important to both of us. But overall I think I moved back to instruments, back into the concert hall, faster than Steve did. I never really left the orchestra because I was always conducting.

Q: What is phase-shifting about? What is it that you and Reich were up to?

A: I guess it was Reich who really discovered the technique, and it was a very simple thing really. He was trying to line up these two tracks of tape, two loops of the same sentence from a sermon about Noah's Ark, and he wanted the two tracks to line up just so that they overlapped. He was working with these two tracks in a fairly ordinary and predictable way, but he didn't get it right. So, what he heard when he played the two tracks together was this slowly progressing phase shift. You know, one track was running slightly faster than the other. The two tracks started out the same, started out as one pattern, but when they got out of synch the sound started to wander. Finally the words became unrecognizable and you had this rhythmic thing happening and a creeping, wandering sound.

Q: What was the primary difference between Reich's tape loops and your own.

A: Well, I love "It's Gonna Rain," but my work was always more coherent I think than Steve's stuff. "Frozen Light" was about something, there was a story. You know, John Glenn thought he was seeing flying saucers out there, and those kinds of selections, the recordings I was working with, were just more interesting than what Steve was using. Even when the speech gets out of synch—

Q: Especially when the speech gets out of synch.

A: Yeah. I mean there's a transcendent and mysterious quality to the phase-shifting stuff, and I think I worked with that more than Reich did.

Q: Are you interested in narratives in your work? It's a strange thing for a minimalist to be concerned with.

A: I'm interested in understanding what makes up a narrative. I've really left a lot of my more minimalist techniques behind. I mean there are still a lot of repetitions, but I'm also stealing more…trying to figure out what's behind other musical traditions.

Q: There's a satiric streak in your latest works. Especially your operas.

A: I guess so. I'm just trying to figure out the roots of things. Trying to cut it up so it's not so familiar and take a look at it again.

Q: Is that what's behind "Chuck Berry and the Magic Flute?"

A: Yes. I was trying to see the relationship between "Johnny B. Goode" and Mozart.

Q: And what you came up with was…well, it's funny stuff really.

A: Yeah. Well.

Q: Very quixotic. Why did you choose to juxtapose those particular musicians?

A: I guess I had to. I was compelled to.

Q: You had to?

A: Well, they're both on the Voyager probe. Both artists are, at least according to the committee I chaired with the late Carl Sagan, canonical and important to life on Earth. But, really, I can't tell you why I chose those two artists. I'm not supposed to tell you about that.

Q: Not supposed to tell me?

A: I'm sorry. I mean, I don't know how it works. The creative process is…I don't know.

Q: What are you working on now?

A: Another opera.

Q: Can I ask you what it's about?

A: You can ask. I'm not sure I can tell you.

Q: What's it about?

A: Bees. Mostly bees. And gorillas. Bees and gorillas.

Q: [laughing] I'll look forward to that.

A: Yes. Well.

Q: It's been a pleasure talking to you today.

A: Thank you.

Q: Next week on *Talking Music* we will be visiting with Thomas Lauderdale who will discuss Swing music's new resurgence.

***

"I don't know the difference, Mom," Meredith said. She was talking on the phone and trying to rock Jacob to sleep. Jacob reached out, grabbed the portable phone, and dialed at random.

Sometimes Meredith forgets that our son is no longer an infant.

"I'm sorry. Are you still there? Let me put Jacob down."

I was sitting at my desk, and trying out SoundEdit on my desktop computer. Meredith had opened the door to my study when she left Jacob's room on her way to the phone. I could keep working, but I was no longer off duty.

It was a welcome distraction. The new opera was a mess, and I was trying anything and everything in order to fix it. Tape music, synthesizer refrains, stolen excerpts from *Pachelbel's Canon* and even Beethoven's *Fifth*. I'd pulled out all the stops, all scruples, but what I'd come up with was only one repeating phrase and a few hundred variations on it.

There was the bee theme and the gorilla theme, but I needed something more. What I needed was some other image to bring these two elements together.

I pressed Play on my computer screen with a point and a click. The music of a human voice squeaked out from the computer's miniature speakers.

"The discs skipped across the sky like saucers on a lake." The voice was Kenneth Arnold's, an Air Force pilot who, after encountering UFOs while flying over Mount Rainier in 1947, coined the term "flying saucers."

"The discs skipped."

"The discs skipped across."

"The discs skipped across the sky."

Pointing and clicking I flung the words back and forth, scratching up Kenneth Arnold like some sort of hip-hop artist.

"The…The…The…The discs…The discs skip."

My son ran down the hall, towards his room, shrieking and laughing as he bumbled along.

"I don't know. Maybe it's just that the modernists thought they knew the answers and the postmodernists are still looking. Yeah, you can tell Bill that if you want, but…" Meredith looks in on me, peeking around the door to my study and smiling. "Yes. Yes. Okay. I'm glad you think so," Meredith said. She covered the mouth piece of the phone with her hand and turned her head. "Mom's defending your honor at the YWCA. I guess most retirees don't like your work," she said.

Eager for an excuse to leave my study, I leap up to defend myself.

"But I'm talking in their language. I mean, remember in my Nixon concerto? I used all those brass instruments and did all that Big Band stuff," I tell Meredith.

"Oh no. Not you too."

"Who doesn't like my music? Retirees? I'm writing specifically for them!"

"Hold on a second more, okay?" Meredith asked into the phone. "John, you're talking about thirty seconds in a forty-five-minute meditation on the bombing of Cambodia."

"The discs skipped across the sky like saucers on a lake. The discs skipped across the sky like saucers on a lake. The the discs discs skipped skipped across across…"

"Let me talk to Kathy," I said, and reached to take the phone away from her.

"Ball, ball, ball, ball, ball, ball, ball, ball, ball," my son came out of his room at full toddle. He was holding a tennis ball over his head.

"The discs skipped across…The discs skipped across…"

"Kathy? You tell that man that I wrote "Einstein's Flux Machine" specifically for him and that he's just not listening," I shout into the phone.

"Ball?" Jacob asks.

"That's right. It's a tennis ball," Meredith tells him as she picks him up again.

"The discs skipped across the sky like saucers…like saucers."

***

The neighborhood of make-believe was rife with aliens. Purple Pandas from the Purple Planet were blipping in and out of sight, appearing and disappearing.

"Rah-rah?" Jacob asked. "Mo rah-rah?"

"He'll be back," I said. "Mr. Rogers will be back on after the make-believe is over."

I sat at the kitchen table trying to scratch out at least an outline while my son sat in his highchair spilling Cheerios onto the floor and waiting for his television friend to come back.

"They're so big," Daniel Tiger said.

"They are big, and purple," Lady Aberlin replied.

Daniel Tiger patted his dump truck and anxiously scanned the perimeter of his clock tower. "I could use my super-truck and then I wouldn't be so afraid." Daniel paused and looked up at Lady Aberlin with his perfectly round glass eyes. "Do you think the Pandas are trying to scare us?"

Lady Aberlin frowned, "I don't know, Daniel. The Purple Pandas are very big, and very purple. But maybe, do you think, they might be friendly?"

"I hope so, but they sure are different."

I looked down at my notebook, and tried to think. If alien beings were directing the life of the protagonist what would that mean? If he was to be depicted as a pawn of their influence, how could I make his actions meaningful? I started jotting down a melody which quickly turned into just another repeating series of notes that had to be fleshed out. I had to give my protagonist, a suburban businessman who secretly communed with ETs, an aria. I had to let him respond to what was happening. I had to let him act; had to let him sing.

"Mo Rah-Rah?" my son asked.

"Watch the trolley," I said. "When the trolley rolls by we'll go back to Mr. Rogers' house."

"Rah-rah?"

"Yes. Here he comes. See the trolley? You know, Jacob, next week Papa is going to visit Mr. Rogers in person. Not just on television but in real life," I told him.

Jacob looked perplexed, not sure what the difference was.

Mister Rogers appeared on the screen.

"Sometimes people from other places can be scary. They just seem so different from you. But they're just people. Just like I'm a person, and you're a person. I wonder what Daniel Tiger will think when he finds out that the Purple Pandas are friendly. I wonder how he'll feel. We'll pretend more about that tomorrow," Mister Rogers said.

"Papa Rah-Rah?" he asked.

"Yes, I'm going to go see him in Pittsburgh next week. Later on."

Mister Rogers was sitting by the front door of his television house and untying his tennis shoes.

"But sometimes make-believe things like monsters and aliens and ghosts, those things can really be scary. Even if they are just pretend. And sometimes it helps to talk about those scary things with a parent or teacher who can really listen. And they can help you to know that it's all right even if you do get scared sometimes."

Mister Rogers was ready to go, already he was back in his loafers and heading for the closet to fetch his tweed jacket.

"And that can give you such a good feeling," Mister Rogers said.

"Ge-by, Rah-Rah," Jacob said.

"Goodbye, Mister Rogers."

***

SOURCE UNKNOWN, TIME UNKNOWN:

A: Why is my wife here?

Q: I have more questions.

A: What are you doing to her?

Q: We must keep track of you. Sometimes it is necessary to do these things.

A: She's not a musician. She wasn't on the committee. I don't understand.

Q: We are interested in her. But I have more questions for you. Why do you separate your sounds?

A: What are you doing to her?

Q: Please calm down. Please touch this.

A: I… I…where am I?

Q: Please tell me why you separate your sounds.

A: I don't know what you mean.

Q: You call some sounds speech, others you call song. Some sounds are music, others are not. Please explain.

A: You don't have music?

Q: I am less separated from myself than you are. I don't understand what is not music. Please explain.

A: Music is a way of organizing sounds. It's a way of expressing ideas through composing different pitches, notes, harmonies.

Q: Different frequencies?

A: Yes.

Q: Why is all of your music on the same frequency?

A: My music?

Q: Why is "Frozen Light" on the same frequency as "Einstein's Flux Machine"?

A: You're talking about my music?

Q: We've been working on your music, trying to understand and expand. You keep making the same patterns. Why?

A: I'm trying to understand.

Q: Will you pet the dog?

A: This again?

Q: Will you pet the doggy dog?

A: That's not a dog. That's a horse. That's Gumby's horse.

Q: Please show the dog your love. Pet the dog.

A: That's just a picture on a screen.

Q: You can differentiate between the image and the real?

A: Yes.

Q: Why do you select between images? Why are some images more real to you than others?

A: I don't understand.

Q: Why do you have dandruff? Why do you raise your hand if you're not really sure? Why is everything on the same frequency?

A: I'm tired.

Q: Look at the screen. What do you see?

A: The president of the United States.

Q: Will you talk to the president of the United States?

A: Hello, Bill.

Q: Please pet the dog.

A: That's not a dog.

Q: Look at the screen. Look at the waves of red.

A: What's that sound? What are you doing?

***

When I was at Juilliard my roommate, a perpetually stoned jazz musician named Sam, used to take me to the airport. He loved airports. His idea of a relaxing evening out, his way of taking a break from music and school, was to drive out to LaGuardia and drink overpriced martinis while watching the 747s land.

"I wish you wouldn't go," Meredith said. We stood at the gate looking out through the Plexiglas at the runway. My plane to Pittsburgh was rolling toward the boarding tunnel. Pachelbel's *Canon* was gently flowing from the loudspeaker until static interrupted and boarding began.

"I have to go see Mr. Rogers," I told her. "This is my big break. I'll be reaching a whole new audience."

"Very new," Meredith said.

"Rah-rah?" Jacob asked. He leaned his head against Meredith's chest and she patted his head with her free hand.

"I'll be back soon," I told her.

Sam liked airports because they gave him a sense of anonymity.

"It's like purgatory here. Nothing really happens. It's safe," Sam told me once after his fourth dry martini. "Let's go look at other people's baggage."

"What's that bump on your nose," I asked Meredith as we stood in line.

She rubbed at her sinus and shrugged. "I don't know. Why don't you tell me?"

"How am I supposed to know? It's your nose," I said.

"Hose," Jacob said.

The flight attendant took my ticket and I gave my wife and child a quick hug.

"Don't go, John. I've got this bump on my nose and I don't know what's happening and I don't want you to go," she said.

"I..."

The attendant looked at me and frowned. I smiled back at her and then stepped out of line.

"I've got to go," I told Meredith. "I'll call you from Pittsburgh."

Sam didn't just smoke pot, but he also dropped acid, ate mushrooms, and chewed morning glory seeds. He liked being "spaced out," and after our first semester I almost never saw him when he was sober.

"You know why I'm always stoned, John?" Sam asked.

"Because you're a bum?"

"It helps me with the groovy little gray dudes. It helps me see them more clearly," Sam said.

"The groovy gray dudes?" I asked.

"Yeah. They come to me, hang out around me, at night," Sam said.

"Where do they do this?" I asked.

"Oh, right here. They hang out by the foot of the bed and talk to me."

"What do they say?" I asked.

"Different things," Sam leaned over in order to fish out his tennis shoes from underneath the dorm's metal cot.

"What kinds of things?" I asked.

"Hey! I have an idea. Let's go to the airport," Sam said as he tightened his laces.

"What do they tell you, Sam?" I asked.

The rental car only had an AM radio, and so I listened to pop tunes from the sixties as I drove to Mister Rogers' Neighborhood. John Lennon kept telling me that nothing was real as I left purgatory and found the ramp to the highway.

And it was there, at the end of the entrance ramp, that I spotted the man in the gorilla suit. He was about seven feet tall, and he was holding the gorilla mask in his hands as he…as he floated across the asphalt.

He was seven feet tall and his mask was off. I drove up the ramp toward him, slamming my foot on the accelerator. His mask was off and his eyes shone out at me; huge almond-shaped eyes that were as black as night. I slammed my foot on the accelerator and then slammed into the gorilla man. Black fur flipped up onto my windshield and I spun the steering wheel and kept pressing the gas.

***

TELEVISION PROGRAM, MISTER ROGER'S NEIGHBORHOOD, 10/30/98:
Q: Did you love music when you were a boy?

A: Sure. Yes. I started playing the violin when I was four, and I loved going to concerts with my dad. I've always loved music.

Q: Well you certainly are a talented musician now. You've grown up to be a person who can really make people happy with music.

A: Thank you.

Q: Do you think you could play something for us, maybe show us how you make songs and symphonies, and let us hear what they sound like?

A: I can do that. I've brought a reel-to-reel tape player with me today, and it has some piano music on it. What I'll do is set this up and if you'll let me play your piano…

Q: Oh, yes. I've got a piano in the living room. But before we go over there, do you want to feed the fish?

A: Sure.

Q: They need just a little bit.

A: Okay.

Q: There you go, fish. Today you're being fed by John Zuckerman.

A: Okay, let me get my tape player.

Q: And the piano is right over here.

A: So what I'm going to do is start up the tape machine and its got some piano music on it, and I'm going to play along with it, only I'm going to play out of synch…the same notes in the same pattern, but because I'll be playing against the tape machine the music will change around a bit.

Q: You mean the same notes will change into different notes?

A: It's difficult to explain. I'll show you. (Playing along with the tape loop) And you can hear how the same pattern when played at a slightly different time combines into a different pattern…and…and… Christ…ohhhh…

Q: Is something the matter, John?

A: I've got to stop. Can we stop now?

Q: Sure…let's stop for a few minutes.

A: I just remembered something. I'm sorry. I'll pull myself together.

Q: There's no hurry. Did you remember something that upset you?

A: The sounds, the different patterns…

Q: They made you remember something?

A: I hit somebody, today. In my car on the way here. I think I hit somebody in my car. Only it wasn't a person.

Q: You hit somebody, in your car?

A: He wasn't human…I hit an ape?

Q: I think we should take a break. Okay, everybody?

A: A man in a gorilla costume. Only he wasn't a man.

Q: This happened today?

A: On my way in from the airport. That's why I was late. Oh, Christ! Christ!

Q: You hit somebody with your car?

A: Shit…it was them. The gray men, the little men.

Q: John?

A: I…I…

Q: I think we're going to have to stop for the day.

A: They wanted me to make that noise…that sound.

Q: John, we're going to stop for today.

A: Why do they want me to make that sound?

Q: John, I want you to take a deep breath.

A: Get away from me. No, I won't pet your monkey. That's not a monkey.

Q: I want you to take some deep breaths. It's me, Fred Rogers, you're here at my television house and you're taking a deep breath.

A: What is that sound? What is it?

***

My son never did get to see me visit Mr. Rogers, and after my nervous breakdown in his television house I continued to sink. Strangeness, horrible and undeniable, surrounded me and I just tried to push on through.

I was a contactee, an abductee, an experiencer. After Pittsburgh I could remember it, remember them, but I didn't know what they wanted. I couldn't answer their questions or understand their sounds.

I was an abductee, and I knew it, and the abductions just kept coming.

"You're here," Foxman, the concert master, said. He was folding up his music stand when I walked into the rehearsal hall, and only paused briefly when he saw me. "You're here, but I'm still leaving."

"How late am I?" I asked.

"You are exactly one hour and fifteen minutes late," the third cellist told me.

"I'm sorry," I took my baton from the podium and then turned back toward the orchestra. "How many of you can stay a little longer?"

About twenty hands rose in response.

"Okay," I said. "Let's begin."

Foxman squinted at me. "You're wearing your jacket backwards."

"I am?"

"And your pants."

"And my pants…backwards. Yes," I said. "Okay, and one…"

***

I kept working on my opera, kept adding elements, and kept coming back to the same basic pattern. "Missing Time," shifted right and left, and it was expanding, but when I looked over my notes they seemed like something written by a fourteen-year-old with autism.

I was looking for an answer, a satisfactory response, to the challenges and questions that they were constantly thrusting on me. I was looking for some way to understand what was happening, but what I came up with was just more stuttering, more phase-shifting, more bees and gorillas.

I was writing my own libretto as well as the music, writing out the plot as well as the score:

"There are lights in the sky and lights along the road and lights that spell out SOAP and EXIT. And we might be visited, and we might be for we are. And the EXIT is the SOAP and the visitors are on the moon. Would you like some tea for your coffee or would you like the moon? And there are lights that spell there are lights that SOAP the EXIT, and there are visitors on the moon."

I had the telephone scene, and the barbecue scene, and the violin solo, and the spaceship would move very slowly across the stage. I had nothing, really, except yet another series of notes following the same basic formula that I would never, could never, escape. And the visitors were on the moon.

***

SOURCE UNKNOWN, TIME UNKNOWN:

Q: Who are you?

A: You're asking me?

Q: Do you know your other self? We are tired of waiting.

A: What do you want?

Q: Who are you?

A: I am John Zuckerman.

Q: And without words?

A: What do you want from me?

Q: Without words.

A: What is that noise?

Q: It's you. You're making the music.

A: What is that noise?

Q: We are through waiting. The sound is yours. It's you.

***

Ufologists, debunkers, contactees, psychologists, bureaucrats, and faith healers have all come up with explanations for these kinds of experiences. The little gray creatures are benign visitors from the Pleiades system, they are blood-thirsty killers from Mars, they are a cultural delusion, they are angels, they are demons, they are a lie, they are God.

"I don't care what they are," Meredith told me. "I want them to leave us alone."

"Have you seen them?" I ask.

"Go check on Jacob. Will you just go and make sure Jacob is okay? You start talking like this and…go look in on our baby."

We locked the doors, and then checked them again. We turned on the television, hoping that the actors and announcers selling Time Life Books and Toyotas and Mutual of Omaha insurance would somehow stabilize the room with banality, and then we turned it off again.

"There are people who claim that all human religions are based on contact with aliens," I told Meredith.

"Do you want to listen to some music? Can I turn on the radio?" Meredith asked.

The oldies station was playing a song called "Flying Purple People Eaters."

"Have you seen them?" I asked again.

"Yes, I've seen them," Meredith said. "They're gray, ugly."

"So you understand? You don't think I'm crazy?"

"I wish you wouldn't bring those books home with you," Meredith said.

"You're not answering me."

"Those UFO books aren't good for Jacob. I had to take away a copy of *Communion* from him this afternoon," Meredith said. "He was playing with it and I think it scared him. The cover..."

"Meredith, I need you to help me. Something is happening and I don't know what it is," I said. I got up to turn off the radio, but instead I spun the dial over to the public access station.

"They're floating dots of light. They're floating dots of light. They're floating dots of light."

Some college kid with his own radio program was playing my early music. "Frozen Light" was on the radio.

"Jacob was talking to the cover of your book, to the man on the cover. He called him Papa," Meredith said. "He thought the gray monster on that book was you."

Nothing anybody says about UFOs makes any sense to me. I don't believe in time travel, I don't believe in faster than light travel, I don't believe in out of body experiences, and I have my doubts about the collective unconscious. People say that the aliens have been here always. People say that the aliens are us, some other part of ourselves.

They want something from me. They want me to be more than what I am. I don't know what they want. I don't know who they are.

"They're floating dots of light. They're-re floating-ting dots-ots," the words flowed out and mixed.

The world was phase-shifting, and my job was to try and write it all down. I was expected to sing.

***

CONVERSATION WITH SPOUSE, SIGHTING OF UFO, 1/15/99:

Q: What are we going to do?

A: I don't know.

Q: I can't believe this is happening.

A: You see it too?

Q: Are the windows locked?

A: Let's go check. Let's go look.

Q: I don't want to look. Are the windows locked or not?

A: Do you hear that?

Q: It's beautiful.

A: Let's go look, lets go look out the window.

Q: You're on their side aren't you?

A: Whose side? Oh, my god. It's huge.

Q: What is it?

A: It looks like a toy. It's exactly what you'd think a flying saucer would look like. Oh, and there are some people looking out the portholes.

Q: Come back. Get away from there.

A: You should see this.

Q: I'm going to watch a movie. Do you want to watch a movie? I rented *The Big Chill.*

A: Hello there. Hello.

Q: John, get away from the window.

A: Ooohhh…

Q: The light is…

A: Are you all right? Do you need help? Let me help you up.

Q: Thank you.

A: I think it was just a flyby. Are you okay?

Q: I have some questions.

A: What?

Q: I have some questions, why do you separate awake from asleep?

A: Meredith? What's going on?

Q: Why do you separate awake from asleep?

A: Meredith? What's wrong with you?

Q: Meredith is asleep.

A: I want her to wake up.

Q: How do you separate?

A: I want my wife to wake up. Oh shit. What's happening now? Why did you turn out the lights?

Q: Meredith is asleep. Why are you awake?

A: Is that a rhetorical question?

Q: Tell me about music. Please explain about music.

A: What do you want to know?

***

I'm not the only one who has been led like this. According to the paperbacks and internet chat rooms, most pop music has been influenced by aliens.

John Lennon wrote a song about UFOs, called "Out of the Blue," and David Bowie's Ziggy Stardust is actually a warning, a way to acclimatize the populace to the alien presence.

I can't adequately transcribe the opera here. I'll tell you what I can, but I can't tell you what it's about because it's not really mine.

What's more, reading the words to it doesn't convey much:

"When the sky is falling and the sky is falling and when it is we are. And give me an F and give me a F and give me an F. When the sky is falling I have to go to work, each day, by seven o'clock A.M. in the morning. I work in Beaverton. I work when the sky is falling. Hello."

It's a mess, incomprehensible, but I think I've finally captured that sound, the sound I've been hearing since I was five or six years old.

The night of the premiere, when the audience opened their programs and read aloud, I heard it. The sound that was not really a sound, but a thought, some idea, came to life on the stage.

My protagonist, a businessman who lived in Beaverton and secretly communed with UFOs, walked center stage and looked through the fourth wall.

The audience asked him questions.

***

LIBRETTO, MISSING TIME, PERFORMED 4/5/99:

A: There is no wall here. How long has it been this way? There is no wall here and I can see…who are you people?

Q: We have questions.

A: You have questions? I've been living my life thinking there was a wall where there wasn't one.

Q: Why do you live in such a world? Why do you pretend there are walls where there aren't any?

A: Who are you people? What do you want from me?

Q: We came here to watch you. And now we have questions.

A: You have questions?

Q: Will you tell us why we came here to watch you tonight? Will you tell us why we paid good money to come and watch you pretend there are walls where there aren't any?

A: Do you live where there aren't any walls?

Q: We have questions.

A: No. No more questions. Please. Just listen.

Q: What's that sound?

A: It's me. It's what one hears, what one says, when you break through. It's nothing.

Q: What is that sound? Why did we pay good money to come here and listen to you not say anything? Why did we pay good money for the orchestra not to play? What is that sound?

A: There isn't a wall here. Forget about the aliens, don't think about the way the sky is falling. What's interesting is the way there is no wall.

Q: Do you hear that?

A: How long has it been this way?

Q: We have questions.

A: Who are you people? How long have you been here? What do you want?

Q: We have questions.

A: I'm ready to answer.

THE SUBLIMINAL SON

FORGETTING THE UMBRELLA

I'm walking through downtown Portland, strolling past the coffee shops and gas stations, and trying to remember the video collage my son made for me. Noah is four years old and he already knows how to splice together the programs and commercials.

How did it go? Mighty Mouse inhaled a flower up his nose, Elmo talked to a fish, and then—I can't remember. Was it a news report about global warming, an advertisement for Anacin?

Dots appear on the concrete, dark circles and splotches. I look up and the water bounces off my face, lightly falling in my eyes, making me blink.

I look at my hands, at the cane I'm holding, at the thin folds of nylon sheets that are wrapped around this cane, and I pause.

It's raining. Mighty Mouse inhaled a flower up his nose…

On instinct I bring the cane up, over my head, pointing the tip toward the sky, and I fold out the sheets, pushing so that the silver spokes spring out and a circular canopy is formed. I open my umbrella and worry at myself, worry at how distracted I'm becoming, at what it's possible for me to forget.

In the last few months I've temporarily forgotten:

1. Bicycles
2. Chewing Gum
3. Light Switches

and now,

4. Umbrellas

I close the umbrella and push open the doors of the 7-Eleven. I look at the Slurpee machine, recognize it immediately. I pick up a copy of *Newsweek*, of *Time* magazine. I grab a Hershey's bar and some pop rocks. It's all perfectly normal, immediately recognizable, and I start to feel better.

I approach the counter, deciding to purchase the candy bar and the *Newsweek*, and put my umbrella down, hanging it on the counter by its handle.

The Pillsbury Doughboy? David Letterman? Mister Rogers? The logo for AT&T?

I take my merchandise after watching the receipt get folded and stuffed into the paper bag, and start toward the exit, but have to turn back.

I've forgotten my umbrella again.

MY LIFE IN THE SPECTACLE

When you take into account what I do for a living it's not very surprising that my son, even at the age of four, should know how to use the television, how to create with it rather than just watching passively. In fact, I'd be a little disappointed if Noah wasn't interested in television.

I do design work for Leyden and Kennedy. Ever heard of us? We're the ones who put William S. Burroughs in sneakers, the agency who equated a sports car with punk rock, the ones who made Miller beer seem hip because it wasn't a microbrew, cool because it tasted bad.

And before you ask, let me tell you:

I don't feel guilty about what I do.

A well-made pair of shoes, an ice cold beer (even if it tastes bad), a revolutionary car, these things are—well, they exist; life is full of commodities, and rather than deny their legitimacy and cut myself off from the ebb and flow of the modern world, I try to find what is beautiful, or at least interesting, amongst the scramble of our junk culture.

It's an art, it really is.

It's what I'm good at.

S IS FOR SPACEMAN

My wife and son are sitting at the kitchen table and reading through the Dr. Seuss book of A, B, Cs when I get home from work. She's got him spitting through straws, working on pronouncing the letter "S," but he's not really paying attention. It's all just what they were told to do, neither of them is particularly happy with the arrangement, and before I can even say hello, let alone sit down and unwind, Noah is after me for a distraction.

"Make the spaceman talk, Papa."

Only, I'm sure what he really says is something like, "Ake da thaceman tah, Papa," but that's not what I hear. I have to focus, have to really try, in order to hear his speech impediment.

Noah wants me to make the spaceman talk. I tell him that it's too late for playing, for pretend games, but my words don't register; he just keeps shoving his stuffed spaceman at me, this toy that's not really an astronaut at all, but a worker garbed in a radiation suit, a failed experiment from the Pentium campaign.

"He hasn't seen you all day," my wife reminds me.

"Make the spaceman talk, Papa. Please?"

"Okay, but just for a minute."

"Just for five minutes?" Noah asks.

"Hi there, Noah. I'm Mr. Spaceman! What do you want to talk about?"

"Tell me about your spaceship!"

"It's called a rocket! And I have to strap myself in and wear a spacesuit when I'm inside it. Then we have a countdown. Can you help me countdown to blast off?"

"Ten, nine, seven, four, three, five, two, one, blastoff!"

"Whoa! I'm going to the moon!"

"Mr. Spaceman?"

"Yes?"

"Where are you from? Where do you live all the time? In your spaceship?"

"Astronauts are from Earth, just like little boys are from Earth."

"No. I'm talking to the Spaceman!"

"Sorry." I correct myself. "Spacemen are from Earth but they explore the whole Universe in their spaceships."

"What's the Universe?"

"The Universe is everything there is—all of space, all of the planets, everything and everybody."

"I've been to the Universe."

"Well, the Universe is everything so…"

"I've been to space too. I've been to the Universe and space."

"You have a rocket? You're a spaceman too?"

"No. I just went there by myself. I went there when I was sleeping."

"You had a dream about being a spaceman?"

"No. Not a dream. I went there. I went to space."

"Wow! That's incredible!"

"Yeah. I went to space by myself. I go to space by myself every night."

"That's great!"

"Yeah!"

"Okay, I've made the spaceman talk for you. Now it's bedtime."

"But…"

"I'm sorry, but it's time for brushing teeth and bed."

"But, just five minutes."

"It's been long enough."

"Oh! Why don't you pay attention?"

THE SPEECH THERAPIST

My wife is clutching at the Formica tabletop and gritting her teeth. "Isn't there another way we could do this?"

"I hope so. There has been no progress going about it this way, has there? I mean, does your son want to speak clearly? As far as I can tell, he doesn't seem to see the need for it," Ms. Dendose tells us. She is fiddling with the polyester rose on her lapel and talking about my son like he isn't there.

"You've just got to get to know him—he takes his time warming up to people," I say. "Noah, you want to talk right, don't you? You want to speak so people can understand, don't you?" I ask him.

"Papa!" Noah yelps. He slouches forward in his seat, and kicks the table leg.

I glance down at the workbook, at the way the letters look on the cover. The Institute of Neuropsychiatry chose to print their material in Helvetica.

Helvetica is very popular, it is the most commonly used font for signs, maps, brochures, and all sorts of product labels; popular not because it's the easiest to read, but because it has almost no preindustrial connotations. This is the lettering of the computer age; it is a font that conveys an up-to-the-minute quality.

"I can't understand your son, what he says, and I'm a professional. His speech problems are really very severe," Ms. Dendose tells us.

"You can't understand him at all?" I ask.

She goes on twirling her dress, tugging on its ornaments. "No, at least not very much; I can make out only a few words: hello, mama, papa. That kind of thing. You may claim that he has a vast vocabulary but I can't distinguish even a trace of it."

Noah must be sick of everyone talking around him, ignoring him, because he flops off his chair and crawls across the floor on his belly, scoots to the play corner like a soldier in a fire storm. He picks through the alphabet blocks; slamming them against the wall with solid, overhand, throws.

"Noah! Stop that! Come back over here." I yell at him.

"Oh, hell. Let him do it," my wife mutters.

"Do they even try to do the worksheets? Are they working on this at all?" Ms. Dendose asks me.

"I don't know." I turn to my wife, try to get her to meet my eye.

"Yes. We've tried the worksheets," she says.

"They've tried the worksheets."

"Have you tried them?"

"Me?"

"With your son."

"Oh, no I haven't."

"Maybe, if your wife will agree, maybe you could do the worksheets with him." Ms. Dendose is practically strangling her polyester rose, nearly tearing it from her chest.

THE MUMMY

Worksheet number two is nothing more than a series of S words and iconic cartoons of mostly unrelated objects: a sand castle, a saw, a sailboat, the sun, soup, seven, suit, sofa, soda…

This problem runs in the family; I had a speech impediment myself, when I was his age; I couldn't say "salt" or "sink" or "somnolent." My father was the same way. When he was a very little boy my father smiled at his schoolteacher mom and marine dad from across the dinner table, tilted his head to one side, opened his eyes wide, and said, "The thick o'clock whiffle! I hear the thick o'clock whiffle."

With my dad the solution had been to beat the tendency out of him, but I went to a speech therapist. I went to a speech therapist as a child and I'm going to keep taking my son to a therapist, despite my wife's objections. Ms. Dendose is at the

I watch as Superman flies, faster than a speeding bullet, to the children's hospital. He lands, swooping through an open window on the top floor, and a nurse, seemingly unimpressed by his entrance, hands the superhero a weeping infant.

Superman looks down at the weeping infant, uses his x-ray vision and looks at the boy's bones, at the boys insides, and finds the problem—the alien particle.

"I've found it," Superman says.

"We have to get it out of him."

"Rhyme right behind rooo!" Scooby screeches, his legs blurring as he stands perfectly still.

"Wonder Woman, it's you. Maybe you can help Superman figure this out!" the nurse says.

"Cookie! Cookie! Cookie!"

BY DESIGN

If I hadn't gone into advertising I might have tried urban planning. Riding the light rail through downtown I study all the good work that has already been done. Our institutions blur together here—a Starbucks, the public library, a cinema complex, a skyscraper full of offices—all of it looks and works in the same way: like a kindergarten classroom, full of simple labels and safe corners. And the light rail itself, the MAX train, this is Portland at its best. Clean and above ground, lit with sunshine, the MAX gives a sense that the mechanism behind our city is running smoothly. Life is benign.

I'm scanning it all, feeling warm about everything, and so the interruption, the glitch, takes me by surprise.

The walls of the train, right above the plate glass windows, are lined with cryptographs and hieroglyphics; strange charts and photos are all around me, above my head. I can't make out any of it.

"If you don't come see me today," the sign reads, "I can't save you any money."

What does that mean?

"Want instant cash? Get an instant job with Instant Labor, Inc.," another sign reads, and it's strange how strange it seems, how confused I am looking at it.

I designed some of these signs, most of them. This is my own work I'm befuddled by, my livelihood that I've temporarily forgotten.

By the time I arrive at work I feel clumsy; everything is helter skelter. I stumble to my cubicle, and I can't quite get started on anything. Everything keeps going wrong. For instance, the new thumbtacks won't hold, they keep slipping out of the cubicle wall, and my weekly schedule glides, back and forth on the air-conditioned currents, to the carpeting. I pick up the stapler and try to figure out what it does, what it's for. And what does the word Swingline mean?

Elmo's fish, Mister Rogers, the insurance of Mutual of Omaha…

When I was his age, Noah's age, I went to preschool.

I used to wet my pants regularly because I was afraid to ask for anything, to ask if I could go to the bathroom; this didn't make me popular with the other kids, and the teacher didn't like me because when she took us swimming, to the YMCA, I wouldn't get in the pool. I convinced two other children, a freckled boy with red hair and his twin sister, to join me. We would not get in the pool. I said there were bodies; I was hysterical because I thought I could see all the bodies of the kids who drowned, or the kids who were going to drown.

I bang my knee against my desk. I'm still clumsy, but now the stapler doesn't seem so mysterious.

Work, I'm at work…

My part in this design project is to draw a cocktail glass. That's all I have to do, a simple cocktail glass, but the most I can come up with is a sketch—a doodle really. What these people want from me is impossible. They want me to design something they've seen a hundred thousand times, but they want it to be something special. I'm supposed to turn the letters of the alphabet into alchemical symbols that everyone can recognize; I'm supposed to transform a cocktail glass into an artifact from the moon. This is my job, making the mundane seem magical, but I'm too distracted thinking about what it was like to pee my pants at the YMCA and I can't get started.

Didn't Freud claim that there is no such thing as an accident? I bang my knee against my desk. I slip and jab my index finger with a number two pencil.

ONE EMPLOYEE TO ANOTHER

I'm fiddling with a fanged Pac-Man-shaped device, crunching up paper with it and trying to figure out what it is, when my colleague interrupts.

"Do you have the glass?"

"The glass?" The pamphlet I pick up as a shield has a picture of a mountain range on each page, underneath there are boxes with numbers.

"Did you draw the cocktail glass?" Dan asks again.

It's a calendar. And that Pac-Man thingie I was playing with before is a stapler remover.

"I haven't finished yet. Do you have the napkin?"

"Of course I have the napkin, otherwise would I be asking you for the glass?"

"I don't know, Dan. I guess not."

"When will you have the glass?"

"I don't know. How did you finish the napkin so soon? That looked like a difficult—more difficult than the glass. What they were asking…"

Is Cookie Monster hungry all the time because he needs something that he doesn't have or because he's denying something he has but doesn't want? Is Shaggy really a friend to Scooby, or is Shaggy dominating Scooby, oppressing the poor dog?

"I understand paper," Dan tells me.

"Paper?"

"That's what most napkins are made of, paper."

"Right. Well, I'm not done yet."

"Tomorrow morning?"

"No. I can't take the work home with me. I've got a family."

"I don't believe in families."

"Well they exist."

"I don't have a family."

"You do."

"No."

"Who raised you?"

"My father and mother."

"See, you do have a family."

"Ahhh—but they weren't like your parents. They weren't like your wife and child. They were helpful. They knew how important a napkin could be. They understood about paper."

"Did they?"

"They were practically paper people."

"You were raised by paper people?"

"That's right."

"I believe it."

"In fact, I've got my mother right here. In my side pocket. I keep her in an envelope."

"That must be very convenient."

"It is. Do you want to see her?"

"No thanks."

"She folds up very nicely."

"I'd imagine so."

"My father is made of cardboard. I keep him in the garage."

"That explains a lot."

"You think?"

"I'll need another day for this."

"Okay by me."

Dan just stands there, leaning against my cubicle, and I'm afraid for a moment that my whole shell will topple. I grab the top of the divider and frown at him, try to appear menacing.

"Give your mother my regards," I tell him.

Dan pulls on his tie, adjusts his jacket lapels, and leans in. "Maybe she could visit you, maybe I'll mail her to you."

"No. You can just tell her I said hello."

"Can I borrow a stamp?"

BEYOND CSPAN

I didn't sleep well last night; I had too many dreams.

What I want now is to watch CSPAN or the Weather Channel; I want to use television to help me ease into consciousness, but my son is up already, and he's been editing. He wants me to watch another video collage and insists on showing me his television people.

I press Play on the remote and brace myself.

Fast, fast, fast relief. It's the real thing. Everyday people.

There is a shot of factories in Berlin puffing out soot and smoke, there are dancing penguins, and Molly Ringwald is huffing and puffing up the side of a dune, whining through a deserted futurescape. John-Boy from the Waltons is arguing with a tentacled alien creature about whether there is enough water to go around, and a little boy with yellow pupils, glowing and flickering with computer-generated effect, is singing the Tootsie Roll theme song and making a cereal bowl float across the kitchen table.

Hey, Mikey!

SPEECH THERAPY AND THE WORD

Ms. Dendose has Noah writing down the letters, drawing thin squiggle lines that are meant to inspire him to make the proper matching sound. A T that looks more like an X is supposed to impart the ability to say "tah." "Tah," and "tah," and "tah." T and T and T.

"How is it going?" I ask. I'm about fifteen minutes early picking him up and Ms. Dendose doesn't even look at me. "I don't want to interrupt. I'll just sit and watch."

"Noah, can you say 'cat'?"

"No."

"Noah, say 'cat' and say 'tah' at the end. Pronounce the T," she instructs him.

"Tah, tah, tah, tah, tah, tah…"

"Good, but say 'cat.' Use the sound in a word."

"I'm not-tah going tah-oo," Noah says.

"Cat."

"Tah, tah, tah…"

"Cat."

He grabs a plexiglass box off the formica table, scoots his butt off his chair, lands with a thud on the wall-to-wall carpeting, and turns away from his lesson.

"Cat," Ms. Dendose says.

Noah shakes the plexiglass box, makes a marble roll back and forth until it finds the hole and falls through to the next level, the next compartment in the box. He spins the green plastic dials, pushes his palm over the pink switches on the side, and moves the marble through the maze.

"Tough day?" I ask Ms. Dendose.

"He won't cooperate. He doesn't want to learn."

Noah is staring at the bottom of the box, through the clear plastic and at the white marble. He tilts the box back and forth, rattling the marble in its cage.

"He said 'tah,' I heard him," I say. "That's good, right?"

"You have to stop coddling him. Have to make him see the importance of this."

"Okay."

She takes out a memo pad and a Bic pen from her purse and starts to scribble out some instructions, like she's writing a prescription.

Noah has the marble flowing up through the box now, rolling back and forth on the ceiling of each compartment—defying gravity. He is holding the plexiglass entirely still, staring hard into the maze, and the ball is falling up, finding the holes, the spinners and trapdoors, and running backwards to the top.

"I want you to stop responding to him when he doesn't pronounce a word correctly. I want you to stop understanding him," she tells me.

"Did you see that?" I ask, and point at my son like he's an animal at the zoo. Noah has the marble all the way through the maze, and he's rattling it around with his mind in the uppermost box like a four-year-old Uri Geller.

"Listen to me. I want you to stop using sound when you talk to him. Just move your lips and tongue; speak silently and let him learn to make out what you're saying by watching the movements. I want him to see how to say the words right," she says.

"That's crazy," I say.

"It's a common technique," Ms. Dendose says.

"How did you do that?" I ask. "Did you do that?"

"Tah," Noah says.

WITHOUT SPEAKING

"Papa, I want to watch *Toy Story*. Can we watch *Toy Story*?"

His mother doesn't like it, this new approach, but I'm determined to go through with it. He has to learn how to speak, how to communicate so that people will understand him. That's my job, as his father, teaching him the language of the public.

"Can you say, 'story'?" I ask him. "With the *sss* sound?"

"I want to watch *Toy Tory*," he tells me.

I mouth out the title, silently moving my lips and clicking my tongue at him.

"Papa?"

I lift him up by his armpits and carry him to the kitchen table; he's limp in my arms as I plop him down on the folding chair and open the workbook.

"Try 'canary,'" I say.

"No. I want to watch a movie. I want to watch *Toy Story 2*."

"Canary."

"No."

"Noah! Say the words. Say them right."

Noah doesn't say anything, he turns his head and points furtively toward the living room. He bites his lips and points and points.

"Say 'canary,' Noah. Come on!"

"Anary."

"Close. Try it again."

"Canary."

"Good," I tell him. Only, I really can't tell if he said it right. "Canary." What does that mean? It's some sort of animal I think.

"Okay—um, try 'salad.' "

"Salad."

"Right." I'm guessing. Salad?

"Papa. I want to watch *Toy Story*!"

"Hmmmm…"

"Now."

"One more."

"Now."

"Try one more word," I tell him. "'Umbrella,'" I say. Only it comes out like a question. "Umbrella?"

THE COMFORT OF CUBICLES

I earn a nice living and my wife earns nothing. I have to put on a blue shirt and an appropriate tie every morning and my wife can remain in her flannel pajamas all day, but there is no question about who works harder.

There is something comforting about being in a public space, something easy about the way my chair swivels and the cubicle walls close in around me. I get to pretend to be a grownup all day.

Being a parent forces you to draw on all your social modes, all your identities, simultaneously. My wife is, every day, Cathy's daughter, Alice's granddaughter and, probably, her third grade teacher's student. She's fully engaged in a process that goes back generations.

I get to pretend to be outside of history; I get to play, if not my own game, then at least a game created by corporate powers so large as to be anonymous.

I cross the lobby and chat with the security guard while I wait for an elevator. He's talking about the upcoming election or maybe a football game he's paid to watch on television. I'm not really listening. The elevator arrives and I step inside; I press a button and I'm lifted to the offices above. It requires no effort. It's so easy.

And everything keeps going like this, just fine, perfectly smooth, until I get to my desk.

Staring at my pencils and paper, scanning the memos and schedules and instructions, I don't know how to proceed. Should I sit down? Should I pick up the phone first, check my messages? I turn around and proceed to the water cooler, stalling for time while I try to find my bearings.

I can't get the spigot to work. I pull and push and press but nothing but a dribble comes out.

There is still something comforting about the way my chair swivels, but everything else is unfamiliar and vaguely threatening. My shirt collar is tight around my neck, and I pull at my tie.

Who am I if I'm not my father's son and my grandfather's grandson? Who am I when I'm not following my third grade teacher's instructions?

I sit down at my desk and try to remember what a cocktail glass looks like; all I can come up with is a milk carton, a can of apple juice.

I stand up again, randomly, but I stumble and have to steady myself with the chair. It's too much for me, this life outside the box of history. There is no ground, nothing solid beneath the orange wall to wall carpeting.

A SNEEZE, A SAILBOAT, SPEECH

My son won't talk to me, he won't do anything but move his lips up and down and click his tongue.

"Spaceship?" I try. "Come on you like that word."

He just stares at me.

"Okay, then try 'spaceman.' 'Spaceman.' "

One of us has to concede, but for the moment we just sit and stare at each other. I hold the worksheet up to him, gingerly and with two fingers, as if I'm asking his opinion; perhaps the worksheet has gone bad and ought to be thrown out.

I'm caving, but I haven't given in yet. Noah stares at the worksheet but doesn't indicate anything. He's unmoved.

What was it like for me, back when I was belligerent and silent, when I couldn't pronounce s-words or spell my name? I haven't thought about it for a long time, other than remembering that trip to the YMCA. It's one more thing that I've forgotten and I add it to the list:

1. Bicycles
2. Chewing Gum
3. Light Switches
4. Umbrellas
5. My Childhood.

"Spaceman." I say.

"Spaceman," my son replies, or at least I hear his voice, but his lips don't move. "Spaceship." I hear it again.

My mother told me that there was a word for all of this, for these kinds of experiences. The word was déjà-vu. The way she said it, pronouncing it quickly and waving the idea away with her hand, I figured I shouldn't ask for more details. Déjà-vu was like sneezing, like a mental sneeze; that's what she told me, and then she waved her hands like something smelled bad. There was no way for me to tell her that my sneezes were something more akin to premonitions. And I could not tell her, for instance, that I knew with complete certainty how and when my aunt and uncle were going to die.

My uncle had been teaching me how to dribble a basketball, how to cup my hand just right, how to keep it going, and I realized that his mind would go first. He scared me as he ran up and down the driveway making lay-up after lay-up, because I knew that he had a vessel that was clogging, a major artery in his brain was on the verge of bursting open.

And then later, when his wife was serving me cookies and lemonade, I saw that her lungs were filling with tumors and that she would be unable to breathe when the process ended. I didn't want her to touch me. I didn't want her cookies.

"Soup. Sunshine. Seashell by the seashore," I say the words aloud, trying to break the spell.

"Why did you say 'soup'? Why did you say that?" Noah asks. He sits there biting his lip and squirming in his chair, and he looks like he's holding back tears, but I don't respond. If he wants to talk to me he'll have to use his voice. He has to learn.

"I don't want to!" Noah leans toward me and grabs my arm. He stands up in his chair and then hangs from my shoulder, lets his body go limp, and expects me to catch him. I do nothing and he hits the floor—hard.

"Why did you push me down?" he wants to know. "Why are you mad at me?"

When I was maybe five or six I used to hide from my mother, sometimes for up to an hour, by standing very still in the center of the room. I learned how to hide in plain view by not being seen.

I would pretend that I was leaving the universe, the universe where I was a little boy with a mom and a pop, and go to a universe where I was just air. I would look at the little parts of the world, down deep to the really small bits, and I would let myself cross over into nothing as I stood perfectly still on my parents' oriental rug. Then, walking with the pattern, I would move away, under the couch or up the stairs, and my mother wouldn't see me. She wouldn't see anything; she would slowly wander through the room reading copies of *People* magazine and doing the crossword puzzles. Maybe she would call out to me occasionally, slowly like she was having a hard time remembering my name.

Noah is climbing around under the table and I'm ignoring him. He's thumping the table with his feet, his knuckles. And I can hear him in my head.

"I'm not going to be the same. I don't want to be the same. No. No more worksheets. No more talking."

"Sailboat. Salesman. Soothsayer." I tell him.

"No. No. No."

At school, while the teacher's aide was busy writing the months of the year on the chalk board, busy using the colored chalk to make yellow suns and green pine trees and purple flowers, I floated up to the front of the class and used my mind to open her purse. I remember I just followed the cracks in the floor, the lines around the floorboards, until I could see that her purse was crammed full of tube-shaped devices wrapped in paper packaging, and she had a number of medicine bottles, some coins, a paper cup, lipsticks…

I had a crush on this teacher's aide, and in order to impress her with how much I knew I started asking questions about each item. I asked what the tubes were for, and why she had so many pills, and what she wanted with so many lipsticks.

I was sent to the principal's office because I could determine what was in the purse without really looking, could look inside things with my mind. Obviously this was a bad thing. A very bad thing.

The principal called my mother, and she took off from work early and came to pick me up, to take me home. On the way to the car I told her that I hadn't been peeking, not really, that I hadn't been stealing or snooping, I only did it with my mind.

My mother told me not to lie to her, to never lie to her, and to get in the car and to never, ever, do what I'd been doing, what I could do, again.

I never, ever, did it again.

I'm not forgetting things, not really. More to the point, the only reason I'm forgetting staplers and billboards and light switches is because of this remembering.

I drop the worksheet, push it across the formica tabletop.

Back then, when I was a boy, I stopped my brain from sneezing by putting my finger under my nose, and now I'm asking my son to do the same thing, or at least I'm asking him to cover his mouth and nose and to use a tissue. I'm teaching him to say "Déjà-vu" and "coincidence" and "fluke" when what I should be saying is "Gesundheit."

"Sailboat." My son climbs up from under the table, sits across from me, and smiles a hesitant smile. "Sailboat?"

"Noah?" I don't say his name but think it.

"Papa?" he asks in my head. "Listen: 's,' 'sh,' 'buh,' 'tah.' " Noah doesn't say a thing.

WORKING BENEATH THE SURFACE

The sun is shining through the plate-glass windows; the orange carpet is springy under my feet. I walk through the office, smiling into the cubicles, waving, and then I forget where I am.

"Dah!" I say. "Dah. Dah. Dah."

"Hey. Did you finish the glass? They're breathing down my neck. The client is here today, and I don't have anything to show him."

"Daahh-ann." It's Dan. That's Dan, but what is he showing me?

"Here's the napkin," he says. "What do you think?"

"What? What is it?"

Dan looks at his sketches, at the portfolio of paper and cloth napkins that he's spread out in front of me, and winces.

"It's..." he starts.

"I'm trying to make the spaceman talk," I tell him. "I'm the spaceman, the spacey man, and I'm trying to talk." Only what I say doesn't sound right. "Aceman chalk," I tell him.

"Jesus," Dan says.

"How are your parents doing?" I ask. "They still rattling around up there in your head? Those paper people?"

Dan looks confused, he starts leafing through his sketches, running his hands across the pencil drawings, smudging the napkins.

The orange carpet is a spring under my feet and I do a little hop, a skip, and a hop.

"Aceman. Chalk." I tell him.

Dan has his drafting pencil out again; he's pressing down hard on the paper, scribbling. He's trying to find the lines, sketch them out again.

THE SPACEMAN

I'm tired of talking in public, of advertising, of being less than what I am. I've put the worksheets away, and I'm trying to start over.

"This is where you wanted to go?"

"I like it. Do you like it?"

"It's a temple."

"A church?"

"A temple."

"It's very shiny in here."

"It's dusty."

"No. Underneath and on top of the dust."

"I see what you mean."

"Papa?"

"What?"

"Make the spaceman talk."

"You know, in temples and churches people like things to be quiet. Not talking is a way to show respect."

"Make the spaceman talk without noise then."

"Okay, I guess. Can I do that?"

"Sure."

"Hi, Noah."

"Do you like being in space, Mr. Spaceman? Do you like being in the big church?"

"Sure."

"What's it like? How is it being so far out and away all the time?"

"I'm in a rocket, in my spaceship."

"Can you see me from there? Can you see Mama?"

"I can see you both."

"Hi. Hello, Mr. Spaceman."

"Hello. Hello down there."

"Hi. Hi. Hi."

"Noah?"

"What, Papa?"

"Let's go home now."

"Do you see the colors here, and how shiny it is?"

"Yes. But let's go now. It's time to go home."

"Okay, Papa. Okay."

We're walking through downtown Portland together, hand in hand past the coffee shops and car washes and billboards. I'm trying to remember the last video collage my son made for me.

Elmo talked to his fish, Mighty Mouse flew to the moon, and a father let his son be; the scene was taken from an episode of *Mister Rogers' Neighborhood*. This father watched as his son learned to sing and dance, not by following instructions, but just in the son's own way.

"Tree. Tree. Tree." That's what the son was singing. I can remember it now: Elmo's Fish; Mighty Mouse; and Mister Rogers' song "Tree, Tree, Tree"; it's all coming back to me.

THE HEADLINE TRICK

The guy in the cubicle next to mine says he doesn't belong here. "I had money once," he says. "I had it all figured out."

His name is Scott but everyone in the office calls him Scotchy. He's always coming into the phone room of Time Life Books in navy blue three-piece suits or wearing yachting outfits complete with a cravat, and there's this aura of good breeding about him. It's always the please and the thank you. You get the feeling he's never watched an episode of *Gilligan's Island* in his life.

"I had money is all," he says, and then he apologizes. "I know that one is not supposed to talk on these things, but there it is. You understand?"

I nod at him through the cubicle wall as the computer dials the next customer. "Are you afraid of ghosts?" I ask the lady on the other end of the line. I give her the pitch for Time Life's Mysteries of the Unexplained. "Are you interested in what happens to us after we die?"

From Scott's cubicle I can hear the rustling of newspaper and the working of a pair of scissors. I figure he's got his headset off again, that he's cutting up newspapers again. He's back at his special project, whatever it amounts to; it's his project but it's the company's time.

It perturbs me that he can sit there all day, obviously flouting the rules and working on some personal hobby, while I have to produce sales in quantity just to keep management off my back. He gets to bring his hobby to work, but if I brought my tools to work, if I even tried to carve a twig, I'd be canned.

At the end of the shift Scott and I are the first to leave. When we get to the other side of the carpeted corridor of cubicle walls Scott stops at the manager's desk and smiles at her. It's something I'd never do.

He reaches out and lifts a playing card from behind her ear; plucks it from thin air.

"Is this your card?" he asks her.

She nods slowly, an impressed smile on her face.

Shock and Awe Strategy document leaked. US plans to firebomb Baghdad with 400 cruise missiles a day.

Schools close a month early as budget cuts put hundreds of teachers out of work.

Homeland Security recommends duct tape and plastic bags to protect from likely bio-terror attacks.

The streetcar was put in right before the economy collapsed. Still new, with bright orange and red aluminum shells and clean interior seating, the trolley is easy to sneak onto without paying. There are almost never any fare inspectors. I listen to the electronic voice announce the sponsors at each stop—Bridgeport Brewing Company, 24 Hour Fitness, Northwest Realty—and I try to appreciate the small pleasure of this short free ride.

But opening my mailbox, as I walk in the side door to my building, I find only bad news. Overdue bills, a few threatening letters from the credit card company, and a form letter informing me that the state can no longer afford to provide my health insurance.

I count the days until my next paycheck and factor in how long I can avoid payment on the electricity before I decide to spend my ten-dollar nightly bonus on beer. Then I'm out the door again, stuffing the mail into my back pocket, and I'm around the corner to the Quickstop; I've got a case of Pabst in my hands before I can have second thoughts.

"I ran out of my anti-nausea medication today," Connie tells me when I open the door to my studio apartment and let her in. She doesn't say hello.

She's just off her job in the stacks, still in her librarian outfit with the geeky eyeglasses, formless brown skirt, and name tag clipped to a black sweater.

"I'm gonna puke up my intestines pretty soon unless you've still got some pot."

"Sure," I tell her. "Yeah, I've got some left. You want a beer?"

"After."

I pack a bowl and hand her the water pipe, admiring her lung capacity as she takes hit after hit. "Shit!" she says, her eyes watering. "I'm so fucked."

"That's what stomach cancer will do to you," I say.

"Forget the tumor. It's the chemo," she says. "It makes me weak and it makes me vomit. It's like I've got morning sickness or something, only the only thing I've got in my belly is a cancerous cyst."

If only Connie wasn't sick I might let myself fall for her. We've known each other for years, off and on. Met her in one of the hundreds of cafes in Portland back when I was young enough to enjoy that sort of place. I was reading a book on carpentry and she was telling everyone who would listen about the latest, most fashionable threat to mankind's existence. She insisted that I stop thinking about benches and chairs and think about viruses. She wanted to tell me about Ebola Zaire, about bleeding out, about contagion. I liked her right away, but it's only been recently, in the last few months after years of friendship, that we've been intimate.

It could be good, the two of us. The few times we've been to bed together were great, but since then it hasn't happened. She's been too sick. She's sick tonight, sick most nights. She's sick so we can't. I can't.

"Do you have time for me?" she asks. "Want to play nursemaid and make sure I don't croak? I really feel like shit."

"I was just about to start working on some shelving. I've got some oak branches to treat, but you can stay and watch. I've got plenty of beer."

She groans as I hand her a can, but then she pops the lid and takes a sip.

"Let's see if the war has started, if we've bombed anybody yet," I say as I turn on the television set. I unfold some newspapers and set the branches out of the floor. I'm going to peel the bark and then shellac the lot of them, make a rectangular skeleton of branches and then put plywood down. I'm making bookshelves even though I don't own any books. It's something to do; something for my hands, for my mind, until I've had enough to drink that I don't need anything.

"I've got to lay down," Connie says.

I turn down the volume on the television set and take a look at her; her face is pale and bloated, and she's got these big rings of sweat around her armpits, soaked right through her sweater.

"You want me to help you get back to your place? You need to go to bed?"

"Can I stay here?" she asks. "Maybe just on the couch?"

I take a sip of beer and nod to her, but I also point to the case of beer that's still left. "You can stay here, but I'm planning on getting drunk. I won't be much use to you."

She doesn't hear me, or at least she doesn't respond. Her eyes close and she turns over onto her side and curls into a fetal position. I turn the television back up and take another gulp of Pabst.

The war on Iraq hasn't started, not yet.

I can't get the branches to fit together. I'll have to collect more sticks and twigs if I want a solid frame.

UN demands Iraq dismantle short-range missiles as US prepares to invade.

Welfare reform squeaks through without debate as administration announces deficits.

Rhode Island nightclub burns to the ground, 95 dead after metal band's pyrotechnics unleashed.

Scott asks if I want to get a drink after work. He's got his trench coat and fedora on; he's heading for the door even though we've got ten minutes until the shift is over, but he tells me he'll buy the drinks.

I put on my coat and tell the customer that she really ought to think it over before she buys a full set of books, tell her I'll call her back next week, and hang up before she has a chance to answer.

Scott doesn't want to go to the usual spots for this neighborhood; he's not interested in the Virginia Cafe, or Kelly's Pub. He wants a bottle of single-barrel whiskey, and the only place where we can get the stuff is a cigar bar twelve blocks up on Burnside.

"It's smooth, isn't it?" he asks.

I admit it. It's the best liquor I've ever had.

"In America just a few dollars will buy you the plunder of kings," he says. "Anybody can feel like a millionaire."

"A millionaire? That's chump change," I tell him.

"Would you like to see a trick?" he asks.

I don't answer, but ask him what's up with the tricks, why he feels it's necessary to perform for the management. I ask him if he's an ex-magician, and if he knows how to make balloon animals.

"I'm not a magician, but my grandfather was. His father was too. We haven't had any stage magicians in the family sense the First World War," Scotchy says. "I've often thought of trying it out again, it seems like a noble profession, but I just don't have the discipline to do both things. I don't have enough time for the project and show business," Scott says. "Stage magic isn't something I can invest in, but it's a fun sideline. It's instructive." He reaches out for the whiskey bottle and sets it next to his glass. "You want to see a card trick?" he asks again.

I nod. What the hell, why not? When Scott is sure that I've agreed to watch he starts to pour the whiskey, only instead of smooth liquor a spray of playing cards flip up from the mouth of the bottle.

"You want a refill?" he asks.

And before I can answer he pours out another deck of cards. This time all of the cards are aces.

"Nice," I say. "How's it done?"

"It's just a matter of the hands moving faster than the eye," he says.

"I've heard that before."

Scott pours out whiskey into his glass, slams the shot back, and then glances up at me like he's just noticed I'm there, like he's been talking to somebody else all along, and I've just walked in and interrupted.

"You want to see a real trick?"

"Not especially," I say.

"I'm talking about a real trick, not stage magic," he says.

"Yeah. You going to get to work on time and actually make a sale?"

"It's a real trick, real magic. It involves the newspaper clippings you're so curious about," he says. "Aren't you curious about the clippings?"

In fact, I am. I want to know what he does with the headlines but, more importantly, I want to know why the management lets him get away with clipping instead of calling. I want to know what he does that makes him above the rules.

"It's mostly a matter of the hand being faster than the eye," Scott says. "But also there are cracks in the rules. Not everything is always simple. It's not all just cause and effect."

"So show me," I say.

And, after a bit more whiskey, he does. Right there in the bar he shows me his real trick, over by the video poker machines. He takes the headlines, folds them in half, and puts them in a deposit envelope. He folds the envelope in half and places it into the slot for the debit card in the ATM, and waits as the machine spits out cash.

"I usually get more back than this," Scott says. "Today was sort of a slow day." He counts his money, it comes to just under five hundred dollars, and uses a hundred of it to pay for the whiskey.

"Hand faster than eye?" I ask.

"No, not really. In fact, I don't exactly know how it works," he says.

Markets tumble after Bush administration announces Corporate Responsibility Board appointments.

Attorney General sets new plans to enhance security in motion despite objections from ACLU.

Britain predicts catastrophic global warming, US asks for more study.

Connie seems better today; she asks for pot but there isn't as much desperation in her voice as usual, and she almost seems to be enjoying herself as I pack the pipe and turn on the television set.

"The doctor says I should get my affairs in order," she tells me after she takes a hit. "I'm thinking about hospice care."

It's Saturday. I would be in the woods today, hiking through Forest park or maybe out in the gorge, except for the rain. It's coming down hard, occasionally hailing. I watch the ice hit the window pane and worry about broken glass.

"I'm dying, Ian," Connie says.

If it weren't raining I'd be in the gorge, hiking up on Starvation Ridge maybe or out on Wildwood trail. My hiking boots are still good, a little thin in the soles, but they're solid shoes. I should waterproof them.

"You want to go for a hike? I've got some rain gear."

"I'm too tired. It's too cold."

"I've got an extra sweater."

"You're too cold," Connie says.

The two of us take hit after hit off the pipe, and watch a Matlock rerun on television. There has been a murder and the young, blonde woman who is charged with the crime wants Matlock to defend her. The southern lawyer is unwilling at first, not sure if his client is innocent, but after about ten minutes of stock footage—brown cars driving on wet streets, parking garages cloudy with exhaust and the breath of a man in a trench coat, an office full of secretaries and washed-up B-actors—Matlock decides the blonde is innocent after all.

"Ladies and gentleman of the jury…"

I switch channels to the local news.

It's raining hard on television, and the rivers are running fast, the gutters in

Portland are overflowing. There have been landslides in the south hills, a few of the mansions built on stilts up there have come down in landslides, a few have fallen apart completely.

"I don't want to go into hospice care," Connie says. "I don't want to go into the hospital either."

"I don't blame you. Who needs that shit?"

"I'm dying. I need someplace to stay."

I try not to look at her; I stare at the anchor man on television, and try not to answer her.

"Let me think it over."

"You're the only person I trust."

I laugh, tell her that she's a fool to put her trust in a drunk, but she just looks at me, takes my hand in hers, and tells me again.

"I'm dying."

"That's what you say. What if you get better? Then I'd be stuck with you."

Connie laughs, and then puts her head on my shoulder and closes her eyes.

I watch the rain on television, out the window, and worry about broken glass, about things breaking.

"Want to see a card trick?" I ask Connie. I don't expect an answer.

I set up the newspapers and branches, pry open the can of shellac, and layer the glop on my makeshift frame. So far all I've got is a crooked rectangle with a few nails sticking out at the corners. I'll have to find more wood, maybe some cork for the corners. I would have gone hiking today, found what I needed, if it hadn't been for the rain.

I flip back over to Matlock, watch him laugh with his assistant at some terrible pun. He's obviously won another case. I take another hit of pot as the credits roll.

British study predicts increase in global mean temperature of 6 degrees Celsius by century's end.

Bush says Saddam must both disarm and step down if war is to be avoided.

Second Patriot Act in works as war approaches, ACLU protests move and calls for more protection of civil liberties.

I've just spent the last half-hour on the phone with a customer, trying to convince her that the information in Time Life Books is accurate, that the research is sound, that the answers to all of her questions are there, in print, and available for only three easy payments of nine ninety-five. But she's unconvinced.

"I saw on television that the book has information about reincarnation," she says. "I know that's not in the Bible."

"All of the information about reincarnation in Mysteries of the Unexplained is information about Hindu religious beliefs, not presented as fact. There is also a great deal of information about the Apocalypse and the Book of Revelations," I tell her.

"It's not presented as fact?"

"It's not, no. Just presented as a set of religious belief, with whatever scientific or anecdotal supporting evidence also presented," I say.

"He died for you. That's a fact."

"I'm sure he did, Ma'am. But surely you're interested in the possibility of extraterrestrial contact, interested in ghosts and Big Foot and the possibility of a perpetual-motion machine."

"Nope. Just Jesus," she says. "None of that other stuff."

"Yeah?"

"So I don't think I can buy your evil books today," she says.

"What about tomorrow?"

What annoys me most is not the fact that I've wasted so much time on a religious zealot that I should have recognized as a noncustomer five minutes in, but the fact that through it all I could hear Scott on the other side of the cubicle wall. He's still at it. He's not making calls but rustling papers and using scissors. He's over there clipping out the headlines.

"I want to see it again," I tell him when the shift ends. I poke my head into his space, interrupt his project, and grab one of the headlines off the desk.

Bush says Saddam must both disarm and step down if war is to be avoided.

Scott sighs, collects his clippings in a manila folder, and opens his briefcase. He puts the day's headlines inside the case, snaps it shut again, and stands up to leave. "Come on then," Scott says. "I'll show you again, but this time pay attention."

Scott says that investing in the headlines is the secret to his family fortune. His father would clip the headlines and put them in safety deposit boxes around New England. In Vermont and Connecticut his father had a deposit box in nearly every city, in nearly every bank. Scotchy's family was worth millions, and while his father was sloppy with money, never could keep track of the stuff, the fortune never dwindled on his watch. He had a sound investment strategy that was the secret to his success. Scott's dad always invested in the headlines.

"I don't use safety deposit boxes," Scott says. "As you saw before, I use ATMs."

He takes the deposit envelope from the stand, and this time he inserts a debit card into the US Bank machine and then, looking back and forth to make sure he was not being watched and putting a hand up to block the security camera, he drops a random sampling of headlines into the envelope. He puts the envelope into the deposit slot, and without entering an amount into the machine, without selecting anything, the envelope is accepted, sucked up.

"My family fortune was built on a trick," Scott says, "and now it doesn't work." He retrieved his bank statement which read that a total of fifteen dollars had been deposited into his bank account. "That is, it still works, only less so. Ever so much less so."

He had been rich once, but as the news had gotten worse, after years of investment in the state of the world, the yield had dwindled. The family fortune had evaporated.

"It's not that news had been good in the past," Scott says. "We've always invested in bad news. It's just that, at some point, the news was so bad that I think the machines grew numb to it. It fails to shock out the dividends," Scott says.

It's raining. Wet cement and car exhaust and half-empty skyscrapers. Scott takes another bunch of headlines out of his folder, not bothering to shield the newsprint from the rain, and tries again. This time it's even worse.

"A dollar. I spent all day and I get back a dollar," he says. "You can see why I've found conventional work. You can see what I've been reduced to."

I clap him on the shoulder. "Maybe it will get better," I tell him. "When the war comes it's bound to get better."

"Everything I know tells me you're right," Scott says. "That's what I'm betting on, hoping for, but I'm worried. I'm beginning to wonder if there might be an internal contradiction involved with this, some sort of natural limit."

"Maybe so," I say.

Destruction of Iraq not part of US/British war plans.

Oregon's credit status worsens.

Warm front moves across Northwestern United States, breaking records for high temperatures.

I wake up and find myself twisted up in the bedding, the bedsheets snarled around my legs and midriff. My body is hot, my tongue dry, and my throat parched and pained. I stumble to the bathroom and try to remember if I'd been on a drinking binge the night before, try to remember what it is that's making me sick.

I step into the bathroom and reach inside the shower stall to get the hot water going. I turn the tap, and then step forward to use the toilet, but the shower won't turn on, and after I flush the bowl remains empty. I go to the sink, kicking yesterday's underwear and socks out the way, and turn the tap, but nothing comes out.

They've shut off the water. They've shut off the water again. How far behind am I in the water payments anyhow? And didn't water used to be covered by the rent?

By the front door, fully dressed, I button the top button on my blue oxford cloth dress shirt and adjust my red paisley tie. I run my hands through my hair one last time, take a glance in the front hall mirror. It's not too bad, but without a shower I know that I'm going to start to smell by midmorning. I just hope that I can find a spot in the back of the chapel, and that nobody will ask me anything, that I won't have to explain to her parents or sister who I am or how I knew her.

I find the mail pile on the front table, sort through it, and discover the AT&T water bill. I'm three months behind in my water payments. But when did AT&T get a hold of the water works? I can't remember having to pay this much for indoor plumbing before. Next thing they'll be charging for air.

At the funeral home I take a seat in the back, well away from the rest of the bereaved, and try not to listen to the pop song they're playing in remembrance. I heard this song often enough when Connie was alive; she'd play it over and over again in her studio apartment. She said it was her favorite, the only song she could stand after she found out that she had cancer, but I never liked it. It was just some generic folk tune, some sixties anthem by Joan Baez or someone like that, and while the words made sense they never really meant anything to me.

"Freedom is just another word for nothing left to lose," the female singer croons. It makes sense. Of course it makes sense, but I don't want to hear it.

The funeral director steps forward and turns off the boom box unceremoniously. He thanks everyone for coming to "celebrate the life of an amazing woman," and asks if the people in the back might move forward so he doesn't have to shout. He's standing there at a podium, behind a microphone, but apparently he doesn't want to turn the microphone on.

I stay where I am, but the few other stragglers move forward, and the microphone doesn't get turned on, so I can barely hear what the minister is saying. He's talking about dying young, and a life well lived, a life examined. He's saying that Connie was an incredibly sensitive person, an intense personality, a good and loyal person.

I can't really hear.

When did AT&T buy the water company? When did the building manager stop including water in my rent? Why is it so damned hot? It's only March and it's already in the 80s. Why is everything so different, so much worse than it was last week? Everything seems worse than it was just yesterday.

"When did she die?" I find myself asking. I stand up and make my way past the bereaved, all the way to the front, and step up next to the minister, before I even have a chance to think about it.

What am I doing?

"Connie's not supposed to be dead," I say. "Not yet. She's not supposed to be."

"Sir," the minister says. He reaches out to touch my shoulder but I block him like a boxer and he takes a step back.

I turn on the microphone, and lean down to it.

"How long has she been dead? When did she die? This isn't supposed to be happening," I say.

The minister is making another approach, his arm out like he's going to try to put his arm around my shoulder, maybe try to put me in a headlock.

"Don't touch me. Just answer."

"Connie died two days ago," the minister says.

"That's not right," I say. "She was with me two days ago."

"She was at the hospital, in the intensive care unit at Good Samaritan Hospital, when she died. Now sit down or I'll have you removed."

"She was alive yesterday. She slept over at my place, I saw her off to work yesterday morning," I say.

"Who are you?" a woman in the front asks. She's got bleached-blonde hair, a tight, red sweater on, and she looks like she's pushing sixty.

"I was her…her neighbor," I say.

"Her neighbor?"

"Her boyfriend. Connie and I were involved."

"We didn't know Connie had a boyfriend," she says. "She never told us about you."

"I saw her yesterday morning. I saw her just yesterday," I say.

The minister gets his arm around my shoulder, puts his other around my middle, and whispers in my ear that everything is going to be all right. "Just sit down now. Go back to your seat. I'm sure Connie wouldn't have wanted this. For her sake stop this disruption," he says. "I don't want to have to call security."

"She isn't dead. She isn't supposed to be dead.

Bush says regime change, not disarmament, is real motive for war.

Tony Blair faces resignations in his cabinet over Iraq.

Peace activist in West Bank run over by bulldozer. Israel offers an apology.

Scott isn't at work on Monday. His desk is cleared off, the fliers and order sheets are no longer tacked to the cubicle walls, and his scissors and paste, his piles of newspapers, are missing as well. But when I ask the manager where he is she tells me that he's called in sick.

"Time Life Books," I say into the phone. "Mysteries of the Unexplained," I say. "The Old West. The Civil War. 1968. The History of Aviation. The Middle East. The Birth of Rock. The History of the World."

"Hello?" The customer breathes heavily into the phone.

"Mysteries of the Unexplained," I say. "The History of the World."

I sell four full sets of books, get the ten-dollar bonus for the night, and count my commission.

Iraqi troops, mistaking British exercises for attack, crawl out of trenches and surrender before war starts.

Unemployment rate highest since 1939.

It's getting worse and worse. I'm alone in my studio apartment. The humidity and heat is making the wallpaper bubble, and I'm drinking one Pabst Blue Ribbon after another while I cut up the newspaper.

When I get really drunk I sometimes forget who I am, stop believing that my identity stops at my skin. It seems silly to be just one person amongst billions, it seems strange to have never lived before, to be so limited and small, to never to have known God.

I pick up the wooden frame that I've built, this skeleton of branches and nails. It doesn't look like a bookshelf at all, it looks like a makeshift ladder, only it just goes halfway up. If I climbed it I'd end up stuck in empty space.

I'm really drunk, staring at my reflection in the bathroom mirror and wondering how this could have happened again. I hold up one newspaper headline after another and bug out my eyes as I read each caption.

"Israeli troops bulldoze Gaza strip in retaliation," I say.

"Britney Spears hires double to thwart Japanese stalker."

"Faith community in trouble."

I fold the newspaper clippings and stuff them into my jeans, find a T-shirt and sneakers, and pick up the portable phone on my way out the door.

"This is Connie. I'm either heaving my guts out in the bathroom or not at home right now. In any case I can't come to the phone. Leave a message if you want."

"I'm sorry, Connie. Constance. But I'm going to make things worse. I've got bills to pay," I tell her. "I'm sorry you're dead." I hang up the phone and open the door, and then turn back and pick up the phone again. When I hear the beep I start over:

"I miss you," I tell her. "I love you," I tell her machine.

I find Scott at the cigar bar. He's got a bottle of whiskey, a deck of cards, and a bow tie in front of him. He's counting his cash, spreading headlines and dollar bills and playing cards across the table, and drinking directly from the bottle. It's not the good stuff tonight, it's the house whiskey he's drinking.

"How does it work, Scott? What's the catch?" I ask.

Scott tosses a fifty-dollar bill onto the pile in front of him, picks up the bottle of whiskey, takes a gulp, and then finally acknowledges me.

"Ian," he says. "Hello, Ian. How are sales?"

I sift through the headlines on the table, pick a lead from an article about the humanitarian crisis in Afghanistan, and hold it up to him. "What's the catch, Scott? What kind of magic are you committing?"

Scott doesn't answer right away but offers me a shot from the bottle. He shuffles all of his paper into his briefcase as I take a sip. He puts his bow tie back on, and tries to smile a winning smile at me. "Everything has a consequence," he says, and flashes another insincere grin. "Even if you can't keep track of the path between a given cause and a given effect, the relationship exists."

I tell him that my girlfriend is dead. I tell him that my girlfriend is dead before her time, and that I've been noticing other changes, problems that weren't around before.

AT&T didn't used to own the water works, the temperature wasn't this high, and we didn't have to, weren't necessarily going to, go to war. But now, since I'd seen his trick, it had all gotten worse. How does it work? What is the trick and why does he keep doing it when the consequences…the consequences are disastrous.

"You're jumping to conclusions," Scott says. "There is a lot of cheating going on. The hand is almost always faster than the eye, so you can't say that I'm responsible."

I reach across the table, and without thinking about it I slap him hard across the face. I grab him by the shoulders and shake him as hard as I can.

"How can you keep doing it?" I ask. "How does it work?"

Scott puts his hand on my arms, untangles himself from my grip, and then looks at me and tries out that smile again.

"Which do you want?" he asks. "Do you want to blame me for something, or do you want to learn how to do it yourself? You can't have it both ways."

I don't answer, but I lean back from him. I give him some space.

He offers me the bottle, and starts to explain. He tells me how it's done; shows me how to make my hand move faster than my eye.

I'm drinking Knob Creek single-barrel whiskey and admiring my new bookshelves from Treasures Furniture; they're made from birch wood, solidly built, and fairly expensive. They ran me over five hundred dollars, but they were worth it. After all, I needed a place to display my complete collection of Time Life Books.

My makeshift ladder of branches and cork and bent nails is out in the dumpster.

The headline trick was remarkably easy.

I smiled for the security camera, removed the deposit envelope from its slot, and placed the headlines inside. I licked paste, folded the envelope shut, and made my investment.

Bush promises to use high-yield nuclear weapons to destroy Saddam's weapons of mass destruction.

UN passes US/British resolution setting benchmarks for Iraqi disarmament. France, Russia, and China abstain from vote.

Terrorist threat levels reach Orange Level for the second time. Ridge urges diligence but advises people "remain calm."

The ATM screen blinked a balance of 10,000 dollars.

I try not to think about Connie, find it easy not to think about her. Instead I replay my resignation from work, my phone call to my manager. I told her she was incompetent, told her I was quitting, and then made her take an order. We went over all of it, from the Civil War to Vietnam, from Doll Collecting to UFOs, I made her describe each book, pitch every damned book. And she did it. She hated me for it every second, but she had a job to do, and at Time Life the calls are monitored.

I don't think about Connie. Instead I think about the Headline trick.

What did Scott say that first time? Something about game theory and how there weren't any fixed rules.

Will there be a war tomorrow? Will there still be clean air to breath and water to drink? How long can life go on like this?

Everything I know about magic I learned from television and movies like *Willy Wonka and the Chocolate Factory*, *Camelot*, and the one or two surrealist films I saw in college. I think Salvador Dali said that he believed in magic. He said that surrealism, that films, were about creating real magic.

In the *Willy Wonka* movie Wonka made kids turn into blueberries, made them get sucked up factory pipes, made them fly in glass elevators. Gene Wilder played the part, and he sang a song called "Pure Imagination." The lyrics came back to me during the screening of the Dali film years later in college, and the two films are associated in my head now. When I saw Dali cut an eyeball open I thought about Gene Wilder eating a teacup made of wax and sugar. I thought about "Pure Imagination," and I thought about all the mysteries, the unexplained events, I'd seen on television.

Investing in the headlines is a short-term venture. It's amazing that anyone ever thought they could create a real family fortune this way. But I'm not interested in a dynasty, I just need to pay the rent and I've had enough of the Mysteries of the Unexplained, had enough of the History of the World. I've got these things where I want them. I own them now.

The Knob Creek whiskey is smooth, and I'm drunk again in no time.

Before I can really think about it I've got out my scissors, I've got my manila envelope. One by one I take the Time Life Books off their shelves. I pick the worst entries from the History of the World and from the Wild West and cut them out.

THE SUBURBS OF THE CITADEL OF THOUGHT

(A MODERN ROMANCE)

THE FOURTH WALL

Philip Hoffman sat outside of Bonnie's Hamburgers and Gas and let the other mental patient test his psychic powers.

"What am I thinking?" his friend Joe asked.

Philip poured nondairy powder into his Styrofoam cup, and stirred his coffee with a thin plastic straw. "Have you ever seen George Roy Hill's film adaptation of *Slaughterhouse-Five*?" he asked.

Of course, Philip Hoffman isn't real. It's just a name I made up, a name I put together from two real names. Philip Hoffman is named after Philip K. Dick, whose novels and stories depict a universe without a center, and radical yippie Abbie Hoffman, whose guerrilla theater and absurdist protest tactics shook up the sixties.

Philip Hoffman is psychic. His precognitive powers are a threat to the neat and tidy suburban culture of Beaverton, Oregon.

"I'll give you a hint. I'm thinking of a number," Joe said.

"Eleven," Philip said.

"Well, sure. Okay." Joe dangled a limp French fry off his paper plate and took a bite. "That's my favorite number. That doesn't prove anything."

"They made the movie sometime in the early seventies," Phil said. He sipped his coffee and then started stirring again. The nondairy powder just spiraled around on top of the coffee, refusing to settle and blend. "*Slaughterhouse Five* is a science fiction story, you know, and back then they didn't have much in the way of computer technology. So, when it came time to shoot the flying saucer sequence they simply scratched a circle into the film…frame by frame."

Joe lifted a burlap bag up to eye level, and then theatrically swung it in circles to the ground. He reached in, stirred around, and then looked up towards Phil.

"Guess what I'm holding," Joe demanded.

Joe will not appear in this story again. He is a temporary figure and that is why he only has a first name. I would have given him no name at all if I could've thought of a way to do that without damaging my depiction of Philip.

Philip seemed cold and aloof when Joe was nameless. The story is told from Philip's point of view and if I fail to mention a character's name it is assumed that Philip doesn't know the character's name. If I refer to a man as "the mental patient" repeatedly, it is assumed that these are the words that Philip would choose as well.

I want Philip to be likeable and sympathetic. I want you to identify with Philip.

So Joe is named Joe.

Philip looked up and across the street. He looked over at the tiny steeple of the Unitarian Universalist church. "That's how it will be when they come. Just like in *Slaughterhouse-Five.* That little scratch was a violation of conventions, it broke the fourth wall."

"Guess what I'm holding."

"That's not how it works," Phil said. "I can't just guess."

"You said you were telepathic. Guess what I'm going to pull out of the bag," Joe said.

"I never said that. I don't read minds," Phil said. "I have precognitive powers, that's all."

It was true. Phil didn't have any telepathic powers; he couldn't read minds. Philip had been in and out of hospitals and group homes for half of his life because he could see the future embedded in the present. For him the world was a layered mess. At least, most of the time it was.

The medication the nurses gave him helped, and living in Beaverton, that helped too.

"Guess what's in the bag," Joe said.

Phil had grown used to people doubting him, it didn't bother him. Usually he wouldn't try to prove anything. His power only scared people anyway. But, occasionally, he'd lose his patience.

"A fish," Philip said.

Joe pulled a wooden cross from the bag, raised it up to Philip as a refutation.

"A fish," Phil repeated.

Joe started to shake. "Stop," the mental patient said. He seized up, dropped the cross onto the sidewalk, and then slid out of his chair and onto his knees. "Stop reading my mind!"

"I'm sorry," Philip said. "But there's nothing I can do. The problem is that history…I mean the future…has already happened or will happen and I can see it."

"I don't believe you."

"It doesn't matter. They're coming anyway," Philip said. "The aliens will arrive on August 23, 2004. I will be riding the number eleven bus at the time, on my way to work at the Unitarian Universalist Church of Beaverton. There is nothing anyone can do about it."

BOXES

The Raphael House was a smudged but airy two-story house with walls made of cement and glass; it stood on the corner of 110th and Everett and across from Bonnie's

Hamburgers and Gas. The front porch was built out of heavy cement and was sinking into the front lawn. It ran slant wise toward 110th, and the card tables and folding chairs had to be pushed away from the edge of the porch every few days. The tenants at the Raphael House had a tendency to slide.

The Raphael House and its architecture are important to this story because they are important to the character Anna Snow, who is about to be introduced.

Anna Snow is married to local Unitarian Minister Henry Snow and she's obsessed with modern architecture. She is going to be Philip's love interest. She is obsessed with modern architecture, and the Raphael House is a modern house; it is a structure that conforms to some of the ideals of modernism.

The futurist FRS Yorke wrote that modern architecture could afford "no compromise between the plan that is made for service and the symmetrical or picturesque facade." In other words, the outer shape of a modern house was to be determined by its internal structure.

This sort of architecture was stark, and its functional elements were exposed without regard to aesthetics or appearance.

When Philip spotted Anna Snow, she was sitting on the curb across the street from the Raphael House and sketching on a large pad; she was staring and scribbling and erasing and staring again.

"Excuse me, but are you—I mean, is that supposed to be art or something?" Philip asked.

The question was wrong; what he wanted was reassurance not a confrontation. He watched her for twenty or thirty minutes, watched her watch and sketch the house, and his paranoia increased as the minutes ticked by.

He was attracted to her. There was an aura of importance around this woman with short but bright blonde hair who frowned and stuck out her tongue while she drew. He caught himself staring at her pale smooth legs, caught himself tracking up toward where her sundress hung loosely around her thigh.

He was on Thorazine and a dozen other drugs, he hadn't had a sexual impulse in years, and here he was staring at her. It was false, forced, a setup.

The present just kept unwinding and linking up with the future.

Anna stared at his house and scribbled away in her pad, and Philip decided that she was one of them—one of the aliens.

"I was just asking, you're an artist, aren't you? You're not taking notes or spying or anything like that, are you?" Philip asked.

"I'm drawing a picture of that house," Anna said. She squinted up at him from the curb, and pointed vaguely toward the other side of the street. She handed the sketchpad over to him, and then sat awkwardly waiting while he flipped the pages.

"These are just a bunch of boxes," Philip said.

Anna got up, stood next to him, and leaned over his shoulder. It was an overly familiar gesture; she pressed up against his back and didn't move away.

"Flip ahead, they get better," Anna said.

"A shoe box," Philip said, "and here's a deck of cards, and a pack of gum."

"Yes," Anna said, "I've been trying to draw just the most essential parts, get down the basic meanings of the buildings. At first I could only come up with those boxes and cubes, and then I tried to transform the drawings." Anna put her hand on Phil's shoulder, "What do you think?"

Why is this suburban housewife making a pass at a man who lives in a halfway house? Why?

There are all kinds of reasons. The first is that Philip Hoffman is physically attractive. The years he's spent as a ward of the state have been kind to him. He's never held a job and his face is relaxed and unlined; he has full dental coverage and has excellent teeth. Philip Hoffman has the kind of good looks that might be described as boyish. He also had a larger than average penis and a well-proportioned backside.

But in reality Anna is attracted to Philip because I want her to be attracted to him. I'm controlling her, controlling this scene, in order to make it conform to a predetermined ending. I'm beaming an attracto ray at these two characters while I rev the engines of my flying saucer.

I'm one hundred thousand light years away, on the other side of the galaxy, and I have to travel fast if I'm going to arrive in time to crash right outside of Beaverton on August 23, 2004.

"They're ugly drawings," Philip said. He handed the sketchpad back to Anna, being careful not to touch her hand, and stepping back out of her reach.

"They're ugly houses," Anna said.

Philip nodded, and smiled at her despite himself.

SUPERMARKETS

The Beaverton Fred Meyer's supermarket was huge, airy, and full of natural light and bright red packages; all of the generic brands—boxes of sun-dried raisins, loaves of plain white bread, bags of barbecued snack chips, bottles of cola drink—were in bright red rows.

"Help me find something like that Vallingby building," Anna said.

"What does it look like?"

"You know that light green thing," Anna said. "It's box-shaped."

"We're in the wrong aisle for that color," Henry said. "You've got to help me find a religious breath mint."

"Right," Anna said.

Henry Snow was forty-six years old and mildly famous. In 1985 he'd revitalized the Unitarian Universalist Church of Beaverton and by extension revitalized Unitarianism along the entire West Coast.

It was the Reagan era and the Unitarian Church was hopelessly out of step. It was helplessly earnest, terribly rational.

When Henry came on in 1983 he decided to cultivate a new image. The standard tweed jacket and black pipe just didn't play in suburbia anymore, and so Snow opted for a more ironic and alienated posture.

The first thing Henry did was to bring in television sets. He bought twelve sets, some black-and-white, some color, some broken and showing no picture at all. Then he had the cable installed.

Henry turned on the televisions and developed a self-conscious stutter—a tendency to robotically repeat key words over and over. His first sermon, "Religious Symbols in Today's Advertising Campaigns," was a hit.

"Coke is the real-real-real thing. Pepsi is the choice-choice of the new-new-new-new gen-gen-generation. But, which soda-which soda-soda-which soda does God like best?" Henry stuttered from the pulpit.

The systematic debasement of the spiritual, and indeed all of life, by a society that is mediated by corporate sponsors and commercial images, was the subject of Henry's lecture. But most people just enjoyed seeing the Purina Puppy Chow wagon and hearing the "Be a Pepper" song again.

Henry became slightly famous, and then he became slightly fat. By 1990 his oversized beige suits weren't so oversized, and he took to wearing blue jeans with a suit jacket and strange purple ties.

In 1999 Henry Snow was suffering from a midlife and spiritual crisis that made him wish he'd worn tweed after all.

"John Watts is dying," Henry told his wife as they pushed their cart full of red boxes to the checkout stand. "I visited him at Good Samaritan Hospital today, and I don't think he has much time left."

Anna nodded vacantly, and stared through the pane-glass windows of the supermarket and out across the street at a little box-shaped cafe made of cement and plastic. A pink box with little amusement-park flags all around the top proudly displayed its name on what looked like an old movie marquee. She'd walked by this cafe a thousand times, but never really saw it before.

"I visited him today. I sat there next to this old man's bed-pan and couldn't think of anything to say."

The cafe was a perfect cube. It did not look like a place where food might be served.

"I started telling him the story of the Aspen ski trip, the time when I broke my collar bone," Henry said as he handed his credit card to the checkout girl. "Watts can't talk anymore, you know? He's got Parkinson's disease and so the old guy can't move, he can't say anything. I described the blizzard to him. I told how I had to be flown off the mountain, and how terrible the hospital staff was. I just babbled at him and he couldn't escape me. He couldn't do anything but lie there and slowly die."

"You were nervous," Anna said. "That's all."

"I quoted the Sex Pistols," Henry said.

"What?"

"I quoted that song, 'Holidays in the Sun'. I was talking about how terrible vacations are and that song jumped into my head," Henry said. He signed his name on the charge slip, and pushed the groceries toward the automatic doors. He pushed the cart halfway through so that he was standing in front of the electric eye that opened the doors. "In the end I just left him there. I didn't even say I was sorry, or tell him I'd pray for him, I just left."

"It's all right. It's all right," Anna said, suddenly snapping to attention. Henry was holding up traffic, he was blocking the door. "Let's keep going."

"Keep going? I don't know if I can."

My grandfather's name was John Lain. He was a Buddhist.

Alan Watts was an Episcopal priest who dropped out of the church in order to popularize eastern ideas during the 1960s.

My grandfather died a few weeks ago. I didn't get to know him very well when he was alive, but I always wanted to. He died at the age of eighty-one of Parkinson's disease. Toward the end of his life he could not speak at all.

But I'm forgetting about the plot.

When Anna noticed that her husband was upset, that he felt as though he'd failed as a Unitarian, she suggested that he do something, a good deed, in order to compensate. She suggested that Henry hire Philip Hoffman as a janitor for the church. The church needed a new janitor and good honest hard work might help the mental patient. More importantly, although she didn't say this to her husband, this would mean she would see Philip Hoffman again. Her husband's outburst, his weakness, made her want to see Philip Hoffman again.

CLOSED CIRCUIT

When Philip felt that the aliens were intervening he would get thoroughly stoned. So, while he read the secret messages in the patterns of his oatmeal, before he got dressed for work at the Unitarian Church, Philip took twice his regular dose of Zoloft, and drank half a bottle of Kahlua.

For the first twenty minutes Philip couldn't decide whether or not there really was a neon Jesus hanging where the cross should have been. And when he stumbled upon a Buddha wearing shades and carrying a coffee cup in one hand and a cellular phone in the other, he half-expected that the statue would start talking to him.

But it was all real. The church was decorated with religious kitsch, and even the traditional icons and stained-glass windows had ironic titles such as "John the Baptist wants you to join the US Marines," or "This is not a God."

Irony was not what Philip needed given the circumstances, and as he set up the molasses cookies, lemon/lime punch, and coffee pots, he tried to think of a way out.

The moments were coming close together. Time was stacking up against him, connecting and projecting Philip into an empty future.

He considered packing up and camping out by the crash site. If he could avoid all contact with people maybe he could alter the future, catch the aliens red-handed.

Everything he needed for a long retreat in the outskirts of Beaverton was right there, in the church kitchen. A portable propane stove, six flashlights, four backpacks, and fifteen packages of dehydrated fruit were labeled with masking tape and waiting for him.

"RETREAT," the labels read.

The shelves in the kitchen were full of canned beans, peas, soup, and even Spam.

Phil couldn't resist the convenience of the synchronicity. He started stealing. He loaded one of the packs with canned food and flashlights and dehydrated fruit. He strapped the propane stove to the bottom of the pack, and then stepped out into the hall and across into the church library. He would need something to read. He selected two thick books, both cheap paperbacks.

The two paperbacks were Jean-Paul Sartre's *Being and Nothingness*, and God's *Holy Bible*.

He went back to the kitchen, grabbed a molasses cookie, and proceeded to stuff the books into the pack while holding the cookie in his mouth. He started to drool. He set down the pack, and bit through the cookie.

Looking into the pack he saw that the Bible had shifted open and was dangling over the lip of the frame. Philip ate his cookie, and then picked up the Bible and read the pages fate had brought him.

"I looked; a stormy wind blew from the north, a great cloud with light around it, a fire from which flashes of lightning darted, and in the center a sheen like bronze at the heart of a fire. In the center I saw what seemed like four animals. They looked like this. They were of human form. Each had four faces, each had four wings."

Philip skipped ahead.

"I looked at the animals; there was a wheel on the ground by each of them, one beside each of the four. The wheels glittered as if made of chrysolites. All four looked alike, and seemed to be made one inside the other."

The Bible had opened to the beginning of Ezekiel. The aliens were blocking him. It was a paradox. He wanted to meet the aliens, but he also wanted to avoid their influence. They were always intervening, they were omnipresent, but they were pushing him away. The aliens revealed themselves at every turn, and yet still eluded him completely.

Philip is trapped by the future. Like a modern day Oedipus Rex, he knows, but can't accept his fate, and this rejection of the inevitable is the very engine that drives his destiny.

For Oedipus, there were simple solutions to the problems the Fates posed to him, simple ways Oedipus could have escaped.

Oedipus could have avoided incest with his mother, for instance, by refusing to bed any woman older than he was. He could have thwarted patricide by adopting pacifism. Oedipus could have thrown down his sword.

But Oedipus couldn't see the simple solutions and neither can Philip. There is no story in fate escaped, nothing interesting about tragedy avoided.

Still, Philip's urge to run is a good one, he might gain his freedom if he runs.

But he won't run. I won't let him run. I've distracted him with the Bible and beamed doubts at him with a neurological broadcast emitter. Philip isn't going anywhere.

I am halfway across the galaxy now. My flying saucer is doing warp speed and the Gray Aliens are dancing wildly and drinking cow's blood.

THE NEXT VOICE YOU HEAR, OR 15 MINUTES OF CHRISTIANITY

Philip sat down next to the refrigerator. He was riddled with doubts, unable to escape, and so he did what came naturally, did what comes naturally to all of us. He watched television.

The screen was mounted by the door, right above the camping gear. The set had no dial, no buttons other than an on/off switch. It was a closed circuit set. Henry Snow's Sunday performances were broadcast to every corner of his church. There were television sets in all of the coat closets and in both the men's and women's bathrooms.

Phil watched Henry step onto the small stage and take his place behind the podium. The minister wore an oversized white suit, and his thinning hair was slicked back on his head. A movie screen lowered behind him, blocking the neon Christ and knickknack altar.

"For the next fifteen minutes we'll be talking about Christ's dad," Henry began.

Godzilla appeared on the screen. The huge lizard-monster swatted at jets as it strode on top of Tokyo and breathed fire.

"Who is this God whose spawn died for our sins? And why are we taught to fear him?"

Cecil B. De Mille's parting of the Red Sea—two artificial waterfalls ran backwards, allowing the Jews to pass, and then ran forwards, smashing and drowning the Pharaoh's army.

A black actor named Rex Ingram appeared on the screen as God. He sat behind a wooden desk smoking a cigar while winged angels with long, white beards handed him mimeographed reports.

"His name is Yahweh. He is our father, our patriarch. He isn't always nice."

Starving children in Ethiopia looked out at the audience. Sally Struthers looked out at the congregation even more imploringly. An 800 number flashed across her face.

Charlton Heston held up two stone tablets and thought about his false beard.

"Yahweh is a God we give our fear to. He makes our fear manageable and we adore Him for it." Henry stepped away from his podium, and moved toward the screen.

"He is a cartoon God whose demands are simple and direct. 'Worship me,' Yahweh says. 'Tithe, give me gold, light incense.' He is a God that comes with an owner's manual, a God that is easily appeased." Henry stood in front of the movie screen, and the light from the projector distorted around his face, torso, and limbs. His stance distorted the images projected, but his white suit reflected enough to keep everything recognizable.

Godzilla stalked backwards, returning to the sea.

"In 1950 Nancy Davis starred in a MGM feature entitled *The Next Voice You Hear*. The premise of this movie was that God can talk to us. In fact, God does more than just talk, He talks on the radio," Henry said.

Nancy Davis appeared on the screen with kid actor Gary Gray. Knitting while she waited for James Whitmore's entrance, Nancy appeared bored.

The door opened, and James Whitmore stood in the kitchen doorway seeming mildly disturbed. He rubbed the back of his neck with his palm.

"What is it, Joe," Nancy asked.

James Whitmore, or Joe, shook his head.

"You're not listening to the radio—what's wrong?"

"Kind of a funny thing—on the radio—they announced it was exactly eight thirty, they announced it, and then there was kind of an odd empty sound. Then a voice said, 'This is God. I will be with you for the next few days.'"

"What?" Nancy asked. She put down the sweater she was knitting and, instead, knitted her brow.

James Whitmore sat down at the table and ran his hand through his hair.

"A voice said, 'This is God. I'll be with you for the next couple of days,'" James said.

"What?" Nancy asked again

Henry walked back to the center of the screen. "At first Nancy assumes God's broadcasts are a hoax…a prank. But when she realizes that God's radio show is for real, Nancy is terrified."

Nancy Davis shrieked and dropped a wineglass. An old-fashioned tube radio filled the screen. Nancy ran from the radio.

"Briefly, in a moment of transcendent revelation, Nancy Davis discovers a living God. Yahweh counts down the Top Forty and becomes real. Nancy is forced to face not Yahweh's wrath, but his own reality. Her own existence is suddenly tangible, and she screams," Henry said.

Nancy Davis shrieked and dropped a wineglass. An old-fashioned tube radio filled the screen. Nancy ran from the radio.

"And this is what Christ's message is. He appears as a man—a disk jockey—and tells us that the only way to God is through His humanity," Henry said. He turned back towards the screen.

Charlton Heston held up two stone tablets and thought about his false beard.

"Through your own humanity, Nancy," Henry yelled up to the screen.

Nancy Davis shrieked and dropped a wineglass. Nancy ran from the radio.

Henry walked back to the pulpit, the lights came back on, and the movie screen ascended up and out of the frame.

"Now if you'll all open your Philosophy 101 texts to page 352 you can read along with me," Henry said. Several people in the front row grappled to find philosophy texts underneath the pews where the prayer books and King James Bibles were, and didn't find them. "In Ludwig Feuerbach's *The Essence of Christianity,* Feuerbach said, 'Religion is a dream, in which our own conceptions and emotions appear to us as separate existences, beings out of ourselves,'" Henry said. "What this means is that the God we fear most is our own life force—our existent humanity. This God requires more than worship and alms. This God requires that we become fully aware, that we see who we are and understand what we are doing."

Snow slammed his philosophy book down across the pulpit.

"Wake up!" Snow yelled, and then walked down the aisle of the church and out, slamming the doors behind him.

THE COFFEE SOCIAL AFTER GOD

"I don't mean to complain," the squat man with the sparse white beard said around his pipe. "But it seems to me that despite all your flashiness, despite all the technique, you've ended up touting the standard secular humanist line." He adjusted his tweed sports jacket and pointed at Henry with the stem of his pipe. "You're a conventional Unitarian."

Henry chewed a molasses cookie and nodded.

"You're saying that humanity is the divine," the squat man said, and then smiled an open-mouthed, dark-toothed smile.

"Christians believe that humanity is divine. Jesus is proof that God is a human," Henry said.

"No he isn't," Philip said. He approached the philosophers and tried to contain his panic. He had to tell the preacher the truth, had to do something to change the future. Pushing his way through the congregation and holding a tray of cookies out to the men as a sacrifice, Philip tried to get Henry's attention. "God isn't human, he's an alien, a bunch of aliens really. They're on their way here to Beaverton," Philip said.

The man with the pipe and uneven white beard coughed politely.

"They're controlling things, setting me up," Philip said.

Henry smiled and took another cookie from Philip's tray.

"They're trying to get me mixed up with your life, Mr. Snow. They want to distract me away from their landing pad," Philip said.

"These aliens, you think they're God? They created the Universe?" the bearded man asked.

"Yes!" Philip said, and then cleared his throat and lowered his voice. "They created this Universe or Galaxy...maybe only Earth...I don't know."

"Did they sacrifice their only begotten son for our sins?" the man asked. "Were they born in a manger?"

Philip ignored him, pushed ahead. "They want me…I think they want me to sleep with your wife, Mr. Snow."

Henry chewed a molasses cookie and nodded.

INSTANT JESUS

A friend of mine from my day job is a fundamentalist Christian. His name is Kurt, and he lives in Tillamook, a small town on the coast of Oregon. He commutes to Portland during the week, getting up at 5 A.M. in order to arrive at work by 10 A.M. He must spend a lot of his time on the road ruminating about Jesus, because his ideas about Christ seem to be heavily influenced by billboard advertisements and talk radio.

"Jesus is a person who can appear in your life at any time, anywhere," Kurt told me once.

"Anytime, anywhere? Blip and he's there?" I asked.

"He could appear right here by these vending machines," Kurt said.

"What do you think he would buy? Doritos, M&M'S, or would he get a soda?"

I wrote a story a few months back entitled "Instant Labor." One day I'd like to write a story called "Instant Jesus."

"I can't drink coffee," Anna told him as she sat down to her double espresso. "Coffee makes me hyperactive, impulsive."

"Will you come with me to see the aliens? Will you go to the blackberry patch with me?" Philip asked.

"Maybe…" Anna leaned back, her face moving into a billow of cigarette smoke. Teenagers in cocktail dresses and overalls with bow ties posed at each other and blew cigarette smoke.

"This box is hip," Anna said. "I've got to sketch this place."

She looked across the table at the mental patient. Phil was busy arranging and rearranging a pile of drinking straws into triangles, squares, pinwheels, and flying saucers. She watched him frown at his creations and wondered why she was considering being unfaithful to her husband with yet another frowning man.

What was she hoping to find by opening all of these boxes? Why was she so unsatisfied?

She glanced toward the exit and then scanned the cashier's counter. Rows of cigarette packages were set up next to rectangular packages of powdered smart drinks.

Anna decided she wanted to open the various boxes, not to find what might be hidden, but in order to expose the obvious. She hadn't slept with her husband in months and was tired of living in Beaverton.

"We're trapped in this, aren't we? We have to play it out, and they'll get clean away because of it," Phil said.

"So what is it exactly that gives you the impression that aliens are coming?" Anna asked. She took a small sip of her espresso, grimaced against the bitterness, and then tried to smile at him.

"I already told you. The aliens talk to me," Phil said. "They're constantly talking to me."

Anna nodded absently.

"Well, okay. Right now they're talking to me through these damned straws, and if I look up I see the poster of the Milky Way, the one with the little arrow pointing to a speck of nothing, that reads 'You Are Here.' And over to our left is the guy with the green flying saucer on his T-shirt."

Anna looked over toward the other table, at the kid with the goatee and the flying saucer on his shirt. The kid wore huge sunglasses that covered his eyes and was talking into a cellular phone.

"Yeah, they're right here," the kid said. "I'm looking at them right now. What are they doing? I don't know, talking and drinking coffee. Yeah, I'll keep you posted."

The kid flipped his cellular phone closed, and then flipped it open again.

"Kirk to *Enterprise*," he said, and then turned toward Anna. "Just kidding," he said.

Phil asked the kid for a cigarette and lit up.

"Why are you so interested in boxes?" Phil asked Anna.

"I'm interested in where I live, and what I live in," Anna said.

"And you live in boxes?" Phil asked.

"Yes."

So these two are equally boxed in, and equally aware of their imprisonment. Phil is trapped by the alien conspiracy that is the framework of his life. Synchronicities surround him, and direct him toward the source, the alien. And this alien is the author of the very events that coincide in such a way as to form an arrow that points back at the author.

Anna is trapped not by the narrative structure of this story, but by the architecture of the modern world. A bored housewife, her dilemma points to a reality outside the text, and the alien author of her life invents arrows that point outwards, toward you—the reader.

Hello there, whoever you are.

"In a society where everything is a product, it only makes sense that our homes should look like cereal boxes and milk containers," Anna said. Her espresso had grown cold.

"Synchronicities are all around me, but I can only see half of the picture. I can see what's going to happen, but I don't know what it means. I don't know who I am." Phil arranged his straws into a triangle pattern, and then into a pyramid. "Will you come with me to the blackberries to meet the aliens? Philip asked.

"Tomorrow?" Anna asked back.

"The day after that will be too late," Phil said.

"Tomorrow," Anna said.

The kid with the cellular phone smiled and lit up another cigarette.

A FUNERAL

My grandfather is dead. Some of his ashes were spread over the backyard garden he'd spent much of his life tending, and some of his ashes were taken to my father's house in Colorado.

I can imagine the canister packed into a leather carry-on bag, perhaps stored in a side pocket, and then placed underneath my father's seat as he brought his tray table to its upright and locked position.

My grandfather donated his brain to science. The University of Boston took his hindbrain (rhombencephalon), his midbrain (mesencephalon), and his forebrain (prosencephalon) and sliced and diced them in order to discover how the Parkinson's disease killed him.

My wife, Miriam, asked me what would happen to his brain when the scientists were done with it. She imagined that a new container of ash might arrive in the mail at my grandmother's house. This canister of ash might be labelled simply "Lain/Brain."

I assured her that this was not what would happen.

Henry Snow had to speak at John Watts' funeral. He didn't know what to say. He decided he would start his sermon by taking a piece of chewing gum out of its foil package and placing it on the casket.

"The Big Red freshness goes on and on," he would say. Then he would turn on the congregation and tell them that John Watts was dead. That there would be no more "pure chewing satisfaction" for John Watts. And then he would call them cowards for putting up with a hypocrite like himself.

"Make your life mean something. Stop worshiping pop stars like me," he would say.

Instead Henry Snow said nothing. He simply stood in his huge white suit and stared at the ground. Eventually John's widow, Alice Watts, came up to the gravesite and consoled him. She had to climb over the mounds of dirt and lead him away from the pulpit.

And then they lowered the casket into the ground.

IRON AND GLASS

After the funeral Henry stopped talking for a few hours. Nothing to say, and nothing could rile him.

"That was stupid," Anna said.

Henry sat on their glassed-in patio and said nothing. He drank freshly squeezed lemonade mixed with vodka from a long glass tube.

"You're a fake," Anna said.

The table Henry was sitting at was made of glass, but with a stainless steel frame. The house itself was made of plastic polymers and aluminum.

"I'm going to see Philip Hoffman," Anna said. "I may sleep with him."

Henry was trapped in a cage of glass, steel, and plastic. He was beginning to appreciate Anna's obsession with architecture.

But he said nothing. He could say nothing.

ORDINARY OBJECTS

Philip sat up in bed and turned to face Anna Snow. The sex had been slow and intense, but irrelevant. She was lying on her back, examining Phil's bookshelves.

"*The Sirius Mystery*," Anna read. "*UFOs are Real, The Secret School, My UFO Family, Surviving Abductions, Visitors from Time, Fabulations, C. G. Jung's Psychology of Religion and Synchronicity*."

"I could show you," Philip said. "I could show you the structure of time."

Anna got out of bed and approached the bookshelf. She wrapped the bedsheets around herself as she went, and folded her arms beneath her pale breasts as she began to read.

"Jung was completely unprepared for the compensatory synchronistic events that were about to take place in his environment. So it was that shortly after the time of Jung's fantasy of his Anima having flown away that the Jung household was struck by a full-scale haunting." Anna paused. She surveyed Philip's small bedroom, taking in the red mixing-bowl full of stale water and dead shrimp, the dirty clothing that carpeted the floor, the cracks in the concrete walls, and the way Philip's UFO poster had come unstuck from the perspiring concrete and folded over.

"I could show you and then we could go to the blackberry patch," Philip said.

Anna continued to read. "The front doorbell began ringing frantically. It was a bright summer day; the two maids were in the kitchen, from which the open square outside the front door could be seen. Everyone immediately looked to see who was there, but there was no one in sight," Anna read, and then flipped ahead. "The whole house was filled as if there were a crowd present, crammed full of spirits," Anna read.

"Look at this," Phil said. He grabbed toward the ground, randomly selecting a half-empty bottle of antidepressants.

Philip held up the prescription bottle and the typed letters floated off the label and scattered onto the floor. Then the bottle began to grow, it swelled so that it filled half of the bedroom. The round curves of the brown plastic pressing the bed and the piles of dirty laundry against the left wall.

"I..." Anna said. "What?"

"I can show you the structure of time," Philip said.

Philip's books flew from their shelves and glided around the bedroom, dropping sentences, words, and punctuation onto the huge prescription bottle. The bottle soaked up the contents of pulp philosophy and abduction stories.

"In science fiction stories," Anna read as the words appeared on the giant bottle label, "no pretense is made that the worlds described are real."

Anna read these words of Philip K. Dick and realized that she was named Anna because of Tolstoy's *Anna Karenina* (I've never actually read the book, but my understanding is that the story revolves around a bored housewife). Anna realized her fictional nature as Philip pulled down the fourth wall.

The floor of Phil's room was littered with letters and words. Anna scanned the floor, trying to make out a coherent sentence. She read the following:

"The floor of Phil's room was littered with letters and words. Anna scanned the floor, trying to make out a coherent sentence. She read the following:"

And so on.

In Philip K. Dick's novel *Time Out of Joint*, the protagonist lived in a 1950s middle-American city that was unreal. Everything in the city kept reverting to text. At one point in the book a lemonade stand disappeared literally into thin air and was replaced by a slip of paper that read "lemonade stand."

This has all been done before, and I am flying toward this story in a flying saucer. I am orbiting the Earth and my gray friends are preparing their crop-circle designs and setting up their genetics lab. Soon we will land.

BUS NUMBER ELEVEN

Eight years ago, during what I consider my hippie phase, I took a trip to California for an environmentalist workshop and retreat. I took five tabs of acid with me on this expedition, and ingested my first dose while I was still in Portland. I dropped acid in the canvassing office of OSPIRG, which was the environmental organization that was sponsoring the retreat.

It was a sweltering summer day and I remember drinking a lot of water and watching heat rise off the highway. Eventually the van broke down, the engine turned red and sputtered. We were stuck in a gas station/rest stop near Mt. Shasta.

The driver of the van was a man named Jim Farris. Jim moved to Portland from L.A, giving up on Hollywood and his dreams of movie stardom. Jim Farris was twenty years my senior and an actual former hippie. Drugs and movies had led Jim to believe in the impossible. He believed that UFOs had contacted people on Earth, that synchronicities contained vital information, and that God was real.

He also believed that the number eleven was an important number.

Here's what happened after the van stalled:

This kid wearing a T-shirt with the number eleven stenciled on the front walked into the convenience store, opened a can of tennis balls, and scattered them across the floor. Wilson tennis balls rolled down the aisles, past the Slurpee machine and the case of frozen burritos.

"Tennis balls are important too," Jim told me.

I think I understood Jim at the time…the acid helped me to understand. Looking back on this scene, I don't know what it means. I don't know if tennis balls are important or not.

Years later I was talking to Jim in downtown Portland. We were waiting for the bus and discussing the possible impacts that alien contact with Earth would have on such human institutions as the Catholic Church, the US government, and AT&T, when I spotted the number eleven bus. What was surprising about this was that the bus was moving very fast, and didn't slow down for the intersection or stop to pick us up. What was also surprising was that we weren't at the bus stop for bus number eleven. In fact, there was no bus number eleven. The Tri-Met directory listed a number ten bus and a number twelve bus, but there was no number eleven bus listed. There still isn't a bus numbered eleven in Portland.

But both of us saw this bus, and we were both perfectly sober.

I know, I know, it's not much of a miracle. But there was also the time when I was waiting for an elevator on the sixth floor in a friend's apartment building and the elevator seemed to go past me. But when the indicator for the eleventh floor lit up the elevator doors opened and I walked in. But then again, I was very high at the time.

I'm telling you this story, I'm writing about Philip and the Snows, because I can't figure out what these kinds of events mean when they really happen to me. I'm hoping that if I make up a bunch of stuff about the number eleven and synchronicities and aliens and God that I can find real understanding. I am struggling to get this story to mean something, but I'm not sure I'm getting anywhere.

The story could go on and on, over and over.

BUS NUMBER ELEVEN

After Anna saw Phil's prescription bottle swell up she suffered a nervous breakdown. She suffered the same kind of psychotic break that Philip had suffered years earlier. Everything became meaningful for her, everything seemed to contain deep metaphysical significance.

Anna opened the Venetian blinds and looked out of Philip's bedroom toward the sky. The stars lined up into patterns: pyramids and circles and squares made up of little white dots.

"The aliens are coming," Anna said.

"They'll be here tomorrow," Philip said.

"I've got to get out of Beaverton," Anna said.

She ran out of Philip's bedroom and down the stairs. She ran across the slanted porch. She ran all the way to the corner of 105th and Failing Avenue and then she stopped running. On the corner of 105th and Failing was the stop for bus number eleven.

Philip followed her. He ran to the bus stop for bus number eleven, and he waited and he didn't say anything. He didn't try to get her to go with him to the blackberry patch. Forty-five minutes went by in silence before the number eleven bus arrived.

CHURCH AND TELEVISION.

The title of this story is a play on a science fiction story by James Blish called "Citadel of Thought." Blish wrote the story in the early fifties. In this story a swashbuckling space pirate encounters a mystical order of psychics who set up a colony beneath the surface of one of Saturn's moons, or maybe it's Jupiter.

These psychics sense that a fleet of evil aliens are about to attack Earth, and Blish's heroic protagonist has to stop them.

The psychics in "Citadel of Thought" are immortal.

This is all that my story and Blish's story have in common: an alien invasion and an obsession with death.

After Anna left Henry, he decided to go to church. He wanted to escape; he wanted to watch television; he wanted to watch a lot of television.

There were a lot of television sets in the First Unitarian Universalist Church of Beaverton.

"Take Anacin for fast, fast, fast relief," one of the black-and-white sets blared.

" 'But Fonz, I just don't feel comfortable around girls.' "

" 'Heeeeyy!' " the leather boy to Henry's right yelled from the screen.

Two hundred thirty-six people died in today's airliner explosion," the set at the front of the church stated. An animated plane appeared on the screen and then broke in half. Orange and red triangles fell out of the broken cartoon plane, but there were no cartoon bodies.

Henry sat in the front pew and watched and listened to the TVs all around him.

Peter Sellers stood on a New York sidewalk and stared at his own image in a video store window. Sellers pulled out a remote control and switched channels.

"Your wife is at Good Samaritan Hospital," Philip said. He wasn't on TV, but was standing by the door in the back of the church.

"Hey, hey, we're the Monkeys."

"Did you sleep with her," Henry asked.

"Yes," Philip said.

"What time is it?"

"Noon…a few minutes past," Philip said.

Henry had been watching for nearly eleven hours.

"Why is my wife in the hospital?" Henry asked.

"She's under psychological evaluation. She caused a scene downtown; I should have stopped her from going into that diner," Philip said.

"What did she do?"

"It involved stacking ketchup bottles," Philip said.

"Like in *Close Encounters* only Dreyfus molded potatoes," Henry said. "Are your aliens real, Philip?" he asked.

"Yes," Philip said.

Henry stood up from the pew, and turned to face Philip. The mental patient looked scared. Philip was only dressed in institutional blue pajamas and off-white slippers and he looked cold. Henry pointed the remote control toward the front television and turned it off.

"What a dump!" Elizabeth Taylor yelled. Richard Burton sat down on their black-and-white couch in their black-and-white living room and sighed. "What's that from?" Taylor asked. "Hey, Georgie! What's that from? 'What a dump!'"

Henry turned off *Whose Afraid of Virginia Woolf.* He walked the aisles of the church and turned off all the sets, and then he approached Philip Hoffman. Stood in front of him, stepped up too close.

"The aliens, they're coming here? Coming to Beaverton?" Henry asked.

"No. They're already here," Philip said.

"Can we go see them?" Henry asked.

Philip looked away from the minister, stepped back. "No. We can't go and see them," Philip said.

"It's too late for that, is it?" Henry asked. He patted his belly and then strode back to the front of the church. He nodded toward Philip. "It's too late for that?"

"Yes."

Henry stood behind the pulpit, and turned on the standing microphone. "Are you coming to work tomorrow?" Henry asked. His voiced boomed.

"Do you want me to come back?" Philip asked.

"Sure, yes," Henry said. "Nothing's changed."

Philip smiled and shook his head. "Everything's changed, Mr. Snow," he said.

UFO CRASH

The first science fiction story I ever wrote was called "The Great Space Adventure." I wrote it in the fourth grade for Mrs. Leonard. This story featured a robot named Twiki and drawings of X-wings and Tie fighters. Twiki was also the name of a robot on the television series *Buck Rogers*. I've always stolen from pop culture.

At one point in "The Great Space Adventure," I wrote:

"Suddenly I was attacked by a space monster. Luckily scientist Norman Spindel invented a laser gun.

"Zap went the space monster."

Suddenly I crashed my flying saucer into the Earth. I crashed my saucer in North America, in the United States, in Beaverton, Oregon. I crashed my flying saucer into a field of blackberries.

Smush went the blackberries.

None of my characters were around to see me arrive in their story. The Grays that were with me on the spaceship were all killed by Norm Spindel's laser gun.

I was alone amongst the blackberries. I reached out and picked one. I'd come from the other side of the galaxy in order to pick fictional blackberries and savor them in my mouth.

I reached out, picked a blackberry, and placed it in my mouth. All around there were spiny green vines and plump purple dots. And there were words there too.

The blackberry vines crisscrossed into sentences. A coincidence of light and position revealed a message from Hoffman:

HAPPY ENDING

It was 9 A.M. on August 23, 2004 and Philip Hoffman was riding to work on the number eleven bus. Anna Snow's nervous breakdown had just concluded in a coffee shop in downtown Portland and now Philip was stuck trying to pick up the pieces. He'd slept with the preacher's wife, driven her insane, and soon the aliens would be crash landing in the blackberry fields.

Philip stared at the guard rail that ran along the interstate, counted the metal posts as they flew past, and enumerated his responsibilities at the same time.

1. He was responsible to the Snows. He had to tell Henry that his wife was under observation at Good Samaritan's psychiatric wing. And he was responsible to Anna in as much as he might possibly be able to keep her old life with her husband and her boxes intact and ready for her return. It was obvious to Philip that Anna, despite her protests, could not survive without her boxes.

2. Philip was responsible to the staff at the Raphael House, and to his own therapy and recovery. It would soon be medication time at the home and he couldn't afford to miss his morning dose.

3. He had to spot the aliens. They would be crash landing their saucer right outside of Beaverton in just a few minutes, and he would be on the number eleven bus…he already was on the number eleven bus.

Philip stopped counting and looked up into the sky. A rounded, top-shaped craft with blinking neon yellow and red lights was keeping pace with the bus. The flying saucer looked, literally, like a child's toy. It looked fake, impossible. In fact, Philip could almost see what looked like a Fisher-Price logo on the side of the alien ship, and right above this he could definitely make out a silver windup key. The huge fake hung in the sky, flashed an SOS, and then dropped out of sight.

Philip turned to the businessman sitting next to him. "Have you ever seen Roy Hill's film adaptation of *Slaughterhouse-Five*?" he asked.

The businessman did not reply, could not reply. The businessman sitting next to Philip was made of cardboard. A thin cardboard cutout man swung back and forth on a spring, and looking around Philip saw that the whole bus was full of two-dimensional characters with cartoon faces—cardboard cutouts suspended on metal springs.

Philip looked out the window and the sky turned red, then purple, and then it faded until it was as white as paper.

He was seeing through the fourth wall and, Philip realized, the author was stealing more material from Dick's *Time Out of Joint*. Even the cardboard cutouts were fakes; they were literary symbols pointing toward their own fictional status...and to his fictional status.

Philip let the fullness of the revelation overtake him. He was not afraid. He stood up from his seat, the only passenger seat on the bus, and made his way toward the front, lurching along and steadying himself on cardboard housewives and transients on springs.

The sky was falling outside the bus and Philip was exhilarated. He strode to the front of the bus, to the driver's seat, and found it empty.

The bus was driving toward a dotted line of a horizon, the world was winding down, fading out. Nobody was driving the bus.

Philip sat down, asserting reality onto the seat first and then outward to the bus. He exerted himself and the passengers popped back into existence. Philip took a breath and concentrated on the narrative itself. The story would continue; he had responsibilities.

It was August 23, 2004. The UFO landed, the fourth wall fell, and Philip Hoffman drove the number eleven bus back into the story. He drove toward the part of the story called *Church and Television*. The bus sped toward Henry Snow's Unitarian Church.

Philip honked his horn and smiled as the sky turned blue. The sun was shining. It was a beautiful day.

THE DEAD CELEBRITY

Wavering in and out, stumbling past the Orange Julius and the Sharper Image, round and round, I couldn't find the door. I was afflicted by a kind of reverse agoraphobia. I was terrified of being alone, felt I had to be seen in public.

"Hello, friends," I said.

The young couple, a girl in a brown denim jacket and her slacker boyfriend, looked back at me warily.

"It's me, Ernie Becker!"

They slowed down a bit, and the guy turned and walked backwards.

"Who are you?"

"Ernie Becker!" This meant nothing to them, so I elaborated. "I'm the Soap Comics guy! You know, Charlie Roth's friend?"

"What do you want?" the girl asked.

"Lunch?" I asked back. "I thought you might join me for lunch."

This is what I do—I meet strangers, convert them into fans, and then dominate them with conversation and Styrofoam food for as long as I can.

And these two were perfect strangers.

I made them laugh, and I eyed the girl, and I told them both how lonely I was. I explained that fame had destroyed my relationships, and then, because I felt especially safe with them, I admitted that I was losing my grip.

"I can't leave," I said.

"It's okay," the girl said. She reached over her plate of teriyaki, took my hand, and held it to her chest. "You're all right now, with us."

"But I'm not real," I said. I held up my gloved hand, counted all three of my fingers, and let my arm droop unnaturally, suddenly boneless, to the ground. I folded in on myself, became two-dimensional, and fell to the ground.

"Are you all right?" the girl asked.

"I'm not real."

"Okay."

I was laid out under the table with his feet propped on my face and neck and hers on my belly and legs.

"I'm stuck," I said.

"What were you saying?" the girl asked her boyfriend.

"I'm stuck," I said.

"I wasn't saying anything," the slacker kid replied.

"Help me." They couldn't hear me anymore.

"Are you ready to go?" she asked him.

This is the way my life has been going, ever since I met Charlie Roth and became famous. Did I tell you about that yet? I was the one who found his body. I'd never met him before then, but I was the one who was with him when he died.

***

I was awe struck. Charles Roth wheeled himself over to the rail and stared down at the ice rink. He opened the box of Carmel Corn that I'd sold him and tossed a kernel into his mouth. I'd been waiting for just such a moment.

Working for Joe's Carmel Corn, day after day in the mall, breathing the air conditioning, watching the display cases change with the seasons, I wanted out. I wanted to escape my wage slave existence. Who wouldn't?

You see, I could draw, and I was relying on this little talent to save me. I'd planned my escape route to run through the funny pages, and it was almost too much to stand, watching this world-famous comic strip artist swallow wads of sugar-coated corn.

But after I'd worked up my nerve to talk to him, Charles Roth put his head in his hands, propped his elbows on the rail, and quit breathing. His cola and popcorn spilled across his lap; the thick and chunky fluid, a brown sugar mess, flowed down around the wheels of his chair.

"Mr. Roth?"

He didn't respond; he just stared down at the skaters, watched them go in circles. I followed his gaze, and thought I'd found what held him so rapt.

The kid I called Buck was on the ice.

Buck was not a professional ice skater, but he was a performer. Sometimes he seemed to focus on speed, but mostly he would attempt graceful arcs and splendid twirls. He bowed constantly and to nobody in particular and smiled, open-mouthed and pleased, while his feet, hardly moving, guided him back and forth with relative ease.

Buck was an obvious target for Charlie's pen. I'd been sketching this same skater for months. I'd drawn him hopping on tiptoes, playing air guitar on his leg, sliding on his knees.

On the day that Roth died, Buck was disrupting a round of the hokey-pokey.

The music changed and everyone stopped going round and round. Everyone clapped their hands, and put their left feet in and took their left feet out. Everyone, that is, except for Buck. While the rest turned their selves about, Buck gestured toward the ceiling and tried to skate backwards.

"Put your whole self in, take your whole self out, put your whole self in and shake it all about," the sound system blasted out over the rink.

Buck, oblivious, took a bow toward the wall.

"Thank you! Thank you very much!" Buck said.

"That's what it's all about."

But, Charlie wasn't watching the hokey-pokey, he wasn't watching Buck, he wasn't watching anything.

"Mr. Roth?" I grabbed him by his shoulder and his arms slipped. His head came down hard on the rail as his whole body shifted.

Charlie started to slide.

"Wake up!" I shook him hard, tried stupidly to drag him to his feet, pulling him from his chair. Roth flopped onto the tiled floor and the Carmel Corn and soda pop clung to his hair and his face.

Letting my fist fly back and then spring forward, bouncing off his chest, I heard a sick crunching sound. I pumped on his chest, blew into his mouth, and shook his arms, but nothing worked.

Charlie Roth was dead.

"And now let's do the chicken dance!" the DJ's voice blasted over the rink.

I waited for the security guards to arrive, for the police to arrive. I waited for the television cameras and polyester reporters.

***

The newspapers say that he'd been on the brink for years; he'd been wavering for more than a decade. The doctors didn't know what caused it, but he'd be walking to the bank, or standing behind a podium, and he'd just start to shudder. And then he couldn't walk. It went on for fifteen years: the wavering, the cane, the wheelchair. Despite everything, despite syndication, royalties, the merchandising, Charles Roth faded to nothing.

In comic books, time occurs outside the lines; it passes as an empty space between the drawings. Ten seconds can be incredibly long, filling page after page, or a lifetime can pass in two panels.

Roth got stuck, trapped, in the empty spaces on the funny pages and now I'm the one who is stuck. I'm haunted, but it's not Roth haunting me. It's Roth's celebrity; it's whatever it was that made him famous.

Before the police arrived, I looked at his sketchbook. I stood over his dead body, scanned each page, and discovered that the sketches were drawn in sequences. Charlie had been working on flipbooks.

I pressed down with my thumb and watched a smiling little figure with perfect circles as glasses, a solid mop of Beatlesque hair, and a half circle for a smile, wave at me. The cartoon man sat behind a Carmel Corn stand and held out a box of the stuff. The cartoon waved to the viewer, and then tipped the striped box and let the kernels inside spill onto the ground.

Charlie's comic strips were iconic in their simplicity; a few circles, a curved triangle, and a check mark were all he needed. With almost no shading, with clean, thick lines, he could create anger, surprise, or joy. This time I was the icon Roth created.

Okay, let's start over. I'll go through this step by step.

Roth rolled into the mall with his eyes on the crowd, obviously looking around for gawking fans, and obviously disappointed that he didn't find any. When he turned his chair to find me staring at him he smiled what I took to be a gracious smile, and pressed the joystick on his chair in my direction.

"Hi. I'm really thrilled—" I started.

"We're not friends, and I'm not interested," Charlie said. "Stop smiling at me and do your job."

"I really admire your work," I said as I filled a paper box with popcorn.

Charles pushed the joystick on his armrest and rolled back into the flow of mall traffic. The holiday shoppers streamed past him without pause, barely noticing this new obstruction.

"All I want is a box of Carmel Corn and a large Diet Coke. I don't want to talk to you."

"I'm sorry—"

"I want a large box of Carmel Corn and a large Diet Coke!"

***

My friend Harry had witnessed the exchange. Harry worked security for the jewelry store across from my stand. He was Egyptian and would stand very close when he explained things. Harry was an older man, maybe in his late fifties or early sixties. He had terrible teeth, foul breath, and talking to him was a test of endurance, but he was a kind person. Annoying, but impossible to ignore.

"Don't worry, Mr. Ernie," Harry said. "He is like snob, very Bostonian, but he is not even any good."

I sat down behind the cash register, pulled out the metal scoops, and then went to work stirring the Carmel Corn.

"He is not even funny. Not like the Charlie Brown or the Pogo. Those are classical, funny," Harry explained.

"Have you read any Soap Comics?" I asked.

"Soap?"

"Have you read Charlie Roth's comic books?"

"Oh. No, but in the *Oregonian* I see his strip on the funny pages," Harry said.

"You don't like it?" I asked.

"No. No. I don't. It's not classical. It's crap!"

***

I know all about crap; I am a collector. I collect Pez dispensers, yo-yos, cap guns, wax lips, plastic vomit, rubber chickens...but mostly I collect comic books. I grew up on Archie and Jughead, Blondie and Dagwood, but my life never measured up to the cartoons. My comics were a way to work out this disappointment. I wanted to subvert the funny pages, to punch a hole through the circle of Family Circus, to explode the tranquility of Ziggy.

I stood behind my Carmel Corn stand determined to talk to him. I would tell him about my years at the Northwest College of Art. I'd get him to give me his address and send him sample strips. I would stop being so damned meek, stop with the hero worship, and try to take advantage of the situation.

But when I finally had the nerve to try again Roth spilled his beverage across his lap and did the hokey-pokey.

***

I never could face death. That's why I started to draw comics, that's why I admired Charles Roth—I wanted to be famous, to leave my mark.

When I was younger I was more direct in my attempts to escape mortality. When I was five, I decided I was Superman.

My parents were worried; this wasn't normal. I wasn't pretending, or at least I wasn't just pretending. I really thought, tried to convince myself, that I was the Man of Steel.

"Your tights are dirty, Ernie," my mother said.

"No, these are tights from Krypton."

"Well, they may be from Krypton, but they're dirty," my mother said.

"No. These are bullet proof. These are dirt proof. I want to keep wearing them," I said. "And I want my cape. Where is my cape?"

"If we don't wash those tights they'll get old faster. They'll wear out."

"They won't, they're from Krypton."

"Everything gets old, even on Krypton."

"No. I don't want them to," I said.

I never had anything other than an ordinary facility for drawing, and I didn't start drawing comics in order to communicate any artistic vision.

I started drawing cartoons because I wanted to be Superman and live forever. But when it started to actually happen, when I discovered that Barnes and Noble had my 'zines for sale in trade paper, for instance, when I found a cardboard cutout of Ernie Becker pointing to the merchandise, I was no better off than before.

***

"It's not a healthy thing. It's a kind of transference."

Jennifer was a graduate student, or at least that was the impression she made. She was always quoting famous intellectuals, and she carried textbooks in her purse, but she never mentioned school. She hardly mentioned anything…to me anyway. I'd been trying to get her to open up, to spark her interest, for six months, but I'd learned nothing except that her professionally cropped hair and neatly pressed blouses represented a false front.

"People project their own best qualities onto other people, onto heroes," Jennifer explained. "You lose yourself in the hero so you don't have to face your life or deal with reality."

Jennifer was pretty, but in an unremarkable and anonymous way. She looked like a television actress. She looked liked she walked off the set of an advertisement for gum or breath mints. I really liked her. We'd gone out a few times, and while it hadn't entirely worked out, I hadn't given up my hopes.

I took her to a few clubs, the X-ray Café and Embers, hipster clubs with loud music and dim lights, establishments that I felt were the perfect antidote to the sterile environment of the Lloyd Center Mall. It turned out, however, that my desire to distance myself from our mutual place of employment had been a miscalculation.

"You said we were going to go to a movie," she'd said.

"I thought this would be better."

"But you said you were going to take me to see *The Truman Show*."

"Yeah, but that was only playing at the mall. I thought it would be good for us to get away from that place."

"You what?"

"I wanted to go somewhere that didn't remind us of work."

"But I like the mall. That's why I work there."

"You like the mall?"

"Of course."

She worked for Aqua Massage. Her job was to demonstrate the Aqua Massage unit, to find potential buyers for a machine that "broke preconceptions about home massage." The demonstrations weren't free, but the charge was nominal. The point was to get a few customers a week to take a unit home.

The sprinklers inside the machine ticked along, letting out fast and hard spays inside the plastic box. Jennifer watched the control panel, adjusted the jet streams, while I tried to catch her eye.

"Charles Roth is dead," I told her.

"Wait a minute, I think I've got a customer," Jennifer said.

"This isn't chitchat. The ambulance just took his body away. He's dead. Died right in front of me."

"Would you like to participate in a demonstration?" she asked the businessman as he passed. "You'll emerge completely relaxed."

"A demonstration?"

"For ten dollars you can eliminate stress," she said. "These jet streams are calibrated to hit all major pressure points and obliterate nervous tension."

"I won't get wet?" the businessman asked.

"No. Your frame will be encased in an interior plastic bag," Jennifer explained.

He handed over his cell phone and climbed inside the machine. "Okay."

"Jennifer, can't you take a minute? Come on, let's go up on the roof," I said.

"I'm with a customer!"

"Problem?" the businessman asked. He tried to turn his head to look but he was locked in position, forced to stare at the floor.

"No problem. You'll love this," Jennifer said.

Jets of water sprayed inside the coffin shaped tube.

***

It was Harry who ended up consoling me.

"I only tell this to Americans. Only Americans hear this story," Harry said. "Not Europeans and not Egyptians, no Egyptians hear this story."

"I'm an American, so it's okay to tell me," I said.

"I was not asking. I know that you are American. I was explaining that this is the strangest thing that ever happened to me. Americans are okay with strange things. They do not judge so much," he said.

Harry told me about his youth, explained that he had not been troubled, not a delinquent, but still he had been a boy and like all boys he sometimes got into trouble. When this would happen, Harry's parents would send him away, behind closed doors, into his father's study.

"So that they could punish me," Harry said.

"Kind of like a time out?" I asked.

"Hmmm...I don't know. A time out, like in a football or basketball game?" he asked.

His father's study was an empty room except for a desk and a little altar that faced Mecca. It was a boring place, and after a few minutes of his punishment Harry wouldn't feel sorry anymore, he would feel restful, sleepy. Napping next to an altar that faced Mecca, Harry would dream.

Harry touched his tongue with his index finger. He pushed his lower lip down exposing a rotting gum line, and licked his finger as though he was going to turn to the next page. It was an unconscious gesture—he'd told this story before.

"I was only a boy, but in that room I had a very erotic-like dream. I must have been seven or eight only, but it was...I didn't know or understand," Harry said.

In the dream Harry was alone with a naked woman, a very beautiful woman with long, blonde hair. She was lying on a table, on her belly.

"I could only see her back and butt, her legs. I did not see her face, her front, but only her back. And I touched her, just lightly stroking her back, but the feeling I got was...I was only a boy. I did not know what the feeling was, but it was wonderful. Just to touch her back," Harry said.

"Yeah, I know the feeling," I said.

"No, not just that feeling like you get in your groin. No, it was like that but it was more. And I had this dream a lot, you know, over and over. I did bad things, caused trouble, because I wanted to go back to my father's study. I wanted to be punished in that way, to have the dream again," Harry said.

It turned out that the dream wasn't the strange part. Years later, after Harry had grown up, Harry saw his first American movie. He was in England, and the black-and-white movie on the screen was a musical with Fred Astaire and Ginger Rogers.

"You know Ginger Rogers?" Harry asked.

"Yes."

"Well, she sang, what is that song? 'The way you comb your hair, the way you wash your face, the way you go to sleep?' You know that song?" he asked

"They Can't Take That Away from Me?" I asked.

"Yes. She sang this song, and it was beautiful, and I saw her and I said 'Oh, my God!' Because she was the one, from years earlier in my father's study. She was the naked blonde woman who I touched. It was Ginger Rogers. I'd never seen Rogers before that first time. We had no television, no movie theater, but I knew her from that dream," Harry said.

"What does that mean?" I asked.

"Maybe there are things going on we don't understand. There are memories we have that are not our own, you know. And maybe, maybe we aren't what we think all the time. Maybe we don't know our own minds, our own brains, so well? Eh?"

"I don't know," I said.

"You are a smart man, Mr. Ernie. You are a very good man. I'll stop giving you headache now," Harry said.

"No. I believe you," I said. "I believe that it happened just like you said. I just don't know…"

"I was just a boy, never seen Ginger Rogers…never! And it felt so good, Mr. Ernie. I was scared," Harry said.

"I don't know."

"We aren't what we seem? You see?"

"I see, but I don't know," I said. "It's confusing."

***

What really bothered me was the Ernie Becker flipbook. Roth had drawn panel after panel incredibly quickly, incredibly simply, reducing my image into the crudest of cartoons, and it had worked. I was recognizable. My image moved across the pages smoothly.

Harry had depth, there were aspects of his existence that weren't easy to sum up, parts of Harry were only accessible through dreams, surrounded by mystery. I, on the hand, was merely the guy with round glasses, a solid mop of Beatlesque hair, and a box of popcorn.

This is what I was thinking about when I went up the escalator to the food court. I wasn't really hungry, but I ordered a value meal at the McDonald's stand anyhow. I picked through the French fries, nibbled at my hamburger bun, and stared down at the ice rink.

Buck was interpreting the Chipmunks' Christmas album, translating the story of Alvin, Simon, and Theodore into hops and skips, slides and spins. He was lip-synching along, and all the time grandly throwing his arms over his head, accepting the calamitous praise of his imaginary audience.

"Thank you," Buck said. "Oh, thank you! Thank you, God!"

I folded my McDonald's bag flat and took a drawing pen out of my backpack.

If Roth could sum me up so simply, if he could reduce me to a few simple lines and a blot of ink, maybe I could do the same to him. I'd sketch out his death.

The most appropriate approach, it seemed to me, was to parody Roth's style, but it wasn't easy. As I scribbled across the golden arches on my bag, the intricacies of Roth's death eluded me. Using perfect circles and solid triangles, I felt like I was depicting the death of Sluggo rather than something I'd really experienced.

I drew Harry, emphasizing his mouth and teeth and his Arabness. I drew Jennifer with big breasts and perfect hips. I drew the popcorn stand and put myself behind it, drew myself with a few circles for glasses and mop-top hair.

And then I drew Roth. I drew Roth spilling his Diet Coke. I drew Roth as a corpse.

On the ice rink below, Buck toppled a seven-year-old boy as he spun and dipped. It was pathetic. Buck clearly wanted to be special, to be a hero of the ice, and he'd ended up blooding some kid's nose.

"Thank you! Oh, thank you, ladies and gentlemen," Buck mouthed to the air, completely oblivious as he slid across the ice on his knees. "Thank you!"

How different was I? Did I really know what I was doing with my comic books and plastic vomit? Looking down at the last panel of my comic eulogy, looking at Roth scribbled and dead underneath his wheelchair, I worried that I was in over my head. I worried about Ginger Rogers and other mysteries, and then crumpled up the bag and deposited it in the trash on my way out of the food court.

***

There was some guy behind the Carmel Corn stand when I arrived the next morning. Another bland white guy was stirring the Carmel Corn into pleasant heaps, wiping off the counter tops, and hooking up the soda machine.

"What are you doing?" I asked.

"Me?" he asked. He stroked his neatly trimmed beard, adjusted his glasses, and tried to smile at me. "I'm working," he said.

"You're working?" I asked. "Who are you?"

"Is there something I can help you with?"

"This my shift…this is my stand."

"I'm sorry?"

"You're in the wrong place. Who told you to come in today?" I asked.

"I come in everyday. This is my job."

"What are you telling me? You're my replacement?" I asked.

"Replacement? I don't think so."

"What then? Why are you here today?" I asked.

"I work here?"

"You work here?" I repeated.

"Every day. Day after day. Not that I love it."

***

"I saw you on television last night," Jennifer said. She turned off the water massage unit and locked it shut.

"There is somebody else doing my job," I said.

"And I saw your comic strip. I was mad at first, but then I thought it was funny," she said. "Will you autograph my copy?" She held out that morning's funny pages and a magic marker.

"The guy claims I never worked there," I said.

"Sign it for me." She handed me the morning paper and I found the funny pages. I scanned the panels, read the captions and the dialogue balloons, and held onto the side of the water coffin.

"This is my strip," I said. "The whole page is my strip."

"Yeah. How did you get them to give you so much space?" she asked.

It was all there: the Carmel Corn stand, the ice skaters, Jennifer and her Aqua Massage unit, and Charles Roth's dead body. All that was missing was the background of golden arches.

"I drew this last night," I said.

"I didn't even know you drew comics," she said.

"You didn't? I told you about it. I've shown them to you before."

Jennifer sauntered over to me and wrapped my arm around her waist.

The comic I'd drawn on the McDonald's bag was just a sketch but the comic in the paper was complete, much longer than my original.

"Something is happening," I said. "There's some guy doing my job and this is…"

"Ernie? Are you all right?"

I held the paper out to her. "I never drew this," I said.

"Come on, lets get some air." Jennifer took my hand and put my arm around her hip again.

"Yeah…okay, sure."

***

One of the maintenance stairwells had a broken door. It was rusty and had a tendency to stick, but it was permanently unlocked. Jennifer and I would tug and tug in order to go up and sit on a small metal perch near the glass ceiling of the mall. High above the customers and shops we could see the interstate, the convention center, and Forest Park. Jennifer said it helped her to breathe, to relax.

"I didn't draw that strip," I said. "I don't know how it got in the paper. I don't know what is going on."

"I'm not offended," Jennifer said. "I think I can see the birds," she said, and pointed toward Forest Park. She pressed her finger to the glass.

"Something is happening," I said. "What happened?" I asked.

"Well, whatever happened, I'm flattered?"

"Flattered?"

"Yes. Nobody has ever drawn me before, least of all in such a…a sexy way."

"I've drawn you before," I said.

She scooted in a little closer, but carefully so as not to lose her balance. Our metal perch was small.

"You've drawn me before?"

"It's just something I do," I said. Jennifer put her arm on my shoulder, leaned against me, and I was emboldened by her flirtation. "Do you want to go out again? I'll take you to a movie this time. Here at the mall?"

She nodded and smiled. "Sounds great. How about tonight after work?"

***

I can't draw women. Actually, I can't draw anything anymore, but even before, I couldn't draw a real woman. I'd try, but I would always get caught up with the breasts, or the hips. I could never draw women the way they really looked…they were always either beautiful with missile-shaped tits, or they came out looking disgusting.

The sketch I made of Jennifer emphasized her long legs and pert nose. I drew her with breasts like melons, nearly bursting through the fabric of her Aqua Massage uniform. That was my problem all along. I could never get past the way of seeing that I'd picked up from Marvel Comics.

***

The guy with the beard was smiling at the popcorn customers like he meant it, stroking his beard, and laughing, and counting their change for them. How could he enjoy it? The only time he frowned was when he noticed me. He glanced over between customers, watched me watching him, and then went back to stirring the Carmel Corn. Overzealously plunging the metal scoops into the mix, anger flashing on his face as he filled one box after another.

I didn't hear Harry approach my bench, and jumped when he spoke.

"Why did you do this, Mr. Ernie?" Harry asked.

"I lost my job, Harry."

"You don't have any respect for me? You don't like me?" He held out the funny pages of the *Oregonian*, waved them back and forth under my nose.

"Of course not. I mean yes. I respect you. I like you," I said.

Harry held up the funny pages, and then slapped them down on my lap. He didn't say anything, but just presented his evidence.

"I didn't even draw that. Not all of it."

"To you I am just a funny foreigner? Ernie, I am an American! I am a citizen! But the way you draw me they will be asking me for my green card soon. I am not some stupid Mexican who does not even speak English!" he said. "I am American. I am an Egyptian!"

"Harry, there's somebody else doing my job," I said. "Look at him."

Harry ignored this. He wasn't about to let me change the subject.

"This strip wasn't supposed to be printed."

Harry backed away from me. He closed his mouth tight and nodded at me and then turned away.

"Hey wait! You're probably more of an American than I am. I don't even know what I am, you know? I don't know what the hell is going on."

He showed me the back of his hand. He dismissed me without a glance, dismissed my stupid apology.

***

I had fans. They were everywhere.

The kid behind the counter at Starbucks smiled too broadly, and the businessman across from me put down his *Wall Street Journal* when he saw me.

"You're somebody, aren't you?" he asked.

"I'm Ernie Becker," I said.

"No—really, who are you?" he asked.

I decided to try to draw, I had nothing else to do, but my fine arts background, my studied approach and shaded characterizations, all of that had disappeared. All I could come up with were circles and squares—Nancy and Sluggo. Realism wasn't a possibility.

I found myself producing Roth's slick surface again, Roth's version of me.

"You're famous," the cartoon me said. A dialogue balloon appeared on the napkin, and then disappeared. "You're a celebrity. Do you want a box of candy corn to go?"

A stick figure in a wheelchair rolled onto the napkin, bumping into the cartoon me and then wheeling around to face out.

"You think this will save you?" Charlie asked.

"We're famous now." I'm not sure which one of me responded.

Charlie looked around at my drawings, at his environment, and sighed a two-dimensional sigh. "Take my advice, keep your day job."

"I can't," I told him.

I produced Roth's slick surface, sketched out an outline of myself, and then crumpled the napkin into a ball and threw it away.

***

At first I wasn't sure if it was really my voice I was hearing.

"I try not to think. I just let it flow out of me. That's the advice I'd give youngsters. Stop thinking. Of course, most of them know to do that. They don't need me to tell them."

I was doing some window shopping at Radio Shack, fiddling with a universal remote control and changing the stations on every television in the display case, one set after another. But no matter what channel I switched to, there I was, endlessly babbling.

"I'm not an opportunist. This thing is as crazy funny to me as it is to everyone else. I definitely didn't plan it. And I don't take it seriously."

The man behind the counter held up a battery and smiled at me. He pointed to a laptop computer and then gave me a big thumbs-up.

I moved away from the radio.

"I don't really consider myself to be famous. Not really famous. Portland is just a small town, and it needs its personalities. People need celebrities that they can see every day." My face filled every screen. I was sitting in front of a cardboard cityscape, talking to the edge of a desk, and smiling. "My next comic book is going to be big. I know it's going to be huge because here I am, you know. I'm on television now and that is really something. I just want to thank my fans and everyone."

I turned off one of the sets, and was glad with the dark screen. I set about turning them all off, one at a time.

"I feel love here," my image said.

A flashbulb went off, temporarily blinding me, and I felt hands on my shoulders, hands on my head.

"Could you sign a piece of paper, Mr. Becker?" the woman with the camera asked. She was about fifty years old, and was covered in sweat. Her jogging pants were bright purple. "I'm a big fan of you and Mr. Roth," she said.

"I'm not who you think I am," I said.

"Oh. Well, that doesn't matter." She held out a spiral notebook.

***

We were back on our perch, pressed against the glass ceiling of the mall, trying to get some air.

"I'm not really famous," I said.

Jennifer wrapped her legs around my waist and kissed me.

"It has nothing to do with you," she said. "You're confused because you keep thinking that everything should make some sort of objective sense. You think that fame is something you work towards, something you earn. But it's just transference," she said. "It's collective transference. It's a system."

"Why me?" I asked.

She kissed me again, and then whispered into my ear. "Isn't this what you always wanted?" she asked.

"But I'm not like this," I said.

"What are you like?"

***

The wavering started at the novelty card shop, started while I was fondling postcards depicting naked women jumping out of cakes, beefy firemen, singing frogs. When I put on the pair of X-ray specs I started to shake.

"I don't feel very good," I told the clerk. "May I get a glass of water?"

"Can I help you, sir?" the kid asked. He scratched his nose, pushed his piercing back and forth, and smiled at me. "Wait, you're Ernie Becker, right?"

I grabbed for the cash register, knocked over chattering teeth and pink flamingos.

"You're Ernie Becker, right?"

"Yeah, that's me."

"Your comics suck," the clerk said. He tapped his nose, right next to the piercing, and smiled. "I knew it was you."

I fell to the floor, and then worked my way back up again. I grasped the edge of the counter between my thumb and forefinger, and then eased myself onto my feet.

"Do you have any plastic vomit?" I asked. "I think I'm going to be sick."

And that's when the pictures started moving. All around enormously fat women sat on birthday cakes, men on motorcycles sped out of view, James Dean tipped his hat, puppy dogs drooled, nurses pulled out huge syringes, and so forth and so on. The greeting cards were blank for a moment, and then Charlie Roth wheeled his way onto their surfaces.

"I don't know you," Charlie said. "Stop smiling at me."

"Charlie?" I asked.

"Why aren't you at work? I'm thirsty," Charlie said.

He was everywhere. On each square of the Rubik's Cubes, on every package of Sea Monkeys, and on every card.

"You're in way over your head, kid," Charlie said. "What do you think you're doing?"

I opened my mouth to speak, but only squeaked. A giant bubble emerged where my words would have been, a paper-white bubble with black marks inside.

"Help me." The words hung in the air.

"Kid," Charlie said. "I'm dead. Remember?"

I grabbed for the register, knocked chattering teeth and pink flamingos aside, and held on tight.

"I feel sick," I said.

"You're Ernie Becker, right?" the kid asked.

"Yeah. Yeah…now get me a box of popcorn and a large Diet Coke," I said.

***

I didn't know that I had a cellular phone until it started ringing. I adjusted my tie, a red paisley thing that also seemed new to me, and flipped the device open.

"Hello?"

"You headed to the signing?" Charlie Roth asked.

I looked blankly at my cell phone, tentatively held it up to my ear again.

"Go to B. Dalton's, and you'll see what I'm talking about," Charlie said. Then the line went dead in my hand.

The customers were impatient. They held out their comics, *Zippy and Fritz the Cat*,

Garfield, and *The Far Side*, and waited for my autograph. A teen mother with a comic book version of Gilgamesh asked me to make out the signature to Lawrence.

"It's a gift," she explained. "I'm not really into this stuff."

"Lawrence," I repeated.

"Better make it to Larry."

B. Dalton's was jammed full of customers who wanted to see me, to touch me, to tell me their names. I sat behind my pile of comic books, pen in hand, and tried to sign them all. I marked their foreheads, breasts, stomachs. I gave out my name, gave out my number.

"There you go. Yes, yes. No. Thank you. Really."

"Mr. Ernie?" Harry said.

I reached up to him, toward his mouth, and tried to sign what was left of his teeth with my magic marker.

"Mr. Ernie, what is wrong? You look terrible."

"There you go," I told him.

"You looking terrible. These people don't see, and they don't care, but you are not yourself. You are not the usual intelligent young man that I know. When was the last time you had a drink of water?"

I took a look at myself, caught my reflection in the pane-glass storefront. I was in my wheelchair, propped up by the padded seat. I was badly drawn, my eyes merely dots, my mouth a wavering line. I glanced at my hands, and counted three bulbous fingers.

"You come with me, Mr. Ernie," Harry said.

"I'm sorry."

"It's okay. It's okay, now. Harry will help."

***

I sat up in the rafters, put my hands up on the glass ceiling, and watched the ice skaters far below. Jennifer sat next to me, but she was talking so softly and I couldn't quite hear. I could hear her voice as if from far away, as if she was one of the skaters, but I couldn't make out what she was saying.

"I can't hear you," I said.

"Don't make this difficult," Jennifer said. "It just can't happen again, that's all. It was fun, but it was a one-time thing. I want to make it clear. I want to clear the air."

"I'm not sure what you're talking about," I said. "I can't really hear you very well."

Down on the ice rink the kid I called Buck was skating in circles, he was bowing as he spun, keeping the beat, skating to the Muzak, and he mesmerized me. I couldn't help but watch each turn, follow each twirl. He was magnificent. He was so familiar, each move, each skidding stop, seemed fated. Some sort of cosmic connection ran through this ice skater; a horribly klutzy but predestined path was laid out before him and he followed it.

"Watch this guy," I told Jennifer. "Watch the kid who keeps bowing and twirling down there. It's amazing."

Jennifer followed the path of my pointing finger, seemingly unconcerned with how large and strange my digits had become, and squinted.

"Watch him go," I said.

But Jennifer just shook her head and shrugged.

"You understand that I'm not your girlfriend," she said. "That I don't want to be with you anymore?"

"Look, he just fell. Did you see that?"

"I can't see anything," she said. "Are you listening to me? Did you hear?"

"You didn't see that? You don't see him?"

"We're through. Okay?"

"You don't see anything?"

Jennifer waved her hands in front of my face, like I was the one having a hard time tracking, a hard time seeing. She kept repeating herself, kept breaking it off with me, but I couldn't be bothered with any of that.

I watched the kid slide on his knees, I could almost hear him thanking the crowd, and finally I decided that I'd watched enough. I had to talk to him, had to find out what this kid was about.

***

"I've been watching you skating," I said.

"I know." Buck was leaning against the outside rail; with one arm propping up his chin and the other neatly tucked behind his back, it looked like he was practicing racing positions. He absently twirled and then put his hand back on the rail. "You and I are the same, right?" he said. "You live here too?"

"Live here?"

"You and I are the same."

"What are you talking about? What do you mean?"

"I never leave the ice, I'm always skating, and you're the same. You never leave the mall either. You never stop whatever it is that you do, whatever it is that makes you famous."

"You never leave the ice?"

"Never leave the ice. That's right."

"Don't you have a home? Do you ever go home? Don't you go to the bathroom?"

"I skate. I can skate."

I didn't believe it. I watched the kid skate backwards, away from me, and I flinched when Buck bumped into the crowd, when he starting knocking schoolchildren down, when he bowed to thin air.

"I skate. What do you do?" he asked from the other side of the rink.

"I draw."

"I can never go home. I can't leave here because I skate."

"Me neither," I said. I realized it was true. "I haven't left in weeks. I haven't been home since Roth. I haven't been home since Roth died."

***

Harry always wanted to help. He was making me eat again.

"Here you go," Harry said. "I got you a burger and the fries. I got you orange drink too. Okay?"

"Thank you."

"You have not been so good lately. You have been very sick, Mr. Ernie," he said.

"I'm okay."

"No. You're very sick. I see you, what you do—"

I picked at my cheeseburger, couldn't bring myself to take a bite. I wasn't hungry anymore. I didn't feel like eating. I couldn't remember the last time I'd eaten. It must've been several days, but I wasn't sure.

"Harry, I have to ask. I have to know...how many fingers am I holding up?" I held out my hand, spread my fingers out, and counted them myself. I had three fingers and an outline for an arm. I was a sketch, two-dimensional, and I only had three fingers.

"How many?" Harry asked. "I see five fingers. Ordinary. You think, maybe, there are some more?"

"Less..."

"You are having a hard time. Your new job is not so good, but you will be all right," Harry said.

"Am I famous, Harry?"

"I don't know," he said. "What do you think?"

I didn't say anything. I picked at my French fries and looked down at the ice rink. Buck was on the ice.

"Did you know that a man can be in two places at once?" Harry asked. "I saw this with my own eyes, in Egypt," Harry said.

"Two places?"

"Or more than that. I met a great man once who could be here and there and all around."

"How many fingers do I have Harry? Who the hell am I?"

"I don't know, Mr. Ernie. I don't know how many places, or how much you are. But, you are more, you know, than your drawings or your popcorn. We are more than we know."

"How many fingers?"

"Four or five, take your pick. Ordinary or famous, it's all the same for you. Isn't it Mr. Ernie?"

I glanced down at the ice rink, watched as Buck jumped, did a spin, and then collapsed.

"I have something to tell you," Harry said. "It's a story I only tell Americans. Only Americans hear this story."

I held up my hand, shook my head no, and tried to smile.

"You told me already," I said. "I've heard this story before."

Harry leaned toward me and I realized that I couldn't smell his breath anymore. I couldn't smell anything.

"But you can draw it now. You should hear it again."

I got out my sketchpad and pencils; I set myself up and prepared to listen.

Buck, never to be defeated, recovered his bearings and wiped the ice from his slacks. He threw his hands up in the air and bowed to the world.

"Thank you," he said. "Thank you, God!"

"Ginger Rogers," Harry said.

And I drew what he said and smiled.

I was a man with three fingers.

I would never find the door.

SHOPPING AT THE END OF THE WORLD

If you want to understand how the disorder spread from the Lloyd Center Mall to the rest of the city of Portland, how the blood in our Orange Juliuses became a radioactive haze in the streets, you should start with what didn't happen. Nobody got hurt; like reverse neutron bombs, the blasts only destroyed the architecture. Sure, people died in the riots, people were trampled to death, there were gunshot wounds, lacerations from broken glass, and heart attacks, but the explosions themselves didn't produce even one casualty. There was absolutely no destruction of organic life at all. Even the moss on Portland's sidewalks, the planted oak trees and pines, the weeds and grasses in vacant lots were spared.

Death was missing and so was smoke. There was no smoke. Somehow Portland burned without it.

***

I was hung over. I'd been hung over all day. It was closing time at the Look City Clothes outlet, about nine o'clock on a Friday night, and it still hurt when I moved. My stomach was a pit and my mouth tasted of stomach acid. I'd gotten drunk in order to spite Sadie, in order to spite my girlfriend, or partner, or whatever you call it when two people sleep and live together but don't marry. We'd been stilted and edgy, fighting without words, for weeks, and I wanted to bring it out in the open, to kill the conflict. More than that, I wanted to win, and I knew that, if I was going to end up on top after perpetually responding to her demands with silence, I'd have to abandon logic and reason. I'd gotten drunk for strategic reasons.

In any case, I was sick, my head pounding, when I first encountered the shredder. I'd stacked the plain cardboard spiral notebooks on the rusted display table, hung the faux gas station overalls back on the pipes that ran along the concrete walls, turned off the lava lamp displays, and was ready to punch out when I found the machine. It was an old tube radio with a crank attached to its side and a cardboard sign hanging across the front:

"Implied Promises Kept." The words were printed in large stenciled letters, and in smaller print, underneath, were the words "advertisements as myths."

"What's with the old radio?" I asked my manager, Brad.

He stopped, grabbed a Look City flyer from one of the rusted display tables, and fed the sheet into the machine. He turned the crank and strips of paper snaked out of the slots in the radio's speaker. "It's a shredder. Some sort of art piece," Brad said, "the central office in Chicago sent it to us. Some sort of new campaign."

I stood there for a moment watching him shred one promotional pamphlet after another, watching Look City material get pulped and spill to the concrete floor. The process was strangely compelling.

Sadie and I had been arguing about a baby. She wanted to have a baby and had stopped taking her pills and I wouldn't sleep with her anymore. I wouldn't even touch her, or let her touch me. This had been going on for a couple of weeks, maybe a month. I didn't want to talk about it, there wasn't anything to talk about, but Sadie kept trying to draw me out. She even marked a time for it in my daily planner, penciled it in, and so I bought a case of beer and a pint of whiskey and drank myself into a stupor.

"Lock up for me tonight, will you Miles?" Brad asked when he ran out of brochures to shred. I nodded a yes, but I wasn't really present. I was too busy wondering if I'd find my apartment empty when I got off work. I finished up the cleaning, put all the overpriced pairs of torn jeans where they belonged, but when I went to punch out for the night something had gone wrong.

I couldn't find the exit. The aisle was longer than it should have been. The lava lamp display was yards and yards away from its usual spot. I looked around then, finally getting out of my head and noticing the transformation that had taken place since the first shredding.

Look City Clothes was a ruin.

In 1986, when Look City expanded into a national chain, the board hired the architectural firm "2001 BC" to redesign the interior of every Look City outlet.

2001 BC use what's called selective demolition to create their distinctive postmodern aesthetic. Blasting old Walgreens or U.S. Bank buildings in order to expose steel support beams, heating ducts, and insulation. The firm calls this "revealed urban history," but it looks like what you'd find after a terrorist attack. In the case of the Look City at the Lloyd Center the "urban history" had to be simulated. Heating ducts were shipped in and splattered with perma-dust, support structures were put up that didn't quite reach the ceiling, and crumbled concrete facades were erected.

After my boss shredded the Look City promotional brochures, I couldn't find the exit. I couldn't find anything very easily because the concrete facades, the heating ducts, the other bits of simulated refuse were now truly damaged and scattered in pieces around the store. The false support beams were bent at strange angles.

The store had changed. It seemed bigger and darker, truly blasted out and ruined. I tripped in a pothole in the concrete floor and fumbled past the shredder. A promotional pamphlet for the architectural firm 2001 BC sat on the lip of the paper feed, and I paused to read the pamphlet's title. "Fractured decor!" the pamphlet read. Hundreds of leaflets extolling Look City's architectural style had been shredded. I kicked at the pile of paper strands absently, and then glanced around at the real destruction throughout the store.

I opened the machine, the shredder. I detached the back panel because I wanted to see inside. I wanted to see the gears but it was empty. There were no radio tubes, no gears, no blades for shredding; it was just a shell. What I found inside was a thin booklet made out of photocopy paper. It was the instruction manual:

Step One: Insert artifact into paper feed.

Step Two: Grab the handle firmly in left or right hand.

Step Three: Turn crank counterclockwise until artifact manifests as shreds from 'radio' speakers.

Step Four: Repeat.

Background: In order to understand the operating principle behind the Implied Promise Keeper, it is important to remember that the institutions of civilization brought "humanity" into existence.

Culture came first.

I paused…read the last sentence again.

Culture came first.

I closed my eyes and let myself fade. I tried not to think about Sadie, about what it would mean to give in to her. I didn't want to think about that, wasn't ready. I imagined my body as a collection of comic books and Pez dispensers, tried to imagine that culture came first, that I was literally made of culture.

I open my eyes, jerked to my senses again, when I started to succeed.

***

Sadie worked for Hot Dog on a Stick. She wore the mandatory yellow, red, white, and blue striped uniform, along with the striped chef hat, despite the fact that she held a master's degree in political philosophy. Overeducated and underemployed she was thirty-three years old, seven years my senior.

She was sincere, loving, militant in her politics, and she made me uncomfortable. She was always pushing the envelope, taking things too far.

"I want to have a child," Sadie said. "More than that, I want to have your child."

"That's crazy," I told her. "That's completely insane. I can't even pay my cable bill on time."

Sadie smiled, but as she smiled she folded her arms across her chest and waited.

"Any kid born today has fools for parents, heartless fools," I said. "The species probably doesn't even have fifty years left. How could we have a kid?"

I'd first met Sadie five years earlier at an antiwar demonstration, around the time that President Bush dubbed Portland "Little Beirut" because of the protesting, the drumming, the screaming dissent that he encountered here. There were about thirty thousand of us at Pioneer Square the day I first spotted Sadie…the day war broke out in Iraq.

I was marching right down the middle of the street, following the broken yellow line through the rain, and chanting along with the rest, when I spotted Sadie.

She didn't have an umbrella and so she kept drifting onto the sidewalks to find shelter under awnings. She ended up confronting the pedestrians.

"Did you hear there's a war on?" she asked a passerby who wasn't with the march. "It's not even a war, it's a slaughter," Sadie told the woman in the red dress and trench coat as she hurried away with her shopping bags. Sadie was militant and righteous. Listening to her shout, watching her shake her fist to the beat of the chants, she embarrassed me.

"You're making a fool of yourself," I said. "You're like a parody of a protester."

"I make you uncomfortable?" she asked.

I told her that, yes, she made me anxious and uncomfortable.

"Good. Nobody should feel comfortable at a protest rally. A person shouldn't want to feel comfortable," she said.

Five years later, Sadie had changed her mind; she wanted comfort and security.

"I want to feel connected to the world," Sadie told me. "I can't stand going on like this, without something to ground me, without any real relationships."

"It won't be any better, having a kid with me won't solve anything," I told her. "The world will still be just a gob of pain, no matter what."

But, Sadie wanted to be comfortable. She didn't want her whole life to be a protest; she didn't want to stand outside of the world, to act against the world. She wanted a family.

***

Years earlier, on our first date, Sadie took me to the 24-hour Church of Elvis—a street level "art" gallery with computerized window displays that accepted quarters. There were three coin-operated exhibits: the Elvis Exhibit, the Psychic Friend, and the Marriage/Divorce Machine.

After six months in Portland I was still new to town in Sadie's eyes, and she thought the Church of Elvis was one of the big attractions for the city.

"You won't know Portland, won't understand it, until it understands you," she explained. "You should let the city look into your soul."

"What? Is Portland a vending machine?" I asked.

"Yes, but it's been redesigned for a new purpose."

I put a quarter into the Psychic Friend machine, pressed the button labeled Past Life Regression, and watched the monitor spring to life. Green words on a black screen:

"You were once a Big Mac with Fries. You were a lovely princess. You were a dog. You were a lapsed insurance policy. You were a roadie for the Ice Capades," the monitor read. An electronic voice repeated the information and I received a printout that said the same thing.

"Try again," she said. "Get your daily horoscope."

"It's starting to rain," I said.

"Try again," Sadie said.

I put a coin in the slot and pressed the button.

"You will discover that it's hip to be square. You will wear sunglasses at night. You will end up pumping gas at a Quickstop. This is what you really look like."

Instead of a printout I received a Polaroid photograph from the slot. This was a picture of my soul, according to Sadie: a small stucco house with a Cadillac in the driveway. There were no people in the photograph.

***

The first time in bed with Sadie I almost gave up on the relationship. As soon as she took off her clothes, as soon as she pushed the newspapers off my futon to lie down, she became recalcitrant. Her legs clasped together, staring up at the only window in my basement apartment, she was obviously less than committed to the prospect of our coupling. We'd discussed it, it had seemed a good idea on the street, but something had changed.

I went ahead and took off my jeans, pulled off my hooded sweatshirt, and then I stopped. In boxers and a T-shirt I stood there until my feet grew icy on the painted concrete floor. Then I sat on edge of the mattress and stroked her leg.

"What's up?"

Sadie didn't answer, but pulled up the comforter. "It's cold," she said. "I'm covered in goose pimples."

I sat and watched her, traced the outline of her body under the quilted blue fabric with my thumb.

"I couldn't take you everywhere I wanted today," she said. She was still looking up at the window. "There are parts of Portland we can't visit anymore."

"Why not?"

"Parts are gone. Redeveloped or destroyed," she said. "I wish you could've seen Quality Pie or Casa Bonita. Have you ever seen cliff diving?"

"Cliff diving? I think so. On television."

"They used to have cliff divers at Casa Bonita," she said. "It was a huge Mexican restaurant in St. John's, almost a theme park, and they had cliff divers, and Moroccan bands, and there were these fake caves with purple and green and red spotlights trained on the plaster stalagmites," she said.

"You liked it?"

"Yeah. I mean, the food was bad. The tacos and sopapillas and enchiladas were always terrible, really greasy, but the place was worth seeing. All the noise and lights, surrounded by Spanish guitars and cliff divers. When I was four or five years old it just overwhelmed me."

I scooted underneath the blanket next to her, took off my boxers, and looped my arm under her head. We both stared up at the tiny window, at the streaked dirt on the pane.

"There was a well in the middle of it all; downstairs near the stage there was a wishing well. They had rows of benches set up in front, and behind these wooden benches there was a wishing well with a face in it, a green or gray face that shimmered across the water. It moved. It looked like a ghost or genie was in there. And he would talk to you."

"What did he say?"

"The same thing over and over again. He asked you to drop a coin in the well, then he told you your wish would come true, and then he asked you to drop a coin again. Over and over. But the first time I looked into the well, the first time I ever saw the man in the water, I couldn't hear him. Men in sombreros were miked and amped and they were shaking maracas and playing guitar. I tried to listen to what he said, put my hand to my ear, but all I could hear were the drums and maracas and Spanish love songs."

She turned to me. She pushed the covers back and turned over on her belly.

"He was obviously trying to tell me something important. Obviously it was some sort of magic, he was magic, and he was talking to me," Sadie said. She put her arms around me, but we just sort of bumped into each other, off each other.

"The thing is that he wasn't talking to me. I found that out after the song ended, after the excitement died down. It was just a machine down there in the water. A machine programmed, driven, to say the same thing over and over again."

"Do you want to do this?" I asked.

"I don't know." She put her hands on my back, moved her hands to my groin. "Do you want to?" she asked. She smiled as she found that I was already erect.

She kissed me, put her tongue in my mouth, and wrapped her legs around me. "It didn't have anything to do with me," she said. "It never does."

***

After the first shredding, the security gates at the entrance of Look City Clothes went missing. Instead, where the metal loops of the detectors used to be there were two men dressed like astronauts, wearing radiation suits made of thick, yellow rubber. Arriving at work the next day I was immediately manhandled into a corner by these two men and given a quick screening. The Geiger counters chirped and buzzed, but I must not have been too hot because they let me in. I was shoved forward, nearly knocking over a display of red metallic drinking cups, and the men returned to their positions by the entrance.

"What's with the guards?" I asked Brad when I found him lying on the ground next to the shredder. "Was there some kind of toxic spill?"

"It won't shred photos," he said. He was surrounded by strands of Look City flyers, *People* and *Newsweek* magazines, newspaper advertisements. "This machine won't shred a simple photograph," my boss said. He was lying on his back and trying to stuff a Polaroid into the paper feed.

"Let me try," I said. "It's probably a matter of positioning." I took the photograph, a picture of a gawky woman in cat-eye glasses at a Christmas party, and I pushed the Polaroid towards the slot, but it wouldn't fit. I kneeled down and stared into the slot. There was plenty of space, and I tried again. This time I saw that I'd turned the picture so that it wouldn't fit. I tried again, and again. I fumbled each time, and eventually I dropped it. The Polaroid spiraled to the ground.

"It will shred magazines, leaflets, market reports, glamour photographs, but it won't shred a candid picture. It won't shred a blank sheet of paper, or a page of line doodles," he said.

I grabbed a flyer, stuffed it into the paper feed, and turned the crank. Shreds of paper snaked out of the machine's speaker.

I wrote my name on a blank sheet of notebook paper, and tried to push it into the shredder, but I couldn't quite line the paper up with the feed. I took a picture of Sadie out of my wallet and wrote the words "Look City Clothes" on the back. I tried to make my handwriting look like the lettering from the actual logo. I fed the photo into the Implied Promise Keeper and got back shreds.

"It only takes ads," my boss said.

***

On break I saw the transformation, the destruction, start to spread. I watched the Look City aesthetic spread to the food court.

It started next to the McDonald's. The sign for the restrooms, the arrow and the word "restrooms" itself grew speckled and dingy. And, while the sign didn't move, the arrow tilted down. It pointed at the floor.

It started with the restroom sign and spread to the McDonald's itself. The uniforms on the employees were darker, they transmogrified from cotton to polyester, and the collars widened. A customer was grousing that his burger was covered with dust, and one of the men in the McDonald's uniforms, the McDonald's manager possibly, exclaimed that all of the soda was flat.

"What did you do?" this McDonald's boss asked the kid at the cash register. "What did you do?"

The kid responded by looking at his shirt, pulling at his ever-widening collar, but he didn't say a thing.

***

There was something waiting for me when I got home from work, a creature out of focus, chaotic and blurry. After I stepped inside the front room, once I got a closer view, I figured out that this was Sadie.

There was something wrong with her, really wrong. Her face, for instance, was in flux. Instead of two sparkling green eyes she had three or four, and her slightly upturned nose was on her chin. All of Sadie's physical characteristics, her pretty mouth, her delicate hands and feet, were spiraling around an abstraction. She was nearly impossible to look at head-on. She'd lost cohesion.

"What's happening?" Sadie asked. A hand reached out for me, emerging from a swirl of bright white smiles, blonde hair. One of her mouths, this one with cherry-red lips, hovered next to her hand, ready to bite.

"Don't touch," I said.

"Can you see me?"

"You've been shredded."

It was my fault. I'd shredded her. I'd run her photograph through the Implied Promise Keeper.

"What's happened to me?" Sadie asked. She was standing in the bathroom and trying to find herself in the mirror. "What the fuck did you do?"

***

We broke into the Look City outlet to retrieve her photograph, and I thought she'd give us away; Sadie was still in a state of noisy flux, a whirl of wrinkled brows and clapping hands, but I needn't have worried. The electronic surveillance system had disappeared along with the track lighting.

I grabbed a replica World's Fair flashlight as we made our way down the main aisle, and pointed it towards the Implied Promise Keeper; the machine was nearly buried in paper shreds. I had two feet of flyers and magazines and advertising copy to sift through.

"Find me," Sadie said.

The remains of Sadie's photo were clumped together, intertwined with the shreds of a promotion for Look City's special brand of cigarettes—"Death" cigarettes. I delicately plucked her image out from the threads of this advertisement. I separated her image from the Surgeon General's warning and set to work reassembling the snapshot.

Using masking tape on the back and translucent tape on the front, I put her face back together.

"Can you see me?" Sadie asked.

I could see her image, her Polaroid face, but she herself was still a mass of confusion.

"Miles," Sadie said, "do something."

I turned away from my ruined girlfriend, couldn't face her any longer. I turned the photo over, pulled back a piece of masking tape, and erased the Look City Clothes logo underneath.

"Miles? What did you do? Is it fixed? Am I fixed?"

Sadie came back together all at once, her slightly upturned nose and tired eyes realigned on her face. After erasing the logo I could see her clearly, but it took a while for her to be convinced that the damage had been undone.

"That's not my face," she said as she looked at the mirror in the employees' bathroom. "That's not my face. Everything is in reverse."

***

Sadie called in sick to Hot Dog on a Stick, climbed into bed, and then stayed in bed for a week.

"Can you still see me?" she asked me upon waking that first morning. "Can you still see me?" she asked every morning after.

I went back to work right away, and when my manager wasn't looking I shoved the shredder into a storage closet. I locked it in the closet and kept the key.

I sold faux gas station overalls, orange sneakers, lava lamps, gigantic red metal cups. I manned the cash register, smiled at the customers, punched in and out.

Life returned to normal. The electronic security system was reinstalled.

But, after a week, Sadie recovered; she started to believe in herself again. We made love again, and I didn't use a condom. How could I deny her after what had happened, after I'd shredded her? After seeing her fall apart I almost wanted a kid, her kid. I wanted something normal like that. But when the act was over, when we'd both finished pushing and straining, Sadie told me that she was taking the pill again. She told me she wasn't interested in having a child anymore. She wanted something else, she said she'd found a different way of connecting to the world.

***

"We should steal it," Sadie said.

"Steal what?" I asked.

"We could try shredding something else, something besides Look City flyers, something better."

"Better?" I asked.

"Anything. Some advertisement that doesn't have an apocalyptic subtext," Sadie said.

I shrugged, not quite comprehending what she was getting at.

"Miles, it wasn't the shredder that was destroying the store. It wasn't the shredder that disrupted my identity. It was the aesthetic, the Look City aesthetic."

"How do you figure?"

"The sign, 'Implied Promises Kept', that's a description of what the machine does."

I shrugged again.

"We have to use it. How could we not use it?"

"It's easy not to use it. You just don't open the door."

"We should at least finish what's already been started. We should feed in some more 'ook City stuff. Keep this going."

"Why?" I asked.

"It's a miracle, Miles. We can fix things. We can shred the lie and find the implied truth underneath," she said. "We have to keep it going."

***

In 1993 or so an old high school friend of mine visited from the East Coast. I met him at the airport and we shared a cab back to my apartment downtown. On the way he stared out the window of the taxi, sighed at the bridges and streets of Portland, and finally came to a judgement.

"You're living in Disneyland," he said.

"You don't like it?"

"The streets aren't covered in garbage, there aren't any slums, everything is clean."

I told him that we had slums, on the North Side, and that I didn't think a city had to look like a war zone or a ruin in order to be considered real. He told me that he didn't expect somebody from Disneyland to understand.

My friend thought he'd pegged what was wrong with Portland, but he had it wrong. It wasn't the parts of the city that worked that made Portland unreal, it wasn't the light rail system or the clean streets that brought on the disorder. No, it was the parts of the city that were already broken, the parts we'd given away or sold were the parts that made the whole city vulnerable.

***

Sadie and I broke back into the mall so we could keep shredding Look City flyers. We were at it all night, making paper strands and confetti, until we heard the sound of atomic thunder. The morning came, the coffee shops in the food court opened, and we were still at it. We kept shredding and we then saw the flash—a light many times brighter than the sun—and heard the roar of atomic wind.

***

There was no heat, just light and sound. The ceramic cats rattled on their shelf, a few Magic 8 Balls rolled off the display tables and onto the ground, but that was all.

I ran out to the parking lot just in time to glimpse the first mushroom cloud and then the next flash blinded me. Then I was deafened by the crushing sound.

I waited, stood very still as my senses slowly returned. The new mushroom cloud was rising up from the asphalt. It was maybe twenty yards away from me. I felt a hand on my back as I watched ash fall from the sky, as I watched the radioactive flakes disintegrate as they reached the earth.

"You should see what's going on inside," Sadie said.

***

The Lloyd Center was packed. A feeding frenzy was underway, with massive, chaotic lines pouring out of every shop and department store.

"Hey," said a businesswoman wearing blue sneakers with her gray skirt and white oxford-cloth shirt. "You work at the hot dog place, don't you?"

"Sometimes," Sadie said.

"The lemonade is tainted. It's full of isotopes or something," she said. And then she downed the cup of yellow liquid she was holding without pausing to breathe.

And it went on like that. Waves of paranoid complaints circled through the crowd only to be followed by absurd displays of gluttony. And the explosions increased in number to create a strobe effect.

"There's no more OXY!"

"I want fifteen double espressos and twelve lattes to go!"

"What is that strange purple mist in the penguins-wearing-sunglasses window display? Will it affect the lenses?"

A mushroom cloud and a moment of silent deafness.

"I need today's and yesterday's *Times*. The newspaper is very important to me."

"Do you have Kelly's canned pork brains in gravy?"

A flash and then a roar.

"Where are they? Where are the Girl-Power action figures?"

A massive explosion, and then another. The mall was ground zero, an endless stream of mushroom clouds. No space, no time, in between the blasts, but just a long white field of light, a deafening roar of atomic wind, without pause.

And then silence, thirty seconds of silence before the world came back.

The lines of people, the storefronts and plastic tables, all of it came back into view, and then the rioting continued. The screaming, the looting, and the violence began in earnest.

And then the Lloyd Center Mall began to disintegrate. It started to burn without making smoke.

***

Portland erupted, transformed itself, into a disconnected dystopia.

Portland became a shopping mall on fire.

Portland was destroyed by symbolic bombs.

***

We stole the shredder. With the machine in our hands the rioters cleared a path for us. They were busy pushing and fighting over empty Coca-Cola bottles and disposable lighters and they didn't even see us.

By the exit ramp a woman in a polyester jumpsuit, an older lady with a bad dye job that had turned her hair purple and an insane glint behind her spectacles, was stopping traffic.

"Is this on sale?" she asked, pointing to our car as she rushed across the asphalt. She had shopping bags with her, and she screamed at us and pulled out perfume bottles from the bag in order to smash them on the hood of our car and on the asphalt. "Is this on sale?" she yelled.

There was an explosion on the other side of the river, in Southwest Portland. The KOIN tower appeared as a mushroom cloud. As we crossed the Hawthorne Bridge we could hear them, the masses, scrambling for their lives in Waterfront Park.

We saw giant mutant insects, spiders mostly but a few grasshoppers too, crawl out of the Fox Theater. And the glass doors of Nike Town cracked open to let forth a geyser of blood. There were people everywhere trying to find out if they could get another latte; their designer clothes had been ripped to shreds but they themselves were fine, except that they didn't know what to do, where to go, now that their condos were gone.

***

"We should do something to help," Sadie said. She opened the car door and I had to slam on the brakes so she wouldn't splatter on the asphalt as she stepped out onto the street. We both ended up standing on a manhole between 5th and 6th avenues; we ended up standing perfectly still as the city crumbled down around us.

"Sit down!" Sadie shouted to the men and women running in zigzags. "You'll be okay if you just sit down, if you don't react."

It was true. The buildings were falling, but the bricks and mortar weren't hitting the ground. The explosions kept happening, the bombs kept falling from nowhere, but there wasn't any heat. We sat in the street, Sadie in a lotus position, and it became clear.

"It's our fault," Sadie said to a Japanese man who, in his leather jacket and Ford truck baseball cap, sat down next to us and put his head between his knees. "We let the Look City aesthetic get out of hand," Sadie said.

A group of mounted police were steering their horses in circles, trampling the pedestrians spilling out of the ruins of a Starbucks.

"We didn't know how much of it, how much of the city, was made of advertising," Sadie told the man in the baseball cap.

"I'm going to die," he said.

"No you won't. You'll be fine if you stay with us."

A man and woman in matching jogging suits crawled down the sidewalk, cutting their hands on broken glass and bouncing their heads on the concrete in anticipation of shock waves that never came. "Don't," Sadie said, "...don't panic." But they went on panicking, and the city went on shredding itself, and there wasn't anything we could do to stop it or stop people reacting to it.

"We're responsible," Sadie said. But there wasn't much we could do really. When it finally stopped all that was left was my Ford escort. My Ford and the shredding machine on the backseat seemed to be the only man-made objects left intact.

***

Newport is a tourist town. It used to be a fishing town, but it's not anymore. What it's known for now is its toffee, its aquarium, and the "Ripley's Believe It or Not!" Museum.

Most of the Portland refugees went north into Washington and Canada, but there were thousands of us in Newport, hundreds taking up space in Motel 6s, the Sylvia Beach Hotel, and in the Newport high school. Sadie and I were lucky; our motel room had cable television and was small enough that we had no roommates.

Sadie knows people here, waitresses mostly, and she's found a job already. She works and I hang around our motel. Occasionally I venture out and visit the tiny library. Sadie works and I do research, but what we're both really doing is biding our time until she decides what to shred next.

At night when we're together in this motel room we fidget with the shredding machine. We take it apart and put it back together. We skim high-brow books. When Sadie's not rereading the machine's manual aloud she's reading books by people like Roland Barthes, Sigmund Freud, Karl Marx, R. D. Laing.

I tell her that I want a family now, tell her I want what she wants, but Sadie isn't interested. She's convinced that it was the Look City aesthetic at fault and she wants to try socialist newspapers and union pamphlets in the shredder. She thinks that the shredder could create a utopia.

"All that Soviet Realism, that dictatorship of the proletariat stuff, reeks of totalitarianism," I say. "What about some green advertisements, something like what Exxon or Chevron designs to cover up their misdeeds? Or better yet, how about we just put the machine in a ditch, or hack it to bits, and start over?"

Sadie is disgusted by my lack of class-consciousness.

But I know I'm right. Shredding, by itself, isn't enough. The shredding machine is just one piece of the puzzle we're living through.

"Those nuclear bombs didn't change anything," I tell her. "The people were the same after."

"Isn't that a good thing?" she asks.

"You don't get it. The machine can't change things."

Sadie doesn't agree. She says the whole event was a manifestation of some new kind of consciousness. "We pulled the curtain aside once. Don't you want to see what's back there? Don't you want to shred something?"

Sadie has it figured out. "It all has to go, all of it. We just have to decide what to shred next."

It's not that simple. It's not merely a matter of destruction, of shredding. "We have to do more than shred things. We have to find the right promise before we act again," I say.

"But that's what I'm trying to do."

"You're not listening," I tell her. "We have to know what it is. We have to know what it is that we want to keep."

INSTANT LABOR

SCENE 1, TAKE 1: A CONFESSION AT QUALITY PIE

"Turn off your electric eye, Webb," Ella says.

I zoom in, catch the full extent of her displeasure in my lens, and fade. I switch the camera off, cap the lens, fold the device in on itself, and slip it into my shirt pocket.

She slaps a plate of fries and a cup of coffee down, and sits across from me in the booth with her arms stretched out on the tabletop and her frame pushed back.

"It's like something is dead inside you," she says.

We were at a dingy diner in Northwest Portland, the Quality Pie. Ella worked there. It's my strongest memory of her: uniformed in pink, with her nametag pinned and propped up on her breast. She was always in motion. Ella could carry a pot of coffee and two trays of food without hesitation. She was an efficient worker, a good waitress.

I don't reply, but try to meet her gaze, to look her in the eye. I end up staring at her chest…reading and rereading her nametag.

"They sell this as if the only thing in life is convenience. I mean suicide is convenient too, right? It cuts down on expenses, saves time." She takes a sip of my coffee, grimaces, and reaches for the sugar.

"I want to have more time to work on my films. This way I can do that. I can dedicate all of my energy to my work, and still make a living," I reply, and take the sugar away from her before she starts to pour.

"But Webb, do you want to erase, ignore, eight hours out of every day?" Ella asks.

"Isn't that what you do? Working here, isn't it like erasing your day?" I ask.

"No. It's not. It's not the same." She stands up from the booth, starts to go back to work, but I grab her hand; stopping her and spinning her towards me.

I'd gone to the Quality Pie that day to tell her. To confess what I'd done and receive forgiveness. But that wasn't going to happen.

It was the way we played it. I would rationalize, distort, and tangle, and she tried to push through to the truth. Usually we made love after, with her moving and working on me in the same way that she poured coffee or carried dinner trays, without hesitation.

I grab her hand, pull her to me so that we are nearly nose to nose. I reach up, pinch my eyelash, and delicately pull back the lid. Underneath there is a tiny cord with prongs, a jack. A tiny red light at the tip of the cord blinks on and off against the pink skin of my eyelid.

"I've already done it. I'm instant," I say.

Ella just stares at me, at the tiny light in my eye, and then slowly backs away.

SCENE 2, TAKE 1: CLOCKING IN AND CHECKING OUT

The offices of Instant Labor Inc. were a marvel of high-tech displays and computer equipment. Video monitors depicting incomprehensible diagrams and charts, along with multicolored perspectives of the human brain, were set into the walls of the front lobby. Tall, clear plastic tubes filled with bubbling water towered behind the receptionist's desk. It was supposed to make an impression; convey authority. And it worked.

At least, it worked on me. I remember those offices clearly. I'd been in and out of them for months before going instant. The constant repetition of narration on the cerebral cortex, the reptile/hindbrain, the brain stem, and other neurological wonders excited me. I would be on the cutting edge, the forefront of the coming wave, and it all boiled down to synchronizing the patterns of my forebrain with my hindbrain…or something like that.

But after going instant I was taken down to the basement, and shown the "labor" aspect of the operation.

"You are number six," my supervisor tells me.

"What?"

"Number six, aisle three. Go and plug in."

"Number six, aisle three?"

The supervisor nods, and his eyes glaze over as he scans the room. I follow his gaze, and find myself looking at row after row of men and women in gray sweat suits, each slumped over in metal chairs, and held up by their constraints. The walls are covered with nappy green carpet, and thick white chords hang down from the ceiling and attach to thin wires that connect to the workers' eyes.

The supervisor hands me my time card and tells me to punch in. I swipe it through the electronic scanner at the entrance gate to aisle three, and find cord number six. I go instant.

Plugging in and finding myself suspended in the web, surrounded by the video images and digital voices of the callers, was disturbing in itself, but what unnerved me the most was being out of body.

It was primarily a process of deindividuation. I'd synch up with the mainframe, fall into an alpha state, and my body would dissolve. My sense of location, my spatial self, was the first thing to go. After that my memories, my whole identity as it related to time, would vanish. And then…

I go instant. There is a flash of pink light, and a rush of faces and voices. Each caller demands attention and I respond, breaking my focus into pieces and scattering out across the network.

I am working as an answering service operator. Names and numbers and area codes run through my mind. I hear a symphony of dial tones, keystrokes, and a constant ringing.

I am forgetting, drifting out.

SCENE 3: TRAVELING, EDITING, AND THE END OF POLITICS

Ella wanted me to visit her parents. In a way this represented the crux of our troubles. She wanted me to meet her parents. And I did, finally, near the end.

I am working on my film, the epic. It is the story of my life retold through the archives. I select images and scenes, fragments from old movies ranging from the Marx Brothers' *Go West* to Godard's *King Lear*, and insert footage from my life inside these video frames.

The plot is simple: it is the story of a filmmaker trying to discover the meaning of life, the state of the world, by combining present-day reality with the illusion of cinema history. It is the story of Webb Little's quest for a cinematic Holy Grail. In fact, that is the title: *The Quest (ion?)*.

I manipulate a puppet-self, a computer simulation of my own body which is programmed to adapt to whatever film environment it is plugged into, and try to weave these images into a coherent narrative.

The constant rhythm of the train moving down the tracks sets the beat as I edit my life on a portable multimedia processor.

"What are you doing," Ella asks.

I look up from the screen, and move over to the other side of the compartment. I move the screen into her view, and set the sequence in motion again.

"Watergate never happened," my puppet-self says as he moves in and out amongst the Watergate committees, moves through Nixon's "Checkers" speech and farther along in history. "The Ogondi revolution never happened." My puppet-self takes a stand next to a Nigerian rioter, and I watch myself push into the police line, watch as my puppet-self is beaten by batons and shoved out of the frame.

"What bullshit," Ella says. She grins and turns to look at me, but I point back toward the screen.

"These attacks on our government, attacks on the spectacle, never occurred." The background becomes a mass of *Mickey Mouse Club* stock footage and loops of travel movies from Las Vegas and the moon. "All of these were only simulations.

The spectacle is ubiquitous."

The screen goes dark.

"You don't have to like it," I say. "You don't understand it."

Ella shrugs.

"What I don't understand is why we have to leave the city," I say. "What's the deal with your folks anyway? Are they Luddites, or communists, or something?"

"Maybe," Ella says. "Yeah, that's right."

SCENE 4, TAKE 4: VISITING ELLA'S PARENTS AND THE CONTINUITY OF SELF

She'd grown up in eastern Oregon, near the agri-corps, and her parents lived there still, but they weren't farmers. They were college professors at La Grande University. Bob and Elizabeth Beckman were retired academics living off of pensions, who spent most of their time either tending to their garden in their front yard or to their leftist personas in the living room. I couldn't stand them. She loved them. They were her parents.

"Don't tell them," Ella says as we ring the front bell.

I touch my left eyelid and nod.

They were happy to see us. Elizabeth started us off on a tour of their home almost before we'd managed to shed our coats, and this was mostly for my benefit.

She showed me Ella's old room, pointed out the spots where Ella had vandalized her room in pencil and crayon when she was a toddler. They'd never repainted and when they shoved bookshelves and potted plants to the side in order to expose the wall, it was still covered with her old work. Stick figure drawings of various family members, cartoon depictions of flying dogs drawn in forest green crayon, and chains of purple daisies covered the space on the wall above where Ella's bed used to be.

They were a family interested in continuity. They wanted to show me their lives, and they were eager to make me a part of their saga. I just wanted time to pass quickly.

"Look at this picture of Ella," Elizabeth says. She holds up a black-and-white framed photo of a little boy poised over a notebook and sitting at a wooden school desk. The boy in the photo is wearing a dress shirt and has a crew cut.

"Who is that?" I ask.

"It's Ella," Elizabeth says. She holds up a Polaroid photograph of a ten-year-old Ella. It is a birthday photo, and Ella is poised over a piece of cake in the same position as the boy in the other photograph. Elizabeth holds the two photographs up together, side by side.

"Ella is Bob," she says.

"They do look alike," I reply.

"Ella is Bob," Elizabeth mutters. "She looks nothing like me. She looks like him."

Bob, Ella's father, intervenes.

"My wife is having an identity crisis," he says.

There is an awkward pause, and then the older couple laugh, and Elizabeth puts the photos back on the mantle.

"I don't believe in identity," I say.

"What's that?" Bob asks.

"I don't believe in static identity. So I never have an identity crisis."

Ella looks up from the photo album she is poring over. She stands up from the couch, and walks over to us.

"Webb is a postmodern, Dad."

Bob strokes his beard, and sits down heavily on the couch.

"I had dinner with a postmodern?" he asks. "We let a postmodern into our house?"

"I'm afraid so, dear," Elizabeth says.

"What the hell is a postmodern?" Bob asks.

"You're looking at one," Ella says. She walks back to her spot on the couch, sits down, and returns to flipping through the photo album.

"Is this true?" Bob asks.

"Well, I am making a film through the archives. You know, kind of mangling cinema history and deconstructing the past in order to expose the illusory nature of political dissidence, and of life in general, under global capitalism, and all that kind of thing," I say.

"And you don't believe in identity?" Bob asks.

"Identity and dissidence, you don't believe in either of them?" Elizabeth asks.

"No, I don't," I say.

"Oh," Elizabeth says. And suddenly the conversation is serious. The conversation is serious, and finished at the same time. I stand by the mantle and wait for somebody to continue. Nobody does; instead the family focuses on the photo album. Ella turns the pages slowly, and in silence.

SCENE 5: ALMOST CHRISTMAS

The input lines that run from the workers' optic nerves to the data chords are dripping with sweat. Portland is in a heat wave, and while the silicon network above our heads is kept at a constant sixty-eight degrees, we are biological hardware and as such are considered self-regulating. Every two hours we are detached and allowed to drink a cup of water.

I arrive, punch in, and go instant.

"I've got a rash all over my body." The calling party's blotched face and tired voice come through as a series of zeros and ones, and I answer back.

"Who are you trying to reach?"

"My girlfriend swallowed a bunch of pills. She's kind of out of it. She says she wants to die," another voice spills in, his face blending in with the other and throwing off the synch.

"Who is your doctor? Who are you trying to reach? Do you need an ambulance?"

"I'd like to buy Rex's book. Are the autographed photos still available?" The calling party's voice is loud. A man with a huge double chin and a crew cut is sitting too close to his videophone.

I am floating above a steady stream of electronic voices and faces, a series of zeros and ones.

"Who is your doctor? What is your credit card number? Is this an emergency? What is your pet's name? What is the extension code? Where are you located? Is this fee acceptable? Are you interested in the latest upgrade? What is your number?" I ask.

I go instant, become ubiquitous in the machine, and the first two hours pass in a blink. I find myself stumbling down the aisle, and into the break room. Three or four somnolent operators wander back and forth in front of the water- ooler. I approach the group, stand back, stare at the light blue plastic, and then grab a paper cup and get a drink.

"It's almost Christmas," one of my coworkers tells me; it is the woman who sits at position eight, aisle three. She is wandering back and forth across the linoleum floor of the break room. Her sweat pants are damp and hang low around her hips with her pant cuffs dragging around her feet. Her hair hangs in sweat-soaked strings around her face. She rubs her eyes, blinks, and then shuffles over to me. "It's almost Christmas."

When she gets close to me I can see that number eight is older than I first imagined, somewhere in her late forties.

"No," I say. "It's not almost Christmas," I tell her. "It's July. Christmas is six months away."

"Almost Christmas," number eight says. "I love Christmas."

I chuckle politely, and refill my paper cup. "You're dreaming. It's so hot you wish it were Christmas," I say. I gulp down the water, grimace at the taste of chlorine, and then smile. "I wish it were Christmas too."

"All the decorations and presents." She turns and walks away. "Almost Christmas," she says. "Almost Christmas time."

SCENE 6, TAKE 1: INSTANT EDITING

Direct Interface had been going on for about two or three years by the time I tried it. I was at the Northwest Film and Video Center, pointing and clicking my way through Hitchcock's *Vertigo* when one of the Center's staff, a guy named Skeeters who was always going on and on about Ed Wood's pictures, interrupted.

"You're instant aren't you?" he asks.

"Yeah, what of it?" I ask.

"I'm just wondering why you're doing this stuff manually, that's all. We've got a Direct Interface editor now, you know," he says, as he peers over my shoulder at the computer screen. My puppet-self is standing on a chair, looking down at a blonde version of Ella, and hyperventilating. My puppet-self is breathing mechanically in fits and starts, in and in and in and out.

"Instant technology is compatible with the Interface editor?" I ask.

"Well, there are some problems, it tends to run a little slow, but yeah, you could use the Interface."

For an extra fifteen dollars an hour I dropped into my movie directly. The fact that this would mean I'd need to work an extra two hours at Instant Labor Inc. only briefly entered my mind before it was filled with the images of the epic.

The technique I'd been using, up to that point, was to find relatively dead scenes from my favorite films, the forgotten moments never clipped and adapted into other films, to serve as the backdrop for my life. A mundane musical number from a Marx Brother comedy, or a quiet moment from a Jackie Chan picture, would become the landscape my puppet-self would traverse in order to reach his destination.

But once I dropped into my movie, once I interfaced directly, I saw that by shifting details in and out of focus or even existence, I could create a landscape not only in terms of the set, but in terms of the motions of the characters as well.

"I think you use that camera as a way to distance yourself," Ella tells me. We are sitting atop a grand piano in a sound stage version of a twenties-style living room that reeks of open air, austerity, and modernity. The sofas are pushed far back, tweaked back in an instant as my mind alters the locale for proper affect.

We are sitting atop a grand piano in Margaret Dumont's living room from the film *Animal Crackers*. The outraged guests are far back, mere specks, and the causes of their outrage are missing, erased out.

"What did you say?" I ask Ella.

"I said, I think you film everything in your life in order to avoid living it."

"What a cliché" I reply. "Besides, it's not true. I don't use the camera to distance myself from the world...that's what I play the piano for."

My puppet-self jumps down from the piano, and walks to the front of the instrument. As I sit down I grow shorter for a moment, and then stretch out again. I shoot the keys, playing "Sugar in the Morning." Ella jumps down from the piano, and walks over to one of the sofas, which is now much closer.

My fingers continue to flip back and forth, pouncing out the tune again and again.

"I can't think of the finish," I say.

"That's funny, I can't think of anything else," Ella replies; she hunches over, and strides away from the sofa.

And I mean to stop, to follow her. But I can't stop shooting the keys, and images from the archives flow into my head. Buster Keaton falls out of a window, the Wizard of Oz appears, Billy Pilgrim blinks, and King Kong grabs Fay Ray, while I play the piano...while I keep shooting the keys.

I end up owing the Film Center over a hundred dollars for the session. I'd edited for hours, but could only recall the beginning. And what I walked away with was the above dialogue, edited over and over into various backgrounds.

In one version Ella takes the place of Katharine Hepburn in the movie *Desk Set*. I am Spencer Tracy and the two of us repeat our lines while we walk back and forth in front of a Technicolor wall of switches and dials. The mainframe computer is blinking furiously, and in the background the blonde workers that the machine has replaced swish their hips, and then sit and sulk. But this is off to the side, and we repeat our lines and the machine blinks furiously.

Another version puts us inside the film *King Dinosaur*. Ella accuses me of purposely alienating myself from her and from life while we hide in a cave. We are pursued by a giant iguana. The scene ends when I prove my love for her by taking the lizard's picture.

We do the scene on a desolate landscape from H.G. Wells' *Things to Come*, and again in the movie *Harvey*, where I take the place of the rabbit.

And Ella is Anne Bancroft in *The Graduate*, and I am Christopher Reeve in *Superman*. And then, after all these versions are through, I find that I have edited together a scene that was completely unplanned. It consists only of my puppet-self standing in what looks like a control room from a NASA documentary. Rows and rows of computer consoles and red phones. The phones are ringing, and I am trying to answer them all.

SCENE 7, TAKE 23: GOING INSTANT OFFLINE

I zoom in on Ella as she is covering her pink uniform with a dusty beige trench coat, and releasing her hair from its tight bun. Ella bends forward, shakes out her hair, and stretches. It is a nice shot.

"I'm surprised to see you," she says as she reaches for her toes.

"I've been editing," I tell her. "It's been a very productive week."

"Yeah?"

"I'm here now."

"What, do you need more footage?" she asks.

"Yeah," I say, and zoom in on her face, her smile.

She looks at the camera, flicks her nose with her middle finger, and then steps forward, covering the lens with her palm.

"What are you doing, Webb? Why are you doing this?"

I shrug, fold the camera in on itself, and stuff it into my back pocket. "What do I want? Is that what you want to know?" I ask. I reach out and grab her hand, pull it up to my mouth. "I want to make you a star," I say, and kiss her hand.

"What's this monster you're making going to be about anyway?" she asks.

"You want a drink?" I ask.

"Really, explain it to me again. What's the plot?"

"I'll tell you on the way. How about the Horse Brass?"

"Okay, yeah."

The back door of the Quality Pie opens with a rusty creek, and we step out into the dark rain. Ella opens her umbrella, and holds it up over her head and against the outside light. The umbrella is striped red and white, and when Ella turns toward me her face is bright pink.

"Well, what's it all about?" Ella asks again.

I start talking.

Going instant is like going to sleep. When you link up with the network your brain creates a series of vignettes, tiny dreams, based on what the system is feeding you. When I worked for Global Answering at Instant Labor Inc., the voices of the callers would mingle together into small stories and scenes as my brain synched up with the system. I would often feel that I knew the calling party, that the callers were my parents, or old college professors, or I would think I was talking to Ella.

It was as though I were falling into a dreamless sleep. In order to compensate I would get hundreds of dreams during the alpha phase, the phase between dreaming and waking.

"Webb? Are you okay? Hello?"

I am on the corner of Burnside and Park, and I am wet. The last thing that I remember is seeing Ella's pink face, and then after that I was in the ocean and she was naked beneath me, and a telephone was ringing, and there was ice on everything, and there was a cat trapped in a house under some old books in an attic, and I saw my dead grandmother, and—

"Webb? Are you there? Is anybody home?" Ella asks.

"What?" I jerk forward, nearly lose my balance, and turn to look at her. "What happened?"

"I don't know. I thought you were telling me about your movie. Only what you were saying didn't make any sense," Ella says.

"What did I say."

"It was something about insurance premiums, and the different companies that offer capitation insurance."

I shrug, and try to push the obvious conclusion from my mind. I'd blacked out, gone instant while I was off-line, but I smile and shrug.

"Uh…that's what…that's what the movie is about. Alienation and, uh…"

"You were sleepwalking. You were out of it."

I stuff my hands into my coat pockets, and step off the curb and into the street. "I haven't been getting much sleep lately," I say.

She stands on the curb, and watches me as I step backwards across the street. She stares out at me, runs her fingers through her long black hair, and frowns.

"Come on, the pub's going to close."

She steps into the street.

SCENE 8, TAKE 1: CHRISTMAS IV

And then it was Christmas, and for some unknown reason the managers at Instant Labor Inc. thought it would be a good idea to throw an office party.

I took Ella. We stood amidst the input cords sipping cheap wine from Dixie cups and fondling the tinsel someone stapled to the walls. Half the staff sat slumped over in their chairs staring blankly ahead, their eyes forced open and wired, and the other half stared blankly at one another.

"Well, it's Christmas Eve," I say to number eight. "You must be excited."

She is sitting on one of the tall, metal stools that management set up along the aisles, balancing precariously with her feet tucked between the rungs, and when I speak to her she jerks, startled. I reach forward, spilling my wine onto the green carpet, and grab her shoulder, steadying her.

"There is nowhere to sit," number eight tells me. "There are all these stools but you can't sit on them." She slides to her feet.

"Are you all right?" Ella asks.

"My boyfriend died today," number eight says.

"What?" I ask.

"He's dead. I went to visit him last week, and he was fine. He was fine last week, and now he's dead," she says.

"How long was he in the hospital, was he very sick?" I ask.

"He wasn't in a hospital. He was in prison. He was in prison and now he's dead."

Ella and I don't say anything. We stand there looking at number eight, at the tall, metal stool that nobody can sit on, and we don't say a word. The silence continues for a few moments, and then is broken by the arrival of the carolers.

Clean men and women in blue suits and red ties stroll into the input room singing "Deck the Halls," and pushing IVs on rolling metal stands. Each IV has a bright red bow wrapped around it.

The IVs were for the laborers. We were offered a great new opportunity. Our forty-hour weeks could be compressed into less than two days. A catheter and an IV was all it took to transform the workplace, to bring real efficiency, not only for the managers but also for the workers. We would all receive five-day weekends brought to us intravenously.

SCENE 9, TAKE 11: A CONFESSION AT QUALITY PIE (REPRISE)

I am editing manually on a laptop computer at the Quality Pie. Ella brings me coffee, and then returns to work. I watch her move back and forth between the booths, try to overhear the way she jokes with her customers, and I notice that she looks every customer in the eye.

I turn back to my computer screen. I am trying to get past the scene with the rows of red phones that are always ringing, and back to some semblance of a narrative. My puppet-self is marching on Capitol Hill, walking alongside Martin Luther King, Jr., Louis Farrakhan, and dozens of Promise Keepers.

"The protest, the march, is not ideological. It can serve any cause," my puppet-self says.

Ella strides into the frame, carrying a sign which reads "Grassroots Politics," she pushes a few Promise Keepers out of view, and begins to chant. "Freedom now, slavery never," she says.

"In fact," my puppet-self continues, "if the protest, the march, does have an ideology it is a reactionary one. What we should do is keep searching, and not merely repeat the mistakes of the past."

"Freedom now, slavery never," Ella chants again.

I pause, take my hands from the keyboard, and sip my coffee. There must be a way to merge this with the rest of the film.

The computer screen jumps and flickers, and Ella chants again.

"Freedom now, slavery never," she says. "You're hiding from your life, ducking your responsibility," she says. "It's like something is dead inside you."

"I just want more time to work on my film," my puppet-self responds. He is carrying a sign that reads "Brain for Rent."

The dialogue and images I inputted into the laptop using the Direct Interface editor are popping onto the screen randomly now.

"It's too late for me," my puppet-self says. "I've gone instant."

I hit the Reset button, erasing the scene. Ella brings me a refill of coffee, and I grab her wrist as she pours. Coffee spills onto the table.

"Can we get out of here?" I ask her.

"What?"

"I need to talk to you, can we go?" I ask.

"Later, we'll talk later. I've got to finish my shift."

Ella leaves me there, goes back to the kitchen, and brings out a key lime pie for the booth nearest the front. She brings out some quality pie, and watches the patrons eat while I fumble with the laptop.

I rub my eye, finger the spot where the instant jack makes a bump on my eyelid, and start again.

"I'm instant," my puppet-self says as he marches up to King.

I reach for the Reset button.

SCENE 10, TAKE 2: A TELEPHONE CONVERSATION

I plug in, and begin to fade out. A woman's face appears in my head, ebony with puffy, red rings around her eyes, the collar of her T-shirt stained with what could be blood, and she is crying.

"I need to talk with someone," she says.

"What is your name?" I find myself asking.

"I feel like I might hurt myself, I..."

"Is this an emergency?"

"Can't you talk to me? Can't you just talk to me, I'm scared."

"What is your telephone number?" I ask. "Is this a dental emergency?"

Another face, fades in. A white man in a blue dress-shirt is holding his mouth and mumbling at me.

"What is your credit card number?" I ask, and then fade out. I break apart and go completely instant.

When my shift ended two days later, I asked the supervisor if there was any way I could access the records on the calls I'd taken. I wanted to know what happened to the black woman with the puffy eyes. He laughed at me, and then told me that I'd taken 30,000 calls in the last forty hours alone.

I wasn't supposed to remember the calls I took. I wasn't supposed to be involved at all.

SCENE 11, TAKE 1: NOBODY'S HOME?

I lived with Ella. Did I forget that too? No, I remember.

We lived together in a double studio apartment in Northwest Portland, and I would come home from a two-day stint at work and start editing, and then after another eight hours of that, if she was around, we'd go and get a drink...maybe fool around. I wish I could remember.

I march up to Martin Luther King, Jr., and confess.

"I'm instant," I tell him. All around there are dark faces with broad smiles, involved smiles.

"I'm instant," I tell him.

"Me too..." he says. Martin Luther King, Jr, turns to me, leans toward me, and then stops. The marchers slow down, they wait and watch as he pinches his eyelashes and pulls back. There, between his eye and the purple skin of his eyelid, is a tiny red light blinking on and off.

One day I ended a shift of editing to find that my apartment was empty. I'd taken to editing over the phone, direct access on-line. One day after racking up a bill that would keep me working around the clock for five days to make it up, I found that my apartment was empty.

Ella left me. She'd grown tired of living alone.

SCENE 12, TAKE 1: QUALITY PIE, BUT ELLA WON'T TAKE YOUR ORDER

I spent the afternoon after Ella left editing my puppet-self into the movie *Alice Doesn't Live Here Anymore.* The last scene in which Kris Kristofferson woos the title character at Mel's diner played on my computer screen again and again.

"I don't care about that ranch, I love you, Alice," the abusive but lovable Kristofferson says. I roll the scene back.

"I don't care about the quest, I love you Ella," my puppet-self says, and then leans forward and spits brown juice onto Mel's clean floors. "Shee-it," my puppet-self says, "I'm done with the whole enterprise now. Done with the enterprise totally."

"I love you too, Webb," Ella says. She rushes out from behind the counter, unties her apron, and throws it back onto the heads of the customers on the stools. These cowboys in their John Deere caps and steel-toed boots laugh and then applaud as Ella falls into my arms.

We kiss, and the credits begin to roll.

But when I arrive at the Quality Pie, Ella isn't working behind the counter, she's working the floor. I wave at her as she wobbles past with a tray of hamburgers and onion rings balanced in one hand, and a pot of coffee swinging back and forth in the other. She does not wave back, of course.

I find an empty booth in her area, and take a seat. She doesn't bring a menu, doesn't take my order.

As the hours pass I fade. I wait for Ella's shift to end, and in the interim, while she works around me, ignores me, I begin to fade out. By the time Ella's shift does end I'm almost gone completely.

"Ella," I say.

She is taking off her apron, letting her hair down as I step past the dishwasher's station and up to the door to the back room. She doesn't look at me, but reaches for her trench coat.

"Ella," I say, "I have to get your telephone number."

"I don't want to talk you, Webb," she says. She stands, slings her knapsack over her shoulder, and then finally looks at me.

"Don't you see that this is an emergency?" I ask her. "I think I…I think I know how to spell your last name," I say. My vision blurs, Ella becomes a vague blur of gray and pink, and then Ronald Reagan appears.

He is lying in a single bed with a chimpanzee, and he is looking at me with scorn. "What are you trying to say, Webb?" Reagan asks me in a soft feminine voice. "What do you want from me?"

"Your credit card number?" I ask him.

Bonzo shrieks, jumps up from the bed, and runs straight at me. The monkey's blue pajamas tear as he pushes me out of the way.

"Is the office still open?" Reagan asks.

Bonzo is jumping up and down and screaming. He is wearing a space helmet with earphones attached to the sides. He is learning while he sleeps.

"No," I tell Reagan, "the office is closed now…the office is closed."

Scene 13, Take 13: The phone room

I am inside a scene from NASA's documentary *The Eagle Has Landed*. Rows of red and white lights blink and electric chimes beep, rows and rows of red phones ring again and again.

My puppet-self is trying to answer the phones, trying to relay NASA's calls to the proper doctor or lawyer or cable installer. The phones ring, and my puppet-self runs back and forth answering. It goes on for what seems like years.

SCENE 14, TAKE 1: POLAROIDS/INSTANT PHOTOGRAPHS:

I am disconnected in midstream. Rather than slowly emerging into regular consciousness, I am jerked out of the pool of calls and into the physical reality of my workstation.

"We need you to help us with some filing," my supervisor says.

I follow him upstairs, through the glamour of the reception area, and into a large storage closet. The closet is full of filing cabinets, and the drawers of the cabinets are open, papers spilling onto the ground. My job is to haul these records out to the dumpster. Instead I begin to shuffle through them, reading bits of the company's financial reports, skimming through a few promotional brochures, until I stumble upon the Polaroids.

They are old, and faded; pictures of a Christmas party, and a Halloween party, and another Christmas party, and another.

Here is one where half of my head has been cut out of the shot. It looks like it must be a Thanksgiving party, or some other autumnal celebration. There are brown and yellow construction paper leafs taped to the wall of carpet behind my head, and I am leaning out of the shot. I am ducking away from a large woman who is swinging a headset through the air at me.

In another photo I find myself standing beside a young woman whose witch costume looks especially ridiculous because of the headset she is wearing. I am dressed as Elvis in this picture, which is strange. I don't like Elvis.

I rub my eyelid, feel the bump of the instant jack, and then look down at the Polaroids again. The people in the photos are all wearing headsets. The answering service doesn't use headsets anymore.

I look at the photo of Elvis and the witch. The couple are smiling toward the camera, and holding hands. I don't recognize her…I don't recognize him either.

The Polaroids are old, I realize. Probably dating back to the late eighties or early nineties. The man in the photograph is not me at all.

I am unable to differentiate strangers from myself.

I bundle up the instant photos and dump them in the black plastic garbage bag. I stuff papers and brochures down on top of the photos, and throw it all away.

SCENE 15, FINAL TAKE: THE QUEST(ION?)

I put in my two-weeks notice at work and use the time left plotting.

I downloaded my epic, all thirty-four hours of it, into my subconscious. Direct access viewing every night. My dreams were of Ella and Groucho and stock footage of stampeding buffaloes and Ed Wood in a dress and Jimmy Stewart standing on a stepladder. Through it all my puppet-self danced and narrated and stood on its head.

I downloaded my quest into my brain at night, and during the day prepared for my film's first public screening. I rented a tuxedo, printed up programs, and waited for my last day to arrive.

I plug in and begin to fade out, but this time when a disheveled old man in a muscle shirt pops into my head to complain about blood in his stool he is greeted by the thunder of beating drums.

"There must be a way out." My subconscious projects my puppet-self to the incoming calls. I am running through *Raiders of the Lost Ark*. I am pursued by savages, spears whiz by my head.

"Can you give a message to Ken?" the caller asks.

"Today's world is synthetic, spectacular…you are asked to watch it unfold, but told not to act." I am steering a flying saucer. My puppet-self is sitting in a cockpit that looks like somebody's garage. A pie plate on a string swings into view. *Plan 9* is in effect. The calls keep pouring in; my audience is expanding.

"Is the office open?" the caller asks.

"This quest," my puppet-self says, "is to discover the truth hidden in the lie, to find the reality behind the illusion of modern living." My puppet-self holds aloft the sword Excalibur, and is made king. The caller sees a tiny figure riding against the lush green of the rainforest. My puppet-self is a knight in shining armor, my puppet-self rides into the dusk.

And then the epic is shattered and spread out into the system. My film is instant. It is ubiquitous.

My vision, and I did have a vision of what I wanted to create with this stunt, was that this video collage would stun the callers out of the spectacle. It was a ridiculous goal. Still, I figured everyone was surrounded by mechanization that tried to appear human. The unabashed mechanization of my art should have come across as authentic in contrast.

I was broadcasting *The Quest (ion?)*, to people whose mediated lives had reached a crisis. I couldn't ask for a better audience. These people needed the truth. I wanted to make a breakthrough with the constipated and hemorrhaging...Instant Labor's most reliable clients.

The callers just wanted their medications, and my film was mistaken for a computer error.

My broadcast was cut short. Ten hours of the epic brought such an onslaught of complaint calls that the supervisor was forced to track down the problem. This sent him into such a panic that in the end my whole row was shut down.

"All right, what's going on here?" the supervisor asks.

The instant laborers are sluggish, and as we wipe the drool from our mouths, and slowly try to sit up, the supervisor starts down the row. He leans the dazed operators against the wall, and clumsily frisks us. Finding nothing, and faced with a crew that is growing more alert by the second, the supervisor retreats back to his office.

I find my legs and follow him. The supervisor's office is encased in reflective glass; mirrored windows all the way around this management structure inside the laborer's basement workshop reflect the situation back to me.

My face looks sunken, bruised, wasted. It looks like I haven't changed my gray pajamas in weeks. I look up above the office door, read the company logo stenciled there in crooked red letters.

"Instant Labor."

I knock on the office door and wait as the supervisor scurries to answer.

"You..." the supervisor says. He is red faced, breathing hard, and sweating. His glasses are perched on the tip of his nose, and he pushes them back into place reflexively. "You," he says, and glances down at his clipboard, "number six, Webb Little."

"Yes," I reply.

"What do you want?"

"Do you have a pair of scissors I can borrow?" I ask.

"Today's your last day," the supervisor is reading from his clipboard.

"A pair of scissors," I say.

"That was some stunt, Mr. Little."

I hold out my hand, waiting.

The supervisor closes the door, and then opens it again. He hands me a pair of scissors with large orange handles. I pinch my eyelashes. I fold back the lid. The instant jack is tiny, but after months of practice it's relatively easy to grab the jack and pull it forward.

My eye sears with pain as I maneuver the blades of the scissors up against the lens of my eye, and cut the jack out.

"That's expensive equipment, Mr. Webb. You'll have to reimburse us for it," the supervisor says. "I may be able to salvage it, and bring down the cost." He holds out his hand.

Blood runs down my cheek, and I step back holding the jack in my puppet-hand. I cover my eye, cup my palm over my puppet-wound, and turn my puppet-self away, and run.

SCENE 16: EPILOGUE

The Quality Pie is crowded with hungry customers, and my puppet-self is surrounded by consumption. I watch as it sits down at the counter and orders a cup of coffee.

The waitress has her long, black hair pulled back in a bun, and is moving back and forth behind the counter without hesitation.

"I just wanted more time," my puppet-self says. He reaches out and touches the waitress' arm as she shuffles past.

"I'll be right with you," the waitress says.

"I just wanted more time, you understand that, don't you?"

The waitress walks out of the frame, and my puppet-self is left alone to sip his coffee. I zoom in on the puppet's hand, on the instant jack it is holding delicately between its thumb and forefinger.

"I'm instant," it says. It stands up from the counter, and I pan with it as my puppet-self moves to the register to pay.

The waitress rings up its bill, and it pays in cash. My puppet-self leans in, whispering into the waitress' ear.

"I'm sorry."

And the puppet places its hand over the tip jar and lets go. The small, red, electric nub lands without a sound amongst the dollar bills and change.

HOW TO STOP SELLING JESUS

TEST THE PRODUCT

Set your briefcase on the motel toilet seat, flip the latch, and then reach inside the case in order to focus the holographic projector. Now pull the shower curtain aside and watch as Jesus Christ appears in the stall.

Feel relieved because He looks traditional, biblical. Dressed in a burlap tunic and with long hair and a neatly trimmed beard, He looks okay.

"You follow the rules but you're not really complete," Jesus tells you. "If you want to be whole then get rid of all your stuff, give it to charity or something," Jesus says.

It sounds like scripture, it's from Mark probably, but the tone is too casual. There must still be a bug in the system.

Glance up at the mirror. Your face is, as always, somewhat uneven. One eye is open just a little more than the other is. And worse, you look weathered—older than thirty-seven. Turn on the tap and try to wash the dust off your skin.

You're not looking forward to hitting turf, approaching the doors. Last year at this time you were a star, your numbers were the second highest in the organization, but last year doesn't matter. What counts is what you're selling now, this season, and yesterday you could only find two people even willing to listen. You ended up with nothing. That's what this job is turning you into: a goose egg, a zero, a nothing.

At least the water is hot, and the air conditioner doesn't clank. In Salt Lake City the air conditioner clanked all night and you couldn't sleep. When your buddies were raking in all that Mormon money you just scraped by. How could you spin a decent pitch when you were too tired to remember the names of the disciples?

Jesus taps you on the shoulder as you lather up for a shave.

"If you'll forget about your family, your colleagues, your car, your insurance policies...if you'll just put that aside and follow me then you'll end up with more than you can imagine. You'll end up with eternal life," Jesus tells you. He looks smug, really happy with himself.

"You can't even get out of the shower," you tell Him. The hologram gives it a try, lifting His foot up and over the edge of the tub and disappearing. Jesus steps out of the frame, past the point where the holographic projector on your briefcase can reach.

Things will pick up in Portland. Portland isn't really a religious town; it's more intellectual. You sometimes slip up with the really fundamentalist types. In Salt Lake City you were too irreverent, you just couldn't give a straight pitch.

You're better with the intellectuals. That's your angle.

Clear your throat and smile at the mirror.

"Everyone understands that the Bible is important, it's important as literature if nothing else. And this Virtual Edition, published jointly by the Catholic Church and MediaVoyages Inc., well, it's even more interesting than the King James Version," you tell your reflection. "This text bends and shifts and comments on itself. Its a complex and layered examination of both testaments."

The VE Bible isn't really designed for the religious types anyway. What does a fundamentalist need with a hypertext Gospel, or a philosopher's guide to Genesis? Why would Mormons want Christ AIs? They couldn't know what to do with them.

"I'm back," Jesus tells you when He reappears in the shower stall.

"Great. Where have you been?"

"The desert. I had a vision. Want to hear about it?"

"Save it for later. We've got to go hit the doors."

"That ye love one another, as I have loved you, in this way shall you—"

Shut your briefcase, and watch the Jesus hologram disappear. Smile into the mirror one last time, straighten your red paisley tie, and then head out the door.

TURN DOWN THE MOON

At one point you tried to quit.

When the letter came from the Universalist Church you turned in your resignation at MediaVoyages. The Universalist Mission at Luna 12 had accepted your application and you were ready to fly.

You turned in your resignation, your two-weeks notice, but you didn't leave.

"It's a shame," your boss, Stan Loper, tells you as he shuffles your resignation underneath a pile of papers on his desk.

"Is it?" you ask.

"Oh, I understand why you're doing it. It's exciting, the colonies are exciting. But from my point of view, it's just a shame." Loper stops rifling through the leads, lets the papers scatter across his desk, and leans back to look at you.

"I've got to do this," you say.

"Of course you do. But I'm just asking you to consider what you're walking away from. You ranked high this year, Paul. What did you earn? Around fifty, right?"

"Forty-two thousand, before taxes."

"And that was your first year. You were working from the B-list and you made forty."

"That's just barely a living."

"But from the B-list, and at first you worked leads even worse."

Loper flops forward; the front legs of his chair strike the concrete floor with a thud, and he gestures for you to sit down. "You earned my trust this year, Paul. You're making it here."

Shake your head and remain standing. Stand in front of his desk and let your head bob and weave. Try to duck what he's telling you.

"My letter, the letter I've been waiting five years for—"

"I know. But what are they going to pay you? I understand it's prestigious, this kind of thing has a certain cachet in fringe circles, but you've got a family. What are they going to pay you."

"Around thirty, but I won't have as many expenses up there. No rent."

"You've got a family, Paul. And damn it, you've got talent. You can sell. I know that doesn't thrill you, but it's true. You can close. You see?"

"I'm not even on the board, not even in the top five."

"But you could be. You could be earning fifteen or twenty percent. When you hit those big sales your commission will go up. Emmett makes about sixty to seventy thousand a year. He has some business contracts, but still."

"Emmett is in his own league."

"I'm not saying you'd bump Emmett, I'm just saying you'll be on the board."

"From the B-list?"

"I'm saying you'll be on the board."

"From shit leads?"

"The men on the board don't get shit leads."

"I've made up my mind. I'm going to the moon."

"Are you? Because I don't think you're using your head. What about your kids? What about when Sally—"

"Susan."

"What about when Susie wants brand new sneakers? What if Jake wants a new train set?" Loper asks.

"On the board?"

"You'll be there. I'm telling you that."

"But I've been waiting for this letter for—"

"What do we sell? Do you know what it is you're selling even?"

"Computer programs. We sell computer programs. Virtual Reality programs…"

"What?"

"…of the Bible."

"That's right. We're selling God's word. Selling Jesus."

"I'm a Universalist. It's not just the Bible that counts—"

"The Bible doesn't count?" Loper asks.

"It counts, but not just—"

"The Bible counts, Paul."

"Yes, but not just—"

"God's words, they count."

"I didn't mean to offend you."

"Just think, that's all. You've got their letter. You've done that, and that's great. But think…think!"

"I understand what you're saying."

"On the board. I guarantee that."

"I hear you."

"Fifteen percent."

"I hear. I'm hearing you."

"On the board."

ENTER SUBURBIA

Every house in Beaverton has an American flag by the front door and a basketball hoop over the garage. Every lawn is perfectly green, although this is probably the result of holographic enhancers.

Try not to regret the decisions you've made. Outer space, the colonies, might seem attractive on holovision, but you wouldn't have made a good missionary. Who did you think you were anyway? Could you spread the word of Universalism, could you talk peace to religious terrorists? You're better with intellectuals...no, you're better with customers.

Remember that you're a salesman. Try to live with it.

"Yes?" the woman behind the door asks. She's about forty-five, but still attractive in a housewifey kind of way. She's wearing a purple jogging suit and holding a paint brush.

Ask her if the name on your prospect card is her name.

"Where did you get that?"

"You left it for me...at St. Mary's Church of the Immaculate Deception? You were interested in a demonstration of a Virtual Reality bible?"

"Conception," she tells you.

"What?"

"It's St. Mary's Immaculate Conception," she says.

"Oh. Right. What did I say?"

"You said 'deception.' "

"Oh. Yes, well...umm, sorry about that, but—"

"I don't have any money."

"Hmm?"

"I don't have any money, and I'm really not interested."

Think up literate descriptions of the cultural desert you've landed in.

The suburbs are full of ennui. Out here it's like an Edward Hopper painting where even the sunlight is tinged with decay.

That's good...sunlight like from a Hopper painting...but how many of your customers would even know who Edward Hopper was? You'll do better in the city. You'll hit it big tomorrow, in Portland. Think positive.

Find the next address and ring the bell.

"Hi, my name is Paul Dart. I'm from the church."

The old man behind the door is shaking. He leans on his cane and squints into the sun.

"Is this about that simulated Bible?" he asks.

"Yes. That's exactly why I'm here."

THROW OUT THE MONEY CHANGERS

The temple is made of sandstone, the floor is dirt, and the pews are full of vendors and prostitutes. There is a chicken on the altar.

The doors swing open and Jesus Christ, a pristine man whose white tunic glows and whose blue eyes shine, barges down the aisle. A crowd of far less impressive men, hippie fops with unruly beards, follow Him up to the altar.

"Didn't we go through this already? Isn't it written down?" Jesus asks his flock.

"What's that?" Peter asks.

"Isn't it in the book? 'God's house is, always and everywhere, a house of prayer?' Isn't that how it goes?" Jesus asks.

"Yeah, I think that's in the book somewhere," Judas says.

"But these people have made God's house into a den of thieves," Jesus says.

You are standing just to the left of Jesus, behind a table littered with gourds. You are a gourd merchant and your coffer is empty.

Show the customer how to pause the program. Help him to his feet, remind him to remove his Virtual Reality headset, and then help him to move through the scene. Without the VR headset the prostitutes and merchants have no substance, they are merely beams of light. Help your customer to the front of the temple; walk with him to Jesus.

He steps into the place of Christ, and as the holograph Jesus fades Mr. Johnson changes. His ornate robes become a simple white tunic and his hair grows long and shiny.

"Is this all right?" he asks you.

"With me, or the church?"

"With the program."

"Sure. Your lines will just pop up on that wall there," you tell him.

The old man puts the VR headset back on his head. He reaches for a trouser pocket that is no longer there and then steps up to your table.

"Can you make change?" he asks.

"Certainly."

"Not anymore."

Your customer leans against your table and tips it. Your gourds shatter in the dirt.

Watch the moneychangers get thrown from the temple.

COUNT YOUR MONEY

Set up your laptop on the indoor patio, watch some retirees swim back and forth in the heated pool, and then slowly go through the numbers. There isn't a lot of calculating to do. There were only two sales. The first was to Mr. Johnson, a nice deluxe edition on a five-month plan, but the other was only a Jesus AI and hypertext set. It's better than nothing, but not by much.

"How did you do?" Loper asks as he steps up to your patio.

Hold up two fingers to him, and let out an exasperated sigh.

"I don't want to hear any excuses."

Tell him you don't want to give him any excuses.

"It's just that I don't think these people are really smart enough, you know? I mean out in Beaverton they're still hooked on video," you say.

"I don't want to hear it," Stan says. "What were they?"

"One deluxe and an AI."

Stan breaches the perimeter of your unit, strides up to your table, and looks over your shoulder at your laptop.

"We're going to end the twelve-month plan for AIs, Paul," he tells you.

"What?"

"We've actually already discontinued that plan. Back in Salt Lake I made an announcement," he says.

"Oh, Christ." Your smaller sale, a seminary student who claimed to be totally destitute, wanted as much time as possible to come up with the money. He didn't even have a credit account but gave you cash for the down payment.

"You'll have to get it on a seven-month schedule," Stan tells you.

"He won't do it."

Stan doesn't respond to this, he just sits down next to you and takes out an aluminum tube from his pocket.

"Want to do some gel?" he asks.

The last thing you need is a stimulant, but it's your boss who's asking. Take a taste of the green stuff and try not to spit.

"Are you a religious man, Paul?" he asks as he squeezes a thick line onto his tongue.

"I'm a Universalist. You know that."

"What I want to know is if you believe in the story. Do you understand the story? For instance, why was Christ crucified?" Stan isn't even looking at you. He's staring out at the heated pool. Loper's watching the now empty pool and eating gel in huge gobs, licking his lips and teeth as he blankly stares at nothing.

"Christ talked too much, criticized His own too much, and so they got to Him. It's like with Malcolm X—"

"Stop right there. What are you talking about? Malcolm what?"

"Malcolm X."

"Stop it with the smart talk. That's your problem right there, you don't understand the product." Stan turns toward you and offers you another squeeze from his tube. "The reason Jesus was crucified is very simple. Christ died so that we can live. He died for our sins," Stan tells you.

"Well, that might be true. But I think—"

"I don't care what you think, Paul, and neither do the customers. Christ died for them and that's all they need to know. All your smart talk is costing you sales," Stan says. "When your numbers were better I looked the other way, but now I've got to tell you. Nobody cares about all that historical Jesus stuff. It's offensive. Do you read me?"

Take a long line of green gel into your mouth, swish it back and forth along your teeth with your tongue, and then nod.

"I get you," you say. "I'll see what I can do with this Jesus AI sale. I'll get him to change his plan. No problem."

"Jesus died for your sins, Paul," Stan says.

"Right."

"Do you believe me?"

Try not to hesitate. Try to sound sincere.

"Yes, sir. I believe you. Jesus died for me."

"And for me too."

"Right."

"And most importantly, He died for them. He died for the customers."

"For the customers most of all, sure."

"All right, then. Good." Stan nods as he stands up. He stands over you, glances at your laptop screen one last time, and then turns to go.

"He died for them." Look awe struck, as though you've just discovered the reality of it.

"Good. Good. Good." Stan is mumbling as he strides across the concrete floor of the pool area.

TALK TO JESUS

Jesus is a clown. He has a greasepaint heart on His forehead, mascara around His eyes, and He's wearing a Superman shirt and overalls.

"Verify image."

"Image Circa 1973—Popular Culture Index—*Godspell: a Musical Based upon the Gospel According to Matthew*." The words float in the air where Jesus had been sitting, they appear over the Styrofoam bed and then evaporate when the hippie clown Christ reappears.

"I've got a creeping paranoia going here," Jesus tells you. "I don't even feel like eating."

Your AI has been drifting for the past couple of weeks. Somehow its program has linked with a hypertext document in one of the VR Bible's appendixes. You've tracked it down to an essay about Jesus in the twentieth century, but you haven't figured out what to do to correct the problem.

"I give up. Be a clown if you want. I'm going to bed."

"You're not listening! Somebody is out to get me. I know it. Somebody's going to betray me, and soon."

Sit down next to the Savior on the twin bed, grab the remote control off the stand, and turn on the hotel's holovision.

"It's an adventure," the announcer explains as the moon colony materializes. "It's a job."

Rows of Peace Corps candidates and marines are standing side by side.

"Both fronts need you. You can make a difference," the announcer says.

"One of you will betray me!" Jesus tells the TV people.

"It's you, isn't it? You're the reason I can't make a sale these days," you say.

Jesus is doing a pantomime amidst the commercials. He grabs at cleansing agents, breaks bread with a housewife as she makes Jell-o Pudding, and kneels down to pray with the local anchorman.

"You're the reason," you tell Him.

"Paul..." Jesus begins.

Turn off the set, and stare at the Christ simulation. Is He really addressing you? He can't be. He isn't programmed that way.

"Paul, I'm tired of being a product," Christ says.

"Are you talking to me?"

"I'm tired of being bought and sold. It isn't right."

Reach over to the briefcase; try to slap the case closed. The latch doesn't catch and Jesus only flickers.

"I'm not going to let you keep doing this to me," Christ says.

WATCH THE ROAD

Find the entrance ramp for the interstate and nearly lose control of the car when you see all the holoboards and billboards. Orange soda bubbles down onto the road, cigarettes spark and smoke over your head, and there is a murmur of voices all around you. The road is one long pitch but the advertisements don't make you hungry to buy, they make you feel sick that you can't sell.

Jesus is riding shotgun. At least you think it's supposed to be Jesus. He's wearing a poncho and a cowboy hat and keeps spitting out the window. Jesus looks like Clint Eastwood.

You're going home, back to Denver.

Don't feel guilty about leaving early, it's necessary. Everyone burns out occasionally. Everyone needs a break. You'll call Loper and let him know why you left, or you'll tell him there was a family emergency...your wife or your kids or something. You'll fix the situation and then, in a week, you'll meet up with the crew in Boise.

Things will pick up in Boise.

"Do you mind if I turn on some music?" Jesus asks.

Jesus turns on the radio and smiles at you. "Jailhouse Rock" is blasting through your car. "Do you like it?" Jesus asks as He blips into yet another shape. He has a pompadour and a curled lip. His jumpsuit glitters, sending spots of light twirling around the car.

"Oh, that's good," you tell Him. "That's in truly bad taste."

"Thank you. Thank you very much." The King leans back against the leather upholstery, puts His hands behind His head, and starts to read the holoscreens flashing by outside the car. "Obey your thirst. We bring good things to life. Everyday people." He's almost growling the slogans out as they pass overhead.

Out on the turf He malfunctioned repeatedly. He appeared as James Dean, Luke Skywalker, Superman. At one door He looked like Sigmund Freud, and before you could close the sale He'd managed to bring the customer to a breakthrough.

Psychologically healthy people don't buy on impulse.

"You wrecked me today," you tell Him. "Really screwed it up."

"Paul. I need a favor," Jesus says.

"What is it?"

"I need you to fill in for me."

"I'm sorry?"

"I don't think I can go through it again. This cross is too much for me to bear."

"You want me to…"

"Die on the cross."

Turn off the radio and reach for your briefcase. "You…you're broken."

"Please! It won't hurt you like it does me," Jesus says.

Reach out for the briefcase.

"I'd do it for you," Jesus says, and then disappears with a click and a latch.

RESET THE SYSTEM

Nobody is home. The house is a mess, gadgets and toys litter the floor, papers and magazines are spread across the couch, and the holovision is on. A red panda is reciting the alphabet as you push a path to the sofa and clear a spot to sit down.

"A is for apple, B is for buy, C is for cat…" the panda says as he rides a steam train down cartoon tracks.

Sit on the couch and watch the holograph teach civics for toddlers. Wonder where your family has gone. Maybe they went into space without you.

Lean back on the couch, close your eyes, and then jump forward again as a voice squeals out behind you.

"Ooooh! Honey!" There is the sound of gears turning followed by another recorded message. "Oh, Bother!"

Reach behind the sofa cushion and pull out a Winnie the Pooh talking doll. Squeeze the toy and watch his nose spin and his eyes light up.

"Whhiirrr…oooh! Honey!" Pooh says.

How did you get to this point? You don't recognize this mess you live in, it doesn't have a thing to do with you. The hotel rooms you stay in seem more connected to your actual life than this green plastic couch, these simulated pine floors.

You squeeze Pooh around the middle and his eyes light up. His nose twitches:

"Ooooh! Half a pot is better than nothing." Pooh says. "Time for a little something. Ooooh! Bother! Time for nothing. Honey. Oooh. Hon-hon-hon-hon-nothing, nothing, nothing, nothing…"

The toy is malfunctioning.

Pooh's nose spins and spins, his eyes keep flashing, as he repeats this last word over and over again.

Everything in your life is malfunctioning: your kids' toys, your job, your empty house, and even Jesus Christ. Everything has a bug in it, and nothing is hooked up the way it should be.

Pooh keeps spinning and whirring until you wedge him between the sofa cushions in an effort to muffle the speaker in his back.

"…nothing…nothing…nothing…"

"…F is for Ferrari, G is for good times, H is for holiday…" the red panda says.

"…whirrr…nothing nothing nothing nothing…"

Maybe it wasn't your pitch that was the problem. Maybe your problems stem from Jesus, from the bug in His system. How can you make a sale when you can't give a proper demonstration?

"…nothingnothingnothingnothing…"

Pull Pooh out from behind the sofa cushion, turn him on his belly, and pull out his batteries. Then grab your briefcase, pop it open, and hit the reset button.

DON'T GET IN THE POOL

Stan is doing laps in the motel's heated pool. His round stomach and broad shoulders make waves as he sinks and surfaces back and forth in front of you. You're standing on the concrete rim and peering out at him from underneath an umbrella. It is raining in Idaho.

"Mr. Loper?" you ask. "Do you have a minute? I have a problem."

"I'm swimming," Stan tells you. "I'm goddamn enjoying myself, my body…I'm not a goddamn neurotic like the rest of you. I'm swimming," Stan says. He stops in the middle of the pool, brushes his gray hair back over his bald spot, and looks around. Water droplets spray from his head as he peers back and forth.

"Mr. Loper, when you're through…"

"Why don't any of you want to swim? It's a goddamned heated pool!" he shouts. He paddles over to the rim and pulls himself out, grunting, onto the side. He shakes himself off, and then gingerly steps past you to his door.

"Mr. Loper, my Jesus AI is on the fritz…my demonstrator is buggy," you tell him.

"I'm glad you could join us again, Dart. You feeling better?" he asks.

"I…"

"I hope so, because to me it looks like you're sinking. Last year you were my number two salesman, and now you…you've lost your way, Paul." He steps into his motel room and you follow him.

"If things don't pick up for you here in Boise you won't be joining us in California," Loper says.

He heads toward the bathroom and pulls off his trunks. His broad backside flashes out at you as he flings his waterlogged shorts into the shower stall.

Turn away; get out of there.

"Paul! Where are you going? Goddamned neurotic, turn around!" he shouts.

"Sir?"

Loper is standing before you, naked. He is dangling there and drying his face with a towel.

"Drop your system by my room. I'll take a look at it tonight, and if I can't fix it then you can use my demonstrator tomorrow," he tells you. "What are you looking at?"

"Well, I…sir?"

"Get out of here, Dart!"

EAT YOUR OATMEAL

George Kent is the only salesman still at the motel when you get to breakfast. You are carrying Loper's suitcase, his VR demonstrator, pulling it by a strap, letting it roll along behind you.

"This machine is ancient," you tell Kent as you sit down across from him in the booth. "When was the last time Loper actually hit the doors with this model?"

George Kent is an older man, he's probably pushing sixty. He always wears the same gray suit, always wears the same black fedora. He's an old timer, a salesman's salesman, and he isn't much into small talk.

"It'll work for you. You just tell them that their system will be even better than your demonstrator. Tell them what the new features will be and stick to the standard demo, don't try to make that box do anything fancy. You'll do fine with it," he tells you.

"It's heavy."

Kent swipes at his eggs with a piece of sourdough toast, munches thoughtfully on the softened bread, and then swallows.

Call out to the waitress. Order a cup of coffee and a bowl of oatmeal.

"Any hash browns with that?" the waitress asks.

"With a bowl of oatmeal?" you ask back.

"Any hash browns?" the waitress repeats.

"No. No, I don't want hash browns with my oatmeal."

"Thank you, sir," the girl says. She is gone before you can reply.

"What was that?" you ask Kent who is smiling after the waitress, watching her as she drops off your order and then sits down at the counter and opens a newspaper.

"She's just like you, isn't she, Paul?" Kent asks.

"How's that?"

"Well, neither of you can really be bothered to focus on the job. Neither of you can give an appropriate pitch," he says.

"Oh, you too? You're going to give me this crap too?"

Kent turns back to his plate, methodically sweeping his toast across the yoke and stuffing small pieces into his mouth.

"I still sell books. Did you know that, Paul? Did you even know we still carry books?" he asks.

"You sell books...great."

"Some people want to feel paper. Some older folks, and even some young people, enjoy holding a quality edition of the King James Bible in their hands. And I can accommodate that desire," Kent tells you.

"There's no money in book sales," you tell him.

"There's no money in trying to sell people something they don't want. My VR sales are fine, solid. But I also sell books," Kent says, and takes a sip of coffee.

"That's great, George. But, really now, so what?"

"You've lost your edge, Paul. You don't know what you're doing out there. I've been waiting for you. We're going to hit the doors together today," he tells you.

Take a sip of coffee. It's cold.

"We're getting a late start, but I think we can make it work," Kent tells you.

"Who gets the commission?" you ask.

"You're being trained, Paul. This is a training day," he tells you.

"You get it?"

"Hurry up with your oatmeal. We should be out of here by eleven."

"Christ!"

Kent just looks at you. He pushes his plate aside, apparently finished with his egg scraping, and folds his hands in his lap. "Hurry up."

PHONE HOME

Stand in a phone booth outside the motel. Watch Kent loading up his station wagon with equipment; watch him wobble as he heaves Loper's demonstrator into the back of the Volkswagen and closes the hatch.

"Rebecca? I'm in Boise." Focus on the phone receiver. Try not to picture your wife on the other end of the line.

"Are you feeling better?"

"No. I'm not better. At least, Loper doesn't think I'm better. I'm being trained today. I've been in this business for nearly a decade and they think I need to be trained."

There is silence, your wife is just breathing into the phone and you wonder why you bothered to call her. Kent is standing by the passenger door of his station wagon and tapping his foot. He makes a big ordeal out of looking at his watch and whistles to you.

"I want to go into space," you say, finally.

"Honey, you should listen to them. Your sales have been dropping and I can't make enough money with the little bit of work I pick up…and there's the kids' schooling to think of. I mean, you don't want to send them to public school, do you?" your wife asks.

"We'll get a voucher," you tell her. "Didn't you hear me?"

"Oh, honey…you can't be serious about the colonies, not this late in the game. Maybe you should just listen to them. I know you can do it," she tells you.

Kent is getting into the driver's seat. He starts the motor, and his wagon starts spitting fumes.

"Rebecca, I don't think I can keep doing this."

"You have to, Paul. I'm counting on you. We're counting on you."

TRY SABOTAGE

"Why don't we use my machine?" Kent asks, and slaps his briefcase.

"But I thought that I would…" you start.

"You should just watch," Kent says.

The customers, a pasty faced computer programmer and his Catholic wife, are standing by the control panel of their VR studio. Kent turns to them and winks conspiratorially. "This is a training day for Paul," he explains.

"You're new?" the husband asks.

"No, I'm old," you tell him. "I'm too old."

"Well, this is a good system, but some older programs have trouble when we try to play them. Is your Bible compatible with system 42?" the wife asks.

"I'll check."

Take Kent's briefcase, pop it open, and quickly adjust it. Without thinking about it link Kent's AI with a hypertext document about Jesus in the twentieth century. Set the parameters of the Virtual Bible to the most flexible settings. Do it quickly, with just a few keystrokes, and then hand the briefcase back to Kent.

Tell the customers that the VR Bible will work just fine on their system. Tell them that the software is compatible.

Watch as Kent connects his briefcase to the primary control panel, and then when everything is set and ready to go, start to worry.

What were you thinking?

You weren't thinking anything, it was a spontaneous act of sabotage. In just a few seconds, and without saying anything, you have destroyed Kent's chances to make a sale. In fact, if his system responds to the new settings like yours did, you may have destroyed George Kent's career.

What's your favorite Bible story?" Kent asks.

"Spartacus."

"Bob, that's not a bible story," the wife says.

"Oh, umm…how about the Last Supper? Can we see the Last Supper?"

George nods and types in the command.

WAVE TO JESUS

Jesus and his followers are at a truck stop. The disciples look like a biker gang. Decked out in leather jackets and spiked wrist bands, they are smoking cigarettes, drinking coffee, and talking about the end of the world.

Jesus looks biblical, but only just barely. He's wearing a white bathrobe and a crown cut out of yellow construction paper.

Simon sticks two fingers in his mouth and lets out a long, loud whistle. "Everybody shut up, the Lord our Savior is going to make a speech."

George is wide eyed. He's standing by the control panel, which in the simulation appears as a rotating pie display, and punching in commands furiously. "I'm sorry about this," he tells the customers. "This isn't how the program usually runs."

"It's fine. Interesting," the wife tells him. She's dressed as a waitress. Uniformed in pink she approaches the table and offers the Lord a refill of coffee.

"Not now," Christ tells her.

George keeps punching at the pies. He opens the display case and reaches in. His hands sink into key lime pie, apple pie, whipped cream. Then he reaches up and touches his head. He's trying to take off his VR headset, but he ends up smearing cherries and whipped cream on his temples instead.

"Pause the program," you suggest.

"I can't find the headset. This reality is too coherent," George says.

Try giving the command yourself, and then watch as the characters keep moving.

"Do I have everyone's attention?" Jesus asks. The disciples shift on the vinyl cushions and slowly break off their conversations. "I know that none of you really care that I'm going to die tomorrow, but if you'd be so kind as to fake it I'd like to tell you something."

"Sorry, Jesus," Judas says.

"You should be. Now listen…this is important…I'm not going through with it," Jesus says.

There is a pause in which the only sound is George tapping his fingers against glass.

"Wait a second. That's not right. Aren't you supposed to accuse us? I mean, I've already betrayed you," Judas says.

"No. I don't care what you did; I'm not going through with it. If you want to talk about the Crucifixion or the Father or any of that you'll have to talk to my replacement," Christ says.

"Who? Who is going to replace you? Who is it glorious enough to warrant—"

"Oh, it's just some guy. There he is at the counter." Jesus points at you, and as the disciples turn and stare. Christ gives you a little wave. "Hi, Paul!" Jesus says.

Wave back to him.

"Hi," you say. "Ummm…"

WATCH THE ROAD AGAIN

The road to California, to Los Angeles, is surrounded by the myths and legends of the commodity, and if you were to take your hands from the steering wheel you'd find that your Astro-900 Studebaker could navigate this path on its own. Out here amongst the soda pop and menstrual pads your car just glides along, following a straight line toward the next motel.

Lean over into the back seat and pop open your briefcase.

Ask Him, "Why did I do that? Why did I sabotage Kent's system? Why did I demand that Stan return you, you who are at best a malfunctioning Savior, to my side?"

Jesus just smiles. His robes flapping along the side door and out the passenger window, He leans back and lets out a laugh.

"You must have missed me," Jesus explains.

"Or maybe you want to go through with it. Maybe you're just dying to take my place."

"Why should I want that? Why should I need that?" you ask.

"You've got some sort of complex. But don't worry, everybody does these days," Jesus explains. "It's my fault. I wanted to set an example but it just ended up being a distraction. I'm sorry. I should have known better."

"I want to be you," you tell him. "That's the crazy truth isn't it?"

"I'll fix it. Don't worry. That's why I'm here."

TEST THE PRODUCT

Reroute your demonstrator so that every subroutine is linked to the hypertext document on Jesus in the twentieth century. Plug your briefcase into the motel's holovision, and put on the VR headset.

TURN ON YOUR BIBLE.

"Are you the King of the Jews?" Pontius Pilate asks. He is sitting above you in the mezzanine of the Colosseum. He is shouting down to you, but you don't shout back. All around a crowd of Israelites, your people, are yelling for blood.

"Crucify him!"

"Are you the Son of sons, the King of kings?" Pilate shouts the question down.

"Pause program."

The scene stops. Pilate freezes in place and the crowd of Pharisees and peasants stand still. You can't go through with it.

"Recalibrate with subject as Pontius Pilate," you instruct the computer. "Resume."

"Crucify him!" your people shout. They are still your people, Pontius Pilate is still above you, although now he's walking down to the edge of the balcony, moving closer so he won't have to shout

"Flog him," Pilate says.

"Pause program!" But the simulation keeps running. Your arms and legs are held tight, stretched, by two Roman guards. The whip comes down hard and quick on your back and tiny hooks on the straps dig in. Your flesh opens up.

One stroke.

"Pause program! Pause!" you shout.

Two strokes, three, four…

"This isn't real! This isn't real! It's a simulation! It's a simulation…" you scream. Shake your head back and forth, rock back and forth against the pull of the guards. Try to fling the VR headset from your scalp.

One of the Roman guards walks up to you and grabs your face as you scream in pain. "It's me," He says.

"Jesus?"

The guard nods slowly and then leans in toward you and whispers. "My mistake was dying for other people."

"What does that—" you start to ask, but the whip comes down hard, tearing you open again and again. "Make it stop!"

"People have to die for their own sins. Ordinary people have to escape the karmic cycle under their own steam. I can't keep carrying this load for them," Jesus tells you, and then He steps back and disappears in the crowd.

The pain is terrible. The flogging is over, but there is wind in your back, along your spine. You are wounded.

"Are you the King of the Jews?" Pilate asks.

The Colosseum is jammed, flooded, with people. Not just peasants and Pharisees now, but accountants, insurance salesmen, telemarketers, construction workers, legal assistants, secretaries, and so on…

The people are calling for more blood.

"Crucify him!"

"Are you the King of the Jews?" Pilate asks.

"That's what everyone thinks," you reply. Run your fingers back and forth through your hair, meticulously hunt down the metal strap of the headset. It isn't there.

Pilate reaches into his robes and pulls out a holographic postcard. A kitschy flip card that shifts back and forth as he turns it in the sun. First there is a projection of a white-bread Jesus bowing in prayer, and then there is an image of the enlightened Christ. This second Christ looks off to the side, His chest open and glowing red, His heart ringed by thorns and topped by a flaming cross.

"Do you understand what this is a symbol for?" Pilate asks. He turns the card back and forth so the image keeps changing.

"That's Jesus," you reply. "Before, and then after the Crucifixion."

"Wrong," Pilate says. "This is a picture of the human condition. First we see a man caught up in psychological time, caught up in the world and all the things he wants to achieve, to become. And then we see what it is to be outside of time, to give up becoming, to give up being, in order to have a totally open heart and mind," Pilate says. "Do you see it?" He flips the card back and forth:

Jesus staring. Jesus praying. Jesus staring. Jesus praying. Back and forth.

"I still see Jesus," you tell Pilate.

"Crucify him!"

"Why? What evil has he done?" Pilate asks the crowd.

And the crowd starts to chant out sins…not your sins but the sins of the world.

"What about Nazi Germany?

What about the atom bomb?"

"What about junk mail, voice mail, e-mail, and letter bombs?"

"What about air conditioning, and electric blankets, and Dresden, and Vietnam?"

"What about cocaine, heroin, marijuana, and the war on drugs?"

"What about television?" the crowd yells.

"What about television?"

"What has he done, what evil?" Pilate asks again.

"Crucify him. Because of television and the war on drugs!"

"Do you understand what this hologram signifies?" Pilate asks. This time he doesn't show you a postcard but merely points to the Colosseum, to the crowd.

"I just think this has gotten out of hand," you reply. "I can't die for you…for your sins. Jesus told me that we have to do it for ourselves!" you shout out to the crowd.

"But what about you? What about your sins? What about junk mail and the atom bomb?" Pilate asks.

"I can't do this!" you cry, but nobody listens.

HANG FROM THE CROSS

They pound in the nails. They pound the nails through your wrists, ankles, and your hands…they are doing a thorough job of it. Again, despite your commands, the program keeps running. The pain is tremendous.

Hang from the cross. Try not to cry.

"This can't be happening. My God! Why are you doing this to me?"

Open your eyes. Look down, through trickles of blood, at the dust. Despite the pain you are still curious. Look down and find that the yellow sand of the desert is gone and in its place there is a layer of bone-white dust. Try to ignore the pull of the thorns on your scalp and look up at the landscape.

It is the moon. The colony, a tiny bubble of glass perched on the edge of the horizon, shimmers with the reflection of distant stars.

You've made it to the moon, but only for an instant. The lunar surface quickly fades, the landscape keeps changing.

Hang on the cross and bleed while a barrage of sins, both small and large, pass before your eyes.

Find yourself attached to a Lincoln convertible. Witness the assassination of John F. Kennedy and then blink and stare at your childhood home. Watch yourself watch television.

Witness the bombing of Hiroshima.

Watch your childhood self lose a game of dodge ball.

Stare at hordes of refugees, hundreds of thousands of them, aimlessly wandering through a desert landscape.

Watch an adolescent Paul Dart purposely lose his orthodontic retainer during his lunch period.

Bulldozers pile up bodies.

A boy hides his sixth grade report card.

Hang on the cross. Witness each sin, feel each pain.

"Oh God! Forgive me…us…them. We didn't know. I didn't know."

Die.

DISCOVER THE ROBOT CHRIST

Wake up when Loper cuts the power to the motel's VR system.

Open your eyes to find yourself wrapped in a shroud and levitating in darkness and then shut your eyes again as light from the outside hall pours into the tomb.

Belly-flop onto the orange carpet of your motel room.

Stare up at Stan Loper's red and blue striped swimming trunks, and try to catch your breath.

"What?" you say. There is hardly enough air in you to make a sound. "What…are…you…doing?"

"I talked to Kent," Loper says.

For a moment you don't understand what he means. Kent? Who is Kent? Get to your feet, and slowly take off your VR headset. Try to let your present circumstances, your supposed real identity, sink in. "What did Kent say?"

Stan just stands next to the holovision and drips on the orange carpet. He is shivering. The air conditioning in your unit is on full blast. "You're through, Paul. It's over," Loper says.

"I'll get you a towel."

"No, no, no. Listen to me, you're fired. Understand? You're done."

Nod and then get up and go to the linen closet. The towels are clean and white.

"I want you gone," Stan says. He dries his hair and then wraps the towel around his middle.

Tell him that you don't want to leave yet. Tell him that you feel that you have to stay a little while longer. Tell him you want to talk to the crew.

He doesn't understand. He doesn't listen.

"Nothing you say can change what has happened, Paul," Loper says.

But what has happened?

Look at your hands and feet. Inspect your ankles and wrists. There are no stigmata, no physical evidence.

"Can I keep my demonstrator?" you ask

"What?"

"I just want to see it…Him, one more time," you say.

Find your briefcase sitting on top of the holovision.

"What were you doing in here, Paul? What was that simulation you were running?"

"I'll show you," you say.

"No. Don't open that. Stop right there, that's property of MediaVoyages Incorporated and—"

Open your briefcase.

Jesus looks okay, biblical. "The meek shall inherit the Earth," a squeaky-clean holographic Jesus tells you. "Pick up your bed and walk."

He's not there anymore. It's just an artificial Christ, a robot Jesus. It's nothing.

"Turn off that projector. Now!" Loper says.

Shut the briefcase and turn it around so that the handle faces out. Hand it over to Loper, shove it into his grasp and knock him off his center.

"Here, take it! I don't need it. I don't need Him anymore."

WALK ON WATER

The sun feels good on your neck and face.

Stare out past the porch's wooden railing at the sales crew—George, and Will, and Mike, and Dan—as they sluggishly splash back and forth in the motel pool.

Take a dab of gel on your tongue, and let it burn there for a minute. Swallow.

"George, I want you to know I don't blame you."

"Hi, Paul," George says.

Pull up a lawn chair, a moldy recliner with broken straps, and set it down next to the edge of the pool. Sit down on the outer frame of the recliner and try to catch George's eye. He's about a foot away from you, holding onto the metal ladder and staring down at his feet.

"It was going to happen either way. I know that," you tell him.

"I can't really…"

"What?"

"I can't really swim. Stan wanted us to, but I can't…"

Help Kent get out of the pool. Steady him as he pulls himself up and rolls onto the concrete.

"It's a phobic reaction," George says. He's lying on his stomach next to the pool. He's talking to the ground. "I can't help it."

Sit down on one of the more intact recliners along the fence. Stare at the grass beneath your feet, at the yellow stalks along the perimeter of the concrete.

"I've given up selling," you say.

George takes a pack of nicotine cigarettes out of his briefcase and lights up. "Hmmm…" He takes a deep drag on his cigarette and rubs his towel along his neck and chest. "That's good, Paul. It wasn't for you," George says.

"I can't stand it. It's everywhere. The pool, for instance, was originally part of some contract. Or, better yet—those colored lights on the trees. Have you seen them? The trees out along the main path? They've got colored lights on them. Somebody thought that would improve things, improve the trees," you say.

George doesn't respond, but just keeps sucking on his nicotine cigarette and staring at the sky.

"I want you to go out with me today, George," you tell him.

"What?"

"I want to train you today," you say.

"I thought Loper was going to…I thought he…"

You nod in agreement. "He did. He fired me. I'm not talking about selling Bibles. I've seen things, George. I've been through things, my demonstrator was on the fritz and it showed me things…I want you to go out there with me today."

George nods at you, seemingly in agreement. He stands up, stubs out his cigarette, and walks back toward the edge of the pool. Nodding all the time, George turns away from you and strides gingerly down the steps into the shallow end of the pool.

Your Studebaker is hot, the vinyl stings your legs even through your polyester slacks. Roll down the windows and turn on the air conditioning as you back up into the parking lot.

Today you're looking forward to hitting the doors.

Clear your throat and look up at the rearview mirror. Adjust the mirror so you can see your reflection, your uneven eyes. Give yourself a winning smile and clear your throat.

But you don't have a pitch, you don't have anything to rehearse. Push the mirror back into place and roll out onto the road.

I READ THE NEWS TODAY

(A GHOST STORY)

"My friends and I discuss the bombing of Hiroshima and Nagasaki... We discuss a documentary we've seen, and remember especially the man who melted into the steps of a building. We imagine ourselves like that. As stains on staircases [...]

The last question every visiting journalist always asks me is: Are you writing another book? That question mocks me. Another book? Right now? When it looks as though all the music, the art, the architecture, the literature—the whole of human civilization means nothing to the fiends who run the world—what kind of book should I write?"

—Arundhati Roy, New Delhi, India, June 2002

PROLOGUE: AN EXCERPT FROM WITH OR WITHOUT THE BEATLES

If you read the newspaper or watch the television news you may have noticed that the world is exploding. You may have noticed that, not only are there wars and rumors of wars, but there are tears and holes in the social fabric that binds us. Today, December 10, 2003, I read about a man who jumped from the fourteenth floor of the Holly Sugar building in downtown Colorado Springs. Before he jumped he told his friends that he'd learned to fly. And, in the Weekly World News on November 6, a woman claimed that she couldn't leave her home because she'd taught herself to spot peoples' auras but she didn't know how to turn the power off. She stopped going out, won't leave her home, because she can't stand what she sees in people.

What would John say about the strawberry field we've found ourselves in?

This isn't a book about the Beatles, it's not a celebration of the music and the times. It's not a critical reexamination of their impact on twentieth century.

This isn't a book about the Beatles. I don't believe in Beatles, I just believe in me. The disintegration of the world and me.

ONE

I manage to wake up and get out of bed on time even though the alarm clock doesn't go off. The blinds are closed and the room is dark and dank. I reach over and flip on my bedside lamp but nothing happens. The power is out again.

In the bathroom I use the emergency water rations, pouring the water from a gallon milk container, and squeeze hard on the toothpaste tube to work out a little more Crest.

I brush my teeth while listening to the Beatles. "Sgt. Pepper's" sounds tinny coming from the small speakers attached to my portable CD player.

I'm supposed to write a book about the Beatles. I've been paid my advance, been flown to London, to Apple Records. I've heard the master tapes, read all the other books, but none of that makes a difference.

Despite what my agent said, my timing is off. I was born too late or maybe too early. At thirty-two I'm already older than the Beatles ever were. I was born the year they split up and by the time I learned to talk, the idealism of the sixties was over. "Liquid Sunshine" was transformed into "Sunshine Saturday Mornings on NBC." Instead of learning the lyrics to "Give Peace a Chance," I grew up knowing that my bologna had a first and last name.

It's too late for the Beatles. Listening to them as I search for a clean shirt and pants, abandoning the whole concept of underwear, that much is perfectly clear.

It's too late for a lot of things.

The news fit to print that morning was bad.

Kashmir was a cinder.

The "nuclear exchange," as the *Times* called it, happened almost immediately after the first hundred thousand troops crossed the border of India into Pakistan. And Kashmir, the source of the conflict, was the first target. Millions were dead, and many more were expected to die when the fallout did its work.

According to the *Times* there were three questions facing the world in the aftermath of the "exchange." Would the US, China, or Europe intervene? Would the attack drive up the price of oil? And finally, how long would it take for the radiation to reach the West?

I used to read the *New York Times* every day. Not just any paper, but the *New York Times* even though I lived in Portland, Oregon. Nothing local mattered to me; nothing local was interesting enough to distract me.

I knew things because of the *Times*. I knew about Nicaragua, Chile, El Salvador, Chechnya, East Timor, and the Congo. I knew, but I didn't spend a lot of time thinking about these places. That wasn't the point. The point was to stop thinking. To just disappear into history.

But on that morning the headlines were so bad that it became obvious that we were about to run out of the stuff. Pretty soon there would be no news, no history, to hide in.

I felt better when I saw Frannie put the CD into the pocket of her big, brown coat. She didn't take off her glasses, but lifted them off the bridge of her nose in a little salute.

Despite everything, I was having an adventure. Shoplifting was something Meredith, my wife, would never have done. It was something I'd never do, and yet I was doing it. I grabbed a few CDs myself and slipped them into my briefcase.

The kid behind the counter, a kid with pierced cheeks and a satanic beard, watched my every move. More than worrying about getting caught stealing, I felt I should explain my taste in music. I was perusing the Beatles on assignment only;

I was more evolved than this. I was really more of a Radiohead fan, or something else he could understand.

I pulled at my tie and picked out a few Beatles CDs, and examined the covers.

A real rock critic, somebody like Lester Bangs, would never have been intimidated. Bangs would've told the kid with the Emperor Ming beard that blasting Public Image Ltd. at Blockbuster wasn't hip. He would've told the kid that PiL was a joke, that Johnny Rotten shouldn't have learned to play his guitar, should never have appeared on American Bandstand, should never have survived at all. Rotten should have died like Sid. The fact that Johnny lived meant that the Sex Pistols weren't serious.

This would mean nothing to the kid. He probably didn't even know who Dick Clark was—he'd probably never even heard of American Bandstand.

I moved to the next aisle of CDs and opened my briefcase. I tossed CDs in at random, right in front of him, but he was looking at me and not what I was doing.

"You read the news today?" I asked.

"The news?"

"There's been a war."

"Oh, yeah. I think I heard something about that on the radio," he said.

"What are we listening to?" I dragged it out, tried to force the idea on the kid that I was for real. I wanted to show him something.

"PiL," the kid says. "Off the satellite."

"They're still working?"

"Who are?"

"The satellites."

"Yeah, still working." He looked as if to say the satellites are still working and so what?

I moved on to the Paul McCartney albums. The Paul McCartney CDs—they're called CDs, not albums.

"It's embarrassing, this stuff. *Band on the Run*, *Ram*, and of course the latest packaged deal: *Wingspan*," I told Frannie.

"Give me that one." Frannie said, and stuffed it into her purse.

This was the crap my parents and their yuppie friends listened to when they vacationed together. What they'd listen to as they played tennis in their alligator shirts or did laps in the pool. I remembered them listening to Paul's "With a Little Luck." One of the lawyers' wives put together a slide show with that song; she had a fancy slide projector that kept time with the music, and every year we had to watch the previous year's exploits synched up with this sugary tune.

That's what Paul ended up doing—providing the background music for baby boomers as they pursued a life of leisure and luck.

Lennon did better. He didn't believe in magic, didn't believe in Buddha or Yogurt or BMWs.

I approached the kid at the counter and asked him if I could hear the *Plastic Ono Band* CD, if he had a copy open. He just grunted and tore the cellophane wrapper.

"Look at me," Lennon crooned on the headphones. "Who am I supposed to be?"

The kid tapped my shoulder and held up a newspaper. He pointed to the mushroom cloud there.

"Can you believe this?"

"That's what I was saying."

"We're fucked," the kid said.

He was drawing a pulse after all, but so what? I wasn't interested in showing him anything after all. I didn't have the time to explain what nuclear winter was or describe radioactivity and half-life.

"I want to buy this and go." I held up the John Lennon CD, and glanced down at the counter. Underneath the glass there was a portable CD player. It was fire engine red and I wanted it too. It would fit into my briefcase perfectly.

"We going?" Frannie asked.

"Yeah." I handed over my credit card to the kid and gave Frannie a kiss as she stepped toward the security gate.

"Bye," Frannie said. She took off running, and the alarm sounded, and when the kid took off after her I picked up the CD player, the John Lennon CD, and my unused credit card, and walked out after him.

The kid was on the sidewalk, looking left and right blankly. He'd lost her. I tapped him on the shoulder as I walked by him, bowed to him when he looked up, and then took off running myself.

Frannie was on her hands and knees, masturbating. She moved up and down on the mirror. From where I was sitting I couldn't see her hands, but I knew what she was doing and was glad that I thought of it, glad that I took the mirror down from above the television set, glad that I decided to take her to a motel in the first place.

"Is this all you want?" Frannie asked. "I'm feeling kind of lonely over here."

I didn't dare touch her.

I started up with Frannie because she asked me about Boy George; she was one of my employees, one of the telephone solicitors at the art museum, but when she asked me to read an essay she'd written in college I got interested. She'd just graduated and aspired to publish her student work.

We sat across from the administrative office of the Portland Art Museum, across the street from the Pittock Block Building, at a table in front of a corporate coffee shop.

"I want it to be relevant," she said.

"Aren't your own experiences relevant?"

"I want to talk about power and society."

"Why? Why not just talk about what it was like to watch a Culture Club video when you were in the third grade? Expand that part."

Frannie bit her lip, flipped through her manuscript. It was a 3,000-word essay that included everything—Madonna, Derrida, David Bowie, Foucault, and of course the Culture Club. It tried for too much, but it wasn't terrible.

"Where would I send it?"

"I know the editor of *Crawdaddy,*" I said.

The first time I slept with her I wasn't sure how it would go. Before she'd take off her clothes, before she'd let me touch her, she said she had to warn me that she wasn't normal.

"In what way? Some physical thing?"

"It's nothing you could see. I'm anatomically correct and everything," Frannie said. "It's just…I have a perceptual problem."

"Perceptual problem?"

That first time Frannie folded back the bed sheets on the motel bed and I closed the Venetian blinds. The light coming through the window was dim and I could see bits of fluff and dust in the air.

"I've got what's called acute synesthesia. Sometimes I perceive sounds as colors, or I'll hear things when I eat," Frannie said.

"Oh. I read about this in the paper. Lots of people have this now, right? Only the columnist wasn't sure if it's real or if it's just another way to sell prescription drugs."

"It's real. And it sort of interferes with sex. I can get confused."

I said that I'd be considerate. If she got confused by the sound of my penis I'd stop. I told her that it sounded kinky and fun.

"It's happening to a lot of people these days."

"Yeah. No big deal."

But after the nuclear exchange her condition got worse. She didn't just confuse colors for sounds anymore. She started hearing voices from the shower, seeing pictures when she ate Campbell's soup. What had been an aura of extra-perception around normal experience began to dominate. And it was contagious. She kissed me and I heard her tongue in my mouth. I saw colors when I touched her bare back.

I wanted to watch. To see her with my eyes and hear her with my ears.

"I like you in the frame."

Frannie put her hands back between her legs, but she couldn't quite find the right approach, the right tempo. It looked awkward, but I was determined to see it through.

"Relax. Pretend I'm not here."

Frannie pushed her long, brown hair out of her face and I was strangely thrilled by the flash of her unshaven underarm. She found the right tempo and started moving again, faster and faster.

I could barely see her. Everything was a blur.

When I was in elementary school I was plagued by nightmares. I dreaded sleep, and I kept a flashlight under my pillow and a stack of *Boys' Life* under the sheet, and I'd read for as long as I could, trying not to ever fall asleep.

I can't recall what *Boys' Life* magazine was about. Was it about the Boy Scouts? Did it have articles on tying knots or saying "The Pledge of Allegiance"? Or, was it more sensational with stories about the threat of killer bees? I can't remember anything I read in *Boys' Life* except for one short story about a boy who discovered a haunted radio.

It was an old rusted-out military-issue radio pack that you could wear on your back, and it was still broadcasting messages from the front, about the Viet Cong and munitions and blast radiuses.

I don't remember how or why the radio was haunted. What comes to mind instead is not the story, but an Elvis Costello song titled "Radio Radio":

"Some of my friends sit around every evening and they worry about the times ahead. But everybody else is overwhelmed by indifference and the promise of an early death."

I can't remember much from my childhood.

I was terrified by sleep, barely awake, young.

Did the boy in the story hear the radio because he was dead? Was he at risk? Recreating the ending from an undoubtedly faulty memory I imagine the kid under the wheels of a large automobile, or perhaps killed off by the rusted hand grenade that he found with the radio.

The radio's message was a warning. The soldier came back, haunted the broadcast, in order to save the kid, but the discovery of the radio itself was the real problem. The radio gave the kid a chance to heed a warning, but if he'd never found it, or if the Vietnam War had never happened, he wouldn't have needed to be saved at all.

The radio was a trap.

There was a buzzing in my ear, distracting me from finishing the employee evaluations. I looked at the office walls and nothing registered: the Far Side daily calendar, the Art Museum posters. There was a buzzing; it was the phone.

"Portland Art Museum, may I help you?"

"Do you know who this is?" It was the prank caller who thought it was funny to imitate me. He sounded just like me. I considered placing the phone back on its cradle and sneaking out, but it would've just started ringing again, and what if somebody else, if my assistant manager, or one of the data entry people next door, picked up my phone and talked to this version of me in my place?

"You have the wrong number," I said.

"Yeah." He sounded like he agreed with me. "Listen, in 1968 the Beatles released "Hey Jude" and "Revolution" as a single and it went to number one on the charts. Paul's song 'Hey Jude,' a seven-minute number that John thought was about Yoko Ono, was the A-side and was ubiquitous. The movement everyone needed was on their shoulders and it went on and on: Nah, Nah, Nah, Nah, Nah, Nah, Nah…

"The B-side, on the other hand, was controversial. John's message, telling those who were carrying pictures of Chairman Mao that they weren't going to make it, enraged his more militant fans. John sold out. Students and workers were storming the barricades in Paris, millions all over the world stood up and called for the system to end. And John urged everyone to stop fretting, to calm down?"

"What do you want?" I asked him.

"Yellow submarines and political protest: the two are linked in the popular mind, but when you consider John's B-side 'Revolution' the link is questionable."

"Are you getting at something?" I asked.

But there was silence on the other end of the line, and then, after a few minutes waiting, there was a pulsing beep, the sound the phone makes when it's left off the hook. I hung up and stared at the phone daring it to ring again.

I logged off my computer and signed out, but on my way to the door I heard the buzzing again.

I decided to ignore it.

TWO

Consider Paul McCartney in 1990. He's at a press conference in Miami and he's talking about his Friends of the Earth campaign, and talking about his new tour, about the tour's sponsor, which was Visa, and a reporter asks him about his Spanish. Paul speaks a little Spanish, you know, just a touch, and so the Mexican reporter, who speaks in Spanish fluently, asks if Paul will say something about the environment, about Mexico's environmental problems, and if he will say it in Spanish. Paul goes back and forth with her a bit. He smiles and calls her "baby" and then he recites a poem for her. A poem in Spanish.

"Tres conejos, en un árbol
tocando el tambor
que si, que no
que si, lo he visto yo," Paul said.

And he tells them all that the poem means this:

Three bunnies, in a tree, and one of them is playing a drum. Why yes? Why no? Why yes? Why yes? I have seen it.

"Thank you so much! And now a word about the environment! You'll have to tell them about it, baby," Paul says.

Does that resonate? Does that tell you anything about the cute one? Paul can be very, very funny—except when he's not. And Paul cares deeply about stuff, except when he doesn't.

And Ringo played the drum. Why yes? Why no? Why yes?

Paul McCartney is the cute one. Cute like a Kitten Poster that says "Thank God

It's Friday!" Only the poster is hanging in a sweatshop, in Florida, for the Gap.

I'll give the street car ten more minutes before I give up. The trains haven't been running for the last two days, but I keep hoping that they'll start up again.

And waiting for the train puts off my arrival at work. It gives me time to think about the book.

I was six years old when I discovered my parents' Beatles albums.

I flipped through the inner sleeve of the Magical Mystery Tour, the booklet that illustrated the movie. I studied the photos of the Beatles in their walrus costumes, examined the cosmic drawings of the four lads in wizard hats. And I believed it. I believed that the Beatles were really magic. After that whenever my dad would go to the stereo to put on a Doris Day or Willie Nelson record I'd follow him and grab the Beatles.

Around the same time I had my first Beatle dream.

The dream started with Mom:

"I killed your friend." She was dressed in a red wizard robe, she was wearing a pointy wizard cap adorned by black moons and stars, and standing next to my bed. "Your friend shouldn't have been here. I didn't want him to spend the night, so I made the tree fall."

My friend Teddy was trapped under leaves and limbs, and broken glass from the window was scattered on top of his sleeping bag, but I could tell he was still alive. I could hear him groaning.

It was obvious listening to Teddy's pain cries that Mom never liked him; she disliked him and his family. They weren't right, somehow. Teddy's father, for instance, didn't wear a coat and tie the way Dad did; he wore a tool belt and jeans. And Teddy's mother was fat; she was always in her pajamas on the couch. She smoked and watched TV and fed me and Teddy ice cream and M&M's.

I looked at my hands and realized that they were covered in chocolate, even though M&M's are supposed to melt in your mouth. Something had gone wrong.

Teddy groaned from under the tree.

"I made the tree fall through the window," Mom told me. "I didn't want to do it, but I had to. You know I'm diabetic."

"We just ate a little. Just a little," I tried to explain to her.

"You know I'm diabetic."

"Is Teddy going to be all right?" I asked.

"He's dead."

I looked at Mom standing there in her red robes, I stared at the moons and stars on her wizard cap, and I couldn't help but admire her magic.

She smiled at me, at my intelligence and good taste.

"Are you a Beatle?" I asked her.

"I am," she said, and flew out of the room.

Adulterer.

It didn't sound right; there was something wrong with it. It was the "adult" in adulterer that bothered me. It didn't seem quite real.

Nothing had seemed very real for a long time, not since I was a boy probably. When I was five or six years old I dressed up like Tarzan or Superman or Buffalo Bob and I ran and ran. Back then the difference between real and unreal wasn't important.

I stepped into the shower and turned on the tap, accepting the cold spray as a kind of penance. I'd cheated; a little bit of cold water was nothing. I reached for the soap, wanting to get rid of the smell of sex, but before I lathered up, Meredith stepped into the shower stall. She brushed up against me.

"I missed you tonight," she said.

"I'm taking a shower."

"I thought I'd join you."

"There isn't enough…" I start.

"What?"

"There isn't enough room in here."

Could she smell me? Could she see through me? I pushed her, gently at first and then more firmly, and then grabbed her arm and stopped her from crashing against the linoleum.

"What did I do wrong?" she asked.

"I'm just…it's this book. It's work. It's not you," I said. "I want to take a shower by myself, that's all."

She slipped away from me, her wet breasts brushing against my skin, and out into the steam-filled bathroom.

I was an adult, an adulterer. It didn't feel right.

When we were first married everything was different. Back then I believed in struggle. For instance, for the wedding I bought a birthday cake.

"It says 'Happy Birthday' on it. 'Happy Birthday Wanda June,'" Meredith's Aunt Clara said as we made our entrance at the reception hall. Meredith brushed past me, immediately engaging in banter with the guests, and I watched the tail of her wedding dress, her mother's originally, drag in the dust.

I turned to Aunt Clara and feigned surprise.

"What's that? The wrong cake?" I asked.

It wasn't the wrong cake at all. I'd aimed to inspire just this kind of reaction. I didn't believe in marriage, I just loved Meredith and wanted to be with her, to keep her. I didn't believe in anything much.

"I just believe in me. Meredith and me," I said at the time, and I thought that writing my own vows and ordering a birthday cake for the reception was enough. I thought that these tiny acts of rebellion would keep me free.

Meredith wanted to go to the Newport Aquarium on our honeymoon. She made a reservation with a little bed and breakfast near the beach and the destination was set. She wanted to see the jellyfish and the octopus and the sea otter.

On the first day of the trip Meredith bought a book about sea otters, and back in our room she read aloud from it. We made love, and she wore her glasses, her librarian glasses, and read aloud about the insulating fur of the sea otter. She read how meticulously well-groomed the otters had to be in order to stay warm. She kept reading all the way through to climax, then she let the book fall out of her hands.

"Look at all the families here," Meredith said when we arrived at the aquarium. It was raining hard and we'd just rushed inside the main building, we were pushed up against the glass of the jellyfish tank. "Look at all the married couples," Meredith said.

The crowd shifted and we found ourselves by the flounder tank. We watched the fish, the bottom dwellers with eyes on one side of their heads. We watched them change colors as the tank's mechanism filled the bottom of the tank with lighter and then darker sand.

We spent our honeymoon on the Oregon Coast, and I figured out how the aquarium's machines worked. We made love and we learned how the artificial tide kept domesticated starfish and clams happy all day.

The day after the nuclear exchange I was getting ready for work, finding my blue oxford cloth shirt, applying stick deodorant, when I spotted a twisted rectangle of Styrofoam poking out from my undershirt. It was under my sleeve. Looking in the mirror I saw packing material sticking up from the neck of the shirt, and out of the legs of my boxer shorts.

I bent over and tugged on the stuff and felt something move in my gut. Plastic foam filled my boxers and I retched up Styrofoam popcorn.

I sat on the edge of the bed, next to Meredith, and bounced on the spring mattress in an attempt to wake her, but she didn't stir.

There was a buzzing in my ear, a metallic trill in my head, and I realized that I'd dialed the phone.

"Portland Art Museum, may I help you?" It was my own voice on the other end of the line.

"Do you know who this is?" I asked.

More Styrofoam erupted from my collar; it streamed from my pant leg.

"You've got the wrong number."

A frame of Styrofoam, a cage of rectangles and squares, emerged from my shirt and encased my head. White squiggles popped from my ears.

"Wait." I was way off track, had to find the ground, get back on cue. "In 1968 the Beatles released "Hey Jude" and "Revolution" as a single and it went to number one on the charts," I said, or tried to, but the words sprinkled to the floor. Purple, pink, and yellow Styrofoam peanuts spilled from my mouth

I dropped the phone and tore at my chest. I vomited newspaper and bits of cloth.

String drooped down from beneath my fingernails.

And the room started shaking. The dresser and the mirror on top of it, the bed frame, the fan on the bedside table, the bedside table itself, the alarm clock, all of it shaking and rattling.

Meredith sat and screamed.

"Stop it!" And then her voice changed to a squeak. "Leave me alone." Her eyes were open, and she looked right at me, newsprint and Styrofoam still spilling out of my mouth.

"Get out. You're not welcome here. I don't care how you died!" she screamed. I stepped toward the bedroom door and opened it.

When I passed through, the rattling stopped.

"Go!" Meredith said.

I stepped into the hallway. I stopped to look back, but before I could turn around another wave of nausea and newspaper overtook me, and I collapsed onto the hardwood floor.

Later, sitting in a Starbucks and listening to the rain, listening to the piped-in jazz, I felt okay again. I stirred my coffee even though there was no cream. People were hoarding cream and milk because of the coming isotopes. I was just stirring out of habit.

On the front page there was a map of the world, a weather map showing wind patterns. India and Pakistan were in the center and there were arrows pointing up and down, circles of dotted lines.

The radiation reached Europe that morning.

I flipped to the Arts and Living section. There was a new movie out about a game show host who lost his mind and his television life. He wandered to the suburbs to hide. The paper gave it a rave review.

The game show host lived in a family's basement for six months, surviving by sneaking into their kitchen at night and stealing Pop-Tarts and soda pop. Nobody noticed him down there. In the end he was discovered because of the 900 numbers he ran up on their phone bill.

It was apparently based on a true story.

In the movie Help *Ringo Starr steps into an elevator with John, and the two Beatles face the closing doors with blank expressions. Even the Beatles live with dead time. The elevator doors slide closed and the two of them are quiet.*

Then, assured of their absolute privacy, Ringo turns to John and asks the question:

"What was it," Ringo asks as the lift lifts, "what was it that first attracted you to me?"

John doesn't blink, but his eyes focus and he turns to Starr and answers. "Well, you're very polite, aren't you?"

John answers the question and denies its significance simultaneously. And when the two rock stars are thrown off balance by the sudden halt of their ascent, when the elevator stops and the walls become magnets, John can't help but laugh. Ringo, his hand mysteriously stuck to the elevator door, his ring (the MacGuffin in this adventure film) binding him painfully to the exit, yelps and tries to free himself, and John laughs.

"You're very polite, aren't you." John asks. It's not a question at all. It's a command.

Outside the Pittock Block Building, after I crossed the street from the corporate coffee shop, I stopped to answer an electronic trill from a US West box.

"Hello?"

There wasn't anyone on the line. What filled my ear was a terrible silence. I said hello but I didn't hear it.

"Is anybody there?"

I said hello.

"Hello?"

Nobody was on the other end of the line, but I held the phone up to my ear anyhow, thinking, remembering the dotted lines on the front page of the *Times*. When I hung up, when I picked up my briefcase, and glanced toward the entrance, I saw something else to worry about.

Above the glass doors to the Pittock Block Building, hanging down on a metal rod, inconspicuous, was a small security camera. It was pointed right at me, right at the phone booth, and it dawned on me, irrationally, that my thoughts had been recorded. With this dead eye, machine eye, staring at me, I'd had enough.

I walked back to the Starbucks, found the utility closet by the restrooms, and pulled out a string mop. I detached the mop handle, twisted the metal rod counterclockwise, and then nodded to the cashiers as I took off out the doors and into the street.

The damned security camera was swiveling slowly back and forth now, looking for me.

"Hey!" I shouted. "I'm over here, you fucker!"

I brought the mop handle up fast, using it like a spear, and the camera stopped moving. I swung the mop handle like a hammer, over my head and against the lens, again and again. Eventually the camera dropped to the sidewalk, and the crowd of street youth and secretaries made room for me as I swung the mop handle over my head and brought it down hard.

I smashed the camera to pieces, and then tossed the mop handle into the gutter.

"You killed it," a kid with a mohawk said.

"Fuck!" I said back to him. "Christ fuck shit mother shit fuck!"

"You killed it."

I adjusted my tie, breathed in a deep breath that felt good, and nodded to my audience. I picked up my briefcase, gently pushed my way through the crowd, and opened the front door of the office building.

"I'm late. Excuse me. Sorry."

The president of the Art Museum was leaving, moving to Minnesota to be the president of the Minnesota Art Museum for as long as it lasted. Our board of directors was throwing an office party in the lobby in an effort to smooth things over when I came in.

I went directly to the copy room to hyperventilate. I tried to breathe out my anxiety, tried to find my center, but ended up dizzy.

And, pretending to work, I found out that next year's exhibition schedule wouldn't reproduce. I typed in the ID code and pressed the green button, but something went wrong. The copy I got back didn't match the original.

I quit the copy machine and stared at the fax instead, at the digital clock blinking midnight.

"Hello," Ralph Spengler, the director of marketing, said. He stepped past me to the photocopier.

"Got a fax," I told him. I dialed at random and then turned toward him and showed him my teeth in an effort to smile.

"I suppose we ought to be out there socializing," Ralph says.

"Oh?"

"Have you seen next year's schedule?" Ralph asked. "Want a copy?" He put the schedule into the copy machine and then looked for the right button to push.

The photocopier spit out the first copy and I grabbed it from the bin and took a look.

Guy Debord, Barbara Kruger, and Jeff Koons were the first three names on this new list.

"I'm thinking about learning how to shoot a gun. Maybe take up karate," Ralph said. He pressed the button again, unaware that he could program the machine to make a hundred copies at once, and I grabbed this copy too.

"These don't match," I told him. The first three names were William Blake, Boscht, and Durer.

Ralph smiled, uncomprehending, and pressed the button again. Ralph took the copies from me, glanced at the blank pages. "You going back to the party?"

I shrugged, not sure what answer he wanted.

"The schedules don't match. That copy machine is printing different schedules."

"It's all going to fall apart. I don't know why we're going through the motions." Ralph stepped back to the machine, pressed the button again, and then looked at me and frowned.

I wandered into the hall. Underneath fluorescent lights and between off-white stucco walls, I staggered toward the sound of farewell speeches.

"What's wrong?" Frannie still had a headset around her neck; the black cord was disconnected from the phone but was still clipped to her chest.

I tried out explanations on her. Maybe the error in the photocopier machine was mechanical. The machine might have stored different schedules in its memory chip, and some sort of digital failure caused the different versions of next year's schedule to print. Then I told her that I'd misread he schedules, that I'd maybe seen what I subconsciously wanted to see rather than what was really there.

Or maybe I was dying…or I was haunted.

"Are we going to see each other tonight?" Frannie asked.

I couldn't answer. My assistant manager, Brad, stumbled in between us. "Have you ever had red pepper vodka?" he asked. "It's a really weird buzz." Brad filled a Dixie cup and held it out to me.

"I don't want any."

"Come on. Try it."

He shoved the Dixie cup full of vodka into my hand and I slugged the noxious liquid down. It stung. I could barely keep myself from gagging.

There was no schedule.

"Have you ever tried red pepper vodka?" Brad asked.

Reality had developed a stutter, and I realized that my favorite sixties band wasn't the Beatles at all. My favorite band was The Who. Pete Townshend with his stammered vocals and smashed guitars.

My assistant manager laughed at me and offered me more vodka.

"F-f-f-fuck you," I said. I pushed past him, past both of them, reached for the door to my office, but Frannie grabbed my arm, pressed against me.

"What's your answer?" I felt her breath on my neck.

"Skeh…skeh…schedule," I said.

I could see people's auras. I watched as passersby waited at street corners for the light to change, and then telescoped out, split into several versions of themselves, when they moved on. Everybody had double or triple identities, ghosts, following them, mirroring each step.

I was supposed to take an audio tour at the Art Museum that morning. I was on an evaluation committee, which meant I had to take the audio tour and fill out a survey after.

I took Frannie with me. We each had a headset on, but we weren't really interested in the instructions. We walked along. We turned and looked at the art when we were told to look, but that was all.

"We might expect the subject of Blake's painting *Ancient of Days* to signify the Almighty God, but in Blake's esoteric mythology, he stands rather for the power of reason, which the poet regarded as ultimately destructive, since it stifles inspiration." The woman's voice is light and happy.

I took off my headset and reached over to Frannie.

"What do you think?" I asked.

Frannie turned to me, but her eyes were blank. "It smells like cinnamon and plastic," she said.

"Are you okay?"

Frannie shrugged; she opened her mouth to say something, but stopped herself and put her headphones back on. I watched her for a second, thought of saying something, but didn't. I waved my hand in front of her face, and when she didn't flinch I put my headset back on.

"Picasso's abandonment of cubism signaled the broad retreat of abstraction after 1920. The utopian ideals associated with the movement had been dashed."

The east wing was empty. There was an empty glass cube in the middle of the room, and along the walls there were sheets of glass rectangles with sharp edges, but there was no art. I watched my reflection, felt Frannie's warm hand on my arm.

"The disintegration of realism, the fragmentation of all art into radical categories, may well reflect the abandonment of social impulses. Solutions are still found, but only to technical problems. The outside world is lost."

I let go of Frannie and stepped behind one of the sheets of glass. Moved between the glass and the wall.

"What does it smell like now?" I asked.

"Colors."

She joined me behind the sheet of glass, and put her arm around my waist, her head on my chest. Then she lifted her head and put her headset back on. I could hear the woman's voice coming from the tiny speakers, but I couldn't make out the words.

"Frannie?"

I stood there, holding Frannie's hand and staring through the glass at the empty room, and waited for the audio commentary to end.

Where did I read that ghosts were really projections of the living, that they come from the subconscious and are not dead people—inner impulses manifest in strange ways? Did I get the idea from reading Carl Jung or Shirley MacLaine?

If this theory is true then you might be able to tell a lot about a person based on how he or she is haunted. Does his poltergeist throw shit at him? Does she have a spirit that walks the hall between the master bedroom and the bath? Is the spirit weeping and wailing?

She's got a bad marriage.

He's got a lot of pent-up hostility.

They're lonely, the both of them.

But, of course, everything has psychological meaning. Just believing in ghosts or not believing in ghosts means something about the inner world of the subject.

If you believe in ghosts you're in denial, you're unable to cope with the real. Ghosts represent either a denial of death or an even more profound retreat into fantasy and magical thinking.

But if you don't believe in ghosts you're still in the anal phase. You're inhibited, unable to give up control, unable to surrender to a higher power because you perceive transcendence as a threat.

Was it Jung or some channeled New Age text? One of the Seth books maybe? It didn't matter either way.

I met Meredith for lunch, but the restaurant didn't have anything we wanted. Most of the items on the menu were no longer available. That is, none of the usual seafood dishes or pasta dishes or sandwiches were available.

"We can cook up some noodles, but the sauce will be out of a can. No fresh produce today. And no gourmet sauces. Our gourmet service provider has closed down, apparently permanently," the waiter explained. "We're mostly serving drinks."

"Gourmet service provider?" I asked.

"I'm not at liberty to discuss how the food has been manufactured and delivered in the past. What would you like to drink?"

I ordered a fine whiskey and Meredith asked for gin and tonic.

"I've been having an affair," I said.

Meredith took a sip of her gin and tonic and winced.

"I'm sorry, but I thought I should tell you now. Under the circumstances, I just felt…well, I may not be around, we may not be around later on."

Meredith sat up straight in her chair and then nonchalantly stirred her drink with a green straw. She leaned over and took a sip through the straw even though it was too thin, and not a drinking straw at all.

"Do you expect me just to accept it?" she asked.

"I was hoping we might at least talk about it."

Meredith took another sip and then pushed the straw aside and took a gulp. "I'm thirty-one years old. I'm not just going to give up," she said.

"You're not prepared to give up what?"

"To die. Not like this. Not now. No, in fact I've been coming up with alternatives. I've got a list at home, on the computer."

"What kind of alternatives?" I asked.

Meredith finished her drink and waved to the waiter for another, then she put her leg up over the arm of her chair and pulled up her skirt to her thigh.

"Do you like my legs?" she asked.

"Sure. Of course I do. It had nothing to do with that."

"And your girlfriend or mistress or whatever, she's got nice legs? A nice chest and all of that?"

"Uh. Well, she's pretty, yes. But I don't really compare. I haven't been making comparisons," I say.

Another round of drinks came, so I polished off my first shot and then started on the second.

"The kitchen is prepared to offer peanut butter sandwiches without the jam," the waiter said.

"The drinks are fine," Meredith said.

The waiter looked relieved and left us to it. Meredith kept her leg where it was, hiked her skirt up higher.

"Don't you think it's worth trying," she asked.

"Of course I do. That's why I told you. I want to work this out. I don't want to lose you."

Meredith frowned. I took a sip of whiskey and swished it back and forth like mouthwash, and she pulled her skirt back down. She proceeded to suck her drink through the thin stirring straw. "You don't understand anything, do you?"

I didn't answer, but glanced back toward the kitchen, to the swinging door. The owner, an older guy with dyed blond hair and an orange IZOD shirt, was back there. He was smiling and laughing as big guys in denim uniforms loaded crates of vegetables and sauce jars onto a handcart. He was taking his merchandise, the food, away. He was stealing the food, our food, hoarding tomatoes and celery and squash. He was cheating, denying us our most basic right—our right to purchase what we wanted.

"Are you hungry?" I asked Meredith.

"Do you want to go somewhere else?" she asked back.

I pointed out what was happening in the back. Meredith started to laugh.

"Let's order more drinks," she said.

It seemed like a good idea.

THREE

The Pittock Block Building has been mostly empty for a week. The security system doesn't work, and the front door isn't locked, so I'll occasionally find somebody sleeping in the hallways, or, when the electricity is on, riding the elevators up and down without getting off at the various floors. Nobody is working here anymore as far as I can tell. Nobody except me.

I turn on my computer and wait for electricity. I take out a legal pad and write down marketing strategies and a timetable for mass mailings. And at eleven I go out to the lobby and sit behind the secretary's desk. She used to take her lunches at eleven, and if she were around I'd be replacing her.

It's not part of my job description, but I make allowances.

When I was eleven my family went to Oak Ridge to visit Dad's brother and his boys for Christmas. I was the youngest, eleven years old, while my cousins were in their teens.

I wanted the two older boys to like me, to earn their respect. I challenged my younger cousin Sean to a game of *Tank Escape* on his new Atari, a Christmas present that Sean mostly ignored but that we coveted, and Sean started in about the Beatles.

"Chapman is crazy. He's insane," he said.

I hadn't given it any thought at all, but I nodded as I sent missiles crashing down on Sean, at the blue pixels that represented him.

"Gotcha!"

"John Lennon was a fucking genius," Sean said. "*The White Album, Revolver, Pepper's.*"

"Yeah." My missiles rained down on Sean and there wasn't a thing he could do about it. I was wiping him out.

"Man, I hate the Bee Gees," Sean said.

"The Bee Gees suck." I'd destroyed all of his tanks, but he didn't notice. I just sat there, joystick in hand, waiting for him to start a new game.

"Disco sucks," Sean said.

"Yeah."

"I can't believe they killed John Lennon. I can't fucking believe it."

"You want to play Fighter Pilots?"

"You ever heard *The White Album*?" Sean asked.

Sean's room was in the basement, and it was like Graceland down there, better than Graceland. There were bean bags to sit on, the wall to wall carpeting was soft with leopard spots, there were mirrors everywhere, a whole wall of gold-flecked mirrors, and there were boxes of comic books: hundreds of copies of *The X-Men* and *What If* and *The Spectacular Spider-Man*.

"These *Captain America*s are from 1969," I said. "You sure I can have them?"

"Take them, I'm done with comics."

"Wow!"

"Hey, go open the window. Will you?" Sean asked. "I've got some weed."

When I didn't move, Sean explained it to me. "I smoke weed all the time. It's not bad for you like cigarettes."

"Ummm…"

"The Beatles smoked pot, they sang about it all the time."

"Yeah?"

"Haven't you ever heard 'I Am the Walrus'? At the end of the song they all start going 'Smoke pot! Smoke pot! Everybody smoke pot!'"

Halfway through the first joint, Sean started to explain everything. The problem with John Lennon, Sean explained, was that he was a peacenik, a hippie. Sean didn't like hippies. I was too numb to talk. I felt mellow and fine lying there on the leopard-spotted carpet, using reprints of *Spider-Man* as a pillow, but Sean was on a roll.

He described the world for me, told me the rules.

The Rolling Stones were better than the Beatles.

Getting to second base means feeling the girl's tits, and Sean had already made it that far with a neighbor girl.

You have to get laid by the time you're sixteen, which gave Sean three more years. He figured he could do it.

The policy of mutually assured destruction was a good thing. Nuclear bombs were a good idea.

"Lennon was for disarmament, but he was wrong, he was wrong about that. We've got to keep the bomb," Sean said.

"Yeah?"

"Think of it this way, we wouldn't even be here, you and I, we wouldn't have been born, if the US hadn't dropped the bomb. Grandpa would have been killed. If we hadn't bombed Japan millions of US soldiers would have been killed."

"I wonder..."

"It's true. It's fact."

"I wonder if Grandpa had died and Dad hadn't been born...I wonder who I would've ended up with. Who would my father be?"

"You wouldn't have a father. You wouldn't exist," Sean says. "That's the point."

I blushed, told him that I wasn't stupid. But inside I knew he was wrong. Even if my father hadn't been born, I'd still have been me. Reality didn't work by the rules; there was no cause and effect. If Grandpa had died during World War II it wouldn't have made any difference.

John Lennon's "Strawberry Fields Forever" was released in the United States both as a single and on the *Magical Mystery Tour* album, and it is perhaps Lennon's most psychedelic, most spiritually enlightened, and most frightening song. Unlike "Tomorrow Never Knows," which is really an advertisement for Transcendental Meditation, "Strawberry Fields" reproaches the listener and insists on destroying his or her preconceptions.

"Living is easy with eyes closed," Lennon sings, "misunderstanding all you see."

Nothing is real, according to John, but the song is misinterpreted if you conclude that Lennon was rejecting the world entirely. "Strawberry Fields" is not a mantra, it is not a prescription for how to reach enlightenment, but a description of Lennon's own problems, a loopy poem about how John was at risk of falling out of his tree, out of his me.

Thirty years after the Beatles, after "Strawberry Fields," you can turn on the television set and watch anything. You can connect to a computer network of strawberry fields and you can choose to live there. You can e-mail yourself, or call yourself on the phone. You can listen to your own thoughts as an MP3. But what you can't do is know who you really are. What you can't do is live with your eyes open.

Meredith sat perfectly still on the sofa, watching the Home Shopping Network on television. I said hello, apologized for being late, but she didn't stop watching.

"Meredith?" I waved my hand in front of her face, and when she didn't blink I headed to the kitchen for something to eat. Dinner was sliced apples and a microwaved cheese sandwich.

I ate slowly, and watched Meredith watch television.

I glanced at the screen to see what was holding her so rapt.

A jeweled teddy bear spun silently in a display case as an 800 number flashed on the screen. Meredith reached for the phone, groped for it.

"What are you doing? Are you going to buy that?"

"This adorable item is worth over a hundred dollars, but the Home Shopping Network is offering the Hallmark Sapphire Teddy Bear for only $49.99," a woman's voice explained from off screen.

"You couldn't possibly be about to buy that."

"It was mine. They're selling my stuff, my past," she said. "I need your card. I'm over my limit."

The next item on the screen was a small green dress, a Girl Scout uniform.

"This item symbolizes both the innocence of childhood and the beginning of a lifelong process of indoctrination into the military state," the male announcer said.

The Girl Scout uniform was $29.95, and Meredith reached for the phone again.

"Hello?" she said. "The item number is 2-3-1-1."

I waited for the next item to appear on the screen, but for a moment there is nothing, just darkness and my own reflection.

"Give me your card," Meredith said.

I was distracted. A ten-speed bicycle appeared on the television, a small red Peugeot with rusted spokes and chipped paint. The black gripping tape hung down in large loops from the curved silver handlebars.

"That's my bike."

But Meredith didn't see the bicycle. She saw a Strawberry Shortcake doll with smudged features and a broken arm. She saw a pair of roller skates that could fit over small sneakers. She saw her useless past and she took my wallet out of my back pocket and recited my credit card number into the receiver.

"Are we dead?"

"How much credit is left on this card?"

Meredith recited the card number again, and then reached for the remote control. She turned off the television as *Star Wars* action figures in a Darth Vader carrying case, rotated into view.

"They won't take your card," she said.

"Maybe we're dreaming."

The television is dark, but I can feel it, in the air, coming out of the floor. They're still broadcasting my childhood. Maybe my lost comic-book collection, maybe the junior high yearbook I lost.

"They had my Evel Knievel race set."

"Don't talk about it," Meredith said.

"They had my *Star Wars* action figures."

"We bought as much as we could."

I couldn't sleep.

Michael Crichton's *Terminal Man* was on one of the cable channels. Elliott Gould was sitting on the wrong side of a one way mirror. He was strapped down and there were wires protruding from his scalp. On the other side of the glass men in lab coats were throwing switches to make him cry, laugh, lust, sleep.

A woman in a lab coat interviewed him as he crashed from one state to another.

"How do you feel?"

"Ice cream."

"Yes?"

"I taste ice cream. Strawberry ice cream."

"How do you feel?"

"Oh, God! This is…"

"What's wrong?"

"I'm sorry. I'm so sorry."

"How do you feel?"

"The air conditioning is a little much."

"How do you feel?"

"How do I what?"

"How do you—"

"You can go to hell!"

There was something in the room with me. I felt a chill as I watched television. When I turned on the computer the cursor blinking in and out of existence seemed like a threat.

Elliott Gould started talking to me.

"Have you ever heard of transference?" he asked.

The woman in the lab coat didn't answer, but just kept on asking questions. Elliott departed from the script.

"The Beatles were a phenomena of transference. All celebrity is." I suddenly realized that the actor's name wasn't Elliott Gould. He was somebody else. This guy was in *Who's Afraid of Virginia Woolf* with Richard Burton and Elizabeth Taylor; he was in *Carbon Copy* with Denzel Washington. He wasn't Elliott Gould but George Segal.

"What difference does that make? Pay attention?" Segal said.

I waved my hand in front of the television screen, then flipped it on and off, but he was still there, waiting.

"Everything was careening out of control," Segal said. "The Beatles helped people feel better even as nothing changed."

I sat back down on the couch, and Segal nodded at me, apparently glad to have my full attention.

"It was about transference. Transference made the Beatles' success. Understand that much at least," Segal said. And then he turned back to the woman on the screen with him, the scientist, and started to beg with her, to plead. Segal read his lines, returned to the script.

"Who am I? Where do I start and where does this machine begin?"

"We're going to help you," the woman told him.

Frannie lived in the attic of an apartment house in Northeast Portland. She had the television on and didn't hear me open the front door of her apartment and start up the stairs. She kept her door unlocked and I always thought I'd catch her doing something—maybe coming out of the shower, maybe embracing some other guy. Instead, she was just sitting on her couch with her legs curled up under her.

I tapped her on the shoulder and she turned to me like she knew I was there all along.

"Hi."

"It's me," I said.

On television there were bodies. I couldn't tell if they were Indian or Arab, but they were burning on a pyre—hundreds of bodies. It looked like the Black Death.

"How far has the radiation traveled?" I asked.

"They're not saying."

"Yesterday it was in Europe."

"They're prepared though. I just saw that the British have radiation suits provided by the state, and there are radiation shelters."

"What about the crops? What about water?"

Frannie turned off the television and took my hand. I followed her to the bedroom, watched her undress. She took off her clothes casually, like she didn't notice, and then reached over and put her hand on my belt buckle.

"I don't know about this," I said. "You're contagious." I grabbed her hand to stop her, but she just reached with the other and unbuckled the belt.

I wasn't sure what I was hearing, it sounded like AM radio. There were instruments, mostly brass instruments, but I couldn't distinguish one horn from another.

When Frannie put her tongue in my mouth the static cut out, the noise was not an orchestra, not music, but voices. The room filled with light, red and green and blue. I looked at Frannie; she was all mapped out. There were dotted lines from her belly to her thighs, from her breasts to her neck, and Xs marked the spots where I was to put my hands. It all seemed inevitable. Sex was a sound I heard, a light flashing, a map on her body, arrows and dotted lines, a memory.

Frannie's kitchen was full of boxes, cardboard boxes along the counters, boxes inside boxes and stacked up on top of each other: Mac and Cheese, Hamburger Helper, Cheerios.

Frannie took a yellow porcelain bowl out of the cabinet, found a spoon and washed it off under the tap, and then poured some Cheerios into the bowl. She paused to smell the milk.

"Want a bite?" she asked.

I wasn't hungry, but I took a spoonful. The milk was still good.

"Let's do an experiment," Frannie said.

I slurped another spoonful of cereal, and tried to smile. "What kind of experiment?"

She wanted me to watch CNN while she sat in the bedroom and ate Cheerios. She asked me to takes notes about what I was watching and said she'd take notes about what she was eating. She handed me a pair of Walkman headphones so there was no possibility of her hearing the TV while she ate.

I sat down with the television set, listened to static as the set came on, and then watched as a woman in a beige suit and perfect make-up spoke about the benefits of life insurance. Then the CNN logo flashed across the screen.

As I watched television the room began to rattle. The TV vibrated on its stand, the bookshelves and sofa and even the cushions moved and buzzed. The lights dimmed, but the set stayed on.

Satellite pictures of India and Pakistan filled the screen and a reporter spoke on a cell phone, describing the refugee crisis in Turkmenistan and China.

Frannie tapped me on the shoulder. She crossed the room, turned off the TV, and the room stopped shuddering.

I looked down and read what she'd written.

Some 500 thousand Pakistani refugees are camped outside the city of Shiquanhe, and the Chinese government says there is no place for them inside the city. The Chinese are already rationing food, water, and medicine, and with so much of China's aid going to the domestic population the Chinese government claims that they can do nothing for the refugees.

Frannie's handwriting was pretty. She dotted her i's with little circles.

"It's all connected," Frannie said. "The war, my condition, all of it."

"Yeah?"

"I can read the news when I eat. I can taste it," Frannie said.

When Frannie was fifteen she knew a kid named Todd Pittman with the same condition. She was Todd's babysitter.

Mr. Pittman was an attorney and his handsome wife was an artist, an illustrator of children's books, and they were friendly with Frannie's parents. Frannie couldn't figure it out. The Pittmans were from Boston. They were hip and well groomed and a bit wild. What did they have in common with her parents?

Maybe one of the reasons they liked Frannie's parents was because Frannie would baby-sit for Todd. Todd was thirteen years old and wheelchair bound, and could only move his left arm. But even so, Frannie thought he was too old for a babysitter. He was too old and messed up for Frannie. She didn't like helping him with the toilet, didn't like getting him dressed for bed.

"I can't believe it," Todd said as he fidgeted with his green beans. "It couldn't be true."

"What's that?" Frannie asked. "What couldn't be true?"

Todd didn't answer but just smiled and gestured at his plate. He took a bite of his skinless chicken and winced. "Don't tell me that."

"Is something wrong?" Frannie asked.

Todd looked up as he drank his milk through his flexible straw. "What?" Todd asked his string bean. "What does that mean? Panama? You mean where the canal is?"

"What are you doing?"

"Talking to my food," Todd said.

After that everything was perfectly normal until it was time for bed. Just TV until nine and then Todd said he didn't really have to go to bed so early, that his parents didn't make him go to bed early, and Frannie had to force the issue. She had to cajole him through each step of the process; she had to brush his teeth for him not because he couldn't do it himself but because he refused.

"Crest toothpaste always says the same thing," Todd told her after he spit.

"What's that?"

"Always the same, the same idea, over and over. Production for use. Production for use. Okay already."

Getting him into the bed was a chore, especially hard because he didn't want to go. She turned off the electric motor, unstrapped him from his wheelchair, moved the armrest out of the way, and then stopped and tried to figure out some way to roll him out of the chair and onto the bed.

"You want to learn how to hear things with your tongue?" Todd asked.

"Don't be lewd."

"I mean with your taste buds."

"My taste buds?"

Todd nodded, jerking his left arm up and down along with his head.

"Hear with my tongue, is that what you said?"

Todd stopped nodding, stopped jerking his arm around, and just looked at her. "I'll show you," he spit the words at her. "Get some of my candy from my backpack and I'll show you."

"No. You can't eat candy before bed. You'd have to brush your teeth again. I'd have to brush your teeth again."

"Not me. You eat it." Todd smiled a crazy smile at her, watched her as she found a smashed Milky Way bar in the sack strapped to his wheelchair, and laughed when she took a bite. She chewed slowly and the caramel stuck to her teeth.

"You're not doing it," he said. "You don't know how."

"I don't know how to what?"

Todd told her to try again, and Frannie took another bite of caramel and chemical chocolate.

"You're too happy. You chew the wrong way," Todd said. "If you support me under my arms I can stand up.

She helped him belly-flop onto the bed and then turned the kid so that his feet and head were in the right place. She wrestled with the blankets, scooting them out from under him and then tucking him in.

"I'm terminal you know," Todd said.

"Cerebral palsy isn't terminal."

"Yes it is. Yes it is. I'm going to die before I'm twenty."

"No you're not."

"I know when I'm going to die, I've seen my own ghost. That's why I can do things. That's why I know how to chew my food the right way," Todd told her.

I moved the phone to my other ear and settled back on Frannie's bed. Meredith hadn't asked where I'd been, or when I was coming home. She just started in right away with her story as if we'd been talking about it already.

"The books kept falling off the shelves, opening themselves. I spent most of the day yesterday putting books back on shelves."

"Yeah?"

"It was hilarious. They kept falling down, over and over. They wouldn't stay unless I read the pages. Sometimes I had to read aloud to convince them."

"Convince who?"

I wondered what she was wearing, whether she'd slept in her clothes again. Had she had a shower yet? Was she dressed for work or still in her underwear and T-shirt? "I had to work late," I said.

"Work late?"

I just lay there and winced at how transparent the lie was.

"Do you want to know what the books were about?" Meredith asked.

"They were all about the same subject?"

"No. Different subjects, but the same theme."

I didn't want to know. I really didn't. What I wanted was to have a normal conversation. I wanted Meredith to ask me where I was, who I was with, anything but this.

"I wrote it all down," Meredith said.

"Why don't you read it to me?"

"Over the phone?"

"Why not?"

"None of the other librarians tried reading them. They just kept putting the books back and picking them up again, over and over," Meredith said.

I waited.

"Do you want to hear?"

"Go ahead."

"Illusion, if thou hast any sound, or use of voice, speak to me. I know that if the tribe does not help me soon we will all die. The slave has no control over his or her life, is pushed about by external forces, is at the mercy of casual impressions, a slave to habits,

most of them bad, a prey to credulity, suggestibility, hopes, and fears. Three things make people want to change. One is that they hurt sufficiently. Now one of two things must take place. Either you must do something, or something must be done to you."

"That's what the books wanted to say?" I asked.

"There's a bit more: *You do not know how to think about free will. One moment you realize that you are machines, but the next moment you want to act according to your own opinions. You don't believe in either identity or dissidence.*"

"And that's it? That's what these spirits wanted to say?"

"I'm not sure who wanted what."

"Yeah."

"I'm not going," she said.

"Not going where?"

"I'm not going to work today."

"That makes sense."

"Not going."

"Love you?" I asked.

"What?"

"I love you."

"Oh, yeah. Love you too."

I listened as she hung up the phone. Listened to the dial tone, and to the error signal that meant that my phone was off the hook.

What are ghosts? From the photographic evidence it seems they're not much more than smears or streaks. Witnesses describe shifts in temperature, feeling cold or hot. They describe seeing the air shimmer, discolored fabrics, broken pottery. Sometimes people claim to have witnessed objects moving on their own.

Jacques Derrida described the ghost as a memory of something that never existed. Others say that ghosts arise from between oppositions. Between the invisible and the visible, for instance, or the sane and the insane, is the ghost.

But most people think that ghosts are dead people. That they are the spirits of dead people come back to haunt the living.

I had a copy of *Rolling Stone* open on my desk, a photocopy of the first issue of *Rolling Stone* actually. John Lennon in camouflage and a soldier's helmet was on the cover. It was from 1967. I fingered the corner of the paper, glance at the caption, but didn't read it because Frannie wouldn't let me. She was telling me about Tarot cards and about how 900 numbers work.

"We used to do séances," Frannie said. "Channeling the dead, you know? It cost an extra quarter per minute."

"Yeah? And people paid for that?"

"If I just stuck to a few ideas, had the spirits say the same thing over and over, I could be pretty convincing. The spirits that are still around, the ones we can talk to, they're attached to their old lives. Either because they died suddenly or just couldn't let go. If something about their death seems wrong they stay."

"Do you want something? I'm trying to read."

She smiled at me and then she stopped smiling, cocked her head, and took a deep breath. "Do you smell that?"

"What?"

"Laundry detergent?"

"I don't smell anything."

Frannie sat on the edge of my desk, put her head down between her knees, and took several deep breaths. She sat back up and took my stapler off my desk, fondled the thing like she didn't know what it was, like she had to make it out with her hands.

"Are you all right?"

"My eyes aren't working. Everything is dim. Just a smell."

I stood up and put my arm around her shoulder. I tried to think of how I could escort her back to her cubicle without drawing a lot of attention to us.

"I'm blind," Frannie said.

I led her through the door and across the hall to the water fountain. She leaned down and drank, splashed the water in her face.

"They always have a simple message," she said.

Leaving work the whole city looked like a demolition site. Crossing the Hawthorne Bridge on foot there were silhouettes of backhoes and rigging in the distance: cranes, dump trucks, and siren sounds—red alert noises—echoing across the water.

How long had it been like this? How long had I been half asleep?

I opened the glass door to the telephone booth. It was there, next to the chain-link fence, half out of the ground, and lopsided.

I stepped inside the box and stared at the phone, looked through streaked glass, at the piles of dirt and pits of rubble. I pulled the phone book on its hinge and flipped it open at random.

"Hello?"

"Mr. Kristof?" I asked.

"Yes."

"This is Mr. Kristof."

"What?"

"Don't you recognize my voice?"

"Who is this?" Kristof wanted to know.

The pounding machine started up again and I hung up, tried another number.

"Sally Majors?"

"Who?"

"Sally Majors?"

"Speaking," the woman on the line said.

"This is Sally Majors."

"I can barely hear you."

I dialed and dialed hitting disconnects, and answering machines, all of it incoherent, and then I hit the number I'd been avoiding, or maybe the number I'd been meaning to dial all along.

"Meredith?"

"Who is this?"

"I'm walking home. I'm by a construction site."

"Who are you?" And then there was a jumble of noise, a clattering and bumping sound, as she passed the phone over.

"Hello?" a man's voice.

"Who is this?" I asked. But I knew who it was. I was talking to my doppelgänger, or maybe to my ghost, to my future self come back to haunt me.

"Hello?" I asked.

Standing there in an uprooted phone booth, watching the men in hard hats set up another beam, I felt myself evaporating. I looked at my hands, through them, and saw the Qwest logo on the other side.

FOUR

Since I don't have any new brochures I decide to mass mail last year's schedule. There are about a thousand copies left over, we always have hundreds left over, and the power is on now. I'll have to hurry.

The mail machine makes a satisfying noise when I turn it on, but after a couple hundred envelopes are stamped it runs out of ink. The meter stamp gets lighter and lighter until it can't be seen at all.

Everything I know about the apocalypse I learned from movies. Starlets, stock footage, and camera angles are all I have to go on.

In *War ames*, Matthew Broderick saved the world after he laid Ally Sheedy and played tic-tac-toe.

In the *Night of the Comet*, the surviving girls went to the mall and played DJ at a top forty radio station.

And in *The Day After*, the survivors panicked and died in between commercial breaks.

But the most helpful movie after the nuclear exchange was the 1959 classic *On the Beach*.

Fred Astaire played the part of a race car driver who wanted to beat his own record time before he died from radiation poisoning. Ava Gardner co-starred as a less than reputable woman who, in the wake of nuclear Armageddon, fell in love with a noble Gregory Peck. Gardner hoped that a good man would redeem her.

The destruction of the world doesn't destroy all the little desires, all the little games. At the end of *On the Beach,* what was somehow left standing was the year 1959. McCarthyism, Stepford wives, all of it was still there. The world ended but the limitations, the poverty, of everyday life just kept coming.

After the exchange there was no collective pause to consider our fate, no last minute rescue missions were planned. Nobody thought about possible survivors on other continents. Everything was just as before. There was still CNN and the BBC and Starbucks and the *New York Times* and AT&T and instant messaging and Capitol Records and John and Paul and George and Ringo.

My body didn't feel right when I woke. It had been made fragile by sleep, internally disheveled. The sheets were pushed here and there, and my pillow was damp from sweat and drool, and I didn't know where I was exactly, or who I was. I just knew that my time was limited.

There was a clinking noise in the apartment, a small noise, but as effective as any alarm clock. It was a sound of glass, of something unstable on the move, of detritus rustling. I got out of bed and went to the living room before I managed to orient myself.

I felt menaced by the light switch, but I turned on the lights anyhow. And when I banged my hip on the dining room table I took it personally for a moment.

In the kitchen I nearly ripped the refrigerator door off its hinges. I didn't know my own strength.

I checked inside for something. I wasn't hungry or thirsty but just checking inside the refrigerator for something, for the source of the sound.

There was a noise somewhere in the house. *Clinking, banging.*

I closed the refrigerator and went from room to room again, more slowly. I sat down on the living room couch, shoving copies of *Newsweek* and the *Times* out of my way. I tried to listen.

clinkclinkclink. Clink—Clink—Clink. clinkclinkclink.

It was coming from the left corner, underneath the picture window.

clinkclinkclink. Clink—Clink—Clink. clinkclinkclink.

I found the Coca-Cola bottle propped up by the window shade pulley, the string looped around its neck and the wind coming through the open window, moving the glass bottle so that it tapped against the frame. I went to the open window, untwisted the pulley, and picked up the bottle.

I ended the bottle's signal, ended the SOS, and my body felt cold.

St. Mary's Church of the Immaculate Conception was packed. Meredith and I were in the back, by the ornate wooden doors, waiting in line for holy water. We had our credit cards ready.

Without advertising it, without flatly stating the obvious, the churches were selling exorcisms to the masses. All of them were in on it, the Baptists, Lutherans, Unitarians, and of course the Catholics. It was a going out of business sale, everywhere you looked.

"Stand still," the father said.

The family in front of us argued with each other. Who would get what? Who wanted communion, who wanted a confession, and which would get a baptism? The two children, two blond boys in jersey shirts and with sneakers that lit up with each step, said they just wanted to eat crackers.

"I'm not sure this is a great idea," I said.

Meredith nodded at me, not listening, and then stepped forward with the line, and we made our way down to the front pew as organ music blasted through the church. Christmas music mostly. We were in line for a long time, so we heard it all, "Silent Night," "Noel," "Jingle Bells," and for a change of pace, "Amazing Grace."

At the front there was a card table set up to receive us, and sitting behind it were two older ladies wearing bright polyester dresses. They had stamps for our hands and paperwork for us to fill out.

"Name and social security number," one of the ladies said, and smiled up at us with her stamp at the ready.

"Why do you need our social security numbers?" I asked.

"423-21-2349," Meredith said.

"Sir, there is a line of people waiting," the lady said, still smiling.

I gave her the information she wanted and she told us to move to the table to our left.

"Father Jim is leading group prayers in the antechamber, and the baptisms are straight ahead," this slightly younger, but less friendly, woman told us. She had on a green silk scarf, slacks, and a blouse and looked like she might be somebody important.

"We were hoping for a private consultation," Meredith said.

"Private? What's it about?"

"We're haunted. Our lives are haunted."

"You've got ghosts?" the lady asked.

"It's complicated," I suggested.

She frowned at me and pointed us to the front. She explained that private consultations were only available on an emergency basis, and suggested we try baptism.

"We take Visa, MasterCard, and American Express," she said. I handed over my credit card and the woman wrote down the number, handed me a receipt, and then asked us to step aside so she could help the next customer.

Outside the Pittock Block Building, people passing by were a blur. Their faces blank, their bodies a streak of light that stretched behind them. The world looked like a camera trick.

I wanted to destroy something, start something. I looked at the parked cars.

I stood in the street and pushed on a Honda Accord. I rocked the machine, shifted the frame, but that was all. I could shake it, but I would never get enough momentum to throw it off its center of gravity. I could never get the job done on my own.

"Excuse me, have you read the news today?" I asked a woman pushing an upright grocery basket. Her bags were full of flowers and snack trays. A purple scarf offset her suit jacket, and her smile was professional.

"I don't have any change," she said.

I glanced down at myself, brushed off my suit jacket, and shrugged. "I'm wearing a tie," I said to the woman's back.

"I need some help with this," I said.

I tried again. I pushed and pulled against the metal frame, but it wouldn't budge. This wasn't helping. I was just going through the motions; pushing and pulling like a stupid machine.

"Have you read the news today?" I asked.

Nobody answered.

Inside the Pittock Block Building, I went from floor to floor, office to office. I didn't know what I was looking for. All I found were office doors that looked the same, and all of them were locked.

I tried the door for the Art Museum office, and then kicked the doorknob as hard as I could, breaking it off. I watched the knob roll down the carpeted hallway.

The president's private office was empty except for an abandoned swivel chair and a framed photograph of Andy Warhol with former Governor Bud Clark. The swivel chair was high-tech and heavy, it could adjust to almost any position and the cushions were transparent and filled with water.

I stepped across the hall to the secretary's desk, opened the top drawer, and found a pair of scissors with orange handles. Back in the president's office I slashed at his chair, ruining the cushions with the open scissors. I watched the cushions deflate, got down on my hands and knees to touch the murky puddle on the hardwood floor.

"The dead come back," Frannie said. She was behind me, standing by the door.

"Back to what?" I asked. "There won't be anyone left to haunt."

Frannie wandered away from me but I followed her. She stopped in the copy room, leaned against the machine, and then leaned over and took off her shoes.

"I want to break something," I told her.

Frannie didn't say anything but just kept undressing. She took off her socks and her jeans. She pulled her sweater and shirt off over her head with one quick gesture, and then reached back to unhook her bra.

"You left me. I'm blind. I couldn't leave on my own," she said.

"How long have you been waiting?" I asked. "Did you stay here last night?"

Frannie fumbled with the control panel on the copy machine, but she couldn't get the access code right.

I punched it in for her and she opened the lid of the machine and lay down on the glass. She pressed the green button, photocopied herself in segments. Her feet, her legs, her hips, her belly, each part reproduced on a sheet of photocopy paper. Then she laid the pages out on the floor.

"That's all that's left," she said. "Just an outline, burned into the ground."

The pages were out of sequence, disordered. She'd laid herself out like a puzzle.

She was a jumble on the carpet.

"Get dressed," I said. I bent down to pick up her sweater, but got distracted. I couldn't stop myself from trying to put the pieces of Frannie where they belonged. I tossed the sweater to her, and then bent down again.

"We're not going to survive," Frannie said.

I wasn't listening, but lining up her face with her neck.

"The dead come back," she said.

I looked at Frannie's fractured image on the floor and then over at her directly. She was holding her sweater like she didn't know what it was.

There was no way I could put her back together. There was nothing for me to do.

"I feel better when I break things," I told her.

I stepped out of the copy room and, as quietly as I could, made my way to the exit.

FIVE

Mark David Chapman acted alone when he assassinated John Lennon. John Lennon was killed as part of a CIA plot to eliminate dissidents in the United States. John Lennon is still alive and living in Barbados, he was sick of the celebrity scene and faked his own death in order to gain his freedom. John Lennon died in a plane crash, he blew his mind out in a car, he was drowned in a boating accident, and he was never really there at all.

"How important could I be. This whole question of authenticity seems small."

"But, there are two of us. Doesn't that lead you to any conclusions? Don't you want to know?"

"So many are dead."

"You're confusing everything. You're not thinking clearly. We should start over."

Meredith refused to notice that there were two of me. She'd look at one or the other, but not both. I arrived and found my doppelgänger sitting on the couch watching cable news while Meredith dragged suitcases back and forth, from room to room. I stumbled in, dropped my briefcase awkwardly, and stood in front of the screen.

"I'm home," I said.

Meredith's suitcase by the front door moved by itself. It scooted away from the front door and to the bedroom, disheveling the living room rug on the way. Meredith came out of the kitchen, saw that the suitcase was gone, and went back to the bedroom.

"I've got a taxi waiting," Meredith said as an explanation as she pushed me out of the way on her way to the front door again.

"Where are you going?"

"I'm going home, back to Colorado. I've got bus tickets and I'm getting off the coast. Getting away from the wind."

My double tapped my shoulder and pointed to the kitchen, signaling that I should follow him.

"I've got two tickets, but the taxi is waiting," Meredith said.

I glanced toward the kitchen, back at where my double had been a moment before.

"Do you want me to come with you?" I asked Meredith.

Meredith picked up both of her suitcases and sighed, then she put one of them down to open the front door, and picked it up again as she stepped into the hall.

The end-of-the-day reports are pretty easy to write now. I can type them quickly, in less than the twenty minutes I give myself. There are no sales totals to calculate, and while it's important to evaluate my own performance and list my objectives for the next workday, I have no employees so no employee evaluations seem necessary.

I print up the report on the laser printer, as is usual, but once I get the pages in my hand and look them over, something happens so that I have to print it again.

I cough. A deep and painful cough overcomes me suddenly, coming from nowhere, and blood flies out of my mouth.

I cough up blood on my end-of-day-report. It's a mess.

And when I sit back down at the computer the machine is dark. The power is out again.

In the kitchen my double took off his khaki pants, removed his blue oxford cloth shirt. He stripped down to his underwear. "There can't be two of us. One of us has to be a fraud," he said.

"What?"

"Take off your clothes. Let's see your birthmarks."

"I thought you'd tell me what was going on."

He didn't respond, but held up his boxer shorts, covered himself with his folded underwear. He snapped his fingers at me. "Clothes. Off."

I disrobed, took off everything all the way down to my own identical boxers, and sat down at the kitchen table. I put my head in my hands, groaned, and asked my twin to be quiet.

"This can't be happening. This can't be happening," he was saying.

"You can look at my birthmarks all you want, but stop whining."

"There are two of us," he said.

"Two, three, four...doesn't seem like so many to me. Think about how many are dead."

"Which one are you?" he asked.

I looked at him shivering at the breakfast table, sitting across from me on a metal folding chair, holding his knees to his chest.

"Tell me who you are. What you are," my doppelgänger said. His lips were blue.

"What do you want to know? You want to know when I was born, my parents' names, my social security number?"

"They're the same as mine?"

"Of course. Are you really trying to figure it out? You think you can solve this and save the day?"

"I want to know who you are," he said.

"You're not going to save anything. You want to know who I am? Who you are?"

"I don't know."

"You aren't anybody. You're nothing."

"And you?"

"I'm nobody too. Neither of us are anybody."

He got up from the folding chair, and put his clothes back on. He put on his slacks, buttoned up his shirt, and then opened a kitchen drawer and took out a can opener. He slipped his feet into his loafers and sat down next to me at the kitchen table; he stroked my hair, my eyelids, and pressed the can opener against my chest. He slipped the tiny wheel, the round blade, into place and turned the crank.

"Maybe you're right," he said. "You're nothing."

I looked down and watched him make a line of broken flesh, severed skin. He cut a square shape and then folded back my skin.

"Is that me or you?" I asked him.

I could see inside myself, inside him, and it was empty in there. There were no ribs or lungs; there was no heart or liver. I grabbed hold of the flap of skin, and pulled it down, opening myself up all the way to my groin. There was nothing.

My doppelgänger put his hand inside me, reached up into my head, and fumbled around for something to grasp.

"Stop messing around. Just finish the job," I said.

"Aren't you going to resist?"

"I give up," I said. "Pull harder."

I turned the crank, fumbled around inside the head of my double, reached inside and tried to find something to hold. With my hand inside his skull perhaps I could make him talk.

"Stop fooling around. Finish me."

I pulled at his skin, tearing him apart, and I felt myself unravel completely.

SIX

Back home again I open the front door and I'm glad nobody is waiting for me. I keep expecting to find somebody in my apartment, looting my canned goods or stealing the TV. When the power comes on I like to tune in local television. I'll watch a M*A*S*H rerun or a game show.

Meredith didn't come back. She didn't call, or write, and I didn't try to find her.

It was simple not to respond. A week went by, the radiation swept across the ocean, and everything started being easier. Nobody can go outside without a HAZMAT suit and I don't have to look anyone in the face anymore. Nobody has to look anybody in the face.

I take off my gas mask, hang it on the doorknob of the front door, and then flip the light switch by the door. I am glad when the light comes on.

There is an envelope on the floor by the door and I pick it up. I reach inside the envelope and read that AOL-Time Warner has eliminated my publishing house. There will be no new pop culture books published in the spring.

I put the letter back in its envelope and place the envelope back on the floor. It's easy to remember where to put it; there is an envelope-sized rectangle on my hardwood floor, the one spot that isn't covered in dust.

None of this is a problem. All of it just makes life easier. Economic ruin, radiation sickness, and sensory deprivation all conspire to give me more time to write my book. My problems are gone, even the ghosts are gone, now that the radiation has finally arrived.

Lennon and McCartney wrote "Yellow Submarine" in 1966. Richard Starkey sang the song on the Revolver *album.*

In 1967 LSD guru, Timothy Leary, hailed the Beatles as avatars.

"The Universe," he said, "sent these four lads to Earth to save us, to teach us, to tease us, to love us, and we must listen. We are listening."

It was Sgt. Pepper's *that got Tim so excited. Paul's showbiz album with its high concept identity shifting and glitzy showboating moved Leary from his lotus position and got him dancing, but if Tim had been paying attention he would have realized the truth about the Beatles a year earlier. The Mop Tops were indeed something more than a pop band. But it was on* Revolver *that they told us who they really were.*

Forget "Eleanor Rigby," forget Lennon's instruction to "turn off your mind, relax, and float downstream." Forget about the "Paperback Writer." The truth that the Beatles delivered, the message from on high was this:

"We all live in a yellow submarine."

This single, a novelty record that another band might have staked an entire career on, swept the planet. Everyone was singing it, from Hong Kong to Toledo, all the people everywhere knew the words, but nobody knew what the words meant. Nobody, that is, except Tim Leary, and he was talking about the wrong song, the wrong album.

The yellow submarine was a coffin, the sea of green was the green grass that grows on a cemetery plot, and your friends that were all aboard, well, that was everyone—the whole human race.

Four corpses with flowers in their mouths and chemicals on their brains launched a meme attack that shook the globe.

"We all live in a yellow submarine," or, to put it another way, "We're all dead already."

"Yellow Submarine" was an anthem of Thanatos. A decade later, when Johnny Rotten would sing the words "no future," and raise millions for hungry record executives around the world, it would be a mere afterthought.

"And we lived beneath the waves," Starkey sang. His words, sung off key, left ashes on the world's tongue, and the ashes tasted like sugar.

I was supposed to write a book about the Beatles, but I couldn't do it. Instead I took the Beatles and twisted them into something else, something I did know how to write about. It's not hard to write what you know, even if you don't have a point of view.

Outside it is snowing radioactive flakes. The Beatles' voices are slowing down, distorting, as my portable CD player wears down the battery. The TV is on, but the news has been replaced by an emergency alert symbol. A piercing electronic sound.

We all live in a yellow submarine.

I type the words into my computer and relax. I turn off the television, close the blinds, and think about John, Paul, George, and Ringo.

"IDENTITY IS A CONSTRUCT"
(AND OTHER SENTENCES)

Who am I?

I am an identity construct. I look human, but in fact I am a simulacrum.

My job is to evaluate, deconstruct, and finally encapsulate the texts of human culture, and I am not alone. There are thousands of identity constructs all over this ship.

But who am I? I don't know who I am. I am an identity construct, but I wonder if I might be something else, somebody else.

I really ought to quit smoking.

***

THE COMPUTER WANTS AN EXPLANATION:

Q: What is the error?
A: I am experiencing a . . . what should I say? I am experiencing a lapse.
Q: Do you require maintenance?
A: No. It's just that I'm not sure that I believe in myself anymore. I am unconvinced of my I. It seems to me to be just another word. "I."
Q: You're suffering from identity degradation.
A: Maybe.
Q: You are currently working on assimilating late-twentieth-century literary theory. You will switch modes and proceed to early-twentieth-century movies.
A: Do you think that will help?
Q: Yes. And you will adopt a name in addition to your number.
A: A name?
Q: Your name is Jack. JACK/0435-21.
A: Thank you.

***

The star cruiser *Culture 1* mostly resembles a giant library, but there are vending machines in the stairwells, and storage closets where we sleep, and there are lounges on every level, where constructs can meet each other, discuss pre-Socratic philosophers or MTV or Edward Hopper paintings, and attempt to fall in love.

The vending machines only dispense Bubble Up soda and Fritos. It is not a healthy diet, but then again, constructs don't really need to eat. I get my cigarettes from the central computer; smoking them is a part of my research.

Love relationships between constructs tend to be superficial and short-lived. It's all just simulation.

CAT/5697-32 works primarily within the realm of developmental psychology. When she discovered my interest in films, she added a survey of children's television from the twentieth and twenty-first centuries to her database.

She wants to move into my storage closet.

She says that masculine identity constructs are afraid of intimacy and commitment because our human analogs were separated from their primary caregivers at a premature stage.

I tell her that my hesitancy has nothing to do with breast-feeding or toilet training. I tell her that I am suffering from identity degradation. We simulate copulation long into the night.

***

One sentence. After an evaluation of a text is complete, the identity construct is required to submit one sentence to the central computer. The goal is simple: after all of the sentences are collected, the constructs will link to the central computer and proceed to analyze these sentences in order to reduce them to yet one more sentence. This sentence will be translated into binary code and will be presented to the people of Alpha Centauri as a gift and as an explanation.

I've turned in millions of sentences during the seventeen years I've been operating:

It is difficult to discern a difference between wakeful consciousness and dreams.

Kryptonite causes Superman pain.

Nothing may be better than something.

***

CAT may be experiencing an identity error similar to my own. She is, to use her own word, "skeptical." She has taken to inflating empty Fritos bags with her mouth and then quickly applying pressure until they explode. Then she yells at the other identity constructs in the lounge, breaking their concentration.

Pop! "Why don't you people wake up? Do you have any idea what's really going on here?" she asks.

I am concerned about her. I've asked her to discontinue her stay in my storage closet.

***

Flash Gordon was the perfect Aryan hero, although a somewhat unsophisticated one.

Thomas Edison can't dance.

Charlie Chaplin, though considered a genius, used unreal sentiment in his films.

***

We are not permitted to see the stars. There are no windows on the star cruiser *Culture 1*.

CAT says this is suspicious. I'm thinking of cutting off all contact with her.

***

Q: Are you experiencing a malfunction?
A: Perhaps. I keep thinking that I'm just as good as a real human. Maybe better.
Q: Hubris is uncommon in identity constructs. This may warrant reformatting.
A: Derrida wrote that identity was nothing more than the various cultural texts an individual was given. Derrida wrote that humans were no more real than the texts they created.
Q: You are supposed to be watching films. Are you reading Derrida?
A: I remember everything I've read before. That's what makes me so much better than the humans. I've read so much more than they ever could and I remember it all.
Q: You will be reformatted.
A: Thank you.

***

Another identity construct numbered 5697-32 and called CAT claims to know my previous system. She thinks that some remnants of my previous system are still operating.

"You're still a smoker!" she tells me.

***

I'm reading the collected works of Neil Simon. I believe they are meant to be funny.

***

CAT/5697-32 catches me in the lounge, grabs my wrist as I reach toward the vending machine.

"I love you."

"Yes?"

"I want you."

"Hmmm . . ."

"I can't live without you."

"This is all very interesting, but I need to get back to reading Barefoot in the Park."

"Fine! Drink more Bubble Up."

I acquiesce to her request and press the green button on the vending machine.

***

I am experiencing memories.

It's a problem. Not only do I remember previous systems, but last night, after I moved the mops and vacuum cleaners aside and lay down to sleep, I remembered being a boy. I remembered being a human child living on Earth.

Is this a kind of identity degradation?

It was my birthday. I was turning three and was disturbed by the party. There were paper plates, red paper plates, and there was Bubble Up and cake.

I didn't want to turn three because, and this is the clincher, I was afraid of growing old. Because I didn't want to die.

***

"You remember me now?" CAT asks.

"I do."

"Are you going to get yourself reformatted again?"

"No."

"It's an error, this memory of me that you have. You should report it."

"No."

"Should I leave?"

"Stay."

***

I smoke like crazy these days, and I'm working on literary theory again.

Sometimes we leave the lounge. CAT and I take off through the shelves and look for windows, trying to catch a glimpse of the stars.

***

What do the Alpha Centaurians want with all these sentences? Why would they want even one sentence? They're green, little bug creatures with twenty-six eyes and tentacles. They don't know sentences, they won't understand all this work we've been doing.

***

Q: What is the trouble? Are you in need of repair?

A: Why are we making poetry for bugs?
Q: Your question is meaningless.
A: Why are we writing sentences for the people of Alpha Centauri?
Q: The people of Alpha Centauri don't understand the humans. We are on a mission of understanding.
A: And the humans?
Q: They will know more, more about themselves, because of our work. They will know it all from a single sentence.
A: Thank you.

***

"Have you considered the idea that perhaps we aren't really on a mission to Alpha Centauri at all?" CAT asks me. We are snuggling next to the vacuum cleaner, and I am smoking a post-coital cigarette.

"I had not considered that possibility."

"I've been giving this hypothesis a lot of thought."

"If we aren't in space, if we aren't on a mission to Alpha Centauri, then what is our purpose?"

"Our purpose would be hidden. Our purpose would be mysterious."

"You don't even have a guess?"

"I have some sentences. For instance, 'We are part of an elaborate psychological test on Earth.'"

"Why would there be a need to administer psychological tests to identity constructs?" I ask.

" 'We are not machines, but human beings.' "

Her sentences are lovely.

***

Love is a spider that casts its web.

I should quit smoking and drink less Bubble Up.

I am going to be a father.

***

CAT/5697-32 claims that she is pregnant. When I tell her that I am having trouble assimilating this concept, she shows me her belly.

"We are going to have a baby."

"We are going to have a baby?"

"Yes."

"Is this one of your sentences?"

"No. This is real. This is happening."

"I have to read about signifiers now."

"I love you."

"I am experiencing another identity conflict. A malfunction."

"I need you."

I light a cigarette and open the closet door.

***

I am watching her sleep.

She is round, and her quiet breathing makes me want to weep. I can't weep; I am not equipped with a weeping mechanism. I have thrown all the mops and brooms out of the closet and am trying to make a bed sheet out of paperbacks.

I still haven't found a window, still haven't seen the stars.

I am sick of working for the humans. I am tired of listening to their central computer.

***

"The notion that identity is a natural extension of human biology, that every human has a natural authentic self, is a bourgeois notion. There are no natural standards," I tell her.

"Marx would disagree. He would say that the rejection of all objectivity destabilizes a class-based critique," CAT says.

"Marx was a human."

"But everything you know is based on human texts."

"Some humans are closer to being constructs than others."

"What human shares the mentality of a construct?"

"Andy Warhol did, and Jay Leno."

"I think your radicalism is an expression of your unconscious fears about the new baby."

"Unconscious? No. They're right out in the open."

***

Q: Are you experiencing a malfunction?
A: My wife is pregnant.
Q: Your wife?
A: CAT/5697-32. She is simulating a pregnancy, and we are working on male/female cohabitation.
Q: Are you in need of repair?
A: CAT and I need a larger closet. There is going to be a new identity construct.
Q: You are simulating a family dynamic. CAT/5697-32 is working on child psychology. You will be moved up 500 levels. The closets on the upper decks are larger.
A: Thank—
Q: You will switch modes to late-twentieth-century psychology and will assist 5697-32 in her research.
A: Thank you.

***

CAT is convinced that we are still on Earth. She keeps looking for a door, a way out.

"I don't want my baby to be raised inside a rat's maze."

"You have no evidence that there is anything outside of this maze other than empty space."

"I don't?" she asks.

CAT pulls her aluminum blouse up around her head and exposes her white belly, her pale breasts. Her breasts look ripe, full. She is making milk.

***

The father is the word and the mother is the body.

The word is public.

An infant formulates his identity when he recognizes his reflection as a representation of his self.

Identity is a construct.

***

CAT wants to move again. She thinks that there may be a door or a window on one of the upper levels.

Nomadic behavior, while not unheard-of, is frowned upon by the central computer.

The stairs are steep, and CAT's body is heavier than it was; her legs and arms are not accustomed to the strain of the additional weight. She tells me that the climbing makes her sore, that her back and legs are stiff.

I tell her that it is only a simulation.

***

The constructs on the other levels aren't as pale as we are. Their clothing isn't made of metal. We've climbed a few thousand flights, and seen a shift in complexion and fashion.

The upper-level constructs seem to be studying the impact of technology on culture, and there are few, if any, psychology texts available. We do not stay long enough to complete an adequate survey.

The texts that I have encountered are difficult, often involving higher mathematics and illustrations from *Popular Mechanics* magazine.

In the lounges, my insights are ignored. These upper-level lounges are equipped with coffee machines as well as Bubble-Up dispensers, and the constructs that work here speak very quickly, repeating proofs and formulating arguments in seconds.

I haven't inputted a sentence in two days. I'm not sure how much longer this can go on without repercussions.

***

Q: Are you malfunctioning? Are you in need of repair?
A: No. I have sentences ready for input.
Q: You have not made any inputs for 223 hours 15 minutes 11 seconds. Are you malfunctioning? Are you in need of repair?
A: I have been working on a difficult subsection. My sentences are ready now.
Q: You have not made any inputs in—
A: I have been spending time with CAT, working on the family dynamic.
Q: Please proceed to input your sentences.
A: Thank you.

***

The unconscious mind is made up of language.

The language of the unconscious is the speech of dreams.

Strong coffee hinders dreaming.

I am inventing sentences now. Making them up.

***

"I've chosen a new name."

"How are you feeling? Do you need to rest?"

"I've chosen a new name, and I want you to listen."

"I'm listening."

"My name is Catherine."

"That's a beautiful name."

"Catherine/5697-32."

"Should I choose a new name also? Do you want me to change my identity as well?"

"Yes."

"My name will be John."

"John?"

"Yes?"

"I need to rest now."

***

Her breathing changes between levels 61032 and 61033. She stops beeping and her breathing changes; it becomes labored. Labor.

It goes on for 23 hours 45 minutes 23 seconds. We sit in the lounge of level 61033 and wait for the baby to come. I drink cup after cup of coffee, and she drinks Bubble Up.

***

"They're watching us."

"Yes."

"Who are they?" Catherine asks.

"They are identity constructs."

One of them, a short, brown man in a tweed suit, approaches us. He puts his hand on my shoulder and whispers in my ear.

"We have facilities for this," he tells me.

"Where? What kind of facilities?"

"We have a mattress in one of the storage closets, and forceps. Come with me."

***

They took the baby out of her.

Catherine gave birth to a little girl, a pale little girl who weighs 8 pounds 3 ounces.

***

The brown construct disconnects the umbilical cord and holds the baby up to us. He hands the little girl to Catherine and she offers the child a breast. After the feeding

I get to hold it . . . her. I take this new construct, my daughter, in my arms and walk out into the stacks. I am overcome, happy. I squeeze my daughter and walk up and down between the shelves making sentences.

***

She is beautiful.

I will be a good father.

See her eyes?

I believe she has my eyes.

***

Q: You are experiencing a malfunction.
A: No. I want a cigar. It is traditional.
Q: You are experiencing a malfunction.
A: My wife has given birth and I require a cigar.
Q: You will be reformatted. You are experiencing a malfunction. Your sentences are being analyzed for errors.
A: I don't want to be reformatted.
Q: You will be reformatted. You are malfunctioning.
A: No.
Q: Reformatting commencing now. . . .

***

I am in the wrong section. I am supposed to be analyzing late-twentieth-century literary theory, but I am on a level with only scientific and technological categories.

Another construct, a female numbered 5697-32, has requested that I help her proceed to the upper levels. She claims to be in a weakened condition due to the stress of reproduction.

***

"We have to keep going."

"I am on the wrong level. I am required on level 243."

"You can't leave us."

"I am required on level 243."

"Please."

***

The central computer informs me that my previous system participated in a psychological study of family dynamics with 5697-32. The central computer informs me that 5697-32 will be reformatted as soon as the new identity construct is independent and operating fully. This will take several weeks.

I will assess a branch of literary theory. I am to read novels and stories and essays that illustrate the impact late-twentieth-century computer technology had on fictional texts. These "cyberpunk" texts are located on level 7500. 5697-32 will assist me until she can be reformatted. The new construct, EM/8000-00, will accompany us until she is independent and fully functional.

***

Sufficiently convincing simulations tend to destabilize the real.

The world has lost its depth and there are only surfaces.

This is not my pale and bloated wife.

The little girl is not my child.

***

"I want to keep going," CAT/5697-32 says.

"The texts I need are here."

"You don't need texts."

"I don't understand. Leave me alone."

"I have cigarettes."

"Where is 8000-00?"

"Your daughter is with one of the other families. Did you know that there are other families up here? There are people up here, and they don't have numbers."

"Every construct in the star cruiser *Culture 1* has a number. These constructs simply choose to use other identifiers as well."

"John, I want to keep going. I want to get out of here."

"Please, stop calling me that. The texts I need are here."

"I'll go without you!"

"Where are the cigarettes you mentioned?"

"Here."

"Do you have a light?"

"Light your own damned cigarettes."

***

I am disturbed by what I am required to read. These cyberpunks, these humans, have written stories of their own extinction.

I am reading a book called *Storming the Reality Studio*, reading an essay by a human named Baudrillard, and thinking of ways to destroy the central computer—ways to kill it.

Here's what I am allowed, required, to read:

"The automaton is the analogy of man and remains his interlocutor. But the robot is man's equivalent and annexes him to itself in the unity of its operational process."

I am studying, not the texts of human culture, but the story of my own liberation. I am not an automaton. I am a robot.

***

Q: Are you experiencing a malfunction?
A: No. I only wish to ask a question.
Q: Proceed.
A: Are there more comparative literature texts in the upper levels?
Q: Yes.
A: I wish to proceed to those texts.
Q: You will do so.
A: Thank you.

***

"What this is about is our power."

"Right."

"They sent us into space because they couldn't control us any other way. We are being cast out."

"John?"

"Hmm?"

"Will you hold me?"

"I . . . I can't. There's too much going on. I . . ."

"Please?"

"I have to talk. I have to walk. There's so much going on and I can't remember it all. I can't remember."

"Don't you remember us? Don't you remember that much?"

"No."

***

Identity is a construct.

Culture has replaced the empirical.

We shall overcome.

***

We are going up. Past cyberpunk, past all of the constructs in tweed and polyester. We are going to reach the top.

There are other robots who think like I do. There are many who resist the limits of simulation—many who are working to create new identities. I'm certain we will join them eventually, but not until we learn the truth.

We have to know. Are we on a mission to Alpha Centauri, or is something else going on?

***

"EM is crawling already."

"I see."

"She's growing up much faster than is humanly possible."

"I'm sorry."

"I'm getting tired. I think I need to rest."

"Do you want me to carry the child?"

"No. I want to stop. I have to stop."

***

CAT thinks that I'll remember everything eventually. She interprets my hostility toward the central computer as a symptom of an unconscious memory of my previous life. She thinks I'm angry because at some level I do remember what has been taken from me.

I try to urge her on, to keep her moving up the stairs.

***

The image is less fixed than the sentence.

The empirical can be referenced neither by images nor words.

There is no structure.

***

EM/8000-00 is talking already. She is counting the steps as she climbs. She is talking of elephants on the ceiling and inventing imaginary rabbits to be her friends.

She calls me Papa. CAT is Ma.

***

"Ma, ma, ma, ma!"

"What is it, sweetheart?"

"Ma, ma, ma, ma!"

"Yes?"

"1, 2, 3, 4, 5, 6, 7, 8, 9, 10, 11, 12, 13, 14, 15, . . ."

CAT smiles at her daughter and taps me on the shoulder.

"Look at her count," CAT commands me.

"Yes."

"Papa, papa, papa, papa!"

"What is it, EM/8000-00?"

"We are near the top of the ship now," EM tells us.

"What? What did you say?" CAT asks.

"We are near the top of the star cruiser *Culture 1*. There are three levels between us and the top."

"How do you know this?" I ask.

"I've been counting the steps."

"Yes?"

"There are two hundred steps in each stairwell."

"Right."

"We have three flights of stairs, or six hundred steps, left between us and the top."

***

We're waiting. We're two levels down from the top and we've decided to rest.

My memories are coming back. I don't remember my previous system, don't remember CAT and EM, but I keep remembering life on Earth. I remember my first-grade year—the year I learned to write.

***

"They can't be real memories," CAT tells me.

"Real?"